Praise for
God Dies by the Nile

A quietly formidable achievement; its understated evocation of tragedy and strength in the face of victimization make it a graceful classic.

Women's Review

Powerfully political.

Poetry Nation Review

'Nawal El Saadawi's achievement is to lay bare the thin flesh and huge passions of her characters.

West Indian Digest

Praise for
Searching

Nawal El Saadawi once again presents a psychological drama that will take you into the depths of a woman's despair. Intimate details and vivid descriptions fill this story of an ordinary person who ends up teetering over the abyss of insanity... This is a novel of Cairo with the languid Nile winding its way through a story of love, guilt, betrayal and redemption.

Miriam Cooke, Professor of Modern Arabic Literature,
Duke University

Searching is an intense exploration of the state of mind of a young Egyptian woman who longs for both professional and personal meaning in her life, but finds herself isolated and adrift in a Kafkaesque world of senseless work. Saadawi creates a hellish vision of Cairo. Her protagonist finds herself utterly alone in a world dominated by casual, brutal patriarchy and a shadowy authoritarian state. This is a disturbing text that makes the reader feel trapped in a world that often feels like a particularly bad recurrent dream.

Jane Plastow, Professor of African Theatre, Leeds University

Praise for
The Circling Song

'To read this book is like looking into a kaleidoscope; as each new element in the story is added, so a new configuration is formed.'

Independent

'Nawal El Saadawi's technique is impressive: at once precise, controlled and hypnotic, even in translation. The style and meaning of the book are one. A song with no beginning and no end, the author tells its universal story.'

Everywoman

'This novel is a powerful example of the kind of anger and desperation to which Arab women writers are beginning to give vent.'

Choice

'Nawal El Saadawi is a legend in her own time. This is an ambitious work indeed.'

American Book Review

'One of Saadawi's most powerful books that we have had the privilege to read in English. Unusual, original and unexpected, it's one of those very rare books which address you in many languages and can take you in many different directions at once.'

Spare Rib

About the Author

Nawal El Saadawi was born in a village outside Cairo, Egypt, in 1931. A trained medical doctor, she wrote landmark works on the oppression of Arab women including *Woman at Point Zero* (1973), *God Dies by the Nile* (1976) and *The Hidden Face of Eve* (1977). After being imprisoned by Anwar Sadat's government for criticising the regime, she founded the Arab Women's Solidarity Association in 1982, before being forced into exile in later life due to death threats by religious extremists. She returned to Egypt in 1996, running for president in 2005 until government persecution forced her to withdraw. Saadawi died in Egypt in 2021.

God Dies by the Nile

and other novels

God Dies by the Nile • *Searching*
The Circling Song

NAWAL EL SAADAWI

Translated by Sherif Hetata, Shirley Eber

BLOOMSBURY ACADEMIC

LONDON • NEW YORK • OXFORD • NEW DELHI • SYDNEY

BLOOMSBURY ACADEMIC
Bloomsbury Publishing Plc
50 Bedford Square, London, WC1B 3DP, UK
1385 Broadway, New York, NY 10018, USA
29 Earlsfort Terrace, Dublin 2, Ireland

BLOOMSBURY, BLOOMSBURY ACADEMIC and the Diana logo are
trademarks of Bloomsbury Publishing Plc

This edition published in 2024 by Bloomsbury Academic

Cover design: Adriana Brioso
Cover images: © Adobe Stock
Author photo © Tom Pilston/Panos Pictures

A catalogue record for this book is available from the British Library.

Library of Congress Control Number: 2024931640

ISBN: PB: 978-0-7556-5160-3
       ePDF: 978-0-7556-5161-0
       eBook: 978-0-7556-5162-7

Typeset by RefineCatch Limited, Bungay, Suffolk
Printed and bound in Great Britain

To find out more about our authors and books visit www.bloomsbury.com
and sign up for our newsletters.

Contents

GOD DIES
BY THE NILE

NAWAL EL SAADAWI

TRANSLATED BY SHERIF HETATA

Introduction

I was six or seven years of age when I heard about a poor peasant girl who drowned herself in the Nile – she had been working in the house of the village mayor. My grandmother whispered something that I didn't understand in my mother's ear. At the age of ten I heard about another girl who fled during the night. She was a servant in the same house, fourteen years old and pregnant. Nobody accused the mayor, except a young peasant who had been planning to marry the girl. He was shot in the fields and no-one was captured. In a dream, I saw the mayor in prison accused of raping servant girls and robbing the women of their harvest. When I told my grandmother, she said it was impossible, that the mayor was a god and no-one could punish him. She said that the mayor exploited the peasants to serve the king's interest, and the king exploited the mayor and the peasants to serve the interests of the British army in the Suez canal. The word 'god' echoed around me but I didn't know its real meaning and I instinctively didn't like it. My parents gave my brother more freedom and more food than me, though I was better at school and helped my mother more. When I asked why, they told me that it is what God said. I felt that God was unjust like the mayor and the king, and that he deserved to be punished, but I kept this to myself.

These women and men in my village inspired me to write *God Dies by the Nile*. Zakeya is not very different from my grandmother and my aunts, relatives and neighbours. In addition to the oppression of colonial rule at that time, women were oppressed by men in the family, in society and in the streets. Poor women were more vulnerable than rich women.

In 1972 I published my first non-fiction book about women and sex. It was banned by the authorities and I was promptly dismissed from my post in the government. I found myself at home with nothing to do but write. I wrote fiction partly because I enjoyed it more, and partly because it seemed less likely to be banned – most of the censors were half-literate civil servants on low salaries, I did not imagine that they would read novels. I sat alone in my small apartment in Giza thinking about my new novel. I don't know why my childhood memory came back to me, especially the image of the mayor and his men sitting smoking by the banks of the Nile, looking at the girls walking past with jars on their heads. The faces of my grandmother and other poor women in my family appeared vividly to me. I finished the novel in two months. Writing it gave me enormous pleasure, a pleasure which sustained me inside prison, and which is more essential to me than breathing.

At that time, Sadat was pursuing his so-called 'open door policy', opening Egypt to foreign, especially American, goods and investment. The result was increased poverty, unemployment, religious fundamentalism and the veiling of and discrimination against women. The Islamization of Egypt went hand in hand with the Americanization. The shops sold imported veils from the USA and Saudi Arabia and prayer mats from Mecca, alongside red lipstick and tight blue jeans. The majority of people in Egypt were deprived of their basic material needs. Our television screens were flooded with religious men preaching chastity, modesty, spirituality and the veil, interspersed with adverts that used naked women's bodies to sell imported foreign goods. For women, the veil and female genital mutilation came to be part of authentic Islamic identity. I found it impossible to be silent. I published my articles in opposition newspapers and eventually found myself in prison, accused of betraying Egypt. One month later, however, in 1981, Sadat was assassinated and I was released by the new president.

God Dies by the Nile didn't escape this climate of censorship and oppression. Like most of my work, it had to be published in Lebanon. My Lebanese publisher in Beirut changed the title to *Death of the Only Man on Earth*. He told me that God cannot die, and when I tried to explain that the word god is a symbol for the head of the village, he said 'Yes, I know, but religious fanatics will not understand this and will burn my publishing house.' This actually happened several years later. In 1982 *God Dies by the Nile* was published, with another fourteen of my books, by a publisher called Madbouli in Cairo. He used the Lebanese title. He said 'They will burn my publishing house if I publish a book with a title like that. God does not die, he lives eternally.'

Thus the book was never published in Arabic with its original title, although it is reprinted to this day. Ten editions at least have come out since I wrote it. I think many women and men still read it. I have received many letters from readers saying that the village in the novel did not differ much from their village. Some men were angry and accused me of mocking Islam and encouraging heresy.

Though it was written more than thirty years ago, I feel that *God Dies by the Nile* still describes the life of peasant women and men in Egypt. The existing regime is no better than the Sadat regime – even worse. Poverty, American neocolonialism and religious fundamentalism have continued to rise. I visit my village every now and then and I see that it still resembles Zakeya's village. Perhaps this is why people still read the book and why publishers still reprint it. The novel has been translated into many languages, including English, and I'm glad that its original title has not been changed. God still dies by the Nile.

Nawal El Saadawi
Cairo, 2006

I

Before the crimson rays of dawn touched the treetops, before the cry of the cock, the bark of a dog, or the bray of a donkey pierced through the heavy darkness, or the voice of 'Sheikh Hamzawi' echoed in the silence with the first call to prayer, the big wooden door opened slowly, creaking, with the rusty sound of an ancient water-wheel. A tall, upright shadow slipped through and advanced on two legs with a powerful steady stride. Behind, followed a second shadow, on four legs which seemed to bend beneath it, as it slouched forwards with a lazy, ambling gait.

The two shadows disappeared into the darkness to emerge out of it again over the river bank. Zakeya's face stood out in the pale light of dawn, gaunt, severe, bloodless. The lips were tightly closed, resolute, as though no word could ever pass through them. The large, wide-open eyes fixed on the horizon expressed an angry defiance. Behind her, the head of the buffalo nodded up and down, its face gaunt and bloodless, but not unkind, its wide-open eyes humble, broken, resigned to whatever lay ahead.

The light of dawn glimmered on the river, revealing the minute waves, like tiny wrinkles in an old, sad, silent face.

Deep underneath, its waters seemed immobile, their flow as imperceptible as a moment of passing time, or the slow movement of the clouds in the dark sky.

In the wide-open spaces the air, too, was hushed and silent. It slipped through the branches of the trees so gently that they barely moved, but it continued to carry the fine, invisible particles of dust from over the high bank of the river, down the slope to the dark, mud huts huddled in rows, their tiny windows closed, their low, uneven roofs stacked with mounds of dry cotton sticks, cakes of dung and straw, then further down into the narrow twisting lanes and alleys blocked with manure, and on to the stream which completed the village contour, where they settled to form a dark, slimy, oozing layer covering its green water.

Zakeya continued to walk with the buffalo behind her, her legs moving at the same unchanging pace, as unchanging as the set look on her face, as the immobile waters of the river to her left, as everything else in these last moments of the night. But to her right there was a slow shift as the mud huts started to pass behind, and the fields emerged before her eyes like a green ribbon laid out parallel to the Nile.

She advanced between the two stretches of green and brown with the same swinging movement starting from the hips and thighs. Overhead, the black night withdrew gradually as the crimson hue of dawn spread out, then, after a while, changed to a glaring, orange light. Suddenly, over the edge of the earth a point of sun shone out, grew slowly to become a disc of fire, then climbed up into the sky. But before the light of day had chased away the night, Zakeya had already reached her field, tied the buffalo to the water-wheel beside the stream, removed her black shawl and put it on the ground, rolled up her sleeves, and tied the tail of her *galabeya** around her waist.

Now her hoe could be heard, thudding out over the neighbouring fields with a steady sound, as it cut deep into the ground. The muscles in her arms stood out, and below the black *galabeya* knotted tightly around her waist, the long powerful legs showed naked and brown in the morning light; the features of her face were still the same, still sharp, still gaunt, no longer pale, but dark with the leathery tan bitten into them by heat and dust, and sun and open space. Yet deep underneath was the same pallor which her skin revealed before and now concealed. Her body no longer stood upright. It was bent over the hoe as she dug away in the soil. Her eyes did not look at the ground, were not fixed to her feet. They were the same. They had not changed. They were raised, fixed to some distant point with the same angry defiance which looked out of them before. And the blows of her hoe seemed to echo with an anger buried deep down as she lifted it high up in the air and swung it down with all her might into the soil.

Its blows resounded with their regular sound like the muffled strokes of a clock striking out the hour. They devoured time, moved forwards machine-like, cut into the earth hour after hour. They never tired, never broke down, or gasped for breath, or sought respite. They went on with a steady thud, thud, thud echoing in the neighbouring fields throughout the day, almost inhuman, relentless, frightening in the fury of their power. Even at midday,

---

* An ankle-length gown or robe which is cut to hang loosely; it is worn traditionally by both men and women, although the style, colours and cloth differ.

when the men broke off for a meal and an hour of rest, they went on without a stop. The buffalo might cease turning round and round for a short while, and the water-wheel would stop creaking for a moment, but her hoe kept on falling and rising, rising and falling from sky to earth, and earth to sky.

The sun rose up in the sky gradually. Its disc turned into a ball of fire, choking the wind, bearing down on the trees, turning everything into solid dryness, so that all things seemed to suffocate, burn in its red fire, and dry up, except the rivulets of sweat pouring down from Zakeya's face and body on to the ground. Beneath the sweat her face was livid like the face of the buffalo turning round and round beneath its yoke.

The hours passed. The sun began to lean towards the earth in a slow, sweeping movement. Its flames no longer burned with the same ire. The heat subsided, and the air stirred, wafting a soft breeze with it from the waters of the Nile. The tree tops swayed from side to side unwillingly, as though spent out. Once more the sky was bathed in a glaring, orange light, gradually swept aside by the sad, grey hue of beginning twilight. The sweat on her face dried up leaving a layer of dust behind like ashes on a dying fire. She threw the hoe on one side, stretched the muscles of her back and stood upright. She looked around for a moment as though awakened in the night, then rolled down her sleeves and untied the knotted folds of her long, black garment before letting it drop down over her legs to the ground. She drew the shawl around her head, and stepped out of the field on to the dusty track. A few moments later she was once more a dark shadow walking back over the same path, with the same steady step, and with the buffalo plodding slowly behind. Now the green expanses of the fields were to her left, and the brown waters of the Nile on her right. In the distance the trees had become slender black silhouettes etched against the greying sky. The sun had dropped below the earth, and to the west, its crimson light no longer fought against the dusk.

The two shadows travelled slowly over the dusty track on the river bank. Her shadow was the same: tall, upright with the head rising straight above the neck. It moved as though advancing to attack. The second shadow too had not changed one bit. It slouched along, completely spent, its step resigned, its head still bent. They advanced over the river bank, two silent shadows in the deepening night. Nothing moved in the whole wide world around, nothing moaned or sighed or cried or even spoke. Only silence in the silent night spreading its cloak over the fields stretched out on the other side, over the waters of the Nile, over the sky above their heads, over everything on the ground.

Slowly the fields swung back behind them, and the huts emerged in front, small, dark, indistinct shadows huddling up for support or shelter against the river bank or perhaps afraid of sliding down into the dust-covered expanse of low land.

The two shadows descended the slope into the ditch, and got lost in the narrow twisting lanes, as they glided furtively along between the houses. They came to a stop in front of the big wooden door. Zakeya opened it with a push of her powerful fist and it gave way with a heavy creaking sound. She dropped the rope by which she held the buffalo. It ambled in through the open door and went on towards the stable. She watched it go in for a moment, then squatted in the entrance to the house with her back up against the wall and her eyes facing the open door, so that she could see the part of the lane which lay beyond it.

She sat immobile, her eyes staring into the darkness as though fixed on something she perceived in front of her. Perhaps what had caught her attention was nothing but a mound of manure piled up near the entrance to her house, or the stools of a child, lying on the ground, where it had squatted to relieve itself near the wall, or an army of ants swarming around the body of a dead beetle, or one of the black iron columns in the huge door on the opposite side of the lane.

The darkness was all pervading, almost impenetrable, but she continued to stare into the night until a moment came when she felt a stabbing pain in her head. She pulled the shawl even more tightly around it, but after a while the pain travelled down to her stomach. She put out her hand and fumbled in the dark for the flat, straw basket containing the week's store of food. She pulled it up to her side, parted her tightly closed lips and began to feed little pieces of dry bread, dry cheese and salted pickles into her mouth.

Her lids were heavy with an exhaustion which was overwhelming. She dozed off for short moments, her head resting on her knees. She could no longer see anything in the total darkness, even when her eyes were wide open. Kafrawi slipped in through the big wooden door and squatted down beside her. She was looking straight at him as he came up, so he thought she had seen him. But although wide awake she had not really seen the man he has become. His body shrinks before her eyes to that of a small boy, and now she is looking at him through her child's eyes, as she crawls on her belly over the dust-covered yard of their house, panting breathlessly, with her tongue hanging out of her mouth. The dust gets into her eyes, and nose and mouth. She sits up and starts rubbing her little fists into her eyes. The next moment she stops rubbing her eyes, and sits with her hands in her lap looking around, but suddenly she sees four black hoofs moving over the ground towards her. One of the hoofs rises slowly up into the air. She can see its dark forbidding underside like the surface of a big hammer ready to drop with all its might on her head. A shiver goes through her, and she screams out loud. Two strong arms reach out to her and lift her from the ground. The feel of her mother's arms around her, the warmth of her breast, and the smell of her flesh are reassuring and her screams subside.

She could no longer remember her mother's face; the features had faded away in her mind. Only the smell of her body remained alive. Something about it reminded her of the smell of dough, or of yeast. And whenever this smell was in the air around her, a strong feeling of happiness came over her. Her face would soften and grow tender for a short moment, but an instant later it would become as harsh, and as resolute, as it had been throughout her life.

When she learnt to stand on her legs, and walk, they allowed her to go to the fields with Kafrawi. He walked in front leading the buffalo by a rope tied round its neck, while she brought up the rear driving the donkey with its load of manure. Her brother remained silent all the way. She never heard his voice except when he urged the buffalo on with the cry 'Shee, shee' or tried to make the donkey move faster by shouting 'Haa, haa' at it.

She remembered seeing her father standing in the fields, but could not recall his face. All that remained of him in her memory was a pair of long, thin, spindly legs, with protruding knees, a *galabeya* with its tail lifted and tied around his waist, a huge hoe held tightly in his big hands, as it rose and fell with a regular thud, and the sombre, heavy creaking of the water-wheel. The wheeze of the water-wheel would continue to go round and round inside her. At certain moments she could feel it stop suddenly, make her turn towards the buffalo and cry out 'Shee, shee', but the animal would not budge. It stood there motionless. The black head perfectly still, the black eyes staring at her fixedly.

Zakeya was about to repeat 'Shee, shee' when she realized the face was not that of the buffalo, but Kafrawi's. He resembled her a great deal. His features were carved like hers, his eyes large, black and also full of anger, but it was a different kind of anger, mingling in their depths with despair, and expressing a profound humiliation.

He remained seated by her side, his lips tightly closed, his back pressed up against the mud wall, his eyes staring into the darkness of the lane, reaching across to the bars in the huge iron door facing them some distance away. He turned towards her and parting his lips slightly spoke in a harsh whisper.

'The girl has disappeared, Zakeya. She is gone.'

'Gone!?' she asked in anguish.

'Yes, gone. There is no trace of her in the whole village.'

He sounded desperate. She stared at him out of her large, black eyes. He held her stare, but there was a profound hopelessness in the way he looked back at her.

'Nefissa is nowhere to be found in Kafr El Teen, Zakeya,' he said. 'She's vanished completely. She will never return.'

He held his head in his hands and added, this time almost in a wail, 'She's lost, Zakeya. Oh, my God.'

Zakeya looked away from him, and fixed her eyes on the lane, then whispered in a mechanical way, her voice full of sadness, 'We've lost her the same as we lost Galal.'

He lifted his face and murmured, 'Galal is not lost, Zakeya. He will return to you soon.'

'Every day you say the same thing, Kafrawi. You know that Galal is dead and you're trying to convince me that he's not.'

'No one has told us that he is dead.'

'Many of them died, Kafrawi, so why not him?'

'But many have come back. Be patient and pray Allah, that he may send him back safely to us.'

'I've prayed so many times, so many times,' she said in a choking voice.

'Pray again, Zakeya. Pray to Allah that he may return safely, and Nefissa too. Where could the girl have gone? Where?'

Their voices like the successive gasps of two people in pain ceased abruptly. Silence descended upon them, a silence heavier than the thick cloak of darkness around them. Their eyes continued to stare fixedly into the limitless night, and neither of them moved. They sat on, side by side, as immobile as the mud huts buried in the dark.

2

The big iron door swung open slowly, and the Mayor of Kafr El Teen stepped out into the lane. He was tall with big, hefty shoulders and a broad, almost square face. Its upper half had come to him from his mother: smooth silky hair, and deep blue eyes which stared out from under a prominent, high forehead. The lower half came from the upper reaches of the country in the south, and had been handed down to him by his father: thick, jet black whiskers overhung by a coarse nose, below which the lips were soft and fleshy, suggesting lust rather than sensuality. His eyes had a haughty, almost arrogant quality, like those of an English gentleman accustomed to command. When he spoke his voice was hoarse, and unrefined, like that of an Upper Egyptian peasant. But its hoarseness was endowed with a mellow, humble quality that belied any hint of the aggression often found in the voices of men cowed by years of oppression in former colonies like Egypt and India.

He moved with a slow step, his long, dark cloak falling to the ground. Behind him followed the Chief of the Village Guard and the Sheikh of the mosque. As they came out they could see two shadows squatting in the dark across the lane. The faces were invisible but the three men knew that it was Kafrawi and his sister, Zakeya, for they were in the habit of sitting there, side by side, for long hours without exchanging a single word. When there was only one shadow instead of two, it meant that Kafrawi had stayed behind in the fields, where he would labour until sunrise.

At this hour they were in the habit of going to the nearby mosque for evening prayers. Once back, they would install themselves on the terrace of the mayor's house overlooking the river, or saunter down to the shop owned by Haj Ismail, the village barber. There they sat smoking and chatting as each one in turn drew in a puff from the long, cane stem of the water-jar pipe.

But this time the Mayor refused to smoke the water-jar pipe. Instead he extracted a cigar from his side pocket, bit off the end, lit it with a match, and started to smoke while the others watched. Haj Ismail could tell from the way the Mayor frowned that he was not in a good mood. So he disappeared into his shop and a moment later came back, sidled up close to him, and tried to slip a small piece of hashish into the palm of his hand, but the Mayor pushed it away and said, 'No, no. Not tonight.'

'But why, your highness?' enquired Haj Ismail.

'Did you not hear the news?'

'What news, your highness?'

'The news about the government.'

'Which government, your highness?'

'Haj Ismail! How many governments do you think we have?'

'A good number.'

'Nonsense! We have only one government, and you know that very well.'

'Which government do you have in mind, the government of Misr* or the government of Kafr El Teen?'

'The government of Misr, of course.'

'Where do we come in then?'

The Chief of the Village Guard laughed out loud and exclaimed, 'Who would dare deny that we're just as much of a government ourselves?'

It was Sheikh Hamzawi's turn to laugh. His tobacco-stained teeth could be seen protruding from his big mouth, and the yellow-beaded rosary swayed from side to side as he slipped it furiously through his fingers.

But the Mayor did not join in the laughter. He closed his thick lips tightly around his cigar, and his blue eyes gazed into the distance over the long ribbon of the river water and the wide expanses of cultivated land, now invisible in the darkness. In his mind he could see them stretching out between the two villages of Kafr El Teen and El Rawla. When he used to visit the area with his mother during the summer months, he never imagined that some day he would settle down in Kafr El Teen. He loved the city life of Cairo. The lamps shining on the dark surface of the tarmac roads. The coloured lights of the riverside casinos reflected in the flowing waters of the Nile. The nightclubs thronged with people eating and drinking as they sat around the tables, the women dancing, their bodies moving, their perfume and soft laughter going through him.

---

* The central government in Cairo which manages national affairs. Misr, here, is Egypt, but also refers to the capital.

At the time he was still a college student. But unlike his elder brother he hated lectures, and lecture rooms, hated the talk about knowledge, and his future. Above all, he hated listening to his brother discoursing about politics and political groupings.

As they sat there plunged in silence, Haj Ismail suddenly remembered the morning newspaper he had left in the shop on the wooden table next to the weighing machine. He disappeared inside again and returned carrying it folded up in his hand. He opened it out under the kerosene lamp, and started to read the headlines on the front page, but his attention was drawn away from them by the picture of a man. It stood out clearly in the middle of the page. The features were familiar and it did not take him long to realize that he was looking at the elder brother of the Mayor. He tried to read what was written below, but the print was too small, and he could not make out what it said. He hesitated for a moment, then moving closer to the Mayor whispered in his ear in as low a voice as possible.

'Has the news you mentioned got something to do with your brother?'

After a brief silence the Mayor said, 'Yes.'

This time Haj Ismail's question expressed concern. 'Has some misfortune befallen him?'

There was a note of pride in the Mayor's voice as he replied, 'No, on the contrary.'

Haj Ismail was so excited he could barely contain himself. 'Does your highness mean to say that he's been elevated to a higher post?'

The Mayor blew out a dense cloud of smoke. 'Yes, exactly, Haj Ismail.'

Haj Ismail clapped his hands together with glee, then looked around at the others and said, 'Our friends, then we must drink sherbet to celebrate the occasion.'

A flutter went round the men seated in front of the shop. The newspaper quickly changed hands going from one to the other. Haj Ismail left them and came back carrying a bottle of sherbet and empty cups.

But the Mayor seemed to be lost in his thoughts. All day he had kept wondering why the moment he had seen his brother's picture in the newspaper a feeling of inadequacy and depression had come over him. He knew this feeling well. It was always accompanied by a bitterness of the mouth, a dryness of the throat which turned into a burning sensation as it moved down to his chest, followed by an obscure and yet sharp pain which radiated outwards from his stomach.

He was a small boy when this feeling first started to come over him. He remembered how he used to run to the bathroom and vomit all the food in his stomach. Then he would stand there examining himself in the mirror above the washbasin. His face was deathly pale, his lips almost yellow, and the gleam which shone in his eyes was gone. They looked dull, apathetic, resigned, as though some cloud had descended upon them and snuffed out their liveliness.

He would wash his mouth several times to dispel the remaining taste of bitterness which lingered behind. When he raised his head to look into the mirror, it was his brother's face that appeared before him. He contemplated the rosy cheeks, the gleam of victory in the eyes. In his ears rang the exultant tones of the voice he knew so well. 'I succeed in everything I undertake. But you have been a failure all the time.'

He would spit out the water in his mouth on to the face smiling calmly at him from the mirror. Then lift his neck, square his shoulders, and addressing it in a loud voice say, 'I am a thousand times better than you.'

Anyone seeing him as he walked out of the bathroom door would imagine that of the two he was no doubt the more successful. His lips had regained their rosy colour, and his eyes were shining brightly. The bitter taste in his mouth had gone, and once more his merry laughter rang out, as he romped around mischievously, teasing his mother who sat in her armchair knitting, trying to pull at the tip of the thread and make the woollen skein roll out. Her haughty blue eyes would flash with an angry light and the curt sentence pronounced with an English accent would sting his pride. 'Your brother is much better than you are.'

Sometimes she would set aside her needles, reach out for the folded newspaper lying on the table next to her, and pointing to a name printed in small letters on one of the pages inside, would say, 'Your brother has passed his examinations brilliantly, whereas you...'

He would stop laughing immediately, as though something had seized him by the throat and was choking him, then swallow several times without responding. And just as suddenly he would realize that he was not really happy, that he had been forcing himself into a merry mood. This feeling of being superior to his brother was just a disguise. The truth was so overwhelming that it shook him to the marrow of his bones. It seemed to exude from every pore in his body with the cold, sticky sweat that now ran under his clothes. It crept into his mouth and nose, reviving the taste of bitterness once more, dropped down with it to his chest, then through a small hole into his belly. He would run back to the bathroom and vomit repeatedly until there was nothing left for him to vomit.

Haj Ismail was sipping his second round of sherbet from the copper cup when he noticed the Mayor spit on the ground scornfully, then he straightened his back, lifted his head, and his eyes travelled slowly over them with a haughty stare. His look seemed to say, 'Compared to me, you people are just nobodies. I am from a noble family. My mother is English, and my brother is one of the people who rule this country.'

Haj Ismail cringed as he sat on the bench, as though trying to make himself so small that he could avoid the eyes of the Mayor. He had been on the verge of joking with him, of telling him the latest stories, but immediately thought better of it. His eyes kept shifting backwards and forwards between the picture of the Mayor's elder brother sitting in the midst of the most important people in the country, his features expressing a haughty arrogance and the small shop with its old, cracked shelves, covered in dust, and the few rusty tins standing dejectedly on them. He tried to tear himself away from the comparison only to find himself lost in the contemplation of the Mayor's expensive cloak, while his hand kept fingering the coarse fabric of his own *galabeya*.

The Mayor's eyes caught Haj Ismail in the act of lifting his cup of sherbet to his lips and draining it in one quick gulp, as though it was a purge of castor oil. He burst out laughing, slapped him jocularly on the knee and said, 'You peasants drink sherbet the way we swallow medicine.'

Now that the Mayor was joking with him so familiarly, the feeling of inferiority, of being of no consequence, which had invaded Haj Ismail a few moments before was largely dispelled. Was not the Mayor cracking jokes with him? Was this not a good enough reason to feel his self-confidence restored, to feel that the social gap between them was narrowing? He felt pleased. Now it was an appropriate moment for him to start laughing, to pick up the thread of merriment where the Mayor had left off, and thus encourage him to go on in the same vein.

'We peasants cannot tell the sweet flavour of sherbet from the bitter taste of medicine,' he said jestingly.

The Mayor was silent for a moment as though turning the words Haj Ismail had spoken over in his head. He began to feel uneasy. They kept echoing in his ears again and again. Supposing the Mayor misconstrued what he had said?

'Your highness, what I meant is that everything tastes bitter to the mouth of a peasant,' he added hastily in an attempt to set things right.

The Mayor maintained his silence. Decidedly, something was wrong. Haj Ismail was now almost sure that he had not been careful enough about what he had said. This time the Mayor could take his last words to be an insinuation that peasants had a hard life, which of course was not at all true. This in its turn might lead directly or indirectly to an even more dangerous conclusion, namely that in the view of Haj Ismail the government was not telling the truth when it repeatedly expressed its concern for the welfare of the peasants, and the protection of their rights. Since the Mayor was the representative of government in Kafr El Teen, such a view could also be taken to mean that as the responsible official he was using his position to exploit the peasants, and to spend the money he squeezed out of them on his extravagant way of living, and his extravagant tastes in food, tobacco, wine and women.

His mind was now in a whirl. He cursed his own stupidity. 'Instead of painting her lashes with kohl, he had blinded her eyes.'*

The best thing to do was to make himself as invisible as he could. But just at that moment he caught a glint in the Mayor's eyes. They were looking in the direction of the river and he turned to see what had caught his attention. High up on the river bank a girl was walking. She held herself upright, balancing the earthenware jar on her head. Her tall figure swayed from side to side, and her large black eyes were raised and carried that expression of pride he had seen so often in the women of Kafrawi's household.

The Mayor moved his head closer to Haj Ismail and said, 'The girl resembles Nefissa.'

Haj Ismail responded quickly. 'She's Nefissa's younger sister.'

'I did not know Nefissa had a sister.'

Haj Ismail realized what was going on in the Mayor's mind, and to curry favour with him said, 'Each one of them is more beautiful than the other.'

---

* A popular saying meaning that sometimes when you try to improve a situation you may make it worse.

The Mayor winked at him and chuckled: 'But the youngest is always the most tasty.'

Haj Ismail laughed loudly sucking in quantities of air through his nose and mouth. He felt in high spirits and was completely rid of the mood of depression which had weighed so heavily on him earlier. Now he was certain that the Mayor's behaviour towards him would not change because his brother was in power. Was he not joking with him as though they were equals, and opening up his heart to him like a friend?

He whispered into the Mayor's ear in hushed tones, blinking his eyes rapidly. 'You are right, your highness, the youngest is always the most savoury to taste.'

The Mayor became very silent. His eyes followed the tall lithe figure of Zeinab as she walked along the river bank. He could see her firm, rounded buttocks pressing up against the long *galabeya* from behind. Her pointed breasts moved up and down with each step. Beneath the tail of her *galabeya* two rosy, rounded heels peeped out.

The Mayor turned round and addressed the Chief of the Village Guard. 'For the life of me I cannot understand how Kafrawi manages to feed these girls of his. Look! The blood is almost bursting out of her heels.'

The Chief of the Village Guard burst into noisy, raucous laughter, gulping in mouthfuls of air. He had suffered a silent torment for quite a while, for it had seemed to him that he was out of favour with the Mayor. Had not the Mayor been talking to Haj Ismail all the time? But now matters looked different. Immediately he felt his mood change, felt himself become gay once more.

'He is stealing from others no doubt. All you have to do is to say the word and we'll push him behind bars.'

He stood up majestically and gave a theatrical wave of his arm. Then pretending to call upon one of his aides, he shouted out loud.

'Boy, bring the handcuffs and chains immediately.'

The Mayor, highly amused by these antics, roared with laughter, and the three men seated with him joined in, including Sheikh Hamzawi who found himself obliged to abandon the water-jar pipe he had been puffing at with zeal all the time, and to laugh more loudly than any of the others, displaying an erratic row of decayed yellow teeth, and jerking the yellow rosary beads frantically between his fingers.

The Mayor waited until the hilarious laughter had subsided before addressing the Chief of the Guard again.

'No, Sheikh Zahran, Kafrawi is not a man to steal.'

Sheikh Hamzawi now found it appropriate to intervene on a categorical note as though he was quoting from the Holy Koran on the sayings of the Prophet Mohamed.

'All peasants steal. Theft runs in their blood like the bilharzia worm. They put on an innocent air, pretend to be dull, kneel down before Allah as they would never think of disobeying Him, but all the time, deep inside, they are nothing but accursed, cunning, unbelieving, impious sons of heretics. A man will prostrate himself in prayer behind me, but once he has left the mosque, and gone to the field, he will steal from his neighbour, or poison the man's buffalo without batting an eyelid.'

He stopped for a moment to cast a look at the Mayor's face.

Reassured that his words were falling on appreciative ears, he went on.

'He might even commit murder, or fornication.'

The Chief of the Village Guard crossed his right leg over his left leg, throwing the fold of his garment to one side in a way that exhibited his new pair of boots, and permitted him at the same time to convey the message that Sheikh Hamzawi was trespassing on ground which was strictly his.

'If we are going to speak of murder and fornication then the Chief of the Village Guard should have plenty to say, but...' Turning to the Mayor with an ingratiating smile he asked, 'Tell me, your highness, you who knows so much. Are people in Misr the same as in Kafr El Teen?'

Sheikh Hamzawi intervened unceremoniously. 'People have become corrupt everywhere, Sheikh Zahran,' he said. 'You can search in vain for Islam, or for a devout Muslim. They no longer exist.'

He noticed an expression of disapproval on the Mayor's face and hastily added, 'Except of course where you are dealing with upper class people of noble descent like his highness, the Mayor. Then it's a different matter.'

He searched frantically in his memory for a verse from the Koran with which to back up what he was saying, but his mind had been dulled by the fumes of what he had been smoking. Undeterred, he made do by intoning sanctimoniously, 'Allah enjoins you to inquire after a man's descent for his roots will always find their devious way to his soul.'

The Mayor pouted his fleshy lips at the Sheikh of the mosque. Why had this man led the conversation away from Zeinab's rosy heels to such weighty matters as religion and faith? He smiled in Haj Ismail's direction and said, 'Tell me, in your capacity as doctor-healer in this village, how is it possible that a dark-skinned devil like Kafrawi should have fathered daughters who are as white as a bowl of cream?'

Sheikh Hamzawi butted in again, attempting to chase away the image of the Mayor's disapproving pout, which was still upsetting his tranquillity. He intoned, 'And Allah doth create from the loins of a man of God a corrupt descent.'

'You have not told me what you think, Haj Ismail,' said the Mayor, ignoring Sheikh Hamzawi's interruption.

The village barber was still busy turning over in his mind the title of 'doctor-healer' which the Mayor had bestowed upon him. It made him feel as though he had been accorded a bachelor's degree in medicine, which put him on an equal footing with any medical doctor in the area. He pulled himself up and gazed fixedly in front of him with narrowed eyes as though lost in deep thought. On his face was the look of a man of science, who has penetrated into the secrets of life and is now endowed with great knowledge.

'By Allah, your highness, and verily it is Allah alone who knows, the mother of Nefissa must have been yearning for a bowl of cream at the time when she was pregnant with the girl. Or maybe she was possessed by a white devil.'

The Mayor was seized with a fit of almost uncontrollable laughter. He threw his head back, giving full vent to his mirth, before turning to the Chief of the Village Guard as though looking for someone to come to his rescue.

The Chief of the Village Guard stood up imitating the same

dramatic stance he had adopted a while before, and shouted into
the night.

'Boy, bring the handcuffs and chains at once. Catch hold of
the devils, boy, and clap them in irons.' Then spitting into the
neck of his *galabeya*, he whispered, 'Let not our words anger
them, Almighty God.'

Everyone joined in the laughter, but the loudest voice of all
was that of Sheikh Hamzawi, who felt that now a special effort
was required to melt the ice between him and the Mayor. Leaning
over he whispered into his car, 'It's a well-known fact that the
womenfolk in the Kafrawi family have their eyes wide open and
are quite brazen, your highness.'

The Mayor gurgled softly. 'Is it only their eyes that are wide
open, Sheikh Hamzawi?' he asked half seriously.

There was another storm of laughter. It was slowly carried
across the still waters of the river, this time sounding carefree, as
though the men were at last rid of their bitterness and melancholy.
Even the Mayor felt better. He had chased away the bitterness
which invaded his heart the moment he saw his brother's picture
in the newspaper. Now he no longer had a need to be distracted,
or entertained. He yawned copiously, displaying two rows of long
white teeth like the fangs of a fox, or a wolf. When he spoke it was
in a tone which brooked no discussion.

'Let's go.'

He stood up, and in the wink of an eye the three men were
also on their feet.

3

She piled up pieces of stone and pebbles in the ditch beneath the slope of the river bank, covered them with earth, and flattened the surface with the palm of her hand. Then, resting her arm on the ground, she sat down with her back to the trunk of a mulberry tree. The earth was fresh against her hot skin. A damp coolness seemed to flow from the tree into the aching muscles and bones of her back. She pressed her forehead and face up against it, licking the moisture that exuded from it with her parched tongue.

The moist trunk of the tree evoked an ancient memory, an old sensation. She could almost feel the warm, wet nipple pouring milk into her mouth as she touched it with her lips. A bead of sweat fell from her forehead onto her nose. She wiped it with her sleeve, then her hand moved up to rub her eyes, but they were dry. She whispered softly, 'May Allah have mercy on you my mother.'

She lifted her face to the sky, and the light of dawn shone in her large black eyes. Her eyes had never looked down, nor did she walk with them fixed to the ground. Like her Aunt Zakeya she looked up with pride and with anger, but in her eyes there was no defiance. Over them now lay a cloud of anxiety, as though she was lost and afraid of what lay ahead of her. Her look wandered into the infinite expanses of sky, slowly plunged itself in its depths. In the distance she could see the horizon, a dark line where the earth met the sky. The red disc of the sun climbed out gradually from behind, and started to pour its orange light into the universe. A shiver went through her body. She could not tell whether it was the lingering cold of the night, or the fear of what was yet to come. She lifted her shawl and concealed her face from the light. In front of her the waters of the river were the same as they always had been, and its banks went on and on forever. She looked back, and looking back what she saw seemed no different from what she saw ahead. The same water, and the same track over the river bank stretching out to an endless end. But she knew this time that somewhere in the limitless space was the village she had left behind. And her mind kept remembering things as though she was back, or as though she had never left. The mud hut where she lived, nestling up against her Aunt Zakeya's dwelling. And just in front across the lane that huge gate with the iron bars, shielding the large house which hid behind from curious stares and probing eyes.

She used to crawl on her belly over the dusty lane. If she lifted her head she could see the iron bars like long black legs, watch them advancing slowly, intent on crushing her under their weight. She screamed out in fright, and immediately two strong arms reached out and picked her up. She buried her nose in the black garment. It was homely and rough, and smelt of dough or yeast. When she nestled up against her breast, her mother put something in her mouth. It was a mulberry fruit, ripe and sweet and soft. The tears were still in her eyes but she gulped them down, greedily swallowing the fruit which was filling her mouth with the taste she loved so much.

Ever since childhood the sight of the iron bars had filled her with fright. She heard people mention the gate and the iron bars when they talked of different things. But they never came close, and when they walked through the lane they sidled along the opposite side, and their voices would drop to a whisper the moment it came in sight. The expression in their eyes would change at once from one of pride or anger or even cruelty to a humble resignation as though they had decided to accept anything which fate might do to their lives. They would bow their heads and look at the ground as they passed by, and if one happened to look into their eyes at that moment not even a hint of anger or rebellion could be detected lurking inside.

Once her legs could carry her around she started to go to the fields, either running behind the donkey, or dragging the buffalo by a long rope tied around its neck, to make sure it followed her wherever she went. And every day she carried an earthenware jar on her head, and walked along the river bank to the bend in the Nile where the girls filled up the empty jars with water. But she avoided passing in front of the iron gate, and took a roundabout way behind the village, making almost half a circle to get to the river bank and walk straight down to the filling place. By now she knew that the iron gate opened on the yard which led to the big house owned by the Mayor, and that the house lay far behind, surrounded by a huge garden with trees and flowers. But somehow her imagination kept telling her that behind the gate was concealed a great giant, a monstrous devil who walked on twenty iron legs which could crush her to death at any moment if she was not careful.

When she grew older, instead of taking the roundabout track to the river bank, she started to follow the more direct route, although it led her right in front of the iron gate. She had grown enough to know there were no devils hiding behind it, and that in the big house dwelt the Mayor, his wife and their children. And yet whenever she heard the Mayor being mentioned, a shiver would go through her. Later, when a few more years had passed, the shiver was still there, but now it could barely be sensed deep down inside her.

But one day her father told her that the next morning, as soon as she had dressed and had her breakfast, she was expected to go to the Mayor's house. That night she could not sleep a wink. She was only twelve years old at the time, and her small mind spent the dark hours of the night trying to imagine what the rooms of the Mayor's house could be like. Through it flitted images of a bathroom in white marble which the children of the neighbours had told her about. They added that the Mayor bathed in milk each night. And before her eyes she could see his wife moving around the house, her skin white and smooth, her thighs naked. The son was said to have a room of his own full of guns, and tanks, and aeroplanes which could really fly. The Mayor too kept coming and going before her eyes as real as she had seen him one day swathed in his wide, black cloak, as he walked along surrounded by the men of the village. She remembered now that each time she saw him she used to run away and hide in the house.

In the early morning even before the red light of dawn had appeared in the sky she woke up, washed her hair, rubbed her heels with a stone, put on a clean *galabeya* and a black veil around her hair, and sat down to wait for Sheikh Zahran who was expected to take her to the Mayor's house. But as soon as he came in sight, she ran quickly away and hid on top of the oven. She kept wailing and shrieking from her hiding place, refusing to budge. At one moment she stopped to take her breath, and heard the Chief of the Village Guard say, 'Our Mayor is a generous man, and his wife belongs to a good family. You will be paid twenty piastres a day. You're a stupid girl with no brains. How can you throw away all the good that is coming to you? Do you prefer hunger and poverty rather than doing a bit of work?'

'I work here in my father's house, Sheikh Zahran, and I work in the fields all day,' she answered in a sobbing voice from her hiding place above the oven. 'I am not lazy, but I do not want to go to the Mayor's house.'

The Chief of the Village Guard abandoned his efforts to make her come down and said, 'You people are free to do what you like. It looks as though you are fated not to enjoy all the good which Allah wants to bestow on you. There are hundreds of girls who would jump at a chance to work in the Mayor's house. But he chose your daughter, Kafrawi, because he believes you are a good, honest man worthy of his confidence. What will he say now when he hears you have refused his offer?'

'I am all for accepting, Sheikh Zahran, but as you can see it's the girl who refuses,' answered Kafrawi.

'Then it's the girl who decides what is done in this household, Kafrawi,' exclaimed Sheikh Zahran heatedly.

'No, it's I who decide. But what can I do if she can't see sense?'

'What can you do?! Is that a question for a man to ask?' responded Sheikh Zahran, even more heatedly. 'Beat her. Don't you know that girls and women never do what they're told unless you beat them?'

So Kafrawi called out to her in a firm voice, 'You, Nefissa, come down here at once.'

But Nefissa showed no signs of doing what he told her, so he clambered to the top of the oven, struck her several times, and tugged at her hair until she was obliged to come down. He handed her over to Sheikh Zahran in silence.

To her ears came the sound of wooden wheels turning slowly over the ground. When she turned round she saw a cart pulled by an old tired donkey coming up the track towards her. The donkey suddenly lifted its head and brayed in a long, drawn-out gasping lament. The cart passed in front of her where she sat on the ground. She looked into the eyes of the donkey and saw tears. The man on the seat of the cart was staring at her, so she lifted her shawl to cover her face. His features did not look like anyone she had seen in Kafr El Teen, so she felt more at ease. She called out to him from where she sat on the ground. 'Uncle, please take me with you to Al Ramla,' then stood up on her feet.

The man eyed her where she stood upright on the bank of the river. He noticed her belly was big, and a faint suspicion crept through his mind. But she looked him straight in the face, and her eyes expressed so much anger, and so much pride that his suspicions were allayed. Her movements were slow as though she was spent out, but she held her body upright. His voice sounded gruff when he spoke.

'Get in.'

She rested her arms on the edge of the cart and with a powerful pull lifted herself up to the seat. She sat close to him, her eyes on the road stretched out before them and said nothing. After a short while he gave her belly a quick sidelong glance, then asked, 'Going to your husband in Al Ramla?'

Her eyes did not blink as she said, 'No.'

He was silent for a moment before coming back to the charge again.

'Did you leave your husband behind in Kafr El Teen?'

She kept her eyes on the road and still without blinking said, 'No.'

His looks were becoming more direct. He examined her big, rough hands resting calmly on her lap. The wrists were bare of bracelets. The daughter of some poor peasant, he thought, who is used to digging the ground, and ploughing. Yet when she looked him in the face he saw something he had never noticed before in the eyes of women who belonged to poor peasant families. It was not just anger, nor was it just pride. It was something more powerful than either of them. He suddenly remembered that when still a child he had once climbed up the fence of the Mayor's house. He found himself looking straight into the eyes of the Mayor's daughter. At that moment the stick of the Chief of the Village Guard landed on his shoulders, and he clambered down as fast as he could. Throughout his childhood years he had dreamed of looking into her eyes. He never understood why this desire had taken such a hold on him. He never spoke to anyone about it. It sounded so strange, so mad, so utterly unheard of that he did not dare voice it aloud.

He turned his head and looked at her. Their eyes met and held each other with a steady stare. She neither blinked nor looked away, as any of the girls from Kafr El Teen or Al Ramla would have done in her place. There was an expression in her eyes he could not define. Anger or defiance or maybe both together. So he shifted his gaze to the road, shook the reins over the donkey's back and thought, 'She does not look like someone who has escaped. Nor does she look as though she is afraid.'

His eyes kept wandering back to where she sat. He could see her bare feet covered with cakes of mud which were now drying. He asked again, 'Have you come far?'

With her eyes still fastened on the road she said, 'Yes.'

Still unsatisfied he queried, 'Walking all night?'

'Yes.'

He was silent for some time. He found it difficult to imagine this young woman walking alone through the night over long dusty roads, or cutting through fields where foxes and wolves and brigands lay hidden. But he said nothing for a while, fixing his attention on the road which stretched ahead of them. Then, as though he had turned the matter over in his mind before speaking again, he commented in a low voice, 'The night is dangerous.'

He pronounced the words in a strange, deliberate way as a man would do if he wanted to frighten her, and see the lids of her wide-open eyes tremble in fear. But she continued to stare at the horizon, watching where they were going with unblinking eyes.

'Night is safer than day, uncle,' she said.

He was silent again. The features of his face remained perfectly still like a child whom someone has struck with a stick just a moment ago, but who refuses to show he is hurt, or to burst into tears. He felt a pressure on his chest, like a strong desire to weep kept back for years, ever since the day when the Chief of the Village Guard had whipped him with his cane. If she had turned to him at this moment and smiled, he would have rested his head on her breast, and wept like a child. Or if he had seen the slightest quiver in her eyes when he gazed into them as the cart started to rock from side to side he might have enjoyed a sense of relief for a while. But she did not quiver and she did not smile. She did not even turn to look at him as though she had forgotten his presence by her side. Even at the rare moments when she did, he felt she was thinking of something else, so important, so big that by comparison he remained as of little consequence as the droppings of a fly. He dipped a hand into his pocket and pulled out a plug of molassed tobacco, or maybe it was a piece of hashish, or opium. He put it in his mouth. His saliva tasted bitter and he swallowed several times, then started to cough violently as though trying to overcome an age-long feeling of humiliation he carried deep down inside him. He bent his head with the deep sadness of a man who has just realized that the only real feeling he has known is this sense of humiliation that he carries around with him, day after day, and night after night.

He closed his lips tightly, and whipped the old donkey several times with the long stick he held in his hand, just as the Chief of the Village Guard would do with the child of poor parents caught playing after school. Now he felt in a hurry to reach Al Ramla, and to be rid of this irksome young woman as soon as he could.

The wooden cart advanced slowly over the winding road, swaying from side to side so much that it looked as though at any moment a wheel might come off. She could hear the donkey gasping and choking as it went along. His breathing sounded slow and monotonous like a clock, like the bumping of the wooden cart wheels as they turned round and round, and the pulse beating under her ribs and inside her belly as though it too was on the verge of breaking down.

She watched the sun rise up into the sky. She watched the fields swing slowly behind, and the compact mass of mud huts emerge from the ground and huddle up against the bank of the river like a mound of earth piled up on one side. Gradually women carrying water jars came in sight as they walked along the river bank moving towards her in a leisurely line. She began to hear a buzzing noise filling the air, for the children had awakened and the flies swarmed through the alleys and over the houses. Long queues of buffalo and cows plodded along raising clouds of dust, and groups of men and women walked by their side. They carried hoes on their shoulders and kept yawning all the time as though the thought that another day was about to start made them wearier than ever.

For a moment it seemed to her that she was back where she had started out, back in Kafr El Teen. She lifted her veil to hide her face but the man sitting beside her spoke to her in a hoarse, ugly voice which said, 'Get down.'

'Is this Al Ramla, uncle?' she asked.

'Yes,' he said without looking at her.

She rested her arms on the wooden cart and started to get down. It leaned suddenly on one side under the weight of her body and straightened up again when her feet reached the ground. The cart regained its balance and he felt it become light, moving more easily over the ground. His heart was beating steadily and he would feel that now it was much lighter than it was before, as though rid of the load which had been weighing it down. He heard her footsteps tread heavily over the ground and whipped the donkey with his stick several times. The cart resumed its slow progress, trundling along over the dusty road. He was on the verge of turning round to take a last look at her, but changed his mind. He fastened his eyes on the distant horizon and whipped the donkey again. It stumbled forwards gasping for breath as it dragged the cart behind it, and the wheels started to turn once more with their slow, monotonous, bumping sound.

Nefissa saw the cart shaking and swaying from side to side, the man's back was thin, and his bones stuck out, and when she looked at him from behind she was reminded of her father. After a while the cart disappeared carrying the man out of sight, but the sound of the wheels crunching over the ground continued to mingle in her ears with the hoarse gasping of the donkey as it breathed in and out. Every now and then these sounds were drowned in a rasping cough like the cough which shook her father every time he inhaled deeply from his water-jar pipe as he sat smoking in the yard of their house.

When she arrived at the mosque she turned to the right and after a short distance was confronted by an area of waste ground which Om Saber had described to her. At the furthest end was a small house built of mud, with a big wooden door. Over the door was a wooden knocker, and close by she noticed the water pump. She worked the pump and drank the water which flowed over the palm of her hand, then walked up to the door. She lifted the knocker several times, allowing it to drop lightly, and heard a woman's voice respond in a long, drawn-out vulgar call like that of Nafoussa, the dancer in Kafr El Teen.

'Who is at the door?'

'It's me,' answered Nefissa in what was little more than a whisper.

The long, drawn-out vulgar call resounded loudly once more. 'Who are you?'

'It's me… Nefissa,' she said.

'Nefissa who?' the woman insisted.

She wiped a drop of sweat which was trickling down her nose and said, 'Aunt, Om Saber sent me to you, Aunt Nafoussa.'

There was a silence. She could hear the pounding of her heart, and the whisper of her breath as she faced the door. Then it swung open by itself, as though moved by an invisible devil.

She stood there as still as a statue. But when she stepped across the threshold she realized that her whole body was shivering.

4

Just before she heard the first cock crow in the dark silence, Fatheya opened her eyes. Or perhaps she did not realize that her eyes had already been open for some time. She could see her husband lying on his back with his mouth open, snoring with a deep choking noise. His breath smelt heavily of tobacco, and his chest kept up a wheezing sound as though phlegm had been collecting in it all night.

She nudged him in the shoulder with her fist to wake him up, but he turned over and gave his back to her, muttering unintelligible words in his slumber. The crow of the cock rang out in the silence once more. This time she hit him with her knuckles sharply on the shoulder.

'Sheikh Hamzawi, the cock has awakened and called out to prayer, and you are still snoring away,' she said irritably.

Sheikh Hamzawi opened his eyes but closed his lips tightly as though he had decided not to respond to her verbal and manual attacks on him, already starting at this early hour of the day. He got up without a word. His wife, Fatheya, was not like his previous wives. None of them would ever have dared to look him straight in the face, or to say anything inappropriate to him, or compare him to any other man in Kafr El Teen, let alone to a cock which had crowed a few moments earlier, and which she had had the impudence to insinuate was better than he.

But he no longer cared how she behaved, even if it went as far as putting the cock on an equal level with him. What mattered was that he had succeeded in forcing her to marry him against her will, and obliging her to live with him all these years even though Haj Ismail's potions and amulets had been totally ineffective in restoring or even patching up his virility.

The first time he had seen her, he was seated as usual in front of Haj Ismail's shop. He glimpsed her supple body as she walked along the river bank carrying an earthenware jar on her head. Turning to Haj Ismail, he had whispered, 'That girl over there. Who's she?'

'Fatheya, the daughter of Masoud,' answered Haj Ismail. 'Her father is that poor man then. No doubt he would be happy to have me as a member of the family?'

'Do you mean that you want to marry her, Sheikh Hamzawi?'

'Why not? I have been married three times and still have no son. I must have a son before I die.'

'But she is young enough to be one of your grandchildren,' said Haj Ismail. 'Besides, how do you know that she will not remain childless like your previous wives?'

Sheikh Hamzawi bowed his head to the ground in silence, but the rosary beads continued to run uninterruptedly through his fingers, impelled by a mechanism of their own. Haj Ismail eyed him with a knowing smile. He burst into a laugh, cut it short abruptly and said, 'It looks as though the girl has turned your head for you, Sheikh Hamzawi.'

Sheikh Hamzawi smiled quietly and looked at the village barber with a gleam in his eyes. 'Verily the look of her revives my spirit. I've always longed for the kind of female she is.'

'Talking of females, female she certainly is. Her eyes seethe with desire. But do you think you can keep her under control, Sheikh Hamzawi? Do you think a man of your age can take her on?'

'I can satisfy not only her, but her father if necessary,' retorted Sheikh Hamzawi. 'It's only what you have in your pocket that counts where a man is concerned.'

'What will you do if the years go by and she does not give you a son?' enquired Haj Ismail.

'Allah is great, Haj Ismail. I am going through difficult times, but they will soon be over. God will breathe his spirit into me, and give me strength.'

Haj Ismail laughed out loudly. 'Those are the kind of things you can say to other people, but not to me, Sheikh Hamzawi. You haven't stopped complaining to me about your condition. How can Allah give you strength? Are you insinuating that God will...?'

Sheikh Hamzawi cut him short quickly. 'Allah can infuse life into dead bones, Haj Ismail. Besides you yourself told me that I can be cured.'

'But you have not been listening to my advice, nor have you followed the treatment I prescribed to you. You've been lending an attentive ear to what the doctors say, and paying through your eyes for their medicines. I told you, doctors know nothing and their prescriptions are useless. But you did not believe me. And now what is the result? You've wasted your money and you're not one step ahead of where you were. Say so, if I'm wrong.'

'Yes, yes, Haj Ismail, but one cannot learn except at a high price. Now I know all doctors are ignorant cheats, and that the only real doctor in the village is you. From now on I refuse to be treated by anyone else. But you must marry me to Fatheya, the daughter of Masoud. If you do that, Allah will reward you generously, because you will have done a service to the man who preserves the holy mosque and defends the teachings of God in this village.'

Haj Ismail burst into hilarious laughter. 'Both I and my children would have died of hunger long ago if we had waited until Allah rewards us.'

'Of course I will pay you, and handsomely. You know me well,' Sheikh Hamzawi said quickly.

'I know you are a generous man, and that you are the descendant of a generous family. But most important of all, you are the man who preserves the faith in this village and watches over our morals. Therefore you must leave the matter in the hands of Allah, and not worry about it any further. I will see to it. You can depend on that. Just follow what I told you to do before. Make constant use of warm water, and salt, and lemon. Burn your incense every night leaving none of it to the following morning, then take the rosary between your fingers and recite a thanksgiving to Allah ninety-nine times. After that, curse your first wife thirty-three times, for were you not fully potent when you married her, Sheikh Hamzawi?'

Sheikh Hamzawi answered in a voice that rang with despair, 'I was as strong as a horse.'

'She managed to cast a spell on you, and I know who prepared the amulet for her. He is not from Kafr El Teen, but I know the secret of his spell, and how to destroy it. The most important thing for you now is to follow my advice, and Allah will bestow his blessings upon you.'

Sheikh Hamzawi lowered his voice to a barely audible whisper and asked, 'When will I spend the betrothal night with Fatheya?'

'Soon, very soon, if Allah wills.'

'What about my having a son, Haj Ismail? I suppose it is impossible?'

'Nothing is impossible if Allah wills that it should not be so. You are a man of God and should know that well. How can you forget that Allah is all powerful?'

The rosary beads ran quickly between the fingers of Sheikh Hamzawi and he gasped, 'May His name be praised. May His name be praised.'

Sheikh Hamzawi rested his hand on the wall and slowly got to his feet. The rosary swayed from side to side in his hand as he repeated 'May His name be praised.' He put on his caftan and his *jiba*,* and adjusted the turban on his head, all the time whispering under his breath. His thin body seemed to bow under a heavy weight as he shuffled towards the door of the house. He heard Fatheya moan in a low voice. He could not understand what was wrong with her these days. She was not the same. She did not even

---

* Garment worn over a caftan, made of thicker, darker material.

get angry with him as she used to do at one time, and spent most of her day in the house lying down. She no longer insisted on visiting her aunt, perhaps because each time he got into a temper and tried to stop her from going out. The wife of Sheikh Hamzawi, as he had explained to her father, was not like the wives of other men. Her husband was responsible for upholding the teachings of Allah, and keeping the morals and piety of the village intact. The wife of a man like that was not supposed to be seen by just anyone. Her body had to be concealed even from her closest relatives, except for her face and the palms of her hands. She was expected to live in his house surrounded by all due care and respect, never to be seen elsewhere except twice in her life. The first time when she moved from her father's to her husband's house. And the second when she left her husband's house for the grave allotted to her in the burial grounds. Apart from that ...

The father shook his head in pious agreement and said, 'Sheikh Hamzawi, you are indeed the most respected and esteemed of all men,' then he gave his consent.

But Fatheya hid herself above the oven and refused to answer anyone, despite all the efforts expended to make her more reasonable.

'God is going to save you from the withering sun in the fields, from the dirt and the dung, from your diet of dry bread and salted pickles. Instead you will spend your days resting in the shade, eating white bread and meat. You will become the spouse of Sheikh Hamzawi, the man who devotes himself to the worship of God, to serving his mosque, the man who leads the people of the village in prayer, and lives a life of piety,' said Haj Ismail at the top of his voice, as though he wanted everyone within hearing distance to know what was going on.

But Fatheya continued to hide on top of the oven and refused to answer.

Haj Ismail looked round at her father and inquired in angry tones, 'Now what do we do, Masoud?'

'You can see, Haj Ismail, the girl is refusing.'

'Do you mean that in your household it's the girl who decides what should be done?'

'But what can I do?' asked the father looking perplexed.

'What do you do?' exclaimed Haj Ismail, now looking furious. 'Is that a question for a man to ask? Beat her, my brother, beat her once and twice and thrice. Do you not know that girls and women are only convinced if they receive a good hiding?'

Masoud remained silent for a moment, then he called out, 'Fatheya, come here at once.'

But there was no answer, so he climbed up on to the top of the oven, pulled her out by her hair, and beat her several times until she came down. Then he handed her over to Haj Ismail and the same day she married the pious old Sheikh.

Sheikh Hamzawi grasped his stick firmly in his hand, and opened the door of his house. Fatheya strained her ears to catch the tapping sound of his stick through the wall as he walked on its outer side. She knew the sound well. It had continued to echo in her ears ever since the night of her betrothal. It pierced through the thick shawl wrapped around her body and head as she rode the donkey to Sheikh Hamzawi's house. She could hear its tap, tap, tap as he walked along the lane by her side. Her

father wore a new *galabeya* and Om Saber, the *daya*,* was clad
in a long, black dress. She could not see the old woman for the
folds of the shawl were worn tightly round her head. She could not
see anything.

But she felt. She felt the burning pain left by the woman's
finger as it probed up between her thighs looking for blood. And
she felt the warm gush and the sticky wet. She did not see the
clean white towel stained red, nor the wound the woman's nail had
made in her flesh. But she felt her virgin colours had bled, for in
her ears resounded the beat of the drums, the shrieks of joy and
the high-pitched trilling of the women.

She moved her hand in under the shawl and wiped the sweat
from her nose and eyes, but it continued to pour out from the roots
of her hair down over her face and her neck to her chest and her
back. Underneath her, on the back of the donkey its rough coat
was becoming wetter and wetter. The spine of the donkey pressed
up between her thighs. She could feel it hard against the wound
which was still bleeding inside. With every step, with every beat
of the *tabla*,† the back of the donkey rose and fell, and its thin
spine moved up and down to rub on her wounds, causing her a
sharp pain every time, and making her lips open in a noiseless
cry. The warm blood trickled out mixing with the sweat which
poured down from her body, and the rough coat of the donkey felt
soaking wet between her thighs.

When they arrived in front of the house which belonged to
the pious and God-fearing man who had become her spouse, they

---

* Local midwife.
† A long, conical drum.

took her down from the donkey, but she was unable to stand on her feet, and collapsed into the arms of those who stood around, to be carried into the house like a sack of cotton.

She realized she had left the streets and was now in the house from the dank, putrid smell of the air inside. Since she was sure that the odour of godliness and moral uprightness smelt good and was pleasant to respire, she realized her nose was to blame for making the atmosphere around her smell like a latrine which was never washed down. She did not know exactly what it was that was wrong with her, but ever since her childhood she had felt there was something impure about her, that something in her body was unclean and bad. Then one day Om Saber came to their house, and she was told that the old woman was going to cut the bad, unclean part off. She was overcome by a feeling of overwhelming happiness. She was only six years old at the time.

After having done what she was supposed to do, Om Saber went away leaving a small wound between her thighs. It continued to bleed for several days. But even after it healed she was still left with something unclean in her body which used to bleed for several days at a time. Each time she had her periods the people around her would have a changed expression in their eyes when they looked at her, or they would avoid her as though there was something corrupt or bad about her.

Later, when she married Sheikh Hamzawi, he too would shy away from her whenever she had her periods, and treat her as though she was a leper. If his hand inadvertently touched her shoulder, or her arm, he would exhort Allah to protect him from the evil Satan. Then he would go to the water closet, wash himself five times and do his ablutions again if he had already done them. In addition she was not allowed to read the Koran or to listen to it being read or recited. But once her periods were over, and she had taken a bath, and cleansed herself thoroughly, he allowed her to pray, and to recite passages from the Koran.

Every night before she went to bed Sheikh Hamzawi made her sit on a carpet opposite him, and showed her how to pray. She did not understand what the words he recited meant, they were difficult words and she kept asking him to explain their meaning to her. But he used to respond in a very discouraging and rough way, insisting that the words of Allah and the rituals of prayer were supposed to be learnt by heart and not understood. So Fatheya tried to memorize them as best she could. The instructions of Sheikh Hamzawi kept echoing in her ears.

'Prayer is built on certain well defined movements of the body, namely: kneeling, prostrating yourself twice each time you kneel, and then sitting up with your feet under the body to recite the testimonial. In addition, there are certain conditions which must be strictly adhered to. In males the body must be covered from the waist downwards to a point below the knees. In females, the whole body should be covered with the exception of the palms of the hands, and the face. At the beginning of the prayer you must stand upright with the face looking straight in front of you, and the feet kept straight on the ground. In the case of males the hands should be lifted and held in line with the ears when declaiming the All Powerfulness and Almightiness of Allah. In females the hands should be held in line with the shoulder bone. The next movement in males is to put the right hand over the left hand and cover the belly below the waist with both the hands, whereas in females the hands are to be placed over the chest.

'Whenever you kneel or prostrate yourself you must do it completely. When you kneel repeat, "I praise thee O Almighty God" three times. And when you prostrate yourself repeat, "I praise thee O highest of all gods" three times. Your prayers become null and void if you say anything extraneous to the words of the prayer, or laugh or soil your cleanliness after ablutions in any way, particularly if you let out wind from the back passage.'

So every evening Fatheya would sit on the prayer carpet and repeat the same ritual. Then she would recite the holy verse of 'The Seat', and perhaps other verses. Her lids would feel heavy, and quite often she fell asleep while kneeling. In her ears echoed the words of Allah and between her thighs crept the hand of Sheikh Hamzawi. She abandoned herself to sleep as though abandoning herself to a man, opening her thighs wide apart and dropping into a deep oblivion right in the middle of the prayer offered to God.

With her ear stuck to the wall, Fatheya followed the tapping noise made by Sheikh Hamzawi's stick as he moved along the lane. She could detect the sound of his foot if it collided with anything on the ground. His eyesight was weak and his stick or his foot seemed always to be colliding with something, or getting entangled in it. It could be a dead rabbit, or a dead cat, or a stone, or a pebble which he would strike away from the door with a sweep of his stick. Sometimes his foot got entangled in his caftan as he stepped over the threshold of his house, making him falter, or his shoe would land on a clod of manure, or the droppings which a dog had left in front of the door since the night before. The rosary would sway furiously in his hand as he heaped curses over dogs and people alike.

But this time his foot collided with a body that was neither that of a dead rabbit, nor of a dead cat. It was moving, and alive, and also much bigger. He was seized with fright thinking it could be a spirit, or an elf of the night. But a moment later he heard a faint moaning, and when he looked down at the ground despite his dimmed eyesight, he could discern what looked like a rosy face, two eyes with tears at the fringes of the closed lashes, and an open mouth with lips which trembled slightly, as it breathed in air with a gasping sound.

For a moment he stood stock still not daring to move. Could it be that Allah had responded to his prayers? Had the amulet of Haj Ismail at last produced its magic effect? This child seemed as though it had fallen from the night sky right in front of his door, just as Christ had come down from on high to where the Virgin Mary had lain down to rest under a tree.

His lips opened to emit a faint choking sound. Nothing was beyond the power of Allah, praised be His name, and clamoured to the high heavens. He continued to stand as still as a statue. His long, narrow face looked even longer than usual, but now it started to show up more distinctly as the pale light of dawn touched it. His eyes were slightly misty, and over one of them was a white spot which shone mysteriously. The yellow beads of his rosary were worn away where his fingers had rubbed against them during the endless hours of a lifetime spent in worship and prayer. But now, maybe for the first time during his waking hours, the beads had ceased to go round.

At that precise moment of the new day the Chief of the Village Guard had ended his night vigil and was on his way home. He came upon the figure of Sheikh Hamzawi standing motionless in front of his door. He had never seen him standing like that before, nor ever seen his face look so long and drawn. It was as though he now had two faces. The upper one was that of Sheikh Hamzawi, whereas the lower face bore no resemblance to him at all, nor to any other face he had seen in Kafr El Teen, nor for that matter, in the whole wide world, although he had not seen much of what was outside Kafr El Teen. It resembled neither the face of a human being, nor that of a spirit. For all he knew it could have been the face of a devil, or that of a saint, or even the face of God himself, except that he knew not what the face of God looked like, since it was not a face that he had seen.

He halted suddenly, and stood there as though turned to stone. His eyes were fixed on the strange ghostlike form the like of which he had never set his eyes on before. For it was not like man, or saint, or devil, or any other of the many creations of God. He saw it bend and lift something that lay at its feet. He felt his fingers close tightly around the huge stick he carried around with the instinctive movement of the village guard. He was on the point of lifting it high up in the air to bring it down with all his might on the head bending low over the ground. But at that very moment he caught sight of a rosy face with traces of tears peeping through the closed eyes, and he heard Sheikh Hamzawi's voice intone, 'Without God we are indeed hapless for without Him we can do nothing.'

'What is this, Sheikh Hamzawi?' exclaimed the Chief of the Village Guard in a loud voice.

'An angel from heaven,' muttered Sheikh Hamzawi.

'And why could it not be a devil, son of a devil?' said the Chief of the Village Guard.

Still almost unaware of what was going on, Sheikh Hamzawi replied, 'It's a gift from Allah.'

Before he had time to finish his sentence, Fatheya had poked her head through the door. 'Say not what you are saying, Sheikh Zahran,' she said in a voice full of anger. 'It is a gift, a blessing from Allah. Only that which is sinful should be condemned.'

She stretched out her arms and rapidly snatched the child from Sheikh Hamzawi who was still standing in the same place, looking as though he did not know what was going on. She closed the door holding the child closely to her bosom. She could feel her breasts tingle as the blood flowed through them, like tiny ants moving deeply in her flesh. She pulled her breast out through the open neck of her garment and pressed the nipple, letting white drops of milk ooze out of the little dark opening. She wrapped her shawl carefully around the head of the baby, before slipping her nipple into its greedy, gasping mouth.

5

The voice of Sheikh Hamzawi soared into the air as the almost invisible glimmer of dawn crept through the sky. It floated over the low mud huts, pierced through the dark walls, dropped down into the narrow winding lanes blocked with scattered mounds of manure, to reach the ears of the Chief of the Village Guard who was now sitting in his house. But this time he had not undressed as he was in the habit of doing the moment he got back from his long night vigil. Nor did he ask his wife to bring him something to eat. He did not even take off his leather boots with the usual quick movement followed by two successive kicks which sent them flying into a corner of the room, as though he was ridding himself of a heavy chain wound around his feet.

He reclined on the mat, his eyes wide open, staring at nothing, his boots securely attached round his ankles. His fingers kept pulling at his long thick whiskers as he was wont to do when he had come upon a dead body lying in some field, or on the river bank, but did not yet know who was the killer, or when a crime had been committed behind his back without his knowing right from the start how the whole thing had been planned.

When the voice of Sheikh Hamzawi went through the village to where he sat, he turned his head and looked at his wife. His lips parted slightly as though he was about to tell her that something important had happened in Kafr El Teen that night. But his wife was quicker to it this time. 'Nefissa, Kafrawi's daughter, has run away,' she said, pronouncing the sentence quickly, almost in one breath, with a jerk of her hand which resembled the kick her husband gave with his foot when he wanted to rid himself of his heavy boots. The news had been whispered to her by one of her neighbours the night before. She spent the long, dark hours tossing and turning on her bed. It seemed to weigh down on her chest with a palpable mass of its own. It oppressed her, and yet carried with it an obscure pleasure, like being pregnant and waiting for the dawn in eager anticipation, for the moment when she could shift this weight to someone else, and enjoy the thrill of telling her man the news that Nefissa had fled before he was told about it by anyone apart from herself.

The name Nefissa rang with a strange sound in the ears of Sheikh Zahran. The image of a small, rosy face with closed eyes and still wet tears around the lids floated in space. For a moment the closed lids opened wide, and he looked into the girl's big black eyes – as they stared straight ahead at something on the distant horizon. His fingers let go of his whiskers, and he gave a sudden gasp like a drowning man when he comes to the surface. His voice rang out.

'Nefissa?'

'Yes, Nefissa,' she said.

Fatheya still sat huddled up close to the wall, with the baby held close to her chest. Its head was swathed in her dark veil, and its lips suckled at the nipple of her breast. If she had not kept her ear to the wall she might not have heard it vibrate with the name Nefissa. She gave a sudden gasp of relief like a drowning woman who unexpectedly finds herself at the surface.

'Nefissa?'

The name Nefissa echoed in the dark rooms, pierced through the walls of mud, crept through the lanes blocked with piles of manure, rose into the air over the low irregular roofs covered in cakes of dung and cotton sticks, higher and higher over the minaret of the mosque and the crescent at its top. Before long it was pounding at the high brick walls and the iron door of the Mayor's house. It resounded in his ears like the summons to prayer tolled out five times a day by Sheikh Hamzawi from the highest point in the village of Kafr El Teen, lying like some dark fungus by the waters of the Nile.

Seated next to the Mayor was his youngest son Tariq. He had just entered college and had come down to the village for his holidays. As he listened to her story his eyes shone with the glint which can be seen in the eyes of a youth barely nineteen when he thinks of a woman's body, with the relief which can come from images and words when the act itself is forbidden. His voice was husky when he said, 'Last week in college we discovered a child in the water closet. And the week before we caught a couple kissing in an empty lecture room. Now here in Kafr El Teen a girl gives birth to her child, abandons it in front of the house of the village Sheikh, and runs away. Girls have no morals these days, father.'

'Yes, son, you are quite right,' the Mayor answered. 'Girls and women have lost all morality.' He accompanied his words with a quick sidelong glance which lingered for a moment on the bare thighs of his wife showing beneath her tight skirt. She crossed one leg over the other with a barely contained irritation, and commented heatedly, 'Why not admit that it's men who no longer have any morals?'

The Mayor laughed. 'There's nothing new to that. Men have always been immoral. But now the women are throwing virtue overboard, and that will lead to a real catastrophe.'

'Why a catastrophe? Why not equality, or justice?'

The son shook his long-haired, curly head, and gave his mother a reproving look.

'No, mother, I don't agree with you when you talk of equality. Girls are not the same as boys. The most precious thing they possess is their virtue.'

The Mayor's wife burst into soft peals of sarcastic, slightly snorting laughter evocative of the more vulgar mirth that could be expressed by the lady patron of a brothel if she had been involved in the conversation. She raised one eyebrow and said, 'Is that so, Master Tariq. Now you are putting on a Sheikh's turban and talking of virtue. Where was your virtue hiding last week when you stole a ten pound note from my handbag, and went to visit that woman with whose house I have now become quite familiar? Where was your virtue last year when you assaulted Saadia, the servant, and obliged me to throw her out in order to avoid a scandal? And where does your virtue disappear to every time you pounce on one of the servant girls in our house? Matters have gone so far that I have now decided to employ only menservants. Pray tell me what happens to your virtue when you are so occupied pursuing the girls on the telephone, or across windows, or standing on our balconies, or don't you know that our neighbours in Maadi have complained to me several times?'

She directed her words to her son, but kept throwing looks of barely disguised anger towards the Mayor. The rigid features of his face convinced the boy that the usual quarrel was about to break out between them, so he quickly switched back to the story of Nefissa.

'Father, do you think Sheikh Hamzawi will adopt the child?'

'It looks as though he intends to do so,' said the Mayor. 'He's a good man and has no children. His wife has been wanting to have a baby for years.'

'Then the problem is solved,' said the son with an air of finality.

'It's not solved at all. These peasants never calm down unless they wreak vengeance on whoever is the cause,' chimed in the mother.

After this parting shot she stood up and went off to her room. The son did not notice the small muscle which had started to quiver below his father's mouth. He pretended he was scratching his chin or playing with an old pimple in order to hide its nervous twitch. His blue eyes wandered away, as though his thoughts had become occupied with something else. After a prolonged silence he said, 'I wonder who the man could be? And whether he's from Kafr El Teen? Which he most probably is. However, he might easily have come from somewhere else.'

'People like Nefissa know nothing outside Kafr El Teen,' commented the boy.

'Why do you say that?'

'Well, you know these peasant girls. They're so simple.'

'I don't think Nefissa was that simple. I've never seen a girl whose look was so brazen.'

'Yes, she was a rather forward girl, and the man must have been pretty rash himself.'

The Mayor said hastily, 'That's why I'm inclined to think that he's not from Kafr El Teen. I know all the men here, and I don't think there's a single one of them who has any guts, let alone the guts to do a thing like that. Don't you agree with me, Tariq?'

Tariq was silent for a moment. The faces of the men he knew in Kafr El Teen started to parade before his eyes. He heard his father say, 'Could you guess who it might be?'

The faces continued to float along before his eyes. Suddenly a face stood out in front, absolutely immobile. Or perhaps it was his eyes which had singled out this face from among the many faces that went by. He examined its features with growing curiosity. And a voice within him began to say 'Elwau.' He did not know why in the midst of all the faces he had seen at one time or another, this face in particular imposed itself upon him. He had never seen Elwau and Nefissa together. Elwau dwelt at the eastern outskirts of the village, whereas Nefissa lived near the opposite limits on the west. But no sooner did he try to think seriously of a man who could plausibly be linked to Nefissa's life than the face of Elwau surged up from somewhere inside his mind. He had never met him face-to-face except once. Now and again he would glimpse him at a distance walking along with his hoe on his shoulder. He was always silent, never spoke to anyone, or turned his head to look at a shop, or a house. Nor was he ever the first to call out a greeting to those whom he crossed on his way, even if it was the Chief of the Village Guard, or the Sheikh of the mosque, or even the Mayor himself.

No one could say that he had been seen with Nefissa or with any other of the women of Kafr El Teen. But every day he could be seen ploughing his field, or digging the soil with his hoe. Even on Fridays, when everybody went to the mosque, to stand behind Sheikh Hamzawi while he led the village in prayer, he would be at work in the field. After sunset he sat on the bank of the river watching its waters flow by, or gazing at the trees standing erect against the horizon. If somebody passed by, he did not look round, and if a person proffered him the usual greeting, his quiet voice rang out in the silence with the words of Salam, but his body continued to sit immobile.

The lips of the boy's mouth moved slightly to pronounce the name Elwau. Yet if anyone had happened to ask him why of all the names he knew in the village that of Elwau in particular had occurred to him at the time, it is doubtful if he could have been able to find an answer. He had met him face-to-face only once. But that one time, it seems, must have been enough for him to see his eyes. And to see his eyes must have been enough for him to realize that they were not the same as the other men's eyes. They were not fixed on the ground, but looked straight ahead of him with the expression of pride, which could also be seen in Nefissa's eyes. He remembered that day now. In what was probably no more than the fraction of a second was born in his mind a link, nay, an unforgettable tie, between what he had seen in their eyes. He could not define what it was exactly, but he knew without a doubt that it was there, deep inside. And it remained with him long after the memory of his encounters with them had sunk into the dark, forgotten recesses of his mind.

But the moment the face of Elwau emerged before his eyes he understood how certain things could never fade away, never die, even if they were no bigger than a drop of water in the ocean, or lasted no longer than a short moment in the infinity of time. So when his father repeated the question he heard a voice within him say 'Elwau.'

And his eyes opened wide with surprise when his father reiterated, 'Elwau?' for he had not yet had the time to open his lips and pronounce the name 'Elwau' or at least so it seemed to him, as he sat there turning things over in his mind. Yet as soon as his father echoed the name, the face he had seen only once before emerged from dark into light, changed from a hazy memory, to a reality in life. His voice rose up from his depths and vibrated with an audible sound in the air outside.

'Elwau?!' it said.

The Mayor pronounced the name again as though to ensure that this time it was transformed into indelible fact.

'Elwau,' he said.

The iron gate opened wide to let in three men. Sheikh Hamzawi, Sheikh Zahran, and Haj Ismail. They filed in, one behind the other, and walked up to where the Mayor sat. No one knows whether they heard him pronounce the name of the man, but they repeated in one breath, 'Elwau.' Their voices echoed in the yard around the house, climbed over the high wall of red brick, cut into the dark mud huts to be repeated in the households before they lighted the kerosene lamps, leapt over the roofs and dropped into the twisting lanes and alleys, creeping along everywhere before the sun had yet had the time to set and light the other side of the earth's globe.

Tariq leaned over the balustrade. Below the terrace the waters of the Nile were crimson red. He watched the sun drop below the distant horizon, and the children playing on the river bank. He could hear them chanting as they wove a ragged line and danced and clapped.

Camel driver, camel driver,
It's Nefissa and Elwau
Nefissa, Nefissa, Elwau is in the basket
Elwau, Elwau, Nefissa is in the field
Camel driver, camel driver
It's Nefissa and Elwau...

His eyes opened wide in amazement, as though he could hardly believe his ears. He turned to his mother who was standing by his side, and almost breathless with surprise, asked in a halting voice, 'Mother, is it really Elwau?'

'How should I know?' she replied in a voice full of irritation. 'Why don't you ask your father, the Mayor?'

6

It was a Friday; the burning disc of the sun like a ball of fire in the centre of the sky, glared down on Kafrawi's head. His eyes seemed to be bathed in the red colour of the sun's rays, and the sweat poured out of him from every pore, streaming down his head, his neck, his chest, his belly and his thighs. He could feel it warm and sticky as it slid over his thighs to his legs, down to the cracked, horny skin of his bare feet. He felt wet as though he had urinated on himself. He slipped his hand under his *galabeya* and touched himself. He could not tell the difference between the feel of his sweat and his urine, nor could he sense whether his muscles were relaxed, or contracted, still or moving. All he knew was that he seemed to have lost all control over his arms and his legs. His body had become a separate part of him, a huge muscle which contracted or relaxed of its own accord, moved or kept still as he stood there watching it, so that he could hardly believe what was happening under his own eyes to this body of his which had always been a part of him. It was as though his soul had left his body and hovered at a distance, or as though another soul which was not his had slipped into his body.

When he saw his bare feet covered in their dry, cracked skin walk out of the field, he wondered at what was happening with amazement. How could his legs walk out of the field like this on their own? He tried to muster enough strength in order to stop them, and for a moment he thought he had succeeded, but they continued to stride slowly out of the field, and out of his control to the only place where the burning rays of the sun could not reach him at that time of the day – to the stable.

It was not really a stable. It was just a shed made of bamboo cane, palm tree fronds and maize stalks, plastered over with mud to form four walls and a roof. The buffalo would lie under it during the summer days and during the winter Kafrawi would spend some of his nights sheltered by its walls.

The buffalo was lying on her belly as she usually did when the weather was hot. Her large, brooding eyes gazed at the dark mud wall, and her jaws moved slowly churning something invisible over and over again, while fine white bubbles of saliva kept coming and going at the corners of her mouth every time she breathed out or in.

Kafrawi's body dropped down on the ground close to where she lay. His eyes fastened themselves on something with the same silent, brooding look. He tried to contract the muscles of his lids and close his eyes in an attempt at sleep. But they remained wide open, continuing to stare fixedly at the dark wall of mud. The buffalo looked at him. Her big eyes were covered in a film of moisture, like tears that had not yet formed. She stretched out her neck coming so close that their heads touched. Then she started to wipe her lips up against his neck like a mother fondling her child. It seemed as though she was trying to say something to him, to ask him what was wrong. He rested his head on hers, wiped his wet eyes over her face, and brought his parched lips close up to her ear. He whispered, 'O, Aziza, Nefissa is no longer here. She has run away.'

And so Kafrawi started to speak to the buffalo, to tell her what had happened. She seemed to answer him, and somehow he could understand what she said. For ever since he had opened his eyes and taken his first look at the world around him, the buffalo had been somewhere close by, either in the field or in the house. Before he learnt to walk, or to pronounce his first words he could see her looking at him with her big, silent eyes as he stood alone in some dark corner crying bitterly as only children know how to cry.

When he began to crawl on his belly over the ground, the first thing he started to do was to crawl in her direction. He could feel her touch his face with her smooth lips. Somehow she could tell when his lips were parched and dry. She would move gradually towards him until her nipple was close to his mouth, and when he opened his eyes he could see the swollen udder with the black nipple hanging down. The smell of her milk floated around him, made him stretch his neck and close his lips over it tightly, and almost immediately he would feel the warm flow of milk in his mouth.

As soon as he could pronounce a few words he called out to her. He named her Aziza, and whenever she heard the name she would turn her head towards him, and her eyes would say 'Yes, Kafrawi.' Every day he pronounced a new word, and she answered with a look in her eyes which said something different each time. Gradually they learnt to understand one another's language. One

day she complained to him that his father had beaten her with a
stick several times as she went round and round tied to the yoke
of the water-wheel. That day he experienced a feeling of hatred
for his father, and refused to eat with him. His father tried to force
him to eat by beating him with the same stick, but he refused
obstinately and went to bed without supper.

When his daughter Nefissa was still a small child she used to
wonder at the way he would talk to the buffalo. 'A buffalo can talk
and understand just as we do,' he said to her many a time. Nefissa
herself had not yet learnt how to speak, but she too seemed to
understand what he was saying to her, and she would assure him
with a look of her big, black, knowing eyes. She nodded her head
and laughed, and sometimes would even stretch out her small
hand and try to play with his whiskers. He opened his mouth,
closed his lips over her smooth little fingers, and pretended to
bite. She gurgled with laughter whenever he did this, and quickly
pulled her hand away. But one day he really bit her finger with his
teeth, as though he was about to eat it up. She screamed with pain,
and backed away from him in fright. And from then on she started
to be afraid of him sometimes, especially when for one reason or
another his face would suddenly turn dark and forbidding, and
begin to look like that of the buffalo. The face of the buffalo could
put fear in her heart also, just as did the face of Kafrawi. She often
played with her and pulled her tail, but all of a sudden a change
would come over her, very much like the change which came over
her father's face. Then her features no longer looked calm and
resigned, but dark and angry. Her big eyes would be filled with
a look which was very frightening, and at any moment she was

capable of lashing out with her hoof, or butting at her with the head. On one occasion she even bit her badly on the leg.

Kafrawi rubbed his forehead against the full udder of the buffalo, opened his parched lips, and took the black nipple into his mouth. He could feel the warm milk flowing down to his stomach. His lids became relaxed, and dropped softly over his eyes. But the milk continued to flow further down to the lower part of his belly, and the upper part of his thighs. He felt something fill up, become swollen and erect, like a strange organ which was not a part of his body. He pressed on it with the palm of his hand, trying to push it back, but it refused to yield. He watched it get out, breaking through the limits of his body and his will, like a part of him over which he had lost control. Slowly it crept over the soft udder, breathing in the smell of female, lapping up the familiar wetness, slid up into the inner warmth and was lost in a great stillness, like an eternity, like death. After a while it tried to slip out into the fresh air again where it could breathe more freely, but the hole closed itself closely about it, like strong fingers intent on choking it to death. It fought for its life, jerked with the mad spasm of an animal caught in a trap, erupted itself of all capacity to fight and collapsed, like tired eyelids on tired eyes surrendering to the deepest of sleeps.

But a few moments later he opened his eyes again to the sound of a terrifying voice screaming out. The voice was not that of anyone human, whether man or woman. Nor was it the voice of some animal being beaten. It was a strange and fearful shriek.

He had heard it once before, a very long time ago. At the time he was lying on his belly on a dusty floor, with his mother squatting beside him. She was passing white flour through a fine sieve, but her eyes were fastened on him in a big black stare which neither blinked nor shifted elsewhere. He could feel them move over his features like the caress of a soft hand. Suddenly he heard the scream. He did not recognize his mother's voice in the awful shriek which rent the air. But his eyes were drawn to her unawares. Scattered all around her and covering her hands, and her face and her hair was a fine powder now spread out in a crimson layer. Her eyes were still wide open, fastened to him with the same fixed stare, but somehow their look was no longer the same, no longer had the expression which he knew so well. These were the eyes of someone else. His mother must have gone out through the open door and would be back any moment. He turned his head towards the door. He glimpsed two narrow, slit-like eyes which he had never seen before. They fixed him with a frightening stare. He bent his head, closed his eyes and dozed off for a while. But he was not really asleep, for he felt two arms lift him up from the ground and carry him away. He thought of opening his eyes to take a look around but he was afraid of meeting the terrible stare of the slit-like eyes, so he left himself to be carried by the two big arms. His face was pushed up against a hard, board-like chest from which emanated a strange odour. His small bare feet dangled down in the air, and swayed from side to side in rhythm with the long camel-like strides of the unknown creature that had snatched him from the ground, and was carrying him far away.

The scream rent the air a second time. He jumped up from where he lay, and without thinking ran towards the spot from which he heard the scream. It seemed to come from the middle of the field of maize, and to have been followed by a slight movement of the stalks around it. But now everything looked as still and as calm as it always had been, and the silence weighed heavily on the earth like the burning red rays of the sun throttling the slightest movement of the air before it even had a chance to stir.

As he came nearer, the field of maize split open suddenly at the same place. In the gap he saw two narrow, slit-like eyes appear for an instant, only to disappear a moment later. They vanished immediately as though the earth had opened to let them through, then quickly pulled them back into its depths, before he had the time to register what he had seen.

He thought he was dreaming. He watched his bare feet with the dark, cracked skin covering their heels walk slowly towards the spot in the middle of the field. His body shivered with some ancient, dark fear buried inside him. He tried to stop his feet, and for a moment it seemed as though they had come to a halt, and were no longer advancing across the field. But he soon realized that they continued to go forward at a steady pace, neither fast nor slow as though driven by a quiet, almost instinctive resolve to discover the unknown hidden somewhere ahead.

He pushed the maize stalks aside with his arms, and saw the body lying on the ground. All around it was a red-stained layer of dust and the wide-open staring eyes brought back a distant image of his mother lying dead on the ground. He put his hands around the face and moved it closer up, so that he could see her better. But the head was shaven like that of a man and she wore a man's *galabeya* around her body. When he looked into her eyes, he felt they were not the eyes of his mother, nor of any human being he had seen in his life. The sight of these strange eyes made him step back in a movement of fright, but before he could cover his face with his hands, and block out the sight, he felt a pair of strong hands clamp down on his back. A babble of hoarse voices interspersed with ugly shouts resounded in his ears. He turned round, and the noise increased. The faces crowded around him, and their eyes were staring, but some time passed before he was able to recognize the narrow, slit-like eyes of the Chief of the Village Guard, Sheikh Zahran.

7

All things seemed to move at the same slow, heavy pace. The red disc of the sun climbed down from the sky slow, ponderous and suffocating as it moved closer and closer to the earth before letting itself drop below the edge. The dark, plodding lines of peasants with their donkeys, cows and buffalo advanced in slow exhaustion over the dusty road to spill like a sticky fluid into the lanes and alleys leading to the houses and stables plunged in a sombre twilight. From the open doorways emanated the mixed odour of fermented manure, human excreta, and dough ready for baking. Before night enveloped the earth in its thick cloak all movement had ceased on the bank of the river, and neither man nor animal could any longer be seen on it. But the five-toed imprints of human feet, the flat rounded hoofs of donkeys, cows and buffalo could still be followed over the dusty trail interrupted now and then by the warm, rounded, freshly smelling clods of dung.

The body lying prostrate on the river bank however was no longer warm. The river breeze thrust against it gently, flapping over the thin, old, worn cloak, and lifting it off the cracked heels of what had once been the man Elwau.

A strong gust of wind pushed the cloak aside and uncovered the lower part of the body. Through his heavy sleep-laden lids, Haj Ismail glimpsed a long, hairy leg rising upwards to a full muscular thigh. He lifted his eyelids with an effort and awakened suddenly, as though a brick had dropped on his head, sat up with a jerk, and looked round, his eyes searching in different directions. When his right eye looked straight in front, his left eye seemed to look behind him, and when his left eye looked to the right, his right eye turned to the left. He had come into the world from his mother's womb with a squint. It was as though for him each thing was split into two, or as though one single thing became two, for while one eye was viewing what he wished to see, the other was always struggling to be free.

He stood up, walked towards the body, and tugged at the edge of the cloak to cover the naked limb. His hand touched the hairy skin, and the swollen muscles underneath. A shiver went through his body. He retreated quickly to where he had been lying propped up against the river bank with the Chief of the Village Guard sleeping soundly by his side. He curled up and tried to fall asleep again, but the hairy muscular thigh kept coming and going before his eyes. While one of his eyes stared fixedly at it in fright, the other fled beneath his lid to hide. His mind went back to a time when he was only ten. His cousin Youssef was older and stronger than him. He had arms and legs covered in hair, and the muscles of his thighs looked like a swelling under the skin. When he saw them the first time he was seized with fright, and tried to run away, but his cousin had locked the door and there was no escape. He dodged this way and that, but Youssef caught him in an iron grip holding him by the back of his neck, threw him to the ground face downwards and wrenched his *galabeya* up over his buttocks. He felt the powerful, heavy body press down on him, and his nose hit the ground so that he could hardly breathe. After a while Youssef got up, opened the door and walked away. He lay there all day without moving, and when his father called out to him from the shop, he closed his eyes and pretended to be asleep. He heard his father's footsteps approaching, and his angry voice calling out again and again. He opened his mouth to answer, but no sound came out of his lips. A moment later a heavy fist landed on his back. He jumped to his feet and meekly followed behind his father to the shop at the corner of the lane where a few old cracked shelves carried packets of tea, or spice, or tobacco, and some cakes of soap.

His father taught him how to count the piastres, put them in the drawer, and then lock it with the key. He also taught him how to weigh tobacco on the balance by putting a piece in one pan, and a small weight in the other, so that the thick iron needle remained steady in the middle, and did not sway to one side.

Before closing the shop in the evening he would seat him on a bench next to him and teach him to give injections and open the abscesses of the people who came.

After the small *Eid* his father went on a pilgrimage to the Hejaz but never came back.* He left him the shop, and a small bag with a pair of pincers for extracting teeth, verses of the Koran made into amulets, needles for injection, a razor for circumcising, and a bottle of iodine which had long since dried up.

---

* *Eid:* Festival following the Ramadan fast. *Hejaz:* Mecca.

Lying on the river bank he felt a painful headache begin to throb at the back of his head. He pulled out a handkerchief from his pocket, and tied it tightly around his head, then closed his eyes and tried to fall asleep, but just at that moment he saw a form which looked like some ghost approach the body where it lay on the river bank. He nudged the Chief of the Village Guard on the shoulder with his fist and said in a low voice, 'Sheikh Zahran.'

The Chief of the Village Guard sprang to his feet and shouted out, 'Who goes there?'

But no one answered.

He looked around carefully through his narrow, slit-like eyes but could see nothing, then started to walk in a wide circle round the dead body, shooting glances in different directions across the maize fields, or along the river bank and down its sloping side. Having failed to see anything which could hold his attention he returned to where the village barber sat cross-legged, but his eyes continued to shoot glances here and there into the night.

'What was it, Haj Ismail?' he asked.

'I could swear I saw a man, Haj Zahran.'

'Come on now! Go to sleep and leave matters in the hands of the Almighty God.'

'But I saw him come close to the body.'

'Who would think of stealing a body?' 'I tell you I saw him.'

'Could you recognize who it was?'

'No, I didn't see him well enough.'

'It must be the devil of Elwau hovering over him.'

'Devil? The only devils in this world are humans.'

He looked at the Chief of the Village Guard with one of his eyes and in a tone of feigned innocence asked, 'Was it a devil that killed Elwau?'

The Chief of the Village Guard answered quickly, 'No, it was Kafrawi.'

'Kafrawi is not capable of killing a chicken, and you know that very well,' said the village barber.

'But when it's a man's honour that's at stake, anyone can kill,' said the Chief of the Village Guard heatedly.

'You can tell that to the villagers, or to the officer who will conduct the inquest, but not to me,' said Haj Ismail. 'I see that this time you want to kill two birds with one stone. But speaking seriously, who is the killer this time?'

The Chief of the Village Guard gave a sharp laugh and then yawningly said, 'Allah alone knows.'

Haj Ismail looked at him again with one eye. 'You know them all without exception, and can name any one of them.'

This time it was the turn of Sheikh Zahran to put on an innocent air. 'Now who can you be referring to, Haj Ismail?' he said.

The village barber chuckled in a knowing way. 'Whoever it is, the officer will be coming in the morning with the police dogs.'

'Do you think dogs know better than human beings?' asked the Chief of the Village Guard sarcastically. 'Everyone says that Kafrawi killed Elwau because of Nefissa. As a matter of fact, quite a number of people saw him kneeling next to his body with blood on his hands. He is steeped in this crime from the top of his head to the bottom of his heels.'

The village barber chuckled again. 'You are really the son of a devil, Sheikh Zahran.'

'I am the obedient servant of him who gives us our orders.' He yawned indifferently. 'In fact, all of us are his obedient servants.'

'All of us serve God.'

'What matters is that we are all servants. No matter how high we rise, or how low we fall, the truth is that we are all slaves, serving someone.'

'We are God's slaves when it's time to say our prayers only. But we are the Mayor's slaves all the time.'

Sheikh Zahran's eyes shone as he whispered in the ear of the village barber.

'Do you know that he does not sleep the night because of Zeinab? I have done my best to convince her but she still refuses.'

'Kafrawi must be encouraging her to refuse. Do you think he has started to become suspicious?' queried the village barber.

The Chief of the Village Guard hastened to refute this possibility.

'No, absolutely not. Suspicion requires that a man be endowed with a brain that can think. But these peasants! They have no brain, and when they do have one, it's like the brain of a buffalo. The problem is that after Nefissa left, Kafrawi has no one to help in the house, or work in the fields except Zeinab. I've been telling him all the time that the Mayor will give him ten whole pounds for her work, that she will eat and drink in his house, and live in the kind of comfort she could never ever dream of. All she will have to do is sweep and clean the house, and she can go home at the end of the day's work. But he won't listen to me. His head is harder than stone.'

'His daughter Zeinab is just as pig-headed as he is. I've done all I can to convince her, explained everything to her in detail, but she's like a mule,' said Haj Ismail. 'I can't see any advantages to her. There's not a girl in Kafr El Teen who has not got more manners and more beauty than she has.'

Sheikh Zahran lowered his voice. 'He's got strange tastes where women are concerned, and if he likes a woman he can't forget her. You know he's pretty obstinate himself. Once he sets his eyes on a woman he must have her, come what may.'

Haj Ismail opened his mouth in a big, prolonged yawn. 'Why not? People like him who live on top of the world, don't know the word impossible.'

'They walk over the earth like Gods.'

'No, Sheikh Zahran, they're Gods all right but they don't walk, they ride in cars. Walking is for people like us.'

'Walking only? You seem to forget that we also sleep on the ground.'

The Chief of the Village Guard curled himself up under his cloak and closed his eyes. Haj Ismail threw a last quick look at the body lying on the river bank before curling up under his cloak in turn. He murmured in a low voice, 'What a shame. Elwau was really too young to die.'

The Chief of the Village Guard heard him and sighed. 'Our lives are in God's hands, Haj Ismail.'

'Yes verily, that's true. It's Allah alone who decides when it's time for us to leave this earth.'

And so they went to sleep with the firm knowledge that the life of people in Kafr El Teen depended on one God ever-present in their minds. They spent many an evening talking to him in front of the village barber's shop, or on the terrace of his house overlooking the Nile. They knew that he burned with such a desire for Zeinab that only death could put an end to it. Sooner or later he was going to lay his hands on her, for like all Gods he believed that the impossible did not exist.

The noise of their snoring rose into the night from under the bank of the river where they had sought shelter. It travelled through the silent night to reach the ears of Metwalli as he lay hidden between the stalks of maize. He emerged out of the field and went straight towards the body. He advanced with wary steps, leaning on his right leg more heavily than he did on the left.

He had a characteristic way of walking, well-known by the inhabitants of Kafr El Teen, very much like a limping dog. An old childhood affliction of the bones had left him with one leg shorter than the other.

He emerged over the top of the river bank. The light of the moon shone down on him revealing a head which looked big compared with the body. His small eyes were buried in a swollen face, and his thick lips protruded under a thin nose. His lower lip hung down towards his chin, revealing its inner smooth belly, and his saliva drooled continuously over it on to the long beard.

If the children of the village had spotted him at this moment, they would have followed behind him shouting out in unison, 'Here goes the idiot.' One of them might even have thrown a stone at him, or pulled him by the edge of his *galabeya*. But he would have continued to walk, paying no attention to them, with the saliva streaming down from his mouth on to his chest, as he moved on, panting and limping like a stray dog. People would meet him moving through the lanes, his wet eyes gazing at the houses and the passers-by with a dull, unseeing look, his thick lips open and drooling the spit of his mouth as he went along. At the end of each day he could be seen sitting near the cemetery at the far end of the river bank, scratching his head and his body, or holding the lice between his fingers before he cracked them under his nails.

If one of the village women passed him by, she would throw him half a loaf of bread, or a corn cob, or a mulberry fruit, aiming it at his open lap. Sometimes she would touch him and say, 'Give me your blessings, Sheikh Metwalli.' Then he would stop scratching, or cracking his lice for a moment, stretch out his hand to her, and take hold of whatever part of her body his fingers happened to touch whether it be her shoulder, her hand, her leg, or any other part, squeeze it, and mutter a few unintelligible words as the white flow of saliva meandered down over his black beard.

It was said that a woman afflicted with paralysis had touched him and been cured, and that he had helped a blind man to regain his sight. He had been chosen by God, knew about sickness, and could penetrate the secrets of the future. Allah had bestowed his powers on him since Allah chose the weakest of all His creatures for His purposes. And so they called him Sheikh Metwalli.

But Haj Ismail, the village barber, chose to describe him as 'the possessed one'; Sheikh Zahran, the Chief of the Village Guard, named him 'the lousy one'; and the children addressed him as 'Metwalli the idiot.' As far as he was concerned, he was Metwalli, the son of Sheikh Osman, who used to recite verses of the Koran over the souls of the deceased buried in the cemetery. But Sheikh Osman was now dead, and all he had bequeathed him was his torn caftan, his turban, a bread basket empty of bread, and an old Koran with half its cover torn off.

Now he was advancing with much less of a limp than he put on when people were around. His eyes had a steady gaze which no one had seen in them before, and every now and then he turned round cautiously. His lower lip no longer hung down over his chin, and the saliva had ceased to flow out of his mouth. Any of the inhabitants of the village seeing him at this moment would not have recognized him.

He was moving towards the body where it lay on the river bank, covered with a cloak. Within a short distance of it, he dropped on his belly and started to crawl over the ground. Reaching the feet, he lifted the cloak, poked his head in underneath, and drew his body slowly up over the legs and thighs.

If the Chief of the Village Guard had happened to open his eyes at that moment, he would not have noticed any change. The cloak still covered the body in the same way. There might have been a very slight movement which rose and fell like some imperceptible wave, but it seemed to be more like a movement of the air than of anything else. Besides no other possibility would have occurred to the Chief of the Village Guard, nor to any man or woman of blood and flesh, or even to one of the devilish spirits that roam around in many places, especially those chosen by the living for the dead. For after all, what was lying on the river bank was no more than a body from which all life had fled, and who apart from the worms which burrow into everything could be interested in the dead?

But Metwalli had lived among the dead year after year, like any worm. Every day he would squat in his usual place at the far end of the village, on the river bank, waiting until the sun had dropped into some deep recess. Then he stood up, descended the slope of the river bank with his limping gait, and walked slowly in the direction of the cemetery to seek his bed among the dead. But once arrived there, before lying down to rest, he wandered between the rows of graves, bending down every now and then to pick up a piece of pastry or bread left by some relative of one of the dead. Even after he had eaten, he remained awake for some time, as though turning something over in his mind before he slept. Then suddenly he stood up again, and walked straight to one of the graves, guided in the dark by a certain smell which he knew so well that he could distinguish it even at a distance, and even if surrounded by other smells. It was the smell of new buried flesh, of warm blood and cells which still lived although the body was dead.

He dug the ground feverishly with his strong wiry fingers, as sharp and as cutting as those of a cat, searching for a piece of meat buried in the ground. With hands trained by this oft-repeated exercise he tore away the shroud of white cloth, rolled it up tightly into a spherical mass, and buried it in a hole dug in the ground. He covered it with earth and left it until he would return to dig it up in the early hours of the next morning while people still slept.

Once over with this task, he turned his attention to the still warm body of the dead. If it was that of a female, he would crawl over it until his face was near the chin. But if the body was male, he turned it over on its face, then crawled over it until the lower part of his belly pressed down on the buttocks from behind.

In the morning Metwalli would disappear from Kafr El Teen. No one troubled to look for him, or to wonder where he could be. But some distance away at Ramla or Bauhout he sat on the pavement of a crowded street, right in the middle of the weekly market bargaining over the sale of some yards of dusty white sheeting which no one knew had served a few hours earlier as a shroud for some dead body buried quite recently in the cemetery of Kafr El Teen.

8

The car entered the village preceded by its high-pitched horn, and followed by a storm of dust, a swarm of children and some stray dogs. Out of it stepped some gentlemen, one of whom was followed by a male nurse carrying a bag, and the second by a policeman holding back a dog which kept tugging at its leash. A group of men were busy walking up and down trying to push the people standing around as far back as they could, or lashing out at the buttocks of the children with their canes.

The whole village of Kafr El Teen had gathered on the bank of the river. The men wore *galabeyas* and each held a stick. The women had wrapped themselves in black shawls. The children were surrounded by clouds of flies, and exhibited bare buttocks and running noses. Everyone was there. Only three people were missing. Zakeya sat squatting as usual in the dusty entrance to her house, with Zeinab beside her. Both were silent, their angry, almost defiant eyes gazing into the lane.

Kafrawi also sat squatting but much further away on the outskirts of the village trying to hide between the maize stalks in a field. From his hiding place he could hear voices coming closer, preceded by the yapping, barking and whining of the dog. He realized that they must have found out where he was hiding, so he stepped out of the maize field and clambered up the bank of the river. Some of the children spotted him and cried out, 'Kafrawi, Kafrawi!', then started to run after him but he ran faster and arrived at the edge of the river. Before the dog tugging furiously at its leash with the policeman running behind it, had time to pounce on him he had thrown himself into the water. He did not know why he was running away, or where he was going.

He was just putting as much distance as he could between himself and something he feared, just going without knowing where to go. He did not know what had happened to him since the moment when he had been lying with the buffalo, until the moment when his body struck cold water.

He heard a splashing in the water and realized that someone was swimming rapidly towards him, getting closer and closer. He lunged out with his arms and legs, straining his sight to see the other shore as though there he would find safety and security. He had forgotten that on the other shore were the orange orchards owned by the Mayor of Kafr El Teen.

On the river bank were gathered the inhabitants of Kafr El Teen. They stood slightly in the background, and in front of them was a group composed of the officer with his dog, the Chief of the Village Guard, some of the village guards, and a few district policemen. Their eyes followed the two bodies swimming in the river, with the zeal of spectators watching a race, and wondering who of the two would be the winner. When the distance between the two swimmers increased the villagers would experience a secret feeling of joy, for they were hoping that Kafrawi would manage to escape, and that the policeman would fail to catch up with him. Instinctively they felt Kafrawi was not a killer, or a criminal. They hated the policeman and his dogs, hated all policemen, all officers, all representatives of authority and the government. It was the hidden ancient hatred of peasants for their government. They knew that in some way or another they had always been the victims, always been exploited, even if most of the time they could not understand how it was happening.

The officer was watching the scene with a cold detachment, looking at his wrist watch every now and then as though he had an important appointment, and wanted to be over with this mission as quickly as possible. The dog also did not seem to care much about what was happening. It was lying on the river bank enjoying the sunshine, the green fields and the expanses of water as though long deprived of a chance to enjoy such natural beauty. The only person who seemed nervous was the Chief of the Village Guard. Every time the distance between the two swimmers decreased, he would shout out encouragingly, 'Well done, Bayumi!'

His voice echoed in the ears of Bayumi like a clarion call, making him lunge out with his arms and legs more vigorously. Why this was so he could not himself understand. He had been assigned the task of capturing this animal, and that was all. Further than that his mind refused to go. From the moment when the order 'Arrest him' had resounded in his ears, he had launched himself in pursuit of the man like a projectile fired from a gun.

Kafrawi's naked body stepped out of the water and leapt on to the shore threading its way through the trees of the orchard.

Bayumi followed close behind, his body also naked except for the pair of baggy singlets which he still wore. He was tall, with wiry muscles, and his face, too, looked hard and narrow with sharp features which remained as rigid as cardboard. It was the face of a policeman expressing neither joy nor sadness, fear nor hope, a face without feeling carrying an expressionless expression which says nothing at all. A face without features like the palm of a hand from which you can glean no feeling or thought, because they have been suppressed for so long that nothing is left any more, or a face made of bronze, or copper like the knocker which hangs on doors, and is used to alert people in the house that there is someone outside who wants to intrude just when they feel most cosy and warm. His body too was hard and copper-like, with arms and legs which ran or swam or walked with a steady, swinging, untiring movement, so unchanging, so enduring that it could hardly be human, hardly come from a body of flesh and blood and bone, but only from a robot with metal limbs and joints.

Kafrawi saw him as he hid behind a tree. His body shook with a strange fear as though he had seen something which was neither man nor devil, neither live nor dead, some evil spirit which was not human despite its human form.

He felt this fear sweep over him like a wave of icy cold water. He could no longer follow his body, understand what it was doing, know whether it was hiding behind the orange trees or threading its way between them. For tracking him down was the frightening shadow, moving at a machine-like pace neither fast nor slow, like the hands of a clock moving steadily towards the hour of execution, so that when the steely fingers closed around his arm he felt his time had come and quietly whispered, 'Verily I do witness that there is no other God than Allah.' Then everything went black and he could no longer hear or see anything. The dark was so stock still that it seemed as though his life had come to a sudden end, and now was the moment ordained for him to go.

When he came to again, and began to hear and see once more, his eyes looked around him in great astonishment. He was squatting in a huge room crowded with people, and they kept throwing glances towards him. In front of him were three men sitting behind something high which looked like a table.

One of the three men was gesturing with his hand angrily, and fixing him with his eyes, in a menacing way. He looked around again trying to understand what was happening. Suddenly he felt a pointed finger jab into his shoulder like a nail, and a thin sharp voice pierced his ear. 'Have you not heard? Why don't you answer?'

Kafrawi opened his mouth and asked, 'Is someone speaking to me?'

The thin, sharp voice cut through the air again. 'Yes, are you asleep? Wake up, and answer His Excellency's questions.'

Kafrawi could not figure out who His Excellency could be, nor could he understand where he now was. He was certainly no longer in Kafr El Teen. He could be in another village, or even in another world. He wondered how they had carried him to this place, and how he had got here.

Suddenly he heard an angry voice say to him, 'What's your name?'

He answered, 'Kafrawi.'

The angry voice came back at him. 'Your age?'

He hesitated for a moment before saying, 'Forty or fifty.'

He heard people laugh and could not understand why they did so.

The angry voice resumed. 'You are accused of having murdered Elwau and it's better for you to admit to your crime, instead of beating about the bush.'

'Admit to what?' he asked.

'Admit to killing Elwau.'

'I did not kill him. Elwau was a good man.'

The voice said, 'Did you not hear that he was the man who assaulted your daughter, Nefissa?'

'I heard them say it was Elwau.'

'After you heard that, did you not think of killing him?'

'No.'

The voice asked, 'Why?'

'I did not think of it.'

'Is that normal for a man whose honour has been sullied?'

'I don't know,' Kafrawi answered.

The voice sounded very angry. 'Is that natural?'

'What does natural mean?'

He heard laughter again. He looked around in surprise. He could not understand why people kept laughing. It occurred to him that they might be laughing about something which had nothing to do with him.

The voice resumed its questioning. 'On that Friday, why did you stay in the fields instead of going to the mosque for prayer like all the men of the village?'

'I've stopped praying since Nefissa left.'

'Why?'

'Nefissa used to look after the buffalo while I went to pray.'

'Did you not know that, unlike the other men in the village, Elwau did not go to the mosque on Fridays?'

'Yes.'

'Did you or did you not know?'

'I knew. Everybody knew that Elwau did not go to the mosque.'

'Why?'

'I don't know why. People say that his mother's grandfather was a Copt, but Allah alone knows the reason.'

The voice asked insinuatingly, 'Did you dislike Elwau?'

'No.'

'Was it not your conviction that a man like him should have carried out the religious rites which Allah has ordained?'

Kafrawi said, 'Elwau was a good man.'

'Do you not know that prayer is a protection against sin?'

'Yes, that's what Sheikh Hamzawi used to say to us.'

'So Elwau assaulted your daughter and committed a grievous sin.'

'That's what was said.'

'And after all that happened, you insist you didn't think of killing him?'

'No, I didn't.'

'Why did you not think of killing him?' 'Elwau was a good man,' Kafrawi repeated.

The voice came back, insistent. 'Don't you care about honour? Don't you care about your honour and that of your family?'

Kafrawi was silent for a moment and then replied, 'Yes, I do.'

The voice said with a note of triumph barely veiled, 'That's why you killed Elwau.'

'But I did not kill him.'

The voice was very angry again. 'Then why were you found near the body?'

Kafrawi was silent, trying to remember, but his memory failed him. He said nothing.

The voice still sounded angry. 'Why did you run away and try to escape?'

'I was afraid of the dog.'

'Do you know why the dog picked you out from all the men in the village?'

'No. It's the dog who knows.'

He heard laughter in the room and looked around in great surprise. Why were people laughing again?

The voice was furious this time. 'Don't try to deceive me. You had better confess. Do you know what's awaiting you?'

'No,' he said.

Laughter echoed in his ears once more. His eyes expressed a puzzled amazement. After a moment he felt the steely fingers close round his arm as they led him away into a long, dark passage. He closed his eyes and muttered, 'I do testify that there is no God but Allah.'

9

Zakeya still sat on the dusty threshold with Zeinab by her side. Both of them were plunged in silence, and their eyes continued to watch the lane with an expression of angry defiance. In front of them there still rose the huge door with its iron bars. It seemed to stand there blocking the way, shutting out the bank of the river and the water which flowed beside it. From time to time the Mayor walked out, tall, broad-shouldered, surrounded by men on all sides. He walked ahead of them with his slow steady stride. In his eyes was the haughty, blue look which he raised to the skies. He never bent his head to look at the ground over which he walked, nor noticed Zakeya and Zeinab sitting on the dusty threshold of their house, thinking over something in silence, their eyes staring in front of them steadily.

Zakeya's hands rested on her lap, over her wide, black *galabeya*. They were big, and the skin on them was coarse and cracked. In her palm lay the deep imprint of the hoe which she held firmly in her clasp whenever she dug into the soil. Her nails were black, and they smelt of manure and of mud. Now and again she would lift them from her lap to hold her head, or

wipe the sticky sweat, or chase away a mosquito or a gnat. Zeinab
sat by her side, her hands busy sifting the corn from the chaff, or
kneading the dung with straw, and cutting it into round cakes like
a loaf of bread. Sometimes she would stand up, lift the earthenware
jar to her head and walk to the river bank. Her body was tall and
slender, her big, dark eyes faced straight ahead. She did not look
at passers-by, or houses on the way, or shops or sheds. Nor did she
smile at anyone, or greet a friend as the other girls or women did.
When she passed in front of Haj Ismail's shop she would hasten
her pace. She could almost feel the blue eyes singe her back.
They gazed at her fixedly, inflexibly, cruelly cutting through her
dress, feeding on the beauty of her legs, on the curving flesh, on
the fullness of her thighs and belly, on the petal-like skin and the
waist narrow and slender above her hips, on her back rising up
like a powerful stem.

She would lift her shawl to hide her face and cover her breast.
But the sharp, inflexible eyes which knew no rest, no quiet, no
tenderness, pierced through her robe as she climbed the river
bank, or descended its sloping flank, slid over her back, and round
her uncovered body to the pointed breasts which moved up and
down with every step, with the beat of her heart and the rhythm of
her breath. She advanced quickly, her eyes fixed straight ahead,
cheeks flushed with health, full lips trembling, her lithe form
wafted through the open spaces as though on air.

When she got home she would lift the earthenware jar of water
from her head, and put it on the ground, then sit down by the
side of her Aunt Zakeya still out of breath. Her heart continued
to beat fast under her ribs, her chest heaved up and down, and

the drops of sweat stood out on her forehead, for they had not yet dried, nor had they dripped down over her face to disappear over her neck.

Zakeya would stare at her silently for some time. Then her parched lips would part and in a low, tense whisper she would ask, 'What's wrong with you, my child?'

But Zeinab never answered, so Zakeya would drop into silence again for a long while before her lips opened again with the oft repeated lament.

'I wonder where you are, Galal my son. I wonder whether you are alive or dead. O God, if I knew he was dead my mind would be put at rest. And now Kafrawi has also been taken away. Who knows if he'll ever come back. O God, were not Galal and Nefissa enough? Did you have to take Kafrawi also? We no longer have anyone left, and the house is empty. Zeinab is still young and I am old. Who is going to look after the buffalo and the crops?'

Zeinab dried her sweat on her shawl and then she said, 'I have grown up now, and I will look after the buffalo, and the crops, and the house and everything else until my father comes back. Father will come back, and so will Galal, and Nefissa as well.'

'Those that go never come back, my child.'

'God knows what difficult straits we're in and He won't abandon us.'

Zakeya muttered in a low tone as though speaking to herself. 'No one is going to come back. Those who go never come back. Kafrawi too. He will not return.'

'My father will come back. You will see. He'll come back,' Zeinab said vehemently. 'He will tell them that he did not kill anyone and they will believe him. Everybody knows my father is a kind man, and could never kill anybody.'

The old woman sighed. 'People here know him. But over there, no one knows who he is. If Galal was here he would have gone with him. Galal knows the people there, and he could have helped him. But Galal is not here. He used to lend a helping hand to everyone, even to strangers, so you can imagine what it would have been like with his uncle Kafrawi.'

'May Allah come to his aid.'

'My child, Allah alone is not enough.'

Zeinab opened her big black eyes wide, and looked at her with amazement. 'God Almighty have mercy on us. God is great and helps everyone. Aunt, why don't you get up, do your ablutions, and pray God to help us.'

Zakeya raised her hands in a gesture of rebuttal. 'I have not ceased praying and begging God to help us. And yet every day our misery becomes greater, and we are afflicted with a new suffering.'

Her voice was not angry. It was distant, and calm, and as cold as ice. Zeinab's eyes opened even wider with astonishment. She was gazing up at the heavens with a strange expression in her eyes. Zeinab was seized with a dark shiver that made the hair on her body stand up. Her hands were shaking as she took hold of Zakeya's hand and held it between them.

'What's the matter, Aunt?' she asked anxiously. 'Your hand is as cold as ice.'

Zakeya did not answer. She continued to stare into space with her wide open black eyes. Zeinab's hand was still shaking as she held her shoulder and pressed it.

'What's the matter, Aunt? Please tell me what's the matter with you,' she implored.

But Zakeya still continued to stare in front of her in silence like a statue. The girl was seized with terror. She clapped her hands to her face in agony and screamed, 'My Aunt Zakeya. O God, something has happened to my Aunt Zakeya.'

Almost immediately the yard of the house was filled with the dark forms of people. They crowded through the dusty entrance of the house, and filled up the yard and the lane outside, coming between Zakeya and the huge iron gate on which she had fixed her eyes. But she could still see the big iron bars moving towards her as she lay on her belly over the ground. They came closer and closer like long iron legs which would crush her at any moment. She licked the dust with her tongue, and a sticky wetness streamed from her mouth, her nose and her eyes on to the ground. She screamed as loudly as she could to make sure that her mother would hear her, and snatch her up quickly from under the long legs of the buffalo that looked as though they would walk over her at any moment. And her mother arrived just in the nick of time to save her from being crushed. It was a strange dream which had visited her many times in her sleep. Other nights she would dream that she was standing on a hill. Suddenly her body fell from on high into the river and started to drown. But she swam with all her might, although she did not know how, and managed to reach the river bank. She was about to lift herself out of the water on to the ground when she found herself in front of a huge iron gate. She was lying on a mat with her husband Abdel Moneim on one side and her son Galal on the other. She opened her eyes to the sound of their breathing. From

behind the iron bars of a window she could see a man pushing a
hand cart filled up with calves' feet and heads, and entrails. Blood
kept dripping from the cart on to the dust. The stranger's eyes were
fixed on her as he came nearer. His long arm stretched out and tried
to pull off the anklet she wore around her leg. When he was close
enough she could see that his eyes were those of Om Saber who
now leant over her and tried to push one thigh away from the other.
Then she pulled out a razor blade from somewhere and proceeded
to cut her neck. She tried to scream, but her voice would not come
out. Then she tried to run, but her feet were nailed to the ground.
When she turned her head, she could see her son Galal sleeping
beside her. She tried to put her arm around him but he seemed to
move out of reach, and suddenly a hand caught hold of her on the
other side. She looked round to find her husband fast asleep, but
he got up at once, and started to hit her on her head, and chest.
Then he kicked her in her belly which was pregnant with child.
She tried to scream again, but her voice did not come out and when
she looked at him he had come very close and was busy tearing her
galabeya down the front till her body was exposed. She could feel
his fingers around her breast, feel them creep down to her belly and
between her thighs. His heavy body bore down upon her with all
its strength, pressing harder and harder down on her flesh, so that
the ground beneath her began to shake. When she opened her eyes
again the face of her husband Abdel Moneim had disappeared and
in its place, right in front of her was the face of her brother Kafrawi.
She screamed out as loudly as she could but no one seemed to
hear her voice. Kafrawi hid his face in the mat and wept bitterly.
She stretched out her hand to him and lifted his head, but when

she looked at his face, it was the face of her son Galal. She wiped the tears in his eyes with the palm of her hand, then washed his nose and mouth with water from the earthenware jar held up by the iron stand in the corner of the room. Around him formed a pool of water and liquid stools but after a short while the ground had started to become dry, but the dryness crept up to her son's body. It shrank rapidly before her eyes, and became the size of a small rabbit, so she dug a hole and buried him in the ground. Just at that moment her husband came back from the fields, and because he could not find his son anywhere he started to beat her again. For it was like that. Every time a son of hers died he would strike out at her blindly, and beat her up with anything he could lay his hands on. And the same thing would happen whenever she gave birth to a daughter. She had given birth to ten sons and six daughters – but the only child who had lived to grow up was Galal. All the others had died at different ages, for life was like that. One never knew when a child would die.

She looked around at the circle of staring eyes, and said in a low voice, 'Galal is the only one that grew up to live. But now he has gone and will not return. Kafrawi also is gone, and Nefissa. The house is empty, and Zeinab is young. And I am too old to be of much use. There is no longer anyone to look after the buffalo, and tend to the crops.'

She heard a chorus of voices say in one breath, 'God is great, Zakeya. Pray to Him that He send them back to you safely,' and without looking at them she replied, 'Many a time have I prayed to God, called upon Him, beseeched Him to have mercy on us, but He never seemed to hear me, or to respond.'

And the voices cried out as though with one voice, 'Have mercy on her for what she has said, O God. Have mercy on us. Thou alone art all-powerful. Without Thee we are helpless, and without strength.'

Zakeya still squatted on the ground, in the same place. She would close her eyes, then open them, then close them again. If she closed her eyes she could see the huge door, or the window with its iron bars, and the man behind it pushing a cartful of calves' feet and heads, and entrails dripping with blood. He tried to pull her by the foot, then by the leg and slaughter her with a big knife. She would open her eyes in terror, and look at the faces gathered around her. The only faces she could recognize were those of her niece Zeinab, and Om Saber, as she sat cross-legged on the ground in front of a tin pot placed over the kerosene stove. White clouds of steam smelling of incense rose up in the air, mingling with the babble of voices and of words she could not make out. She could see the gestures, and the movements of the men and women gathered around, but could not figure out what they were doing there. A group of women were circling around the steaming pot as though dancing. Their breasts and their buttocks shook up and down to the powerful beat of a drum, and the long tresses of their loose hair whirled round and round. Their mouths gaped open as they repeated the slow chant: 'O thou Sheikh whom the spirits obey, let him who carries the evil spirit within him be rid of it at once.' A group of men were shaking and shivering to the beat of the drums. They wore white turbans with a long tail that hung down behind their backs.

Om Saber kept coming and going between the crowd of men and women, her body draped in a long *melaya*.* Her body was short and skinny with flat breasts, but her buttocks were big and shook violently as she whirled amidst the throngs of dancing people. From the front she looked like a man, but seen from the back she looked like a woman. Her quick, energetic movements gave an impression of youth, but her face was wizened and old. When dancing with the men she moved her body and slapped them on the hips in exactly the same way as she did with the women. She danced and laughed, then the next moment slapped her face with her hands and shrieked in agony. When she told dirty stories it was with the same voice as she recited verses of the Koran, or incantations. No one thought badly of what she did. For the villagers of Kafr El Teen she was Om Saber, the *daya*, neither man nor woman, but an asexual being without a family, or relatives or offspring. She lived in a dark mud hut adjoining the hut of Nafoussa the dancer. It was located behind a piece of waste land, near the mosque. No one knew when she had arrived in the village, where she came from, or when she had been born. People did not even imagine she would die, for they always saw her on the move from morning till night, going

---

* A long wrap of black silk worn around the body.

from house to house, helping the women in labour, circumcising the girls or piercing holes in their ears, sprinkling salt in the house the week after a child had been born, consoling wives on the fortieth day after their husbands had died, in fact participating in every occasion for festivity or mourning. At weddings she would lead the *yoo yoos*,* paint the feet of girls and women with red henna, and on the wedding night she would tear the virgin's hymen with her finger, or conceal the fact that it was already torn by spraying the white towel on which the virgin's blood was supposed to pour with the blood of a rabbit or a hen. But when it was a time for mourning her suffering knew no bounds. She would slap her face with both hands repeatedly, scream out in agony, chant a hymn of sadness to the deceased, and wash the body if she was a female. She was always busy solving the problems of girls and women, carrying out abortions with a stalk of *mouloukheya*,† throttling the new-born baby if necessary, or leaving it to die by not tying the umbilical cord with a silk thread so that it bled to death.

All the inhabitants of Kafr El Teen knew her well. She was a part of every household, and no household could survive without her. She brought couples together in lawful matrimony, arranged marriages, found suitable husbands for the girls, and prospective brides for the men, protected the good name of families and the chastity of young females, and helped to conceal whatever could sully their honour, or cause a scandal, or result in a catastrophe, or

---

* A prolonged trilling sound meant to express joy.
† A vegetable used to make a thick, green, garlicky soup. The long, resilient stalk is used in the villages to induce abortions by pushing it into the neck of the uterus.

be looked upon as a sign of disloyalty between husbands and wives. She treated sick people with popular remedies, participated in the rites of *zar*,* danced and sang, slaughtered animals and sprayed their blood, burnt incense, and discovered the hiding places in which people had concealed things. And when it so happened that she was not engaged in any of these activities, she would carry a huge basket on her head and go around the houses selling handkerchiefs, incense, chewing gum and snuff, or telling fortunes, and reading the future in people's cups.

The sweat was pouring out of Zakeya's face as she lay prostrate on the ground, or when she squatted or stood up. She moved from one position to the other in a kind of stupor so that she could not tell in which position she was at a particular moment. All around bodies shivered, and shook, and swayed, falling to the ground and standing up again. Sweat welled out from every pore of their skin. She could tell the women from the way their breasts and their buttocks were shaking, and the men from the movement of the dark whiskers and long beards around their faces.

The sweat continued to pour out of her body in an endless stream. She kept lifting her hand to wipe it away from her brow and face, but each time her hand came away stained a deep red. For Om Saber repeatedly filled her cupped hands with the blood of a cock which she had slaughtered herself, and sprayed it over Zakeya's face and body. One of the men dipped his hand into the blood and took turns at spraying her with it. She felt his hand slip through the neck of her *galabeya*, and cover her breasts with wet sticky

---

* A form of exorcism to rid a person (usually a woman) of an evil spirit by means of a frenzied dance accompanied by incantations and verses of the Koran.

blood. After this many hands crowded in on her body, touching or pinching or squeezing parts of it and spraying more blood until she was soaking in it all over. At one moment a heavy hand moved up between her legs and covered the parts between the thighs with blood. She could not tell whether it was the hand of a woman or a man, but it pinched her roughly. She clapped her hands over her face and emitted a series of shrieks as though she had lost control of herself. She could hear the people around her chanting madly, 'O thou Sheikh whom the spirits obey, let him who bears the evil spirit within him come out with it at once.' The screaming and wailing was mingled in her ears with the beating of drums, and the stamping of feet. Everything seemed to merge into one, sweat and blood, man and woman, features of one face with features of the other, so that nothing was any longer distinguishable. She could no longer tell Om Saber's features from those of Sheikh Metwalli or the difference between Zeinab and Nafoussa the dancer. Zeinab's body seemed to have become taller, its curves were more pronounced, and it swayed and reeled like the body of Nafoussa the dancer. Her hair was undone, and its tresses swung freely in the air in exactly the same way as Nafoussa's hair had gone wild around her head. It looked longer than it had ever looked before, and jutted out in every direction. She tossed it in front of her with a sudden bending of the head, so that it covered her pointed breasts, then threw it back with an upswing of her head, and let its lower ends leap over the moving curves of her hips. Her *galabeya* had split from its tail up to her waist, and when she stamped with her foot it swung open revealing the smooth skin of her thighs and legs. Every time she struck the ground with her foot, the material

rent, and the split crept higher up. Now through the opening
one could see her breast, the lines of her belly, the frenzy of her
dancing flesh. The bodies around her swayed, and reeled, and f
ell, only to stand up again. The men and the women now joined
in one circle which went round and round. In the middle of the
circle danced Nafoussa and Sheikh Metwalli. Each time he moved
his hand, or his knee, or his foot he would touch her thigh, or
her belly, or her breast. She would catch hold of her long hair,
pull it with all her strength, and scream at the top of her voice,
'O thou Sheikh whom the spirits obey, let him who carries the
evil spirit be rid of it at once.' Sheikh Metwalli and everyone else
would join in the same chant, screaming as wildly and as loudly
as they could.

It seemed to Zakeya as though her body was now moving of
its own accord, or obeying a will of its own. She saw her feet walk
towards the circle of people who were dancing. Her body pushed
its way through among the other bodies, and started to move with
them, to shake and reel in the same way. The woollen thread with
which she tied her hair slipped off, and her hair floated down over
her face like some black cloud. She felt a hand touch her breast,
and the strong fingers sink into the flesh with a pain that was more
sharp than the bite of a snake. She opened her mouth wide and
started to scream and to wail in a continuous high-pitched lament,
as though mourning the suffering of a whole lifetime suppressed
in her body from the very first moment of her life when her father
struck her mother on the head because she had not borne him the
son he expected. It was a wail that went back, far back, to many a
moment of pain in her life. To the times when she ran behind the

donkey and the hot earth burnt the soles of her feet. To the times when she learnt to eat the salted pickles and green peppers which the peasants consume with their bread, and felt something like a slow fire deep down inside the walls of her belly. To the time when Om Saber forced her thighs apart and with her razor cut off a piece of her flesh. To the time when she developed two breasts which the menfolk would pinch when there was nobody around to prevent them. To the time when her spouse Abdel Moneim would beat her with his stick, then climb on her and bear down on her chest with all his weight. To the time when she bore him children and bled, then buried them one after the other with the dead. To the time when Galal put on his army uniform and never came back, and the time when Nefissa ran away, and the children's chorus rang out as they sang 'Nefissa and Elwau.' To the time when the car came to the village carrying the gentlemen from town and the dog, then took Kafrawi with them and left.

Her wail went back and back to such times and others she could not forget like a lament which has no end, and sees no end to all the pain in life. It seemed to be as long as the length of her life, as long as the long hours of her days and nights. It went on and on as she tugged at her hair with all her might, tore her garment to shreds, and dug her nails into the flesh of her body as though she wanted to tear herself apart. It went on and on as Om Saber continued to fill her cupped hands with the blood of the slaughtered cock, and spray it over her face, and her neck, and over her body at the front and the back.

'Scream, Zakeya!' she cried out. 'Chase the evil spirit out of your body. Scream as loud and as long as you can.'

Now they were all screaming at the top of their voices. Zakeya and Om Saber, Nafoussa and Zeinab, Sheikh Metwalli and all the men and women of Kafr El Teen who were gathered around. Their voices joined in a high-pitched wail, as long as the length of their lives, reaching back to those moments in time when they had been born, and beaten and bitten and burnt under the soles of their feet, and in the walls of their stomach, since the bitterness flowed with their bile, and death snatched their sons and their daughters, one after the other in a line.

II

But the devil refused to leave Zakeya's body. It continued to dwell within her, to ride on her back, and jump on her chest. She gasped as though out of breath when she sat up, watched him snuggle up against her chest and look at her with the eyes of Galal. She would pull out her breast from the neck of her *galabeya* and try to put her black nipple between his lips. but as soon as she tried to do that the face changed to that of her husband Abdel Moneim. She pushed it back with her hand, but when it looked at her with reproach in its eyes, the features were no longer the same as they had been a moment ago. Now it was Kafrawi's eyes that stared back at her, and filled her heart with a dark panic. A few moments later he had fled behind a door, or a window with iron bars only to return pushing a hand cart in which were piled calves' feet and heads dripping with blood. She could feel her body shrink into her *galabeya*, and would spit* quickly into its neck then call out to her niece Zeinab. Her eyes kept turning this way and that with a frightened look. When the girl arrived she would say to her, 'Zeinab, my child, do not leave me alone. I am

---

* A common gesture amongst poor women which is supposed to chase devils away.

frightened. The devils are looking at me from behind the bars of the window.'

Zeinab looked around but she could see nothing, so she would say to her aunt, 'The window has no iron bars.'

Zakeya would point her trembling fingers to the huge iron door and say, 'It's a window.'

Zeinab's eyes followed her fingers as they pointed to the huge iron gate of the Mayor's house and patted her shoulder. 'It's the door of the Mayor's house. Do not be afraid. Try to get some sleep. I will take the buffalo to the field and come back before sunset.'

Zakeya would catch hold of Zeinab's *galabeya*. 'No, Zeinab, don't leave me alone.'

'But who will go to the field? And who will feed us if I stay here by your side?'

Zakeya answered, 'Galal has taken the buffalo and gone to the field. You stay here with me. Don't leave me alone.'

Zeinab would dry her tears quickly, and say, 'Galal has not gone to the field. I must go to harvest the crop so that we can pay what we owe to the government, otherwise they will take the land away from us, and we will have to beg at people's doors.'

At that moment the voice of a man rang out reaching them across the threshold of their house. 'It's not thinkable that we would let Zakeya and Zeinab be obliged to beg at people's doors. As long as we are here alive in Kafr El Teen this will never happen.'

Zeinab turned round to find Haj Ismail standing in the doorway in front of her. One eye was looking at her, while his other eye wandered in another direction.

She said, 'Haj Ismail, I have to go to our field and, as you can see, my Aunt Zakeya is sick. She no longer eats, nor drinks, nor does she even sleep. All the time she sees things and hears voices, and it makes her very frightened.'

'Zakeya is possessed by a devil,' said Haj Ismail, 'and it will not leave her unless she listens to my advice, and does what I tell her to do.'

'I am prepared to do anything that will make my Aunt Zakeya get well again, Haj Ismail.'

He opened his old bag and extracted a long piece of paper covered with verses of the Koran. He chanted a few obscure incantations, folded the piece of paper and put it in a small dirty pouch of rough white cotton. Then he hung it around Zakeya's neck, chanting other verses and incantations. After that he muttered a few words and started to invoke the name of God and exalt His unlimited power, all the while stroking her head, her face and her chest first with the palms of his hands and then with their backs.

After finishing he wiped his face in his hands and said to Zeinab, who was now sitting close to her aunt, 'This amulet has great powers. It costs only five piastres. And now, Zeinab, listen carefully to me and do exactly what I tell you. Next Thursday, together with your aunt, you are to take the bus to Bab El Hadeed in Cairo. From Bab El Hadeed you will take the tram to Sayeda Zeinab.* There you will find people celebrating her birth anniversary, groups of people chanting hymns to her memory,

---

* A mosque built in memory of the Prophet Mohamed's daughter Zeinab. *Sayeda* is a term of respect used for women.

and many holy people. Both of you offer a prayer to her soul and join in the chanting. Repeat the names of Allah many times with those who are chanting. and spend your night in the mosque in the bosom of our holy lady. On Friday morning raise your hands to the heavens and say, "O God, O God, listen to me. My Aunt Zakeya asks forgiveness for all her sins and will never do anything to displease You. Have mercy on her, You the all merciful." Allah will lend an ear to your exhortations and a holy man will approach your Aunt Zakeya and take this amulet off her neck, then hang it on her again. While he is doing this he will enjoin her to fulfil certain things. After he has finished she is to give him a ten piastre silver coin. Then both of you should return immediately, and do what he has told you without delay. Remember his words exactly, for what he says to you will be the orders of Allah. If you do not obey, the wrath of Allah will pursue your Aunt Zakeya. and the devil will never leave her body.'

Zeinab looked at him and said in a voice which expressed deep feeling, 'May Allah give you long life, Haj Ismail. I am prepared to take my Aunt to Sayeda Zeinab, and to do anything Allah tells me to do.'

On the eve of Thursday Om Saber came to their house at night, and bathed Zakeya's body with pure water from the river Nile. Zeinab tied the corner of her shawl around the few coins some of the neighbours had collected for them to pay for the bus and tram fares, as well as the five piastres for the amulet and a silver coin of ten piastres which was the price she was supposed to pay in order to know what Allah wanted her to do. Zakeya muttered a few words as though talking to herself, 'Even

God wants us to pay Him something. Yet He knows we own nothing, my child.'

And Zeinab answered, 'Do not worry about anything, the good which Allah bestows upon people is without end, and kind people are to be found everywhere. What matters is that Allah should forgive you, and drive the evil spirit out of you.'

12

Before the crimson rays of dawn had appeared in the east, before the cock had crowed, or the voice of Sheikh Hamzawi called to prayer, the big wooden door opened creaking with the rusty sound of an ancient water-wheel. Two shadows slipped out, their heads and shoulders draped in long black shawls. Zeinab's face was drawn and pale under the first rays of dawn. She looked up at the sky with an expression of angry defiance. Moving alongside her could be seen the thin, emaciated, lined face of Zakeya, her big black eyes gleaming in the half-light.

Darkness lifted slightly and the light of dawn glimmered over the surface of the river revealing the tiny exhausted waves like wrinkles on an old, sad silent face that has resigned itself to its fate. Fitful gusts of wind blew the dust off the top of the river bank to the slope below, then further down to the lowland where the huts huddled close together, their roofs stacked with piles of dry cotton sticks, dung cakes and straw, their windows tiny holes like eyes that do not see, their doors of roughened wood, their walls made of mud and clay.

But the big house of the Mayor was quite different. Its walls

were high and built of red brick, its door rose up menacingly
black, with iron bars reaching up to the top, its windows were
made of glass and wooden frames, its roof climbed higher than the
minaret and no cotton sticks, or straw, or cakes of dung were to be
seen on it, for it was made of concrete and always kept spotlessly
clean.

They walked with their eyes fixed on the long road which lay
ahead, leaving behind them, on the dust of the bank, the imprints
of four big feet, each with five toes slightly splayed. Zeinab's
imprints were a little smaller and much clearer for in her legs was
a greater strength. They struck against her garment with a regular
flap. Her eyes gazed along the parallel stretches of water and
green crops which reached out as far as the distant horizon. To
her they seemed endless, and she wondered where Sayeda Zeinab
could be, and where she would find the bus which would carry
them to Bab El Hadeed. Zakeya had started to lose her breath.
She put her arm around her niece's shoulders, and went silently
on without a word of complaint.

At the place where the river curved they came upon a big
mulberry tree. There they found an old man and a young woman
sitting in its shade. On the ground by their side was a small basket.
Zeinab stopped and asked them about the bus. The old man said,
'Yes, my child, wait here with us. We are also going to El Sayeda.'

They sat down on the dusty ground near them, the old man's
eyes kept running between them, then he asked, 'My child, is your
mother ill?'

Zeinab answered, 'She's my aunt. My mother died many years
ago, uncle.'

'May Allah have mercy on her. All of us will die, it's our destiny. But to be sick is another thing. May Allah spare you the misery of being sick.'

Zeinab looked at the young woman sitting by his side. She noticed that her eyes were fixed on something far away, as though she was not interested in what they were saying. She asked the old man, 'Is she your daughter, uncle?'

'No, she's my wife,' he answered. 'She was in good health, but I don't know what happened to her. Almost overnight she started to refuse all food and drink, stayed awake all night, unable to sleep, and got into the habit of talking to herself. She sees things, and screams out in the middle of the night. I took her to one Sheikh after another. They gave her amulets to wear, and we arranged a *zar* for her. I spent all the money I have but nothing worked. So Sheikh Abbas advised me to take her on a pilgrimage to the Hejaz so that she could visit the house of Allah. Allah would forgive her for her sins, and drive away the evil spirit which had entered her body. But I explained to Sheikh Abbas that I was a poor man and had spent all my money on the Sheikhs. I did not have the means to pay for this journey. So he told me to take her to El Sayeda. I would exhort El Sayeda Zeinab to intervene with God on her behalf, and ask Him to forgive her sins. He advised me to take a basket of figs and offer it to El Sayeda. I swear by Allah, my child, that in order to collect the money for this journey I went from house to house begging. Then I bought this basket of figs. And here I am on my way to El Sayeda in the hope that Allah will cure her of her sickness.'

'God is great, my uncle,' said Zeinab. 'He will not abandon her.'

The old man glanced at Zakeya. She was sitting silently with her large black eyes fixed on the horizon as though she was not following what they were saying, or could not hear them. The old man asked, 'Are you taking her to El Sayeda?'

'Yes, uncle,' Zeinab replied.

'Doesn't she have a man to travel with? Don't you have anybody to look after you, my child?'

'We have no one but Allah, and a buffalo which we left behind with our neighbour, Om Soliman. She will feed it in return for the work it will do in her field.'

'God be with you both, my child. May God come to your help, and to the help of all those who need Him.'

Zeinab raised her hands to heaven and said, 'We call upon Thee to stand by our side, O God.'

The disc of the sun climbed higher in the sky. The earth got hotter and hotter, and the air was still. Zeinab rested her head against a tree trunk and closed her eyes to get some sleep, but she woke up suddenly to the noise of the bus. It came to a sudden stop nearby, raising a thick haze of dust. It was leaning heavily on one side as though the slightest touch could make it turn over. Its back was charred and exuded dense clouds of black smoke which mingled with the dust. Zakeya rested her arm on Zeinab as she climbed the steps, and the old man helped his young companion to clamber in. They managed to push their way through, to become a part of the compact mass of bodies and baskets which filled the interior of the bus. They felt themselves enveloped by the hot, stuffy air which seemed to close around them with its load of dust and smoke. Zakeya and the young woman squatted down on the floor amidst the other passengers, near the driver's seat. But the old man and Zeinab remained standing like most of the others. The bus leapt forwards suddenly and Zeinab fell with all the weight of her body on the old man standing behind her, making him lose his balance and land in turn on the passengers standing in the aisle. In less than the wink of an eye those who were upright had fallen on those who were sitting down converting the inside of the bus into layers of compressed air and compact flesh. A moment later the bus started to advance at a slow pace along the summit of the river bank. Those who had fallen down now had a chance to extricate themselves, and stand up, and things returned to normal once more. Zeinab and the old man stood close to one another in the aisle.

The bus continued to reel along carrying its heavy load. The broken windows rattled, and now and again a piece of glass fell off the doors and the chairs seemed to be half-way out of their sockets, and parts were already so loose that they shook with a continuous metallic noise. Since the bus was advancing over a surface which was full of holes and bumps the din was deafening, and it seemed that at any moment it would come apart at its joints. Water kept streaming out between the wheels like urine from an old man who no longer is able to control his bladder and lets it drip down between his tottering legs. The bus was very much like a drunken old sailor swaying and reeling all the way. Puffs of black smoke kept exuding out of it from behind, and at every turn on the river bank it leaned heavily on one side, as though at any moment it might fall into the waters of the Nile. But each time the driver would jump to his feet, haul on the steering wheel with all his might, and save the bus from an imminent catastrophe

just in time, only to find it flinging itself to the other side with the
obvious intent of descending the slope and landing in the ditch,
which at least was completely dry. But the driver, who seemed
well-versed in its antics, would repeat the same manoeuvre until
the four wheels of the bus touched down on top of the river bank
at one time. Then reassured he sat down again, his half-closed
eyes on the road, as though there was nothing he longed for more
than a chance to shut his lids completely and drop off into a sound
sleep while he was driving. His sallow, wizened face stood out
with its worn look against the background of turbaned heads, long
garments, limbs, and straw or wicker baskets.

Zakeya closed her eyes as she sat on the floor of the bus,
overwhelmed by the sight of all these faces, and bodies pressed
up so closely against each other. She had never ridden in a bus
before, nor seen so many bodies packed into so small a space, nor
felt her body shake as violently as it was shaking now. Every now
and then a particularly violent leap of the bus would make her
open her eyes in fright. She felt that the ground was going to turn
upside down and come down on the roof of the bus, or that the bus
was going to do a somersault and land with its roof on the road.
She kept spitting into the neck of her *galabeya* and muttering the
testimony as though for the last time before she died. 'Verily I do
witness that there is no Allah except Allah, and that Mohamed is
the prophet of Allah.' Many other voices in the bus would echo in
her ears, almost gasping in one breath as they repeated the same
words over and over again.

At certain moments it would seem to her that she had died,
and then come back to life in the bus which continued to ride over

the river bank along the Nile. She lifted her head to try and get a glimpse of the river, but the bodies around her obstructed the windows and doors and she could see only the roof of the bus pitch black as though covered with oven soot.

She did not realize that the bus had come to a stop except when she felt Zeinab tug at her hand and say, 'We get down here, Aunt.'

She rested her hands on Zeinab's back and got down from the bus. Her face went very pale, and her eyes seemed to grow even blacker than usual, when she looked around and found neither river, nor river banks, neither mud huts nor muddy lanes, but wide shining streets, huge buildings, cars that raced along one after the other, and trams from which arose a strange clanging, or shrieking noise. The people, too, were different. The women walked along on high heels, and their thighs and breasts were partly exposed by the tight fitting clothes they wore. Gentlemen crowded through the streets in such great numbers that it was difficult to tell how many of them there were. On either side were rows of shops and the movement in the streets was rapid, almost hectic and flowed along unceasingly accompanied by a high-pitched, hectic roar. She held on to Zeinab's hand tightly and pressed her body up as close to her as she could.

'My head's whirling round, Zeinab,' she said. 'Don't leave me. Hold on to my hand. I don't know whether it's my head that's going round all the time, or things around me.'

But Zeinab's head was also in a whirl. Her big black eyes kept looking at what went on around her with a growing amazement. The old man in turn started to lean on Zeinab, while the young woman held on to him tightly. The four of them stood there amidst the flow of passers-by, huddled together for support. Their mouths were gaping in astonishment, and their eyes darted here and there or went round and round with the same frenzied movement as the bustling crowds.

After a while they started to walk along in single file close to a high wall, stepping warily over the ground, overcome by the feeling that as soon as one of their feet touched the ground it would be caught up in one of the churning wheels of the cars which raced up and down. Zeinab asked one of the passers-by where they could find the tram which would take them to El Sayeda. The man pointed to a column rising up from the ground and said, 'Stand here until the tram comes.'

They stood where the man told them. It was a place full of people. When Zeinab looked up she could see long wires stretching overhead above the street. Opposite where they stood was a huge building, and behind the wires was a huge picture which showed a naked woman lying on her back with her legs open, and three men pointing their pistols at her.

She hid her face behind her shawl and said in a low voice, 'Shame on them.'

The people getting on and off the tram kept pushing against one another on the small step which looked as though it could easily give way under the pressure. Zeinab hung on to an iron rail and pulled Zakeya up behind her. Then it was the turn of the young woman, followed by the old man who was hanging on carefully to his basket of figs. But just as he was opening a way for himself, the basket slipped from his shoulder and fell under the wheels of the tram. The old man jumped off after it. Someone screamed, then there were several screams. The figs rolled over the step and were scattered over the asphalt road, to be squashed under the shoes of the people walking along. The conductor quickly blew his whistle and the tram came to a halt.

Zakeya did not see what had happened. She could not tell whether the tram was moving or had come to a stop. She closed her eyes in an attempt to prevent her head from going round and round. When she opened her eyes again her body was shaking with the movement of the tram. Zeinab was sitting next to her, and in front of her was a small window through which she could see the street full of people walking up and down. She could also glimpse the tall buildings on one side. Many of them were covered with huge posters showing almost naked women, lying down, or sitting or standing with their legs apart. In front of them there were always gentlemen and they all carried pistols. She felt that something had happened in the tram, clasped Zeinab's hand tightly by the fingers and enquired, 'What's the matter?'

'The old man,' said Zeinab, 'fell under the wheels of the tram and has gone to the Kasr El Aini Hospital instead of El Sayeda.'

Zakeya gestured with her hand as though pointing to something going on outside the window of the tram way up in the sky. 'Only Allah is all-powerful, my child. Is the world here mad, or is it your Aunt Zakeya who has lost her mind?'

'May Allah make you whole and keep your mind as good as it has always been. Thanks be to Allah you are all right, my Aunt, and Allah will make you even better after you have visited El Sayeda.'

'Blessed you will always be, our lady,' murmured Zakeya.

13

The bodies of Zakeya and Zeinab seemed to become one with the compact mass of human flesh which flowed into El Sayeda Zeinab mosque filling it up and overflowing to the area around, the narrow streets which led to it, the main thoroughfare traversed by the trams that came and went and the big square to which it led. It was a mass composed of human bodies all wearing long *galabeyas*. The women could be distinguished from the men by the black shawls they wore over their heads. The myriad throng walked barefoot, their toes big and flat, their heels dark and cracked, the palms of their hands rough and horny with a groove made in the middle by the hoe, or the plough or the *tambour.** The faces were pale, and drawn, and thin, the eyes black and big, wide open with wonder, or half closed in a kind of stupor or daze, the mouths gaping in one big gasp which took in the air and kept it inside.

Zakeya held on tightly to Zeinab's hand, and she stuck so closely to her that she almost walked in her steps, afraid that the slightest distance between them, even if only a hair's breadth,

---

* A primitive water-wheel turned by hand.

might lead to her getting lost in this mighty human ocean. But
as they moved along somehow people managed to slip between
them and in the flash of an eye Zakeya lost sight of Zeinab. Yet for
some obscure reason she no longer felt afraid, or alone. Everything
around her was now familiar, known, lived before. The *galabeyas*
dropping down over people's bodies were like her *galabeya*, and
the sweat of their bodies had the same odour as her sweat. The
faces, the feet, the toes, the way they walked, and stared and spoke
were things she shared in common with them. She was a part of
this compact mass of human bodies, and it was like a part of her.

She was no longer afraid and her eyes ceased to search among
the crowds for Zeinab. For all the faces she saw were like Zeinab's,
and all the voices she heard reminded her of Zeinab's voice. Even
the words, the way they pronounced them, their very intonation,
the lifting of hands to the heavens, the single unchanging cry, 'O
God, come to our rescue, O God' chanted out in one voice, made
her feel that all these people were Zeinab.

They were sick or blind. They were young or old. They were
children or babes in arms. They were sheikhs of sects, or beggars
or thieves. They were sorcerers, and fortune-tellers, people who
made amulets or recited religious chants. They were saints of God,
intermediaries to His Grace, guardians of the doors to Heaven. All
of them like Zakeya and Zeinab raised the palms of their rough
hands in one uniform movement to Allah on high and chanted in
one voice, in one breath, 'O God.'

Zeinab too had ceased looking for Zakeya. Her face was now
only one of the innumerable faces, a drop in the human ocean, a
single garment amongst a million robes, an invisible particle in

the infinite universe, a pair of hands lifted to the heavens amidst a forest of hands fluttering in the wind, a voice joined to myriad voices in one prolonged, imploring chant, more like a wail of despair than anything else. 'O God, come to our rescue.' The voice of Zakeya too pierced through her lips in a high-pitched shriek which rose from her inner depths, like the cry from a slaughtered neck, or the gasp of a wounded chest.

Zeinab's heart was beating wildly as she cried out 'O God.' It seemed to leap against her ribs, and shake her small breasts under the bodice of her long robe. Her eyes shone with a mysterious gleam like moonlight on a dark, silent stream. She shivered every now and then with a strange fever hidden in her depths, and the blood rose to her face in a virginal flush as though this was the first time her heart had beaten for anyone.

So she cried out 'O God' and with every cry she felt she came closer to Him, so that now He could hear her voice and feel her breath on Him. She, too, could hear His Voice and feel His Breath. Her body had become one with Him, and she shivered with a sudden fear which was more like a deep sorrow, with a feeling of relief more like deep pleasure. She wanted to weep, to shriek with joy, to close her eyes and abandon herself to Him, to savour to the end this feeling of relief, of a body no longer under tension, of a deep pleasure she had never experienced before. But somehow deep inside her there remained a fearful sadness, an exhaustion, an anxiety which prevented her from sleeping, or even from just closing her eyes. So there she sat through the long hours with wide-open staring eyes, almost unaware of what went on around her.

But suddenly she heard someone call out her name, 'Zeinab!'
She realized at once that it was the voice of God. She had called
out to Him all through the night and now He was calling out to her
in turn. She whispered 'O God' and He answered 'Zeinab.' She
moved towards the voice as though in a dream. She did not know
whether she was walking on legs, or flying on wings. The compact
mass of bodies around her, the myriad voices resounding in her
ears fell back, and disappeared, leaving an empty space in which
echoed one voice calling out 'Zeinab.' She saw a face emerge in
front of her from what might have been a thick mist, or a dense
cloud of smoke. It was not the face of a man, nor that of a woman.
It was not the face of a young child or of an old person. It was a
face without sex or age, like that of Om Saber. Instead of the black
shawl she wore, the head was covered in a huge white turban
which reached down midway to the eyebrows concealing the dark
pitted skin over the upper half of the forehead. The skin of the
face also was blotched and pitted as though the old smallpox had
left its marks. The eyes were small without lashes, or even lids.
Just two dark holes staring unmovingly at Zeinab.

'Are you Zeinab, daughter of Kafrawi?' the voice said.

She gasped out a frightened 'Yes.' Deep inside her another
voice asked, 'How did he recognize me amidst all these people?'
But another voice replied almost immediately, 'Praise be to Allah,
for He knows all things.'

'Where is your aunt, Zakeya?' asked the man.

And the voice echoed inside her again. 'He also knows that
my aunt's name is Zakeya. It's amazing...'

She looked round trying to find out where her aunt had gone.

She could see her nowhere. But after a short while she realized that Zakeya's hand was still tightly clasped around hers, and that her shivering body was pressed closely up against her. She could hear her muttering verses and words under her breath.

The man came close to Zakeya, put out his dark, gnarled hand to the neck of her *galabeya*, took hold of the amulet she was wearing between his fingers, and took it off her neck. He recited a few verses, paused for a moment, and then put it back around her neck. Zakeya followed what he was doing intently, with an expression of deep reverence in her eyes, as though she was about to kneel and prostrate herself at his feet. As soon as his hand was still, she bent over and pressed her lips to it with a passionate fervour, muttering to herself. The man abandoned his dark, gnarled hand to her, and turned to Zeinab.

'Your aunt Zakeya is sick. She is sick because you have continued to disobey Allah, and she has encouraged you to do that. But Allah is all merciful, and kind, and He will forgive both of you on condition that you obey, and do what He asks of you. He will cure her of all sickness, if He so will, blessed be His Name on high.'

They raised their hands to the heavens and chanted in one breath, 'We thank, and praise Thee. For Thou art the generous and the bountiful one, O God.'

'You are to spend the night in the bosom of El Sayeda,' said the man. 'Then tomorrow before dawn you are to start out for Kafr El Teen. There bathe yourselves with clean water from the Nile, and while you wash continue to recite the testimony. Once dressed you should do your prayers. Start with the four ordained prostrations, then follow them with the four *Sunna** prostrations. After that you are to repeat the holy verse of the *Seat* ten times. On the following day, before dawn, Zeinab is to take another bath with clean water from the Nile, meanwhile repeating the testimony three times. Then do her prayer at the crack of dawn. Once this is over she is to open the door of your house before sunrise, stand on the threshold facing its direction and recite the first verse of the Koran ten times. In front of her she will see a big iron gate. She is to walk towards it, open it and walk in. She must never walk out of it again until the owner of the house orders her to do so. He is a noble and great man, born of a noble and great father, and he belongs to a good and devout family blessed by Allah and His Prophet. During this time Zakeya should lead the buffalo to the field, tie it to the water-wheel, take her hoe and work until the call to noon prayers. As soon as she hears it she should put down her hoe and pray the four ordained prostrations, followed by the four *Sunna* prostrations. After her prayers are over she must remain in the kneeling position and recite the opening verse of the Koran ten times, then raise her hands to the heavens, and repeat "Forgive me, O God" thirty times. As soon as she is over with this she is to get up, and wipe her face in the palms of her hand, and, God willing, she will find herself completely cured.'

Zakeya bent low over the dark gnarled hand and pressed her lips to it fervently, as she whispered, 'I do thank and praise Thee, O God. I do thank and praise Thee, O God.'

---

* Islamic jurisprudence, used to develop and explain Islamic teachings embodied in the Koran and the sayings of the Prophet Mohamed. The four prostrations mentioned here are not considered canonical but only optional. Practised as an additional rite, they testify to greater religious fervour and should bring more blessings.

While this was going on Zeinab had kept repeating verses of praise and thanks to God. She was so overcome with holy bliss that she forgot to give the man the ten piastre coin as Haj Ismail had instructed her to do. But the man himself now asked her for it. She undid the knotted corner of her shawl with a hand which was still trembling, extracted the coin, gave it to him and kissed his hand as though she was making the offering to God. Deep inside her a voice kept whispering in wonderment, 'O God, he knows Kafr El Teen and our house, and the iron gate which stands in front of it.'

The man disappeared into the crowd as rapidly as he had emerged, leaving Zakeya and Zeinab standing where they were, huddled up against each other in a state of wonderment, and profound humility. Now and again they would look at one another questioningly, as though to reassure themselves that what had happened was real, and not a figment of their imagination, that they had really heard the voice of God, and even seen Him, or at least seen one of His messengers, or saints to whom had been revealed the secrets which were not revealed to others. Zakeya felt her body was now lighter than it had ever been before. The iron grasp which seemed to throttle her all the time had loosened a little. She no longer had to lean on her niece Zeinab, for her legs had regained their strength, and could carry her easily.

Zeinab's eyes became wider and wider with amazement when she noticed her aunt walking beside her as though she could easily manage on her own.

'Aunt, you are better already,' she said in a low voice, full of reverence. 'Look how you are walking!'

And the old woman responded, 'My body no longer feels heavy. O God, verily Thou art generous and bountiful.'

'God is great,' said Zeinab. 'Did I not tell you many a time that Allah would help us, and that you should pray to Him, and be patient?'

'Yes, my child, you always used to say that to me.'

'I disobeyed God and refused to pray, and so did you, Aunt Zakeya.'

'I did not refuse to pray. It was the evil spirit dwelling within which refused.'

'God willing the evil spirit will be driven out of your body when we do what He has ordained.'

'Do you remember all that the sheikh said?' asked Zakeya. 'My body kept shaking, and I am unable to recall his words. I'm afraid we might forget something.'

'Don't worry about anything. Every word he said is engraved here in my heart.'

'May God bless you,' said Zakeya fervently.

14

And so that morning before dawn, Zeinab lifted the earthenware jar high up and poured clean Nile water from it over her head and body. She rubbed her breasts with it, whispering 'I testify that there is no Allah except Allah, and that Mohamed is the prophet of Allah' three times. The water flowed down over her belly and thighs, and she rubbed them in turn, reciting the testimony three times. She dried her long, black hair, plaited it tightly, dressed in a clean *galabeya*, wound the black shawl around her head and shoulders and advanced with frightened, hesitant steps towards the door, before pushing it slowly wide open.

The crimson rays of dawn started to appear above the horizon but the sun had not yet risen in the sky. She fixed her eyes on the spot from which she knew it would rise, and read the first verse of the Koran in a soft voice, repeating it ten times. Then she walked towards the iron gate. She was still frightened, but now her steps were steady, very steady. When she arrived at the gate a shiver went through her body. It was no longer a shiver of fear or doubt, but of deep exaltation. Now she knew what it was that she had to do. Her heart beat fast, her chest breathed full, her body was taut with expectation. Her legs trembled under the long *galabeya* and her large black eyes were raised to the sky, watching for something extraordinary to appear, for the will of God to be fulfilled.

The blue eyes of the Mayor opened wide with wonderment when he saw her appear. From her face and her eyes, from the way she walked with her head held high, he realized at once that she was Zeinab. He rubbed his eyes and looked at her again speaking in a voice which expressed surprise.

'Who sent you, Zeinab?'

'It is Allah Who has sent me,' she said.

'But why did you come this time?'

'Because it is the will of God,' she said as though speaking to herself.

The Mayor smiled, got out of bed and went to the bathroom. He brushed his teeth, washed, then looked at his face in the mirror and smiled again. The laughter was welling up inside him. Speaking to himself in an undertone, he said, 'Devil, son of a devil. What a cunning rogue you are, Haj Ismail!'

When he had finished he came out of the bathroom, and started to look for his watch. He found it on a small table. Its hands were pointing to six o'clock. He grinned and whispered to himself, 'No woman has ever come to me so early in the morning. I must drink a cup of tea first. It will wake me up.'

Zeinab was still standing where he had left her. He walked up to her, and in a voice one would use when speaking to a child, said, 'Listen to me, Zeinab. I want a cup of tea. Do you know how to make tea?'

'Yes, my master,' she said in a tone of voice anxious to please.

'Come with me. I will show you the way to the kitchen. I want you to prepare tea for me while I have a bath.'

Zeinab gasped in wonder when she saw the white porcelain wash basins, the shining metal taps, the coloured walls, the curtains and the stove that lit so easily. She lost herself in contemplation of the kettle which blew a whistle when the water boiled, the cups with engravings and coloured paintings, the silver spoons. Everything around her was new, never seen before, as though she had been transported to another world. She felt that she was now in the kingdom of Allah, praised be His name and revered. Her fingers trembled every time she held something between them. Her heart was beating rapidly, her breast heaved up and down, and her legs kept shaking all the time.

A tea-cup slipped through her fingers and dropped on the floor. She clapped her hand over her chest and shrank to the wall breathing hard, her eyes fixed on the shattered fragments of the cup as though she had committed a terrible crime. The pieces of porcelain shone like coloured crystals over the milk-white floor. The Mayor was enjoying his warm shower when he heard the sound of the cup as it struck the ground followed by a loud, terrified gasp. He smiled as his hand rubbed slowly over his chest and belly with a cake of perfumed soap. He thought, 'How exciting these simple girls are, and how pleasant it is to take their virgin bodies into one's arms, like plucking a newly opened rose flower. How I hate the false sophistication of Cairo women, like my wife with her brazen eyes. Nothing any longer intimidates or thrills her. Her frigid body no longer quivers when I caress her, or hold her tight, or even bite her.'

He came out of the bathroom wearing pink silk pyjamas and walked to the kitchen. He found Zeinab still standing shrunk up against the wall, with her hand on her breast, her lips slightly parted as though she were out of breath, and her eyes fixed on the shattered fragments of porcelain which just a moment ago had been a beautiful cup worth much more than she would ever know.

He watched her thoughtfully with his clear blue eyes, his face looking relaxed and healthy, just as though he were carefully weighing a priceless ornament. Her thick black hair hung in two plaits over her back. She had a fine, oval face tanned by the sun and her timidity was so stimulating, it excited him. Her full lips were a natural red, and slightly moist like a flower in the morning dew. Her breasts were round, firm, upturned with the sharp outlines of healthy flesh. They rose and fell in continuous movement as though impelled by the racing heart which hid behind them. Her eyes were large and black with a trace of tears like a child who has taken fright.

He came close to her and said with a smile on his lips, 'Are you crying, Zeinab?'

She bent her head and answered in a barely audible whisper, 'It fell out of my hand. Forgive me, master.'

She wiped her tears away with her hand. He felt the blood surge up in his body and moved closer, stretching out his hand and tenderly wiping away the remaining tears.

'Do not be afraid, Zeinab,' he said in a low voice. 'The cup, and the owner of the cup, are all yours.'

He was about to take her in his arms but thought better of it. She might only become more frightened if he did that. It was better if he waited until she had become accustomed to her new surroundings, and all the things she was seeing for the first time.

During that time Zakeya had taken the buffalo to the field, tied it to the water-wheel, and started to dig deep into the ground with her hoe. She kept straining her ears to catch a sound even vaguely resembling the midday call to prayer. When the voice of Sheikh Hamzawi finally rang out, the disc of the sun was right over her head, burning down on it, and the sweat poured in a continuous flow, welling out from the roots of her hair, down her neck, and over her back, and her chest. She could feel it trickling down between her thighs and wondered whether it was sweat, or the urine she could no longer keep in her bladder. As soon as the call to prayer died out, she threw her hoe aside, and went to a nearby stream. She washed her face and neck and did her ablutions, then stood on the edge of the stream to pray, kneeling down and prostrating herself with a fervent devotion. She did the four ordained prostrations and followed them with the four *Sunna* prostrations. With her prayers over she remained kneeling, and recited the first verse of the Koran ten times. After that she raised her hands to the heavens and repeated, 'O God, forgive me,' thirty times. She paused for a moment before wiping her face in her hands. Immediately she experienced a strange feeling of relief, very much like a strong desire to sleep. Her lids grew heavy and in a moment she fell into a deep sleep beside the stream.

No matter how burning hot the noonday sun became it could never penetrate through the thick, solid concrete walls of the

Mayor's house. Nevertheless the Mayor felt waves of burning heat running through his body as though he were naked under a white hot sun. He was still wearing his pink silk pyjamas, and sat in the armchair reading his morning newspaper. He glimpsed his brother's picture on one of the pages; quickly turned it over and started to read the news about celebrities and society people. Thus he learnt that Touha the dancer had been divorced, that Noussa the actress was marrying for the fourth time, and that Abdel Rahman, the singer, had entered the hospital to have his appendix removed. He turned over the page to read the sports news, but the pages got stuck, and he found himself looking at his brother's picture again, so he ran over the lines and read that there had been a cabinet change, and that his brother had become an even more important minister. He clicked his tongue in derision. No one knew him better than he did, for he was his brother. And no one knew how stupid a man he was, so slow of understanding, but a real mule for work 'just like a buffalo which goes round and round in a water-wheel with its eyes blindfolded', he thought.

He let the paper fall from his hand and closed his eyes, but suddenly remembered that he wanted to telephone his wife, and ask her how his younger son had fared in the examinations. His hand was about to reach out to the telephone when he heard the sound of water being poured in the bathroom. It reminded him that Zeinab had come to his house at dawn, and that meanwhile she had swept and cleaned the house, so that now all that remained for her to do was the bathroom. A thought flashed through his mind. 'Why not go to the bathroom and have a try?' But he drove it away. Somehow he felt that Zeinab was not like her sister Nefissa who was simple and easy-going, and had not instilled in him the same caution and hesitation he felt in the presence of Zeinab. He could not understand why with Zeinab he was so cautious and hesitant, even afraid. Yes, afraid. Perhaps because she was Nefissa's sister. True, Nefissa's story had remained a secret, but who knew? Maybe this time things would not be concealed so easily. He tried to chase away his fears. Who could find out the things that had happened? He was above suspicion, above the law, even above the moral rules which governed ordinary people's behaviour. Nobody in Kafr El Teen would dare suspect him. They could have doubts about Allah, but about him... It was impossible.

But now he remembered that there were three men in Kafr El Teen who knew almost everything about him. The Chief of the Village Guard, the Sheikh of the mosque, and the village barber. Without them he could not rule Kafr El Teen. They were his instruments, his aides and his means for administering the affairs of the village. But they knew his secrets. They could be trusted to keep them, although deep down inside he felt that they were not to be trusted with anything. If he closed his eyes for a single second they would play a trick on him, or get out of him whatever they could. But he had his eyes wide open, and he knew how to convince them that he could hear them breathe as they slept, and that if any one of them even so much as thought of playing tricks, of wagging his tail, he would cut it off for him, and cut his head off with it, too.

He swallowed two or three times in quick succession. His mouth was bitter and he felt like spitting, like ridding himself of the hatred which for ever weighed down on him. He loathed the three men, and despised them. What made it even worse was the realization that he needed them, that he could not do without them. That was why he was obliged to spend some of his nights talking and joking and laughing with them, and even to convince himself not only that they were his friends, but perhaps his only friends.

He got up from his comfortable armchair, walked to the bathroom and spat into the wash basin, then gargled with water several times trying to rid his mouth of the bitter taste. He looked in the mirror and his eyes fastened themselves on the reflection of Zeinab scrubbing the bath tub so that it shone as clean as alabaster. Her long *galabeya* was wet, and had stuck to her body revealing her breasts and thighs. It was as though she was naked before his eyes. He felt the warm blood rush to his belly and he could no longer take his eyes off her young body.

Zeinab lifted her head bent over the bath and stood upright. She caught the blue eyes of the Mayor fastened on her with a strange look, and stepped back in a movement of fear, shrinking up against the wall as though seeking protection. But her foot slipped on the smooth wet tiles, and in a moment she was lying full length on the floor.

Before she had time to rest her hands on it for support and get up, his arm was already round her waist helping her to rise. The tips of his fingers brushed against her breast, and he felt his hand tremble as it moved stealthily around its smooth contour until it was cupped in his palm.

She gave a half-throttled shriek, part pain at the hard pressure of his hand around her breast sensitive with youth and inexperience, part fright running through her body with an icy shiver, and part pleasure, a strange new pleasure almost akin to an ecstasy, the ecstasy of salvation, of being free of the heavy load which had been weighing down on her heart. Now she could leave herself in the hands of God, deliver her body and soul to Him, fulfil her vow, and savour the relief of having done so.

His hand moved up her legs, lifted the wet garment over her thighs. She heard his voice, hoarse, its tone low and tense with desire whispering in her ear, 'Take off your *galabeya*, Zeinab, otherwise you will catch cold.'

His hands were now sliding up her thighs to her belly as he tried to lift her garment higher. But it was wet and stuck to her flesh. He pulled on it so hard that it split with a rending sound. She gasped, 'My *galabeya*! It's my only *galabeya*!'

He tore the remaining folds from around her body, held her tight, whispering in her ear, 'I will buy you a thousand *galabeyas*.'

He stretched out his hand, opened the tap and a shower of warm water poured down over her naked body. With his own hands he washed off the dust and dirt of the day's work, his hands diligent over her hair, her shoulders, her belly, and thighs and breasts.

He dried her in a soft towel smelling of jasmine, the way a mother would dry her child. She let him carry her to the bed, still and silent. Then he took her in his arms.

15

Just before the crow of the cock rose into the air, Sheikh Hamzawi opened his eyes. In fact his eyes had probably been open for some time taking in the scene which he saw every day, and wondered at with a wonder that was not pure, and unadulterated and innocent but shot through and through with doubt, with a gnawing, aching, never-ending doubt. Yet the doubt itself had a strange quality about it, for most of the time, it was not really doubt, but a deep unshakeable certitude almost bordering on faith that what he saw before his eyes was an indisputable truth, like the truth of the existence of God.

The thin, long finger of dawn crept through a crack in the window and touched the face of Fatheya with an obscure gleam of light. It fell on the half of her face to his side, dim, grey, ashen-like. Her eyes were slightly open as though she were seeing even in her sleep. Her nose rose in sharp lines, and her lips were tightly closed together as though she feared that something might pass through them while she slept. The grey light of dawn revealed her smooth white neck. It ran down to a smooth white breast welling out where he had unbuttoned her garment over the chest.

The child held on to it with its hands, and its lips, and its tightly clenched jaws. She hugged the little body closely in the curve of her arm, with a hold which was tense, as though she feared that some force would tear him away.

Sheikh Hamzawi's look remained fastened to the side of the face he could see with a feeling somewhere between surprise and bewilderment. Was this side of her face so different from the side which the light had not yet reached, and where he would find the features of her face which he knew? What was the difference between the two? He was sure that the features revealed by the light of the dawn were not those of his wife Fatheya. In fact they did not resemble her at all. The nose was her nose, the mouth was her mouth, the neck her neck, the breast was her breast, everything was hers, and yet something had changed, something important but undefinable. He did not doubt for a moment that the woman lying by his side was Fatheya, and that this woman was his wife. He was absolutely sure of this truth, as sure of it as he was of the existence of Allah. And this certitude added to his bewilderment.

Anyone seeing his face at this particular moment would have realized that the man was no longer sure about anything. His eyes were wide open in a fixed stare but near them a small muscle seemed to twitch. The light of dawn pierced through the window and fell on his face. It looked deathly pale and there was a long shadow below it so that the one face looked like two faces. The upper face was his real face, the one which everyone in Kafr El Teen knew. But below it was another face which no one knew, or would ever know because no such face had ever been seen in Kafr

El Teen before. It was not the face of a human being, nor that of a spirit. It could have been the face of an angel or a devil, or even the face of Allah, if anyone had seen it before and could recognize Allah's face when he saw it.

Yet as he lay there, Sheikh Hamzawi was feeling further away from God than he had ever felt before. There were moments when he was very close to Allah, and particularly during the Friday midday prayer when all the men of the village, including the Mayor, would stand behind him, perfectly still, unable to move an arm, or a hand, or a finger, unable to move their lips, or whisper a verse from the Koran until he had done so himself.

At such moments he would feel much closer to Allah than any other man amongst them, be it the Mayor himself. A fine shiver would traverse his body, like the fine thrill of pleasure or of that rare happiness which he had known only as a child on those occasions when he used to throw stones at the other children and watch them run away in fright. During the prayer he would deliberately take his time before standing up, or sitting, or kneeling. Now and again he would shoot a quick backward glance, and observe the Mayor and the rows of men assembled behind him, reverently waiting for the slightest movement of his head, or his hand or even his little finger.

Nevertheless, no matter how much he took his time, or even slowed down the prayer, it would still be over in a matter of minutes, and the men would disperse from around him. Some of them might even tread on his foot as they rushed hurriedly behind the Mayor, carrying an appeal or a complaint of some sort written on a sheet of white paper with the required excise duty stamps stuck in the corner. Under his breath he would curse the 'band of impious rascals' who had no respect for God, and were so busy running after the transient panoply of the earth instead of thinking of the life hereafter. He walked back to his home, a lonely figure, stick tapping on the ground, his yellow-beaded rosary swaying between his trembling fingers. His fingers would tremble even more nervously as soon as he spotted his wife Fatheya. He would call out to her, asking for something in a loud throaty voice calculated to sound more throaty and virile than usual, then cough and clear his chest several times to ensure that the neighbours would realize that Fatheya's husband, the man of the household, was back.

'You've become deaf and blind since that accursed child came to our house. He occupies your whole life, and you care about nothing else despite the fact that he is a child born in sin. I held out a merciful hand to him, but sometimes I wish I had left him to die out there. Ever since the accursed creature, fruit of fornication and sin, has come into our house one misfortune after another has befallen us. People blame me for taking him in, their tongues keep wagging and I have lost the respect I used to enjoy in Kafr El Teen. Even my friends have abandoned me, and the Mayor no longer invites me to spend an evening with him. He has advised me several times to send him to a home for illegitimate children. I've promised to do it, but you refuse all the time. I can't understand why you are so attached to this miserable child.'

His voice would tail off as soon as he had asked this question. He did not understand why she should be so enamoured of the child. As soon as he had thrown the question at her, the rosary would begin to tremble even more violently between his fingers, as though he in fact knew the reason, but would not admit it. But it was a knowing devoid of certitude, a kind of obscure suspicion of knowing what one knew without at the same time being sure of it. The knowing and the doubt went through his body with a deep shiver, as though an icy shaft of wind was dropping down from the crack in the window together with the light of dawn. He could see Fatheya's face, her neck, and the smooth round breast to which the child held so tightly. And the question would start to steal up to him again and crawl over him like the cold, smooth belly of a snake. 'How was her breast giving milk if she had not been pregnant with the child, nor given birth to it?' He had not been the first one to ask this question. He had heard it from somebody else. He could not remember who it was that had asked him. In fact, he was sure it had been a question. Now he thought of it he could recall that it had been just a passing remark pronounced with a whisper. The whisper had made it feel like a sharp knife stabbed into his heart. 'Is Fatheya suckling the child?' He tried to deny that she was suckling it, for he had not seen the child at her breast. Every morning she used to buy buffalo milk for it. But the whispering voice insisted, sure of what it said, with a sureness which brooked no denial.

Sheikh Hamzawi's ears caught the whisper every time he walked along one of the lanes and passed by a group of people. He could see their heads come closer and hear it when it started. He would solemnly pronounce the usual greeting, 'Peace be with you.' Some of them did not even answer. When he passed in front of the shop of Haj Ismail where the Mayor would be seated, surrounded by the Chief of the Village Guard, the village barber and other men, his voice would resound as he said, 'Peace be with you.' There would be a short silence before the answer came back in a low, cold, inconsequential tone, 'And peace be with you.' The voice which answered was not that of the Mayor, nor the village barber. It was some other man who answered. No one among those who were seated invited him to join them. He would return home, walking with his head bowed to the ground to find Fatheya hugging the child. A strong urge to wrench it out of her arms, and throw it out of the window seized him, but each time he would restrict himself to glaring in the direction of the child as though facing a rival so formidable that he did not know how to tackle him.

One night he remained awake until Fatheya fell asleep. He crept on his toes to where the child was lying by her side, and tried to lift it, but although she was fast asleep she held her arms tightly around it. The child as usual was clamped to her breast. She felt him pulling at it and shrieked, 'Shame on you, Sheikh Hamzawi. You are a man of God. He's a small, innocent child.'

'I do not want a child born in sin to remain in my house.'

'Then I will leave the house with him,' she said.

'You are not his mother, and you shall not leave with him.' His voice trembled as he spoke.

'I will not abandon him to the care of anyone else. People have no mercy in their hearts and he's an innocent child who has done no wrong.'

'This child born of sin will bring nothing but trouble to us,' said Sheikh Hamzawi. 'Since he was brought into our home one misfortune after another has happened to us, and to the whole village. The worm has eaten the crops in the fields and I've heard people say he is the cause. No one greets me when I walk along, Fatheya, and I fear the Mayor may chase me out of the mosque and appoint another sheikh in my place. Someone has put into his head the idea that the men of the village no longer like me to lead the prayer, because their prayers might not be favourably received by God since the man who leads them has sheltered a child born of sin and fornication in his house. We will die of hunger, Fatheya, if the Mayor expels me from the mosque.'

'Allah will care for us, Sheikh Hamzawi, if the Mayor chases you out of the mosque,' said Fatheya.

'Allah is not going to make the heavens pour manna on us.'

'How can you of all people say such things about God, Sheikh Hamzawi? Don't you always say that Allah cares for the poor who worship Him? Why would He not take care of us also if the Mayor expels you from the mosque? Have you no trust in Allah, O Sheikh? Have you despaired of His mercy, you who enjoin people never to lose faith? Get up, Sheikh Hamzawi, and do your ablutions and pray God that He may have mercy on you and me, and on all the people in this village.'

So he did his ablutions and prayed. After prayer he would sit on the prayer carpet and recite verses from the Koran. The child would crawl up, sit in front of him on the carpet and look at him with questioning eyes. But the eyes of Sheikh Hamzawi were so full of hatred that they scared him, and he would crawl away screaming at the top of his voice. Fatheya would run up, lift him in her arms and pat him. 'What's the matter, my sweet one, what's the matter with you? Are you afraid of your father, Sheikh Hamzawi? Do not be afraid of him, my sweet one. He's your father and he loves you, and when you grow a little older, he will teach you the Koran, and you will become the Sheikh of the mosque, just like he is. You'll lead people in prayer and give them a sermon on Fridays.'

'You're dreaming, Fatheya,' snorted Sheikh Hamzawi. 'Do you think people here would accept that the Sheikh of the mosque be a man who was born in sin?'

'But it's not the child's fault,' she retorted with insistence.

'I know it's not the child's fault, but people here do not think that way.'

'Why?' she asked. 'Why shouldn't they think the way we do? We're no different to them.'

'Yes, I know, but people are like the waves of the sea, one can never tell when they might become stormy and why. All of them without exception say to me that it's not the child's fault. But when their heads get together, they say something else. These people are unbelievers, Fatheya. They don't have faith in God nor do they worry their heads about what will happen either in this world, or in the next. In their hearts they don't fear God. What they really fear is the Mayor. He holds their daily bread in his hands and if he wants, he can deprive them of it. If he gets angry their debts double, and the government keeps sending them one summons after the other. "Either pay or your land will be confiscated." You do not know the Mayor, Fatheya. He's a dangerous man, and fears no one, not even Allah. He can do injustice to people and put them in gaol when they have done nothing to merit it. He can even murder innocent people.'

'In the name of Allah the Almighty, why then did you keep repeating that he is a man who believes in Allah, and loves doing good to people. Every Friday morning I could hear your voice echoing in the mosque so loudly that it reached me as you made your sermon to the people gathered there, praying to Allah that he bestow long life on the Mayor, saying that he was the best Mayor we had ever had in Kafr El Teen, and that he always sought for truth and justice. Were you fooling people, Sheikh Hamzawi?'

There was a long silence before he replied, 'You know nothing about what goes on outside the four walls of this house. Life in the outside world with people as they are is not easy. The prophet says to us, "Do in this world as though you will live for ever." The Friday sermon, Fatheya, cannot solely be concerned with Allah. Part of it must deal with worldly affairs, and the world in which we live is controlled by the Mayor. We cannot go about our lives if we are in disfavour with him. As far as Paradise is concerned, I am sure that Allah will send me there. Is it not enough that I continue to suffer at the hands of the Mayor and the Chief of the Village Guard in order to protect an innocent child? Or what do you think, Fatheya?'

'Yes, of course,' she said hastily, 'Allah will reward you with many good things because you have adopted an innocent child, and for the protection, tenderness, and care you have given it.'

Taking advantage of the Sheikh's more favourable mood, she sat down next to him and put the child in his lap.

'Look into his eyes, Sheikh Hamzawi. Don't you see how he loves you? Just like a child would love its father. Hold his hand. See how small and soft it is, and how his tiny fingers curl around your thumb as though he's trying to say to you, "Don't leave me father. I am small and weak, and need your help".'

And the child held out its hand and touched Hamzawi's face. The old man bowed his head, abandoning himself submissively to the playful fingers, enjoying their touch as they moved over his whiskers and beard.

One day the child pulled out a hair from his whiskers. He hit him over the hand and said, 'Shame on you.' And so when the boy learnt to speak the first word he pronounced was 'Ame.'* The Sheikh began to seat him on the prayer carpet and to teach him how to recite from the Koran. The little boy would try to lift the Koran but it was heavy, and one day it slipped between his hands on to the floor with a thump. Sheikh Hamzawi shook with anger and bent down quickly to lift the Koran from the floor. He kissed it on one side, turned it over and kissed it on the other, then hit the boy on his hand, saying, 'How dare you throw Allah's book on the ground, you son of sin.' Fatheya came running out at the sound of the child's scream, and when the Sheikh explained to her what had happened she said, 'How can you expect him to understand what you're talking about, Sheikh Hamzawi?'

On another occasion it was noonday and very hot. Sheikh Hamzawi was seated as normal with the Koran in his hands, reading passages from it. Sleep overcame him and the Koran dropped on his lap as he sat cross-legged. The small boy crawled up to him and sat on the Koran. A few moments later Sheikh Hamzawi was awakened by something warm and wet trickling

---

* Baby talk for 'Shame on you!'

down between his thighs. He opened his eyes with a start, thinking that he had urinated on himself, to find the child sitting on his lap. Underneath was the book of Allah all soggy and wet. He scrambled up suddenly, throwing the child off his lap on to the floor, kicked him in the belly and shouted angrily. 'Dost thou pass water on the holy book of Allah, thou son of fornication?'

The boy went pale and could hardly breathe for a moment, as though he was going to choke, or had died suddenly. Then he gave a long wailing gasp which brought Fatheya running up in a terrible panic.

'What happened, Sheikh Hamzawi? What have you done to the child?' she cried out.

Sheikh Hamzawi told her what had happened in a voice which shook with anger. She lifted the child in her arms and screamed furiously at her husband. 'Do you expect the child to realize all this? How can you kick him like that in the belly with your big clumsy foot? Were it not for the grace of Allah you could have killed him!'

'I wish he would die and relieve me of all the suffering I am obliged to go through because of him. I can't stand living in this world any more if this accursed creature is going to continue living in it with me. I'm confined to these four walls like any woman. Nobody visits me any more, and I can no longer visit anybody. And when I walk through the village, people avoid me so that they are not obliged to greet me, or to stop and talk to me.'

On the following Friday Sheikh Hamzawi walked out of his house as usual on his way to the mosque, where he was supposed to lead the congregation in prayer. When he approached the door of the mosque three men stood in his way, and prevented him from entering. He got very angry and shouted at them, 'I am the Sheikh of the mosque. How dare you prevent me from going in?'

'You are no longer the Sheikh of the mosque,' replied one of the men. 'The Mayor has ordered that your services be dispensed with, and has appointed another sheikh.'

'No one can stop me from going in,' shouted Sheikh Hamzawi angrily. 'Allah alone is the one who can prevent me from entering this mosque.' Then he marched straight towards the door. But one of the men held on to his caftan, and pulled him back, upon which he raised his stick and dealt him a heavy blow on the head. The man dropped to the ground immediately, while the other men leapt on Sheikh Hamzawi. One of them struck out at his head with a powerful fist as though he was hitting at the head of a devil, or a snake, while the other man dealt him one slap after the other on the face. He seemed to be taking something out on him, perhaps remembering how his father used to slap him when he was still a young child and say, 'Allah will burn you in the flames of hell for not obeying your father.' The face in front of him now was not that of Sheikh Hamzawi, but of his father. But after a little while it changed again to become the face of Allah who had threatened him as a child that the fire of hell would burn his skin until nothing of it was left, and told him that each time it burnt he would allow another skin to grow on his body so he could burn again once and twice and thrice and ten and twenty times, never endingly. When he saw the face of Allah before him he was seized with a deep panic which made him lash out at Sheikh Hamzawi with a redoubled fury.

The villagers who had gathered to attend the prayer, crowded around instead to watch the fight. One of them tried to extricate Sheikh Hamzawi from the blows raining on his head, but a heavy fist aimed at his face drove him back, and nearly knocked out his teeth. He retreated muttering angrily, 'He who tries to stop a quarrel only gets his clothes torn to shreds.'

One of the men standing around whispered in another's ear, 'The Mayor has removed Sheikh Hamzawi from his job and appointed another sheikh in the mosque. Come, let's go before we miss the prayer.' When he moved off others followed, and as they walked along different thoughts flitted through their minds. Some of them heard a voice within them say, 'Since the decision has come from high up, I have no right to oppose it.' With others, the inner voice said, 'They're all the same, these sheikhs, so what difference does it make? All I can do is pray behind one or the other.'

Only a few men remained outside the mosque. They forgot all about the Friday morning prayer. As a matter of fact, they forgot almost everything else at the sight of the quarrel. They stood there enjoying the spectacle of men fighting, not caring who was doing the beating and who was being beaten as though both aspects gave them an equal enjoyment. It was the peculiar pleasure that men experience at watching a violent struggle between opposing parties, be they human beings, or cocks, or bulls. Some people are even prepared to pay a high price just to watch a fight, and be distracted from the conflicts that go on inside them.

Sheikh Hamzawi's turban fell on the ground and was trodden under the feet of people coming and going. His caftan was now torn to shreds, and blood flowed from his mouth and nose. But he continued to shout out furiously, 'You impious unbelievers. You people who know not Allah. Is that how you strike at the man of God who devoted his life to serving Him all his life, and to looking after His holy house?'

One of the bystanders said, 'If he is the man of God, why does Allah not come to his rescue, instead of leaving him to be beaten up like this?'

'Who said he is a man of God? He is not a man of God at all,' remarked a second.

A third man intervened in defence of the Sheikh, 'How do you know that he is not a man of God? I think he is undoubtedly a man of God.'

'And how are you so sure that he is a man of Allah? I say he is not the man of Allah you say he is,' retorted the second man in an angry voice. But one of the men standing there intervened in the discussion in a way that cut them both short. 'Neither you nor he can tell whether he is a man of God, or not.'

'Then who knows?' asked a man who had been in the thick of the fight just a moment ago.

Another of the bystanders chipped in, 'The Mayor certainly knows. The Mayor is the only one that knows.'

There was a profound silence. No one dared object to what the last man had said. But a small boy who was standing somewhere in the throng piped in a shrill voice, 'How can the Mayor know?' But before he could say anything more, the hand of his father clapped down over his mouth and his hoarse voice ordered, 'Shut your mouth, boy, when there are grown-up men present.'

But the boy's question kept resounding in the mind of one of those who was present. 'Could it be Allah who told the Mayor about such things? But did Allah speak to the Mayor the way he had spoken at one time to the Prophet Mohamed, God's blessing and peace be upon him? Perhaps Allah spoke to saints, and therefore spoke to the Mayor who was a devout man.'

Suddenly the man felt his breath come in gasps. He could not figure out why he had started to gasp since he was only standing like the others watching the fight. Somehow the voice which had spoken within him sounded strange and even frightening, although it had only told him that the Mayor was a devout man. And yet the word devout itself had echoed inside him very much like the mysterious voice of the devil, so that all of a sudden the word 'devout' started to sound more like the word 'dissolute'. He was seized with panic at the thought that he had insulted the Mayor even though he had only spoken to himself. He could not be sure that the voice within him had been no more than a faint whisper. It could have been louder than he thought, and in that case one of the men standing around might have heard it saying that the Mayor was a dissolute man. He nodded his head and waved his hand as though chasing away the devil, muttering to himself, 'O Allah, I do take refuge in Thee against the accursed devil.'

'Yes, it's the devil,' said an angry voice nearby. 'Who would beat up our devout Sheikh Hamzawi other than the devil?'

'But he is no longer the Sheikh of our mosque,' commented a tall man who stood in the small crowd that was still hanging around.

'Allah has nothing to do with the likes of him,' added another voice in support of what the last man had said.

A short man with a meek face who had said nothing so far, took advantage of a sudden silence to ask in a low tone, 'But how can you say that, brother? What wrong has Sheikh Hamzawi done?'

'Don't you know what he did? Don't you live in this village? The worm has eaten our cotton, and we've had nothing but trouble since Sheikh Hamzawi gave shelter to that child of sin in his house. How can we allow a man who adopts the children of sin and fornication to lead us in prayer?'

The tall man was about to say, 'It's not the fault of the poor child,' but he swallowed quickly and kept silent at the sight of the anger glinting in many eyes. He remembered how his father used to repeat always that the children of sin only brought misfortune with them. He heard himself say in a voice which resembled that of his father, 'You're right, brother. The children of sin only bring misfortune with them,' then he swallowed again and rushed off to his field. A voice within him said, 'I'm a coward.' But he braced his shoulders and lifted his head and this time the voice sounded different when it said more loudly, 'He's right, children of sin only bring misfortune with them. Otherwise, why is it that we have had one problem after the other since Sheikh Hamzawi took that child into his house?'

As for Sheikh Hamzawi, he returned home to Fatheya, bleeding from his nose and mouth, his clothes dusty and torn, his head uncovered since he had lost his turban in the fight. Her mind told her that the life of her child was now in danger. She concealed him under her shawl and said, 'We can no longer live in this village.'

'I know no other place to live in,' responded Sheikh Hamzawi in a voice full of despair and exhaustion. 'I prefer to die here rather than in a strange place. There no one will lend us a helping hand.'

'Allah will take care of us, Hamzawi. Do you think He will abandon us to our fate?'

'I don't know,' said Sheikh Hamzawi. 'Allah seems to have abandoned me since I gave shelter to this child.'

'How can you repeat the same things that people in the village are saying?' protested Fatheya.

'Why does that surprise you? Aren't I like other people? Am I not human? I never pretended to be a saint, or a god.'

'What are you driving at, Hamzawi? If you don't want the child to stay, then before the sun rises tomorrow you will not find him here, and you will never see him again in this house. But I also will leave with him.'

'Do as you wish, Fatheya,' answered Sheikh Hamzawi in a weak voice. 'Go with him, or stay here, it no longer makes any difference. All I want out of life is that people should leave me alone.'

'I don't want to leave you alone,' she said, wiping the tears away with her hand, 'but people will give us no peace. Every time something goes wrong in the village, they will blame this poor, innocent child. What has the child got to do with the cotton worm, Hamzawi? Was it he who told the worm to eat the cotton? The brain of a buffalo has more sense in it than the mind of these people here in Kafr El Teen. But where can I go? I know no other village apart from Kafr El Teen.'

A few days passed and Fatheya forgot the questions she had asked herself. People no longer talked about them as they had done before. It looked as though they had forgotten the whole matter, or that what they had done to Sheikh Hamzawi was sufficient for them. And perhaps people would have forgotten. But one day the wind started to blow, and carried with it a spark from one of the ovens in which a woman was baking bread. The spark was very small, about the size of the head of a match, or maybe even smaller. It could have gone out had it landed on the dust-covered ground. But instead it flew on to one of the roofs, and landed while still partly alight on a heap of straw. If a gust of wind had happened to blow strongly at that moment, it might have put it out before it had time to ignite the straw. In fact, the wind went suddenly still, and during this time a small flame caught hold of one straw, so that when the wind started to blow again after a short while, the one straw was burning and the flames quickly caught hold of the whole heap, then moved quickly to the dung cakes and the cotton sticks jutting out as far as the roofs of the nearby houses.

It was not long before the villagers spotted the fire. The women slapped their faces and shrieked, the children screamed piercingly, adding to the clamour, and the men ran around in circles not knowing what to do. The village barber yelled out at them, 'Get pails of water, you animals!' but when the pails were brought the water never got anywhere near the flames. Each family started to count its children, lead the donkey or the buffalo out of the house, or extract the savings of a lifetime from some nook or hole in the wall.

The Chief of the Village Guard rushed off to the Mayor who had been informed of the fire by telephone. The red fire engine arrived after some time, its bell clanging. It was followed by the ambulance moving along behind. By then the children had tired of watching the fire, and turned to the fire engine with its ladder on which one could climb high up into the sky. As soon as it came to a stop they surrounded it on every side, standing on bare feet, their naked bottoms exposed from behind, their noses running in front. Swarms of flies kept settling on their faces or rising in black clouds.

Before the sun had dropped behind the line of treetops on the far side of the river everything in Kafr El Teen seemed to have returned to normal. Here and there wisps of smoke arose from a bare roof covered in black ashes. A child had suffocated in the smoke and lay dead on the mat close to the door where it had tried to crawl, and the frames of some windows were charred and black. On the dusty ground could be seen the imprint left behind by the wheels of the fire engine, but this was soon effaced by the cows, buffalo, donkeys and peasants returning in long lines from the fields after the day's work was over.

Fatheya remained wide awake with her arm tightly curled around the child. She could feel the danger which hovered around them, and kept her eyes close to the wall trying to catch what the villagers were saying. Deep down inside her she knew exactly what was going to happen now. And so when the words which were spoken reached her ears she felt no surprise at all. 'The fire would have consumed the whole village were it not for the grace of Allah. Since that son of fornication and sin descended on our village, we have had nothing but one misfortune after the other. It is time for us to do something about it.'

She felt her heart beating wildly, deep under the weak, distant pulse of the child she held to her chest, wrapped in her shawl. She opened the door slowly to make sure that none of the neighbours would hear it creak, then ran swiftly on bare feet until she had almost reached the river bank, but the eyes spotted her, and surrounded her on every side. She heard a wrathful voice call out, 'Where is the child, Fatheya?'

'He's not with me. He's asleep in the house,' she said, holding the little body tightly under her shawl.

'You are lying, Fatheya. The child is with you,' said the angry voice.

'No,' she said, 'it's not with me.' There was a shiver of terrible fear in the way she pronounced the denial.

She tried to slip away quickly, but a hand moved towards her and pulled the black shawl away, revealing the child as he lay close to her chest with his mouth holding to the nipple of her breast.

'It's my son. Don't take him away from me,' she shrieked with terror.

'He is born in fornication and we are a God-fearing people. We hate sin.'

A big rough hand stretched out in the dark to tear the child away from her, but it was as though she and the child had become one. Other hands moved towards her, trying to wrench the child away from her breast, but in vain. Her breast and the child had become inseparable.

The disc of the sun had by now disappeared completely and was no longer visible behind the line of trees on the opposite bank of the river. The night descended on the houses of Kafr El Teen like a heavy silent shadow, breathlessly still as though all life had suddenly ceased. The men high up on the bank moved hither and thither like dark spirits or ghosts which had emerged from the deep waters of the Nile. During the struggle for the child, Fatheya's clothes were torn away, and her body shone white, and naked, like that of a terrible mermaid in the moonlit night. Her face was as white as her body, and her eyes were filled with a strange, almost insane determination. She was soft, and rounded, and female and she was a wild animal, ferociously fighting those who surrounded her in the night. She hit out at the men with her legs, and her feet, with her shoulders and her hips all the while holding the child tightly in her arms.

Hands moved in on her from every side. They were big, rough hands with coarse fingers. The long black nails were like the black hoofs of buffalo and cows. They sank into her breast tearing flesh out of flesh. Male eyes gleamed with an unsatisfied lust, feeding on her breast with a hunger run wild like a group of starved men gathered around a lamb roasting on a fire. Each one trying to devour as much as he can lest his neighbour be quicker than him. Their hands moved like the quick paws of tigers or panthers in a fight, their eyes lit by an ancient vengeance, by some furious desire. In a few moments Fatheya's body had become a mass of torn flesh and the ground was stained red with her blood.

But after a while the river bank had become the same as it always was at night, no more than a part of the heavy, silent darkness that weighed down on everything, on the waters of the Nile, on the wide ribbon of land stretching along nearby, and on the dark mud huts and the winding lanes blocked with mounds of manure. The men of Kafr El Teen were now back in their houses, lying on the ground near their cattle and their wives like bodies without life or feeling. All except one man, Sheikh Hamzawi, who never closed his eyes that night, nor lay down to sleep. He kept his ear to the wall until all sound had ceased, and a deep silence had enveloped the village; a silence as dark and as terrifying as the silence of death. Then he stood up, walked towards the door of his house and opened it very carefully with a push of his shoulder so that it should not creak. He walked out into the lane, finding his way with the stick which he always used to ensure that his foot would not collide with a pebble, or a brick, or a dead cat which some boy had killed with a sling.

As he shuffled along slowly his stick hit something which his senses told him was not a stone, nor a brick, nor some small dead animal, but something still warm with the blood of life. He stopped short, and stood as still as a ghost, not moving one bit, so that even his yellow-beaded rosary ceased to go round between his fingers. His eyes were fastened on the naked body of his wife lying on the ground high up on the bank of the river.

Fatheya was moaning in a weak voice, and her breast still heaved up and down with a slow, irregular gasping movement. He sat down beside her and took her hand between his own. 'Fatheya, Fatheya, it's Hamzawi,' he whispered.

She opened her bloodshot eyes and parted her lips slightly as though trying to say something, but no sound came out. He glimpsed someone approaching from a distance, took off his caftan, and covered her naked body with it. When the man came nearer, he recognized Sheikh Metwalli and said quickly, 'She is breathing her last. Can you carry her with me so that she can die in her bed?'

Sheikh Metwalli immediately bent over her ready to lift her bleeding body from the ground. But before they had time to take hold of her, she opened her eyes and looked around.

'She's looking for something,' said Sheikh Metwalli in a low voice.

'She's unconscious. Let's carry her to the house,' whispered back the old man, wiping the sweat from his brow.

But when they tried to lift her, the body of Fatheya held to the ground as though stuck with glue. Each time they tried to lift her, she would open her eyes and look around searching for something.

'She won't move. I'm sure she's looking for something,' said Sheikh Metwalli, his eyes probing here and there in the dark. Suddenly his eyes picked up a small shadow lying on the bank of the river, a short distance away. He went up to it, lifted it from the ground and came back carrying the torn body of her little child. Sheikh Metwalli held it out in his arms and laid it down softly on her chest. She curled her arms around it tightly and closed her eyes. And now when they lifted her they found that her body was light and easy to carry.

They carried her as far as the house, and on the following morning buried her with the child held tightly in her arms.

Hamzawi bought her a shroud of green silk and they wrapped her in it carefully. They dug a long ditch for her and lay her softly down in it, then covered her with the earth which lay around. When it was over Metwalli wiped the sweat off his brow. His hand came away moist with something like tears when he touched his eyes. It was something which had never happened to him before, or at least he could not remember himself ever crying except perhaps when he was a child.

Only Allah and Sheikh Metwalli know that Fatheya's body and Fatheya's shroud both remained intact and unsoiled in the burial ground.

16

He rested the big, hot palms of his two hands on the ground, and sat down with his back against the trunk of a tree, stretching out his legs as far as they could go. He had come a long distance, and they ached painfully. He could see his large feet against the setting sun. They were swollen, and the skin over them was cracked and inflamed.

He closed his eyes and tried to sleep, but they opened again. His look remained fastened on the endless ribbon of the river, with the fields rolling out beside it as far as his eyes could see. He was trying to find out where his world of Kafr El Teen began, to spot the first things he could recognize; the big mulberry tree where the river bank sloped down to the ditch, or to smell the odours he could pick out amongst a thousand other things: dust sprayed with water from the village stream, or wetted by the soft fruit of the mulberry tree, or dung mixed with the bran of bread from a hot oven, or his mother's shawl flapping in the wind when he walked beside her, or her breast when he slept on the mat huddled up against her in the winter nights.

For many years he had not smelt the odour of these things.

He had left them behind in Kafr El Teen and gone away. He had never known these odours existed until the day he could smell them no more, until the day he donned his army uniform and became a private. He spent a long time not knowing that he had smelt them before, and they had a place in his life. During that time he slept in a small tent a few miles away from Suez, living with other odours, with the smell of bullets and shells fired from a gun, or burning leather, or conserves packed in rusty tins, or the sand of Sinai when planes unloaded their bombs on it, or winds unleashed their desert storms. But one night he opened his eyes just before dawn and suddenly there was that smell invading his nose. He did not recognize it on the spur of the moment, but it went through him with a strange happiness, like some drug which he might have swallowed or smoked. He was suddenly seized with a yearning to close his eyes and lay his head on his mother's breast. When he woke up in the morning he discovered that he had spent the night with a parcel she had sent him under his head. It was tied in a small bundle, and a colleague of his had carried it with him all the way from his village. Before opening the knot he brought it close to his nose, and for the first time recognized the odour with which he had lived for years in Kafr El Teen without ever having known it.

He breathed in the air blowing down between the river waters and the fields lying alongside, trying to detect the familiar odour of dust sprayed with muddy water from the nearby stream, but his nose failed to catch anything that smelt like it. He threw a searching glance in the same direction but nowhere could he find anything to indicate that he was near the approaches to Kafr El Teen.

He felt that the distance which lay before him might take long hours, or even days of walking. His lids closed over his eyes by a will stronger than his own. When they opened again, after a little while, he found the sun high up in the sky. A few moments went by before he realized that he had slept two days and two nights. He placed his palms flat on the ground and lifted his body upright. The skin of his palms was thick and coarse, and over it was the imprint of the groove made by his rifle. When he had paraded, or stood at attention or held the rifle to his shoulder and took aim it had rested in the groove made by long years of work with the hoe and dug it even deeper than before. When he stood up his body was like a bamboo cane, tall and thin, but his feet were swollen. Pus and blood oozed from the cracks in their skin, and the cracks had dark, muddy edges from miles and miles of walking. The burning disc of the sun was straight above his head and poured its rays down on him, and under the soles of his feet the ground was like hot needles. He could no longer tell where he was, for the Suez Canal was a strip of water and the hot needles under his feet was the silica sand of the retreat from Sinai cutting into his tortured skin.

His breath came in gasps, and before his eyes danced red circles. He closed his eyes to arrest the whirling movement. Suddenly there was an explosion. He knew the sound so well. It was terrifying like thunder, or an earthquake, or both, as though the sky and earth had collided. In less than a second he was lying curled up on the ground, with his chin tucked in, and his head held tightly protected under his arms. Then he crawled quickly over the ground looking for a ditch, or a hole, or a hollow between two sand dunes. There he lay on his belly perfectly still like a man who had died or was frozen.

The sound faded away and was replaced by a silence even deeper than before. He opened his eyes slowly, shooting frightened glances at the sky, looking for something flying high up. But there was nothing. No plane, or burning flame, no smoke, or cloudy greyness. Just the fiery disc of the sun burning down from above. His eyes dropped down from the sky and looked around, and when they ran over the river and the fields he realized he was no longer in the desert. The war was over, and he was returning home on foot to Kafr El Teen. The next moment he noticed that a group of children were gathered around him. They had seen him leap suddenly down the slope of the bank into the ditch. Behind swarms of flies their eyes were opened wide with surprise. He staggered away from them on his swollen feet. He could hear them laughing behind him. A shrill voice cried out, 'There goes the idiot.' Immediately the other children joined in and chanted in one voice, 'There goes the idiot.' Then they started to throw stones at him.

When he reached the outer limits of Kafr El Teen the sun had dropped behind the treetops on the other side of the river Nile. The dark night crept slowly over the low mud huts, and the lines of buffalo and cows slouched along the river bank on their way back home. Groups of peasants walked wearily behind, their backs bent by unceasing toil, their feet worn out from the daily coming and going.

Zakeya was already home. The buffalo was in the stable, while she squatted as usual near the door on the dusty threshold of her house with her back to the wall. She neither moved nor spoke. She did not even move her hand or nod her head. Her large black eyes stared into the night. It made no difference to her whether she kept awake or dozed, whether her eyes remained open or closed, for the night was always like a dark cloak. She did not know when she slept, or when she awoke, she did not know whether what she saw was real, or just another dream, or ghost. She could not tell whether the man who emerged in front of her at that moment was her brother Kafrawi or her son Galal. Her son Galal was not at all like her brother Kafrawi. The last image she had of him was the day they took him away to the army. She watched him walk away between two men. He was young then, and strong, and he walked upright with his eyes fixed on something he could see straight ahead. But the last image she had of Kafrawi was the day on which they had taken him away to gaol. He walked between two men, old-looking and bent, with his eyes on the ground. Yet now she did not know who of the two suddenly appeared before her eyes. The face was that of Galal, but the broken look in his eyes and the back which bent was without a doubt Kafrawi's.

She heard a voice like Galal's whisper in the dark. It sounded weak and spent. 'Mother... don't you recognize me? It's Galal. I'm back from Sinai.'

She continued to stare at him with her black eyes. She could not tell whether they were open or closed, whether this was real or a dream. She stretched out her hand to touch him. Whenever she used to grope for him in the night, his face would seem to fade away, and her fingers would clutch at a dark nothingness. But this time what she held was a hand of flesh and blood, a big warm hand just like Galal's. She brought it close to her face. It had the same smell as her breast, the same smell as her milk before it dried up. It was the smell of his hand, there was no doubt about that.

'My son, Galal, it's you!' she whispered in a weak, husky voice burying her face in his hand.

'Yes, mother, it's Galal,' he said, bowing his head. She touched his head and neck, his shoulders and his arms, his legs and his feet with her big rough hands. She was making sure that there was no wound, no part missing, making sure he was whole.

'Are you all right, my son?' she whispered.

'Yes, mother,' he said. 'I'm all right. And you? Are you well, mother?'

'Yes, my son. I'm well.'

'But you're not the same as you were when I left you,' he said, looking at her with anxious eyes.

'That's four years ago. It's time, son,' she said. 'Time, and you too, Galal, you are not the same.'

'It's nothing,' he said. 'I'm tired from the long distance I walked. It was very long. I need to rest.'

He lay down next to her on the dust-covered ground. She rubbed his feet in warm water and salt, then wrapped them in her shawl. His eyes were wide open, staring at the ceiling of the mud hut. She squatted next to him, and her lips were tightly closed. At one moment she parted them slightly as though about to tell him the story of what had happened, but she closed them again and kept silent. But after a while she heard him ask, 'How is my uncle, Kafrawi?'

She was silent for a long moment before she said, 'He is well.'

'And Nefissa? And Zeinab?'

She hesitated for a moment, then in an almost inaudible voice said, 'They are well. Do you wish to eat something? You probably haven't put anything in your mouth for days.'

She got up and went to fetch the basket of bread, a piece of old cheese, and salted pickles. Then walking towards the door she said, 'I will go to buy you a piece of sesame sweet from the shop of Haj Ismail.'

He realized she was hiding something from him and looked at her with an increased anxiety. 'I do not want to eat. Come, sit here and tell me what's been happening. You're hiding something. You're not the same as when I left you.'

Her eyes avoided his, staring at something in the dark. She was silent for some time, then he heard her whisper, 'Nefissa has run away.'

There was another long silence as heavy and as oppressive as the surrounding darkness lying over the village. Once again her lips parted to let out the same whisper. 'And Kafrawi is in gaol.'

This time she closed her lips as though she intended never to open them again. After a long moment she heard him ask in a low voice which rose from somewhere hidden deep in the dark, 'And Zeinab?'

His voice wavered when he pronounced her name, wavered with a hesitation, with wanting to ask and fearing the answer, with wanting to know and afraid of what would be revealed. A strange feeling had come over him the moment he saw her face, a feeling that something terrible had happened while he was far away. Kafrawi was his uncle, and Nefissa his cousin. But Zeinab had always meant something different to him. Every time he heard her voice calling out to her Aunt Zakeya something within him quivered. When their eyes met he would feel his legs go weak under him, as though his muscles had tired suddenly and needed rest. He longed to lay his head on her breast and close his eyes. If he got a glimpse of her bare legs as she sat with his mother in front of the oven, he would be seized with a strong desire to carry her away from under the watchful eyes to where he could close a door on her and hold her in his arms.

His mother could feel what was going on in him, sense his voice tremble when he called out to Zeinab, notice how his eyes searched for the girl when she was out in the fields. She could feel him burn with an obscure desire when he heard her voice before she came into the house, and watched the warm blood slowly suffuse his dark face when the girl squatted down beside her.

One night when he lay close to her on the mat she heard a stifled groan. She whispered in the dark, 'What's wrong with you, Galal?'

'I want Zeinab my cousin,' he replied without opening his eyes.

'We will marry her to you, my son, when you come back from the army,' she said, patting him on the head like a child.

But now Zakeya stayed silent. He raised his bowed head and looked at her in the dark, and although he could not see her face, he sensed her eyes staring at the iron gate which rose up in the night some distance away from their house.

He asked her again, this time trying hard to conceal the trembling in his voice. 'And Zeinab? What did she do once her father and her sister were no longer in the house?'

'She started to work in the Mayor's house.'

He could not prevent his voice from trembling as he asked, 'What does she do?'

'She washes, and sweeps and cleans the house.'

His whole body started to shiver as he asked again, 'And where does she spend the night?'

'She spends it here with me, my son. She's asleep now, on top of the oven.'

He swallowed quickly. The shiver in his body gradually subsided. He rested his hands on the floor, then paused for a moment before getting up. 'Have you got a clean *galabeya* for me, mother?'

'Yes my son. We've kept the new *galabeya* you had made before leaving for the army.'

He felt as though he was coming back to life. 'Heat me some water. I want to take a bath,' he said.

17

As soon as the Chief of the Village Guard entered the room where the Mayor was sitting he realized at once why he had sent for him. Since the day when Galal had married Zeinab, Sheikh Zahran had been expecting this moment to come. He had voiced his fears to Haj Ismail but the village barber tried to set his mind at rest. 'Don't worry, Sheikh Zahran. Galal has come back from the war a broken man, and he won't dare defy the Mayor. As a matter of fact, he should feel proud that his wife is working for the most important man in our village.'

'You don't know Galal as well as I know him,' said Sheikh Zahran. 'He's one of those stupid men who wax jealous over their wives. And ever since the girl was a child, he's been in love with her.'

'Since he's stupid, he won't be assailed by doubts about anything. It's only intelligent people who wonder about things,' commented Haj Ismail.

'But he's refused to send his wife to the Mayor's house,' said Sheikh Zahran.

'Stupid people like him prefer to eat dry bread and salt, rather than send their wives to work as servants in a house. They think a servant's work is shameful.'

'But this is not just any house! It's the Mayor's house,' objected Sheikh Zahran.

'Stupid people don't differentiate between houses, Sheikh Zahran. To them a house is a house.'

'What do we do if he stops Zeinab from going?'

'Don't start worrying right from now,' said the village barber. 'Maybe the Mayor will have had enough of her by then, and won't want her to go to him any more. You know he gets bored very quickly, and none of these girls has lasted with him very long.'

But the fears of Sheikh Zahran proved to be justified, and the day came when the Mayor said to him, in a voice which brooked no discussion, 'Go, and come back with Zeinab.'

So Sheikh Zahran and Haj Ismail sat in front of the shop smoking the water-jar pipe while they pondered over the problem.

'You don't know Galal like I do,' kept repeating Sheikh Zahran. 'It's true he's an idiot just like the rest of these village men in Kafr El Teen. But we can't be sure that he hasn't learnt a few things since he joined the army, and went to Misr. Don't forget he's lived with soldiers all these years. I doubt if he can be fooled with amulets any more. We have to think of something else from now on.'

'Men in this village are cowards, but they have no shame. Put fear in his heart, Sheikh Zahran. You know how to do that.'

'That's true. But with men like Galal, I prefer to do things without using force. You don't know him well enough. He's not like Kafrawi, and for all you know, he could start creating a lot of problems in the village. Things are getting worse, and people have started to open their eyes much more than before. Prices are rising all the time and the peasants owe more and more taxes to the government. The Mayor is no longer as popular as he was at one time.'

'But you've tried convincing him before and failed,' said Haj Ismail. 'Now you have no choice but to use a bit of force.'

Sheikh Zahran was silent for a long time as though lost in thought. Haj Ismail waited patiently for a while, but then, unable to contain himself any more, he asked, 'What are you thinking of, Sheikh Zahran?'

'I'm thinking of the easiest way. I don't want to use force,' answered Sheikh Zahran.

Haj Ismail looked at him for a long moment before he said in a quiet voice, 'Are you afraid of Galal, Sheikh Zahran?'

The Chief of the Village Guard twirled his whiskers. 'Galal does not frighten me. But somehow this time I feel that something's going to happen. I don't know exactly what, but my mind is not at rest. People have changed, Haj Ismail. The people who at one time could not look me in the eye, now look at me straight in the face, and no longer bow their heads to the ground when I pass by. Just yesterday, one of the villagers refused to pay his taxes and shouted, "We work all the year round and all we end up with are debts to the government." I never used to hear this kind of talk from any of them before. The peasants are getting more and more hungry. All they have to eat is some dry bread and wormy salted cheese. And hunger makes a man blind. It makes him see no one, neither ruler nor God. Hunger breeds heretics, Haj Ismail.'

'They've always been hungry. There's nothing new in that, and the villagers have always lived on dry bread and salted cheese with worms. They've never known anything else.' He fell silent for a moment, and then resumed as though an idea had occurred to him. 'Sheikh Zahran, instead of trying to frighten him, have you thought of trying to tempt him with something really worthwhile? Zakeya and Galal are up to their ears in debt and you are the one who is supposed to collect the taxes they owe to the government. If you suggest to Galal that you might be prepared to be lenient, it could go a long way to making him less obstinate.'

'You have no idea all the things I've attempted with Galal since I found out he'd married Zeinab,' said Sheikh Zahran. 'If I could have stopped the marriage, I would have, but I learnt about it after everything was over. Since then I knew the day would come when the Mayor would send for me to bring Zeinab back, I tried to convince Galal that there was no need for him to stop her from going to the Mayor's house, but he told me that it was she who had refused to go back.'

'Who of the two do you think is refusing?' asked Haj Ismail.

'Most probably it's his influence, since she continued to work for the Mayor until she got married,' answered Sheikh Zahran.

'She must really love him. Or perhaps she feels it's a sin to go to the Mayor's house now that she's married.'

'In any case,' said Sheikh Zahran, 'it's clear that the presence of Galal at her side is an encouragement for her to refuse.'

'Then what did you do after that?'

'After that,' said Sheikh Zahran, 'I tried what you suggested before. I told him we could reduce the taxes he has to pay to the government, but he didn't seem to be interested at all. Now I have no other alternative but to use my authority.'

'But what can you do?'

'He will either pay his debts immediately or else we will confiscate his land.'

'But the land is life to a peasant,' said Haj Ismail. 'If you confiscate it, it's like taking their life. Besides, you might find yourself in a corner if you apply this only to Galal. All the peasants owe taxes to the government so why only him? You had better think of something else, Sheikh Zahran.'

Sheikh Zahran did not proffer any answer. The only way out he could now see was to get rid of Galal in one way or another. He had got rid of Kafrawi by arranging things in such a way that he was accused of a crime and ended in gaol. He continued to scratch his wits in order to find a solution.

Haj Ismail could not hear the questions that were being asked in Sheikh Zahran's mind, but one look at his face was enough to tell him the direction in which his thoughts were moving. They both lapsed into a long silence. All that could be heard was the gurgling sound of the water-jar pipe, or the noise which Haj Ismail made when he cleared his nose and his throat every now and then. The dark night had by now enveloped Kafr El Teen in its heavy cloak, and the air hardly moved over the surface of the river. The sombre mud huts and the winding lanes seemed to sink into a silence as still and profound as the silence of death, as the end of all movement.

18

Zakeya was sitting as still as usual on the dusty threshold of her house, her black eyes watching the lane, and the iron gate with its iron bars, when she heard the noise of many voices, and saw a group of men enter through the doorway, preceded by the Chief of the Village Guard. His voice rang out in the small yard, 'Search the house!'

Before she had time to ask what they wanted, or to understand what was going on, the men had started to move around the small mud hut searching everywhere, behind the doors, on top of the oven, and up on the roof, and in every gap or hole, no matter how small. She stood watching them with an almost dazed look in her wide open eyes. After a while a man appeared carrying a small bundle. He walked up to the Chief of the Village Guard and said, 'We've found it, Sheikh Zahran. He had hidden it on top of the oven.'

The Chief of the Village Guard shouted at the top of his voice, 'The thief! Arrest him immediately. Where is your son, Zakeya?'

'He's in the fields,' she said in a frightened voice. 'What do you want of him? What has he done?'

'Your son Galal is a big thief, Zakeya. He stole this from the Mayor's house,' said Sheikh Zahran, holding out the small bundle. 'Look!' he added, opening it. 'It's full of silver coins.'

She was seized with a feeling of bewilderment soon overcome by her increasing terror at the sight of hundreds of silver coins flashing in the light of the kerosene lamps. But she cried out defiantly, 'My son does not steal, Sheikh Zahran, and he's never been to the Mayor's house.'

Sheikh Zahran's lips twisted into a sneer, which he followed with an ironic, snorting laugh. 'You know nothing about your son, or else you're just pretending that you don't know what he has done. Are you sure he said nothing to you about this bundle?'

'No, Sheikh Zahran,' she answered quickly. 'I know nothing. And my son Galal is certainly not the one who stole these coins.'

The Chief of the Village Guard gave another prolonged snort and asked, 'Then, pray tell me, who stole them, Zakeya, and who hid them on top of your oven. A spirit?'

She slapped her face several times with both her hands and cried out, 'Never, never. My son Galal is not a thief. You will not take him away from us as you did with Kafrawi.'

But they took him. Galal could not understand what was happening. He was taken straight from the field to the police station, in the same *galabeya* he was wearing as he worked. From that moment onwards they kept moving him from one room to another and asking him questions all the time. He walked as though in a dream and from the look in his eyes it was clear that he could not make out a thing of what was going on around him. He felt he was living in a nightmare. He did not know what to answer when they questioned him and all he would say was, 'I don't know anything. I don't know why I'm here. I don't know anything about this bundle. I've never been to the Mayor's house.'

But then they brought the witnesses. One of them was the Chief of the Village Guard in person. There was a witness to say that he had seen him running out of a back door in the Mayor's house. There was a second witness who was sure he had been carrying something which looked like a small bundle. Still a third one maintained that he had called out to him at the time when he had been seen, but instead of answering, he had continued to run until he disappeared through a door opposite the Mayor's house. The Chief of the Village Guard was the last of the witnesses to speak. He said that he had always held Galal in high esteem as a soldier who had done his duty defending the land of his forefathers, and always felt that he could trust him and have confidence in him. But faced with the things which had been brought to his notice, he had been obliged to search the house in which Galal lived. Then after a short pause he added that this was the first time Galal had stolen. He could not understand what had driven him to do so except perhaps that he owed the government a lot of arrears in taxes, and was obliged to pay at least a part of the debt, otherwise the government authorities would have taken the measures that are normal in such cases.

It was clear that the Chief of the Village Guard knew exactly what to say when dealing with the police. He was well versed in their language and they too understood what he was trying to say.

As soon as he was finished the magistrate turned to Galal and asked, 'Have you got anything to say for yourself?'

'I know nothing about this bundle,' he repeated for the hundredth time. The sweat poured from his brow and he looked around him in a daze. 'I never entered the Mayor's house,' he added.

But they sent him off to gaol. He found himself in a narrow room crowded with other people, and he could hardly breathe, or move. When his eyes got accustomed to the absence of light he began to look around. He could see the sallow faces tanned to the hue of dark leather. The eyes were black and large, and they looked at him with the expression of men who have resigned themselves to their fate, and given up fighting a long time ago. For a moment he felt he had seen the face of his uncle Kafrawi. He whispered, 'Uncle Kafrawi?'

But a voice answered in the dark, 'Who's Kafrawi, my son?'

19

When they came to take Galal away, Zeinab held on to his arm and shrieked, 'Don't take my husband away from me. Take me with him.' But the rough strong hands of the men pushed her aside and Galal was driven away in the small van.

She said not one word for three days, nor did she go to the fields, nor lead the buffalo by the rope tied around its neck, as it plodded behind her. She did not even go to the river to fill the earthenware jar with water, or cook, or bake bread. She just sat beside her Aunt Zakeya on the dusty threshold of her house, her eyes silently following the way the van had taken when it carried Galal off to gaol.

On the third day she stood up, went to the stable, took out the buffalo, and left the house leading it behind her. She returned without the buffalo, but between her breasts she was hiding a small handkerchief knotted around a few coins. When she arrived she squatted down beside her Aunt Zakeya without saying anything.

On the fourth day at the crack of dawn she stood up again and went out alone. She continued to walk until she reached the place where the bus stopped. She took it to Bab El Hadeed and then asked a passer-by where she could find the gaol. Along the way she kept asking different people until she reached a station. There she took a train and when she got down walked again until she found herself standing in front of the huge prison door. But the man at the gate told her that visits were forbidden without written permission.

She asked, 'How do I get a permit to visit my husband in the gaol?'

The man explained, and after he had explained she walked back along the same way, took a train and managed to get back to Bab El Hadeed. There she found a tram which dropped her in front of a huge building full of people, and desks, and papers. She entered the building and was swallowed up with the other people. Inside she went from room to room until it was time to leave. And this went on for several days. She felt she was going round and round in an endless journey. After some time the money she had with her was finished. A kind man met her on the way out. He was one of those men who helped women in need to spend the night in the mosque of Al Sayeda. But instead of taking her to the mosque he took her to spend the night with him in his room.

After that no one in Kafr El Teen heard anything more about Zeinab.

20

Since the day they had taken Galal away and Zeinab had gone after him, Zakeya continued to sit on the dusty ground of the entrance to her house without moving or saying a thing. Her eyes stared into the night with a terrible anger like the anger of some wild beast being hunted down. In her mind something was happening very slowly, something like thinking, like a tiny point of light appearing in a dark sky. At moments it would be there and at others it disappeared. She groped in her mind for this tiny star in the infinite night like someone searching for the tip of the thread in a tangled reel of cotton, but it always managed to escape her.

But the darkness of her mind was no longer the same. It had changed. Nor was her mind the same mind it had been before. Something had started to move in it, a tiny flitting thing. And a question kept whispering under the bones in her skull, a question she had never asked before, and which grew louder all the time until it became like a ringing bell. If it was not Galal, and of that she was sure, who was it then?

She suddenly remembered the day when the Mayor sent for Zeinab. Since the girl had married she had vowed to Allah never to set foot in the Mayor's house. Kneeling on the prayer carpet she said to Him, 'I did what Thou willed me to do, O God, and I thank Thee for curing my Aunt Zakeya. Now I am a wife lawfully married according to the *Sunna* of Allah and His prophet, and I will never go there again.' And that night she heard a voice from heaven say to her, 'Yes Zeinab, you are a wife now, and Allah forbids you to go there again.'

It was as though this new awareness had given her a strength which nothing could overcome. No power on earth could any longer convince her to go to the Mayor's house. When the Chief of the Village Guard came to her, she insisted, 'No, I will not go. I refuse to disobey Allah, Sheikh Zahran.'

'But who told you that if you go back to the Mayor's house you will be disobeying Allah? On the contrary, it was Allah who ordered you to go to the Mayor's house, was it not?' asked Sheikh Zahran.

'That was before I married,' cried out Zeinab. 'Now I am a wife and Allah has forbidden me to go there.'

Zakeya was sitting in her usual place listening to what was being said. Suddenly another tiny star lit up in the darkness of her head. She could not grasp anything at the beginning but a slow movement kept going through her mind, and once it started it went on slowly at first, then a little faster. For once she had started to think, it had to go on. She had caught the top of the thread between her fingers and now the reel would keep turning and turning until it reached the end, no matter how long.

Soon another question started to flit through her mind in a subdued whisper which became louder and louder. So in the middle of one night, the night after Galal had gone to gaol, Zeinab felt her Aunt Zakeya give her a violent nudge with her fist, as she lay on the mat beside her. When she looked into the old woman's eyes a shiver went through her spine. They were wide open and something terrible seemed to be going on inside them. She heard her whisper in a strange, hoarse voice, 'Zeinab! Zeinab!'

She whispered back, 'What's wrong, Aunt?'

'I was blind, but now my eyes have been opened.'

'You were never blind,' said Zeinab, shivering all over at the look in her aunt's eyes. 'Your eyes were perfect. But tell me what's wrong?'

For a moment she thought that her aunt had fallen sick again. She clasped her hand and said, 'Lie down, please lie down, Aunt. You are tired. Since they took Galal away you have not slept.'

But the fearsome look in her eyes was still there, almost like a madness, and her voice continued its hoarse whisper.

'I know who it is. I know, Zeinab. I know.'

'Who is it?' asked Zeinab at a loss, and still shivering all over.

'It's Allah, Zeinab, it's Allah,' she said in a distant tone as though her mind had strayed far away.

Zeinab was now shaking violently all over. She took hold of her aunt's hand. It was as cold as ice.

'Ask Allah to have mercy on you. Do your ablutions and pray, so that Allah may forgive us both, and have pity on us.'

'Do not say that, Zeinab. You know nothing,' she cried out in sudden anger. 'I am the one who knows.'

21

Zakeya continued to squat at the entrance to her house with her eyes wide open, staring steadily into the night. Now she never slept, or even closed her eyes. They pierced the darkness to the other side of the lane where rose the huge iron gate of the Mayor's house. She did not know exactly what she was waiting for. But as soon as she saw the blue eyes appear between the iron bars she stood up. She did not know why she stood up instead of continuing to squat, nor what she would do after that. But she walked to the stable and pushed the door open. In one of the corners she noticed the hoe. Her tall, thin body approached and bent over it. Her hand was rough and big, with a coarse skin, and it held the hoe in a firm grip as her big, flat feet walked out of the door. She paused for a moment then crossed the lane to the iron gate. The Mayor saw her come towards him. 'One of the peasant women who work on my farm,' he thought. When he came close he saw her arm rise high up in the air holding the hoe.

He did not feel the hoe land on his head and crush it at one blow. For a moment before, he had looked into her eyes, just once. And from that moment he was destined never to see, or feel, or know anything more.

22

The grey van advanced over the road with Zakeya squatting inside just as she used to squat at the entrance to her house. It sped along streets and roads she had never seen before, or even realized could exist. It was a different world to the world she had known. From a crack in the wood covering the window she could see a river, like the Nile in Kafr El Teen, but to her it did not look like the Nile. The van stopped in front of a huge door. She walked surrounded by the men who had brought her. Around her wrists they had put handcuffs but her large black eyes were wide open. Her lips were tightly closed as though she did not want to say anything, or could not remember words any longer. But every now and then the men around her could see her mutter, like someone talking to herself. She kept repeating in a low voice, 'I know who it is. Now I know him.' In the middle of the night, as she lay on the floor of her cell near the other women prisoners, her lids would remain wide open. She stared into the dark with open eyes but her lips were always tightly closed. But one of the prisoners heard her mutter in a low voice, 'I know who it is.' And the woman asked her curiously, 'Who is it, my dear?'

And Zakeya answered, 'I know it's Allah, my child.'

'Where is He?' sighed her companion. 'If He were here, we could pray Him to have mercy on women like us.'

'He's over there, my child. I buried him there on the bank of the Nile.'

SEARCHING

NAWAL EL SAADAWI

TRANSLATED BY SHIRLEY EBER

FOREWORD BY ANASTASIA VALASSOPOULOS

Foreword

Rawness. Reading *Searching* again, in light of a growing body of work in the Arab world on gender, feminism and social change, is like taking a look at this body from the inside out and seeing it in its raw state. The personal and the political, the body and its context, are constantly in strife, in communication with each other, in tension. Nawal El Saadawi's writing appears affective and effective still. Affective because we, as astute readers, are not permitted to stand still and form tidy conclusions; effective still because the historical context is deliberately unspecified, thus discouraging a located reading that would seek to ground the events in the novel and to explain away the profound questions asked.

Searching tells the story of a young woman, Fouada, who becomes conscious of her life choices after the man she loves disappears. This disruption ignites an intense self-interrogation into the various subjectivities that she inhabits – her role as daughter, as professional, as lover, as human, all come under fire as she roams the streets of Cairo looking for a sign that her life is meaningful, that it does have value and that freedom is a human and humane quality.

Cairo itself is a character in this novel – Fouada walks through the streets, the squares, the restaurants and looks at the buildings and the landscape. What is her role in all this, she wonders. Saadawi convincingly and cinematically draws us in from these wide panoramic scenes into the inner corporeality of Fouada where sensation is embroiled with thought – where the body must try to understand its materiality. Nawal El Saadawi, a well-known activist for women's rights, is also a well-known physician and her interest in the body and its functioning is never far from her creative writing. Pain and suffering are, for Saadawi, first and foremost an assault on the boundedness of the body; on its ability to maintain an order or justice of sorts (one not found in the relations sought outside of it). It is not accidental that our first encounter with Fouada is of her painstakingly examining her sensations; she looks at her face in the mirror and wonders how this face reflects her emotional state. The novel abounds with scenes that move between the constructed reality and order of the outside world and the equally distressing confusion over how the body can react to this reality.

As a writer primarily interested in social circumstances and social consequence, Saadawi has never spent unnecessary time on scene setting and introductory commentary in relation to her storylines or characters – her narration cuts to the quick, to the heart of the matter, and maintains this searching towards a clarity of sorts (I am thinking here of novels such as *Woman at Point Zero*, *Two Women in One* and *Memoirs of a Woman Doctor*). Though she is often described as an author who has not always sought aesthetics over social realism, I find Saadawi's brand of realism a journey into aesthetics itself – a questioning of what type of aesthetics would suit the often poignant circumstances of which she writes. Her deft movement between the internal and the external is an aestheticization of space; of how space can be made knowledgeable and of how external circumstances affect the ability of the body to understand itself and vice versa. Take this scene as an example:

> One of millions, one of those human bodies, crowding the streets, the buses, the cars and the houses. Who was she? Fouada Khalil Salim, born in Upper Egypt, identity card number 3125098. What would happen to the world if she fell under the wheels of a bus? Nothing. Life would go on, indifferent and unconcerned … She looked around in surprise. But why surprise? She really was one of millions … What was so astonishing about that? But it still surprised her, amazed her, something she could neither believe nor accept.

Here, Fouada, and in turn the reader, is being asked to look beyond the bleak overarching reality of Fouada's surroundings and to look instead into the complexity located within the mind that seeks a validation of individuality. This is a constant theme in the novel. Fouada looks with wonder at her name on a hoarding advertising her chemistry lab and shudders 'as though what she read was the notice of her own death'. Sinking deeper into what she calls depression, Fouada experiences a disjointed reality. The searching of the title appears to indicate a searching for words that do not yet exist to encapsulate or describe the variety of unfulfilled desires. In other words, Saadawi seeks to uncover the systems of power that forestall or even prohibit the imagining of another social world – the one that Fouada seeks that is bolstered by a strong sense of social justice. The presence of other characters in the novel – the minister and landlord, her mother, her absent lover – though not always densely portrayed, certainly work to illustrate convincingly how ideology functions. All the characters are a product of the various ideological systems that have produced them and that they in turn feed and produce. Everyone is a victim and a beneficiary of the particular social system – nothing is clear because the way that power functions is not always clear. Fouada ponders these issues through self-reflection:

> She stopped abruptly to ask: But what are feelings? Could she touch them? Could she see them? Could she smell them? Could she put them in a test tube and analyse them? ... She looked around, confused. Were feelings true or false? Why when she looked into Farid's eyes did she feel that he was familiar, and when she looked into Saati's eyes feel that he was a thief? Was that illusion or knowledge? Was it a random movement in the optic nerve or a conscious movement in the brain cells? How could she distinguish between the two?

Saadawi is perceptive to centralize the complexity of the individual, thus forestalling the rather simplistic connection between a villainous society and a central victimized character. Here, knowledge itself is under scrutiny. How do we recognize knowledge and its function? In relation to ourselves, Saadawi seems to be saying; in relation to our desires and needs. How do ideologies gain strength? In relation to others' needs and desires. It is the tension caused by the differences in these desires and the power behind the ideologies that furthermore complicate a fixed notion of social justice. Fouada's mother has dreams that remain unfulfilled; the minister Saati who tries to exploit her has dreams that have been crushed; Fouada has desires that are not compatible with anyone else's, including her lover's whose first love is politics and the pursuit of yet another brand of social justice. Restriction is experienced in many different ways – through gender, through sexuality, through poverty, through political beliefs. I do not intend to undermine the political context that Saadawi is undeniably writing in, that of a restrictive regime that supports corruption, imprisons alternative voices and often turns a blind eye to the shameless denigration of human dignity. Yet Saadawi's novel is neither bound nor restricted by this. Instead, through the use of an often dreamlike quality of internal dialogue, disjointed perceptions and incomplete communications, Saadawi constructs a narrative that powerfully performs a searching of sorts; the search for a voice beyond contextual specificity.

It is tempting to assign an overarching ideology to each of the characters, be it Marxist, neo-capitalist, traditionalist, or whatever, but this would take away from the ways in which Saadawi suggests both the reducibility and the irreducibility of each of the characters into these ideologies, with Fouada orbiting them as a lost soul searching for her way. In many ways, the novel is relevant for readers today as it seeks to transmit frustration and disappointment and to remove the illusion that knowledge is always power. Fouada, for all her insights and knowledge, gives in to the man who most disgusts her. Unable to find a convincing voice with which to express her confusion and her desires, she drifts into Saati's arms like a sleepwalker. However, the novel is keen to remind us of the flitting moments of self-definition, of self-worth, even after it seems that nothing is left.

Searching appears to gesture towards a searching for paradigms within which to understand one's place in the world, how to define and achieve social justice and social equality. Yes, the book is about oppression, but oppression in its many forms – economic, gendered and sexual. Everyone in the novel has a story, a narrative of fear, ambition and disappointment. Through prioritizing Fouada's story, though, Saadawi does make us sensitive to the particular corporeal experience of fear often located in women's narratives. Ultimately, this corporeal fear is nourished by the social uncertainties and confusions that surround Fouada – her place in the world is unclear and her attempt to locate a place within it is filled with uncertainty. Saadawi's text prioritizes this vagueness of searching – a searching that will not necessarily know when it has reached its goal because it does not have the necessary tools to imagine its goal.

I have argued elsewhere on the need to participate in a text's gesturing towards its own construction as a global or universal product. In *Searching*, Saadawi achieves this through the seemingly indisputable language of science – of chemistry. Nevertheless, her achievement is to expand the utility of science beyond its immediate usage and to turn it into a means through which a philosophy of life and society can be measured. In her book *Men, Women and God(s): Nawal El Saadawi and Arab Feminist Poetics*, Fedwa Malti-Douglas argues that Saadawi gains authority through her double role as physician and writer and through contesting the notion of 'natural gender inequality'. Though a physician herself, Saadawi 'denudes medicine and science of part of their magical technological power'. Malti-Douglas argues that in fact medicine becomes 'a repository of [negative] social power' for Saadawi. However, I would like to suggest that in *Searching*, Saadawi posits an uncertainty, rather than a negative position, vis-à-vis the certainty of science. Specifically, Fouada's love of science also represents a love of freedom and creativity. At one of the most poignant moments in the novel,

> Her eyes scanned the sky and the earth. What had she wanted from the start? She hadn't wanted anything, hadn't wanted to succeed or shine. She had only felt, felt there was something in her that was not in others. She would not simply live and die, and the world remain the same. She had felt something in her head, the conception of a unique idea, but how to give it birth?

This 'how' is what preoccupies Fouada – how to voice the desire and creativity, with what language and in what social circumstances? What is the power and weakness in her femininity and the way that she expresses it? What is the meaning of respect and dignity? These are all questions that Fouada cannot find answers to. The novel goes some way to encourage a journey into these thorny and demanding paths – through its gruelling description of pain and loss, confusion and turmoil. Yet it also seeks to turn searching into a poetic endeavour – a searching that reconfigures the questions as it seeks the answers.

Anastasia Valassopoulos
University of Manchester

Part One

That morning as she opened her eyes she felt a strange depression creeping in her veins; stinging ants seemed to be streaming into her heart, where they coagulated like a clot of blood and rubbed against the wall of her heart with the rise and fall of her chest whenever she sneezed, coughed or took a deep breath.

She rubbed her eyes, not understanding the reason for this depression. The sun was as bright as usual, its glowing rays penetrating the window-pane fell onto the wardrobe mirror, throwing a red flame onto the white walls. The leaves of the eucalyptus tree shimmered and quivered like shoals of little fish, and the wardrobe, clothes-stand, shelf – everything was in its usual place.

She threw back the covers, jumping up, and went straight to the mirror. Why did she look at her face the moment she woke up? She didn't know, only that she wanted to assure herself that nothing untoward had happened to her as she slept ... that no white speck had perhaps crept from the white of her eye to invade the black pupil; that no spot had appeared on the tip of her nose.

In the mirror was the same face that she saw every day: brown skin, the colour of milky cocoa; a wide brow on which hung a lock of curly, black hair; green eyes each containing a small black kernel; a long straight nose, and a mouth.

She looked quickly away from her mouth. She hated it, for it was her mouth that spoiled the shape of her face, that ugly involuntary gap as though her lips should have grown more, or her jawbones less. Whether the one or the other, her lips did not close easily, leaving a permanent gap through which showed prominent white teeth.

She pursed her lips and began to look at her eyes as she always did when trying to ignore her mouth. Her eyes had something in them, something that distinguished her from other women, as Farid used to say.

The name Farid reverberated in her head. The veil of sleep was suddenly lifted; she remembered with absolute clarity and absolute certainty what had happened the previous evening. Then she understood the reason for the depression that weighed on her heart: Farid had not kept their date last night.

As she turned from the mirror, the telephone on the shelf by the bed caught her eye. She hesitated for a moment, then walked over to the bed and sat down, staring hard at the phone. She put a finger in the dial to turn the five numbers, then withdrew her hand and laid it beside her on the bed. How could she call him when he had broken their date without apology? Had he broken it on purpose? Was it possible that he did not want to see her? That his love had ended? Had ended as everything ended, with or without reason? And since it had ended, what was the use of knowing why? Besides, was it possible for her to know the reason? She didn't even know why it had started. He used to say that he saw something in her eyes, something he did not see in the eyes of other women, something that distinguished her from other women.

She stood up and walked back to the mirror and again looked into her eyes, examining them closely, searching for that something, and she saw two wide, white ovals in which floated two green discs, a small, black kernel in the centre of each. Eyes like any others, like those of a cow or a slaughtered rabbit!

Where was that something Farid saw? Which she herself had seen? Had seen more than once, inside those two green circles, something that shone out of them distinct and animated, something with a life of its own. Had it gone? How? She remembered neither how it had gone nor if it was from those two green circles it had appeared. Perhaps it had appeared from somewhere else? from her nose, from her mouth? No, not from her mouth, not from that ugly gap …

There was nothing there. She saw nothing appear from any of them. Farid had lied. Why? He lied like anyone else. What was so strange about that? Only Farid was not anyone. He was different, different from others. How? She didn't know exactly. But there was something in his eyes that made her feel he was different. Yes, something in his eyes that she did not see in the eyes of other men, something that shone from his brown eyes, distinct and animated like something alive. What was it? She didn't remember, didn't know, but she had seen it, yes, she had seen it.

She pointed a finger at her eyes, hitting the mirror. She gave a start and looked at the clock. It was eight. Quickly, she turned from the mirror; it was time to go to the Ministry.

In front of the wardrobe she paused again, for the word 'Ministry' had entered her nose with the very air, like a splinter of guilt. She tried to sneeze it out, but, as she breathed, the air thrust it down into her chest to lodge in the triangle beneath her ribs, or, more exactly, the aperture that opened into her stomach.

She knew it would lodge there, graze in that fertile field, eating, drinking and swelling. Yes, it swelled every day and pressed its sharpness into her stomach, which often tried to eject it, contracting and relaxing its muscles to rid itself of all that lay deep inside. But the barb remained, stabbing the wall of her stomach like a needle, clinging with its teeth, like a tapeworm.

She went to the bathroom, feeling a chronic pain under her ribs; wanted to vomit, but couldn't. She leaned her head against the wall. She was ill, a real illness, not faked. She could not go to the Ministry.

Energy spread through her slender body and she turned back to the bed, jumping on to it and pulling up the cover. She might have closed her eyes and slept, but it occurred to her that she must telephone the head of department and excuse her absence.

She pulled the telephone towards her, lifted the receiver, then immediately replaced it, remembering that she had used up all her sick-leave. No illness could excuse her, not even death could give her a holiday. She might claim that every member of her family, one after the other, had died and that she alone remained alive; she was still in her thirties and the head of department would not readily believe the news of her death.

Once again, she dragged her sluggish body from the bed, pressing her fingers into her stomach. She shot a glance at the mirror as she passed, and then dressed. She went towards the door and, opening it, heard her mother's faint voice from the kitchen:

'Aren't you having any tea?'

'I don't have time.'

She went out, shutting the door behind her. In the crowded street her eyes were turned within herself and she saw nothing. She might have walked into somebody or a wall, but her feet moved of their own accord with perfect knowledge, stepping up onto and down from the pavement, avoiding a hole, sidestepping a pile of bricks, as if they had eyes.

They came to a standstill at the bus stop. The dense crowd of bodies jostled her; someone trod on her foot and almost crushed it, but she felt only a pressure on her shoe. She was aware that she was inside the bus only by the vibrations through her body and that curious smell. She didn't know exactly what it was; it was strange; she didn't know where it came from for it did not have a single source, neither the pits under arms nor the dark cavity of mouths nor the flakes of skin that clung to greasy hair.

Something sharp was pressing into her shoulder. She had sensed it before but ignored it since there were many pressures on her from all sides, so why particularly care about her shoulder? But an insistent voice hammered into her ear, like a nail: 'Tickets'. A light rain of spray hit her face. She opened her bag with trembling fingers, for the man glowered at her like a policeman apprehending a thief, muttering something about 'responsibility' and 'conscience'.

She felt her face flush, not because of those two words – alone and out of context they were meaningless – but all eyes were turned towards her, in each a strange look as if in their hearts they too felt accused. But because they knew they would not be punished they were full of secret malice towards the one on whom punishment had fallen.

But she stood accused and as long as she did so she had relinquished all right to respect. Men's eyes took possession of her body the way they appropriated those of prostitutes. Something pushed her. She shrank into her coat, burying her head in its wide collar. Her feet barely touched the ground, delivering her body to the heaving wave of bodies heading for the door. For a fleeting moment she was conscious of violent pressure, like a leaf or a butterfly crushed between books. Suddenly, the pressure relaxed and her body flew through the air like a feather, then hit the ground like a rock.

She got up and brushed the dust from her coat. Looking around, she was delighted to find she was in a place she had never seen before. It seemed that in the moment her body had flown through the air she'd been transported to another world. But her delight quickly faded, for she saw, only a few steps away, the rusty iron railing. The entrenched barb twisted in the wall of her stomach. She opened her mouth to eject it, but hot, dry air thrust in between her lips. A small tear congealed in the corner of her right eye, scratching like a grain of sand.

Looking up and through the iron bars, she saw the black building spattered with yellow blotches that spoiled its original colour. She knew almost certainly that there was a connection between her deep-seated desire to retch and this building, for the feeling always crept upon her whenever she remembered it and grew steadily the nearer she was to it, reaching its climax when she saw it face to face.

She paused in front of the iron gateway, looking around, reluctant to enter. If she delayed for a moment, who knew? Perhaps at that very moment a bomb would descend on the hated building; or someone might drop a lighted cigarette butt in the file store; or the worn-out pump in the head of department's chest would stutter and he would have a heart attack!

But the moment passed and nothing happened. She placed one foot in the gateway, leaving the other in the street. Who knew what might happen from moment to moment? Many things happen from one moment to another. Thousands die, thousands are born, volcanoes erupt, earthquakes bury cities. Many things in life happen from one moment to the next, more than people imagine, for people imagine only what they know, what they understand. Who knows what it means for a rocket to be fired from one moment to another? a rocket with a nuclear warhead? What might be buried if it fell from the sky? Do people know that the sky is jewelled with millions of stars bigger, much bigger, than the earth? That if one of these suspended jewels fell to the earth it would consume it completely? Or would this ugly building alone escape? Would the head of department remain suspended in space above his office chair, licking his fingertips and carefully turning over the attendance register? Such a thing was inconceivable. She smiled, saying to herself, yes of course, it's inconceivable. But her smile froze when she found that – flesh and blood and fully conscious – she had entered the courtyard of the Ministry.

She stopped, tall and slender, staring wildly, in panic, as if her feet had led her to a minefield. Then she sensed some sudden movement in the courtyard. A sleek, black car with a red interior swished across the courtyard as though through water; she was aware that like a huge whale it slid to a stop before the white marble stairs. On each side of these stairs stood a row of statues, each clad in a yellow uniform.

From where had these statues come in that brief moment? Maybe they had always been there and she'd never noticed? There were many things she didn't notice even though they were there. Had she, for example, ever noticed those marble stairs of peerless white?

Her eyes widened in amazement when one of the statues left its place and stepped towards the car. Not stepped in the real sense but twitched and shuddered like a robot, its upper half folded over its lower half as it stretched out a long, stiff arm and opened the car door...

She blinked to expel the grain of sand in the corner of her right eye, but instead it pressed deeper. Through bloodshot eyes, she strained to see what might emerge from the car. First she saw the pointed, black tip of a man's shoe, attached to a short, thin grey-clad leg, then a large, white, conical head with a small, smooth patch in the centre, reflecting the sunlight like a mirror; square, grey shoulders emerged next, followed by the second, short, thin leg ... This body, emerging limb by limb, reminded her of a birth she had seen when she was a child. The car still stood, its curved black roof silhouetted against the entrance to the white marble stairs.

She saw the body laboriously climb the stairs. On each step, it paused, as if to catch its breath, and jerked its neck back. The large head swayed as if it would fall, but it remained securely attached to the neck.

At times it seemed to her as if she were watching this body through a diminishing lens, seeing it as the Tom Thumb of her grandmother's stories. At other times when, as now, she was distracted, this body's reality overpowered her distraction, revealing it as the under-secretary at the biochemistry ministry where she was an employee.

The spacious lobby swallowed him, the car slid away, the statues relaxed and loosened. They walked with flexible legs to the wooden bench by the stairs and sat down. As she passed, they stared at her, blankly, mouths half-open and eyes half-closed. One stuffed a piece of bread into his mouth, another fetched a plate of brown beans from beneath the bench.

She crossed the open courtyard and went to the back of the black building, which was like the back of anything, dirtier, coarser, rougher. She paused before the small wooden door that was covered by a mess of sooty shapes including human finger and hand prints and the letters of fragmented words. She saw the word 'vot…' but dirt had erased the rest.

She walked down the dingy, narrow corridor and climbed the stairs like an automaton; her practised feet jumped over the missing step, her body avoided the iron bar that protruded from the banisters, she reached the fourth floor and turned right to cross the long passageway. She caught the stale smell of urine and turned her head away from the lavatory door; beside it was the door into her office.

She walked over to her desk and sat down. Opening the drawer she took a small cloth and wiped off the dust so that its black skin showed. The skin was torn in places, revealing the desk's white body beneath. She replaced the cloth, looked up and saw three other desks crowded side by side; three mummified heads jutted out above them...

The urine smell lingered in her nose but now, added to it, was another: that of a stale, unaired bedroom. She got up to open the window, but a coarse voice – more like the grunt of a sick animal – said: 'It's cold. Don't open it!'

She returned to her desk, took out a large file and examined the thick outer cover. On it in her own handwriting on a small, white label were the words 'Biochemical Research'. The letters were written with care and elegance, each etched in ink; she recalled how she had pressed the pen on each letter. The pen had been new, the inkpot too, and she could still remember the smell of the ink. Yes, though it was six years ago, she still remembered that smell and the curve of her fingers as she pressed out the letters. She had signed the acceptance for the new job in the biochemical research department and her fingers had trembled as she wrote her name on the official document, the first time she had put her name to an official document, the first time her signature had had an official value.

She opened the file's cover, revealing its yellow interior. Attached to its centre was a thin metal strip from which hung a white sheet of paper with not a single line on it. She closed the file and returned it to the drawer, then raised her head to the sky, but her eyes were stopped by the ceiling. She got up and went to the window to look at the sky through the dirty glass.

Something about the sky relaxed her, perhaps its unfathomable spaciousness, perhaps its deep, steady blue; or perhaps because the sky reminded her of Farid.

She didn't know what connected the sky and Farid but she knew there was a connection; maybe because the sky was always there when Farid was or because it was also there when he was absent? Farid had not come last night. It was the first time he had broken a date. He had not telephoned or apologized. What had happened?

The sky, silent and still, seemed as if in collusion with him. The white clouds continued to drift, unconcerned, and the tree tops were lifted above the distant dark buildings.

Farid was absent for a reason. Everything in life happens for a reason. Things may seem to happen without reason, but sooner or later a reason becomes apparent. But what was the reason? Had there been an accident or an illness or the death of someone close? Or maybe something else? She drummed her fingers on the window-pane. Yes, maybe there was something else – something that Farid wanted to hide. He used to hide things, he hid papers in the drawer of his desk, and sometimes he would close the door when speaking on the telephone.

Such things were normal and unremarkable. Everyone has secrets. Old love letters, unpaid bills, rental contracts on plots of land in the country, a picture of one's mother in a *galabeya** and wooden clogs, or of oneself as a child wearing a *tarbush*† with the tassel missing. Yes, there were always things to hide in a drawer,

---

* An ankle-length gown or robe which is cut to hang loosely; it is worn traditionally by both men and women, although the style, colours and cloth differ.
† A brimless cap resembling a fez.

things one did not always need. Putting them into a locked drawer at the bottom of the desk was blameless. But the long telephone conversations behind closed doors … how to explain them?

She ground the heel of her shoe into the floor and it stuck in a jagged hole in the wood. She tugged to get it out and her shoe came off. She bent down to release the heel, looking around, but the three bowed heads had moved only slightly. She looked at the clock. It was half past ten – three and a half hours before she could leave this graveyard. Sitting down at her desk for a moment, she looked again at the clock; the thin hands had stuck. Tucking her bag under her arm, she got up and strode out.

At the end of the corridor she paused momentarily before going down the stairs. She thought of going up to the fifth floor to apologize to the head of department for leaving early, and put a foot on the stairs. But, instead she descended quickly, shrugging her shoulders and burying her head in the wide collar of her coat.

She soon left the iron railing behind and reached the wide, crowded street, lifting her head from the concealing coat collar. The sun's rays on her back were pleasurable; the pleasure would have been greater except for the weight on her heart. She saw a woman sitting on the pavement, her empty hand outstretched, a young child in her lap. The sun bathed her whole body as she sat silent and still. She was not running away from the Ministry, neither was her heart heavy with such worries.

In the midst of the hurrying crowd, she glimpsed a tall, slender woman who resembled herself. She was walking quickly, pushing forward as if she were about to break into a run but was too embarrassed to do so. A bag swung from her hand, a black leather bag like those carried by doctors or lawyers or civil servants; no doubt it was full of important papers. Its owner waved down a taxi, leaped into it and vanished. She knew where she was going and her movements were light and energetic. Clearly, she was very busy, very engrossed, very absorbed. She had an important job and was happy with it, pleased with herself, felt herself to be important. Yes, that tall, slender young woman was important.

She closed her lips sternly, swallowing hard. Someone important like her would not be idly and aimlessly wandering the streets. She was envious; yes, envy was the word to describe her feelings at that moment. She was unsure of the meaning of the word 'envy' but had inherited it as she'd inherited her nose and arms and eyes. She knew that envy was an extrinsic act, that she couldn't envy herself, that there had to be another person to envy, a person who had to possess enviable characteristics, something important, not important in itself but important to her.

She put her hand into her coat pocket and played with the holes in the silky lining as if searching for something important within herself. Suddenly she discovered that there was nothing important about herself. But it was not exactly a discovery, neither was it sudden, but rather a slow, insidious, obscure feeling, which had started some time ago, perhaps after she'd graduated, perhaps after she'd begun working at the Ministry, perhaps only yesterday when she'd gone to the restaurant and found the table empty, or perhaps this morning when that pointed thing had pushed between her legs as she jumped off the bus.

She swallowed bitter saliva and moved her dry tongue, saying to herself in an almost audible voice: 'Yes, I am nothing.' She would have repeated 'Yes, I am nothing' but her lips tightened and instead the words died inside her mouth where they burned like acid.

She raised her head; her eyes roamed the sky as if in search of something. Yes, she was looking for something. She recalled her mother's voice saying: 'May the Lord make you successful, Fouada my daughter, and may you make a great discovery in chemistry.' She saw the blueness was pockmarked and white clouds drifted indifferently over it. She bowed her head and whispered: 'Your hopes are disappointed, mother, and your pleas are dashed against a silent sky.'

She bit her lip. A great discovery in chemistry! What did her mother know about chemistry? What did she know about any discoveries? Fouada was her only daughter, she laid all her failed ambitions on to her and, unlike other mothers these days, did not think about marriage. Her ambitions were not of the ordinary female type. Before getting married, she had gone to school and perhaps read some stories or a novel about an educated girl who had become great, perhaps the story of Madame Curie or some other memorable woman. But one morning she had opened her eyes and had not found her school pinafore hanging up where she had left it the previous night, and heard her father's gruff voice saying: 'You're not going to school.' She had run crying to her mother and asked her why. The reason was marriage. That was enough for her to hate him from the first glance and she continued to hate him until he died. After his death, while Fouada was still in secondary school, her mother had said, combing her soft black hair in front of the mirror and looking at her slender figure:

'Your future lies in studying, my daughter. There's no use in men.'

Her mother hoped that Fouada would enter medical school, but her grade at the end of the secondary stage was too low.

Perhaps she hadn't studied enough or because in the history class she sat near the window and her eyes wandered to that tall tree laden with large red flowers, like a turban dusted with red copper powder. Sitting in the history lesson, she discovered she loved the colour of powdered red copper, that she loved chemistry and hated history. She could never remember the names of all the kings and rulers who had once governed Egypt; neither did she understand why the living should waste time on the deeds of the dead. Her father was dead and she had perhaps been a little happy when he died, although not for any particular reason; her father had been nothing particular in her life. He was simply a father, but she was happy, because she felt that her mother was happy. Some days later, she heard her say that he hadn't been much use. She was totally convinced of her words. Of what use had her father been.

She saw her father only on Fridays. Usually, he came home after she'd gone to sleep and left before she awoke and the house was quiet and clean, every day except Friday. Her father flooded the bathroom when he took a bath, soaked the living room when he left the bathroom, threw his dirty clothes everywhere, raised his gruff voice from time to time, coughed and spat a lot, and blew his nose loudly. His handkerchief was very large and always filthy.

Her mother put it in boiling water and said to her: 'That's to get rid of the germs.' At the time, Fouada did not know what 'germs' meant, but she heard the biology teacher say in one of the classes that germs were small, harmful things. That day, the teacher had asked the class: 'Where are these things to be found, girls?' The class was silent and none of the girls raised her hand, but Fouada raised hers confidently and proudly. The teacher smiled at her courage and said gently: 'Do you know where germs are found, Fouada?' Fouada got to her feet, head above the other girls, and said in a loud, confident voice, 'Yes, miss. Germs are found in my father's handkerchief.'

* * *

Fouada found herself at home, in her bedroom, sitting on the edge of the bed and staring at the telephone. She had no idea how she had got there or how her legs had carried her on and off the bus at the right stops, how they had carried her from the bus stop to the house or how they had done all this of their own accord without her knowledge. But she gave this matter little thought as she did not suppose this to be a characteristic or distinction peculiar to her own legs. A donkey's legs did the same thing, quietly and silently.

She reached for the telephone, put a finger in the hole and dialled the familiar five numbers. She heard it ring, and leaned against the bedrest, preparing for a long reprimand. But the ringing went on. She looked at the clock. Midday. Farid did not leave the house before one or two. Was he reading in bed? There was a long passageway between the bedroom and the study where the telephone was. Was he in the bathroom and could not hear the phone from behind the closed door? She looked up to the window and saw a branch of the eucalyptus tree playing against the pane. Trees, too, could play. The receiver was still pressed to her ear, the bell was still ringing loudly. Something occurred to her and she put the receiver down for a moment, then, lifting it, redialled the number, carefully ensuring that her finger followed the correct sequence. Immediately the dial stopped after the five turns the ringing pierced her ear like a missile. She pressed the receiver to her ear for a long time; long enough for someone to come out of the bathroom or awaken from sleep. Another idea occurred to her and she replaced the receiver for a moment, then lifted it and called the operator. She asked, was there a fault on the line? A moment later, a gentle voice replied:

'The telephone is in order. It's ringing for you.'

The bell's brazen sound again filled her ear, sharp, loud and continuous. She hung up, leaned her head against the pillow and stared at the window.

Never before had she thought about her relationship with Farid; she had simply lived it. There was no room for both – either live it or think about it. Farid was always busy, spending hours with his books and papers, either writing or reading things, which he put away carefully in the drawer of his desk and locked with a key. He went out every evening and stayed out late. Some nights he stayed away from home. She never asked him where he went, not wanting to take on the role of inquisitive wife, not wanting to take on the role of wife at all. She valued her freedom, her own room, her own bed, her own secrets, her own mistakes –

they weren't really mistakes. Sometimes she loved to disappear and Farid did not know where she was. She delighted to hear words of admiration from a man's mouth, a delicious but never surprised delight, for she was sure something in her was worthy of admiration. But Farid was the centre of her life. Other days she swallowed like a dose of bitter medicine, then Tuesday would arrive in all its wondrous splendour. For on Tuesday she met Farid. Every Tuesday, at eight in the evening in that small restaurant when the weather was warm, or at his house on cold winter nights. How many winters had their relationship seen? She didn't know exactly, only that she had known Farid for a long, perhaps very long, time.

How many winters had passed, how many Tuesdays! And every Tuesday, Farid had been waiting, had not lied once. If he concealed some things from her, he never lied, even when the question of marriage had somehow arisen. Looking at her with shining brown eyes, he had told her: 'I can never marry.' If any other man had said that to her, she might have doubted him or have felt it as an insult. But Farid was different, with him everything became different. Even words lost their familiar, traditional meaning and the names of things might suddenly become inapplicable, meaningless. The word 'dignity' for example. What does it mean? To preserve one's self-respect? Against whom? Against others? Yes. There must be others before whom one's self-respect must be protected.

But between her and Farid, there were no 'others', or any such thing as her self against his self. They shared everything in love, even their selves – she became him and he became her. He protected her rights and she his. Something strange, something extraordinary happened between them, but it happened effortlessly, spontaneously – as naturally as breathing.

Hearing her mother in the living room shuffling towards her door, she quickly got up from the bed and began moving around the room. She did not want her to come in and see her looking solemn and staring into space, like a sick person. Her mother stood at the door in her white headscarf and long *galabeya*, saying in a hoarse, faint voice:

'I see you're wearing outdoor clothes. Are you going out?'

'Yes.'

'And lunch?' her mother said.

Fouada picked up her handbag, ready to leave, saying:

'I'm not hungry.'

Fouada didn't know why she was going out. Only that she didn't want to stay in, but to move, to see movement around her, to hear a loud clamour, louder than that bell that rang, persistently, endlessly in her ear. She left her street and turned right to walk alongside the stone wall to the flower garden. White jasmine glinted like silver in the bright sunlight. As usual, she reached out to pluck a spray, crushing it between her fingers and breathing in its scent. The heavy weight in her heart moved. The scent of jasmine was for her meeting Farid, his kiss on her neck. But now its poignant scent seemed to epitomize his absence, and confused feelings of nostalgia and reality stirred deep inside her. It was all like an illusion, like a dream, that ends when you awaken.

She let the crushed jasmine flowers fall from her fingers, and walked along the narrow street, turning into Nile Street. Suddenly she knew she hadn't left the house without reason or simply to move; she had a particular goal. A few more steps and she found herself in front of the small restaurant.

She hesitated, then entered, crossing the long passageway between the trees. Her heart began to pound, imagining that emerging from the passageway she would see Farid sitting at the white-cloth-decked table, his back towards her, his face to the Nile, his shoulders tilted forward slightly, black hair failing thickly behind his small flushed ears, long slender fingers on the table playing with a scrap of paper or turning the pages of the notebook he always kept with him, or doing something but never staying still.

Yes, she would see him sitting like that. She would tiptoe up behind him, put her arms round his head and cover his eyes with her hands. He would laugh and grab her hands and kiss each finger one by one.

Her heart was thumping violently when she reached the end of the passageway. She turned to the left and looked towards the table. She felt a stab in her heart. The table was empty and naked, with no white cloth. She approached and touched it, as if looking for something Farid had forgotten, a piece of paper he had left for her, but her fingers met only the smooth wooden surface, the wind battering it from all sides, like the trunk of an old tree.

The waiter came over, smiling, but looked down when he saw the look on her face. She walked towards the passage but before turning into it, spun around to look again at the table. It was still empty. She ran towards the passageway and hurriedly left the restaurant.

She found herself in Doqi Street. Seeing a bus about to move off, she jumped onto it without knowing where it was going. She got one foot on the platform, the other hung in the air. Hands reached out to help her on and she managed to push her foot between the others on the step. Long, strong arms surrounded her to prevent her falling, then she found herself huddled with the other bodies inside the bus.

One of millions, one of those human bodies crowding the streets, the buses, the cars and the houses. Who was she? Fouada Khalil Salim, born in Upper Egypt, identity card number 3125098. What would happen to the world if she fell under the wheels of a bus? Nothing. Life would go on, indifferent and unconcerned. Maybe her mother would write her obituary in the paper, but what would a line in a newspaper do? What would it change in the world?

She looked around in surprise. But why surprise? She really was one of millions, really was one of the bodies crammed into the bus, and if she fell under the wheels and died, her death would change nothing in the world. What was so astonishing about that? But it still surprised her, amazed her, something that she could neither believe nor accept.

For she was not one of millions. Deep inside something assured her that she was not one of millions, was not simply a moving lump of flesh. She could not live and die without the world changing at all. Yes, in her heart of hearts something assured her, and not hers alone but in her mother's heart, and her chemistry teacher's – and in Farid's heart.

She heard her mother's voice saying: 'You will be someone great like Madame Curie', then the voice of her chemistry teacher saying: 'Fouada is different from the other girls in the class', and Farid's voice whispered in her ear: 'You have something in you that other women don't have.'

But what was the use of these voices, these words? They had resounded once or twice, vibrations disturbing the air, then they were over. Her mother had said it to her when she was young, a long time ago. The chemistry teacher had said it when she was in secondary school many years ago. And Farid, yes Farid too had told her, but Farid's voice had vanished into the air and he himself had disappeared as if he had never existed.

A fat woman stepped on her foot. The conductor tapped her shoulder to pay for the ticket. A large hand reached out from behind and pressed her thigh. Yes, one body amongst others crowding the world, filling the air with the smell of sweat, one of millions, millions, millions. Unaware, she said aloud: 'Millions, millions!' The fat woman stared at her with large, cow-like eyes and breathed a smell of onions into her face so that she turned away. Through the window she saw Tahrir Square and with all her strength pushed her way out of the bus.

* * *

She stood in the huge square, looking around and up at the tall buildings, their facades plastered with names written in broad lettering: doctors, lawyers, accountants, tailors and masseuses. She particularly noticed a sign on which was written: 'Abd al-Sami's Analysis Laboratory'. Suddenly, something dawned on her, as if a small searchlight had focused in her head. The idea flashed through her mind as clear as a new light. It had always been there, hidden in the recesses, unmoving, but it was there and she knew it.

Now it had begun to move, to emerge from its hidden corner into the field of light. Fouada could read it, yes, written in clear broad letters on the facade of the building: 'Fouada's Chemical Analysis Laboratory'.

That was the deep-seated idea in her head. She didn't know when it had begun, for she merely remembered dates and was not good at calculating time. Time could pass quickly, very quickly, as quickly as the rotation of the earth. Sometimes it seemed to her that it did not move at all, and at others that it moved slowly, very slowly, and the earth trembled as though a volcano was erupting from its depths.

The idea had started long ago. It had occurred to her once when she was sitting in the chemistry class at school. It was not quite so clear but had appeared through a mist. She had been transfixed by a curious movement inside a test tube, colours that suddenly appeared and disappeared, vapours with strange smells, a different sediment at the bottom, a new substance – the result of the chemical interaction of two other substances – with new characteristics, new form, new wavelength. The chemistry lesson ended and she stayed in the laboratory, mixing substances together, observing the reactions with delight, sniffing the gas that rose from the mouth of the test tube, then shouting with joy: 'A new gas! Eureka!'

The slender, bullet-like body of the lab assistant rushed over and, exploding like flammable gas, yelled 'Get out!', snatching the test tube from her hands and pitching her discovery down the sink, cursing the day he had become a lab assistant in a wretched girls' school. He could have been an assistant in a college of science if he had completed his studies. She lost her temper when he threw her unique experiment down the drain and she cried: 'My discovery's lost!' She saw his look of contempt, then turned away and ran from the laboratory. His contemptuous glance haunted her and hindered her experimentation for a long time, and might have ultimately deterred her from pursuing the idea of discovery, but her mind was obsessed with the chemistry class and the chemistry teacher.

The chemistry teacher was as tall and slender as herself, her eyes always smiled and radiated a deeply thoughtful and confident look. It seemed to her that this look was directed towards her alone and not to the other girls in the class. Why? She didn't know exactly. There was no real proof of it, but she felt it, felt it forcefully, especially when she ran into her in the schoolyard, looked at her, then smiled. She didn't smile at all the girls. No, she didn't smile at everyone. That had been the historic day when the inspector had come and the teacher asked a question that nobody in the class – only Fouada – could answer. That day, she heard the teacher say, in front of the whole class and the inspector too: 'Fouada is different from the other girls.' That was exactly what she'd said, no more, no less. It was engraved in her brain just as she had pronounced it, word for word, with the same pauses, the same intonation, the same punctuation. The word 'different' was etched especially deeply, the first syllable emphasized...

Yes, Fouada loved chemistry. Not with an ordinary love like her love for geography, geometry and algebra, but something extraordinary. As she sat in the chemistry lesson, her brain would leap alertly and, like a magnet, everything around her was liable to stick to it – the teacher's voice, her words, her glances; particles of powdered substances might fly through the air, metallic fragments might scatter over the table, particles of vapour and gases might drift through the room. Every particle, every tremor, every vibration, every movement and every thing – her brain picked them all up, just as magnets attract and hold metal particles.

After all this, it was inevitable that her mind turned to chemistry and for everything around her to take on chemical forms and qualities. It was not unusual for her to feel one day that the history teacher was made of red copper, that the drawing teacher was made of chalk, that the headmistress was made of manganese, that hydrogen sulphide gas came out of the mouth of the Arabic teacher, that the sound of the hygiene teacher's voice was like the rattle of tin fragments.

All the teachers, men and women, acquired mineral qualities, except one – the chemistry teacher. Her voice, eyes, hair, shoulders, arms and legs, everything about her was utterly human, was alive, moved and pulsated like arteries of the heart. She was a living person of flesh and blood with absolutely no relation to minerals.

But her voice was the most remarkable thing about her. It had a fragrance as sweet as orange blossom or a small, untouched jasmine flower. Fouada would sit in the chemistry class, her eyes, cars, nose and pores open to the sweet voice, the words seeping in through all these openings like pure, warm air.

One day, the voice brought her the story of the discovery of radium. Previously, it had brought her the names of famous men who had discovered things. She would bite her nails as she listened, telling herself that if she were a man she would be able to do likewise. Obscurely, she felt that these discoverers had no greater talent for discovery than she, only that they were men. Yes, a man could do things a woman could not simply because he was a man. He was not more able, but he was male, and masculinity in itself was one of the preconditions for discovery.

But here was a woman who had made a discovery, a woman like her, not a man. The obscure feelings about her ability to make a discovery became clearer and she grew more convinced that there was something that waited for her to lift a veil and discover it, something that existed, like sound and light and gases and vapours and uranium rays. Yes, something existed that only she knew about.

* * *

Fouada found her body stretched out on her bed with her eyes fixed on the ceiling, on a small, jagged patch where the white paint had flaked off to reveal the cement beneath. Her feet were sore from so much walking around the streets off Tahrir Square. She didn't really know why she had walked, but it was as if she were searching for something. Perhaps she was searching for Farid amongst the people she encountered, because she stared into men's faces and examined the heads of people who passed by in cars or taxis; or perhaps it was an empty apartment she was looking for, because here and there she would pause in front of a new building and stare confusedly at the caretaker.

But now she was staring at a jagged patch of ceiling, not thinking of anything in particular. Hearing the sound of her mother shuffling towards her room, she quickly pulled up the cover and closed her eyes, pretending to be asleep. She heard her mother's panting breath and knew that she was standing at the doorway watching her sleep. Fouada tried to keep still and to let her chest rise and fall with regular, deep breathing. Then her mother's footstep shuffled away from her room. She might have opened her eyes and resumed staring at the ceiling, but she felt relaxed with her eyes closed and thought she might sleep. But then she leaped out of bed, for an idea had struck her. She wrapped herself in a large overcoat and made for the door of her room but then hesitated, walked to the telephone and dialled the five numbers. The ringing was sharp, shrill and uninterrupted. Replacing the receiver, she hurriedly left the house.

She walked rapidly, her feet taking her from street to street. She jumped on to a bus whose number she recognized, got off at a stop she knew only too well and turned right into a small street, knowing that at the end of it was a white three-storey house with a small wooden door.

The dark-skinned caretaker was sitting on his bench at the entrance to the stairs. She was just about to ask after Farid when she caught that inquisitive glance common to all caretakers. He knew her, had seen her time and again going up to Farid's apartment, but each and every time he gave her the same searching look, as if not recognizing the relationship that existed between herself and Farid. She bounded up the stairs, then stood panting in front of the dark-brown, wooden door. The kitchen window overlooking the stairs was open. So Farid was in, hadn't had an accident as she had imagined, hadn't been carried away by the sky. Her heart beat painfully and she considered leaving quickly before he saw her. He had missed their date on purpose, not by accident, and had not telephoned her to explain why. She would have turned on her heel and left except that she saw no light behind the glass peep-window. The apartment was in total darkness. Maybe he was reading in his bedroom and the bedroom light did not reach that far?

She pressed the bell and heard the high-pitched ringing in the flat. She kept her finger on the bell and the sound rang loud and hard in the living room but no one came to the door. She took her finger off the bell and the sound stopped. Again, she pressed it and again the loud, harsh sound reverberated through the living room in the apartment without anyone opening the door. She put her ear to the door hoping to hear the sound of movement or stifled breathing or a sigh, but nothing. Then suddenly, the sound of the telephone ringing came from the study and she leaped backwards, imagining that it was herself calling him from her house. But she was standing in front of the door so it couldn't be her phoning him now. The telephone continued to ring for a few moments, then stopped. Her ear to the door, she heard nothing to indicate the presence of a living being in the apartment. Hearing the clatter of stiletto heels coming up the stairs, she moved away from the door a little and pressed the bell again. From the corner of her eye, she saw a fat woman climbing the stairs. She kept pressing the bell, looking ahead until the woman vanished around the bend of the staircase. She waited a few minutes more until the sound of the thin, clattering heels stopped, and then slowly and heavily made her way downstairs.

She let her feet take her where they would. Thoughts raced through her head almost audibly. Farid had failed to meet her on Tuesday, had not telephoned her and was not at home. Where could he be? He could not be in Cairo or in a nearby town. He must be somewhere far away, where there was no phone or post office. Why was he hiding the reason for his absence from her? Didn't their relationship make it his duty to say? But what sort of relationship was it that made it a person's duty to act in a particular way towards another person? What was it that made it his duty? Love?

The word weighed in her mouth like a stone. Love. What did love mean? When had she first heard it? From whose mouth? She did not remember precisely, but the word had been in her ear all her life. She used to hear it often and because she heard it often, she did not know it, like the feminine parts of herself which she often saw attached to her body and washed with soap and water every day without knowing them. Her mother was the cause. Perhaps if she'd been born without a mother, she would have known everything spontaneously. When she was very young, she learned that she had been born from an opening beneath her mother's stomach, perhaps the same opening through which she urinated or another one nearby. But when she told her mother of her discovery, she scolded her and said that she'd been born from her ear. With this explanation, her mother perverted her natural feelings and many of her intuitions were blocked for a long while. For a time, she tried to create a relationship between hearing and birth, sometimes doubting that the ear was for hearing but rather, perhaps, that it was made for married women to urinate from. She did not understand why she always linked birth to urinating and felt that the two must be related. She continued searching for the site of the opening through which she had emerged into the world and thought she might find out in the history or geography or hygiene class, but they taught her everything but that. She had a lesson on chickens and how they laid and hatched eggs, a lesson on fish and how they reproduced, a lesson on crocodiles and snakes and every living creature except humans. They even studied how date palms pollinated each other. Could the date-palm be more important to them than themselves? Towards the end of the year, she put up her hand and asked the hygiene teacher; but she considered the question to be rude and punished her by making her stand against the wall with her arms up. Staring at the wall, Fouada wondered why plants, insects and animals impregnated each other and this was considered one of the sciences, whereas in the case of humans it was considered something shameful that merited punishment?

* * *

Fouada found she was walking along Nile Street. Heavy darkness covered the surface of the water, the lights of circular lamps reflected on both sides. As it slid along in the darkness, the long and slender Nile looked like the flirtatious body of a woman in black, mourning for a hated husband, beads of imitation pearls dotting the sides of her black gown. Looking around her in the dark, everything seemed dreamlike, surreal. Even the door of the small restaurant overhung with cheap coloured lights projected an eerie, ghostly shadow. She passed by the door without going in, but then retraced her steps and entered. She walked down the path under the trees and at the end turned to look at the table. It was not empty. A man and a woman were sitting there. The waiter was laying glasses and plates in front of them, giving them the same smile that he gave herself and Farid. She turned quickly before he saw her, and left the restaurant.

She walked down Nile Street, head lowered. What had brought her here? Didn't she know that these places were in collusion with Farid, declared his absence and hid him? Hypocrisy and contradiction engulfed her like a dark web. She stamped her foot in anger. What had got into her? Farid had left her and vanished, so why was she hovering around his places? Why? She must banish him from her life just as he had banished her from his. Yes, she must.

The very thought seemed to calm her and she looked up at the street. But her heart lurched violently for she had seen a man coming towards her who walked like Farid. She hurried towards him. His shoulders were hunched slightly and he moved slowly and cautiously. The same movements as Farid! They came closer and closer. He swung his arms in a particular way, not like Farid did. When he was a few steps away, she opened her mouth to gasp: 'Farid!' but the light of a passing car swept the shadow from a face that was not his. Her heart fell like a lump of lead and she shrank into her coat. The man nodded his bald head suggestively. She turned away and hurried off, but he walked behind her, whispering half-formed, incomprehensible words. She turned off Nile Street into a side road and he followed, continuing to stalk her from street to street until she reached the front of her own house.

She opened the door panting. Not hearing her mother's voice, she tiptoed across the living room to see her mother through the open door of her room asleep in bed. She was lying on her right side, her head wrapped in a white shawl and raised on two thick pillows, her thin body hidden under a folded woollen blanket.

Fouada went into her room and closed the door. She stood motionless in the centre for a while, then began to get undressed. She put on a nightdress, took off her watch and put it on the shelf beside the telephone. As her hand touched the cold telephone, she shivered and looked at the time. It was midnight. Was Farid at home? Should she try and call him? Shouldn't she stop this pursuit? She could always dial the number, and if he answered she could hang up. Yes, he would not know who was calling.

She put her finger in the dial and turned it five times. The familiar ringing sounded even louder in the quiet of the night. She covered the earpiece with the palm of her hand, thinking that the loud ring might awaken her mother. The bell continued to screech in her ear like a hungry animal, its echo pounding in her head and bouncing off it as though it were a wall of solid stone.

She replaced the receiver to stifle the screeching, threw herself on the bed and closed her eyes to sleep. But she did not sleep. Her body remained outstretched on the bed, her head on the pillow. She opened her eyes and saw the wardrobe, the mirror, the clothes-stand, the shelf, the window and the white ceiling with the jagged patch from which the paint had fallen. She closed her eyes and let her chest rise and fall with deep, regular breathing. But still she did not sleep. Her body remained, with all its weight and density, on the bed. She turned onto her stomach, burying her face in the pillow, pretending to lose consciousness. But she remained conscious, her body stretched out under the coarse woollen cover. She rolled over onto her left side and opened her eyes, seeing nothing except the darkness. She imagined that her eyes were still closed or that she had lost her sight, but a faint strip of light presently appeared on the wall. She pressed her head into the pillow and pulled the cover over her eyes, but still could not sleep. The familiar weight of her head remained on the pillow. A soft hum began, very softly at first, then it gradually grew louder until it became a sharp continuous whistle like the ringing of an unanswered bell. She imagined that the telephone receiver was by her ear and put her hand under her head, but found only the pillow. The humming stopped when she took her ear off the pillow, then began again. She held her breath for a moment and the source of the sound became clear. It was those familiar repeated beats of her heart, but on no previous night had they been as strongly audible as a hammer nor so continuous. On any other night, she put her head down on the pillow without hearing anything and in a few moments was fast asleep. How did she used to fall asleep? She tried to find out how she slept every night, but suddenly discovered that she did not know. Her body felt heavy, as if shackled with chains, and then she lost consciousness. She remembered that once or twice she had tried to find out how she lost consciousness in sleep and had opened her eyes before drifting off, hanging on to the very last moment of consciousness to see what was happening to her, but sleep always overcame her before she found out.

Really, she knew nothing, not even the simplest things. She did not know by intuition and did not learn from repetition. How many nights of her life had she slept away? She was now aged thirty, every year had three hundred and sixty-five days, so she had slept ten thousand, nine hundred and fifty nights without knowing why.

She pressed her head into the pillow. The humming echoed in her head, a head as solid as stone, a head that knew nothing, did not know where Farid had vanished, did not know why she had gone to the college of science, did not know why she was working in the biochemical research department of the Ministry, did not know what chemical research to do, did not know the old, deep-seated discovery which had to be found, did not know how to sleep. Yes, an ignorant solid head of stone that knew nothing and was only able to repeat this empty echo, like a wall.

It seemed to her that a heavy, high wall had fallen on her and that her body was being crushed into the ground. She felt water surround her from all sides as if she were swimming in a deep and wide sea. Although she didn't know how to swim, she swam with the utmost skill as if flying through the air. The water was deliciously warm. She saw a huge shark glide under the water, its great jaws open, in each jaw long, pointed teeth. The beast came nearer and nearer, its mouth opening into a long dark tunnel. She tried to get away but couldn't. She screamed in terror and opened her eyes.

* * *

Daylight was filtering through the narrow slats of the shutters. She lifted her head from the pillow and, feeling dizzy, put it down again. Then she reached out and took the watch off the shelf. Glancing at it, she jumped out of bed and dressed quickly. She gulped down the cold cup of tea her mother had prepared and went out into the street.

The cold air struck her face and she shivered and moved her arms and legs briskly, but suddenly felt a pain in her stomach and slowed down. She pressed her fingers to the soft triangle beneath her ribs and located the pain, deep inside her flesh, gnawing at the wall of her stomach like a worm with teeth. She didn't know the reason for this strange pain which attacked her every morning.

She waited at the bus stop, but when the 613 to the Ministry came, she stood still and stared at it. As it moved off, she realized that she ought to be on it and ran after it, but couldn't catch it. She went back to the stop, feeling a sense of relief. She would not go to the Ministry today. All her leave had been used, but what would happen if she didn't go today … would it change anything in the world? Not even her death or flesh-and-blood absence from the world would change anything, so how important would be her absence from the Ministry today? One blank space in the old attendance register with its tattered cover.

The world around her brightened at the thought. She looked at the people contemptuously as they ran panting for the buses, blindly hurling themselves onto them. Why were these fools running? Did any one of them know how they slept last night? Did any one of them know that if they fell under the wheels and died or if the whole bus overturned with them and everyone inside and was submerged in the Nile, did they know that this would mean nothing to the world?

Another bus stopped in front of her. There were some empty seats, so she got on and sat down beside an old man. He was holding yellow prayer beads between his trembling fingers, softly muttering 'Oh Protector! Oh Protector! Lord protect us! Lord protect us!' from time to time peering from the windows up at the sky through encrusted, lashless eyes. It seemed to Fouada that some catastrophe had just that minute befallen the man so she smiled at him gently to console him, but he took fright and cowered into his seat away from her, his thin body pressing up against the window. 'How much fear there is in the world!' she said to herself and turned away.

On the other side, a young woman stood beside her. The bus was now packed with standing passengers. A waft of perfume came from the woman, on her face that familiar layer of powder, on her lips that blood-red coating. Her body was slim and so short that her stomach bumped against Fouada's shoulder as she sat, but her buttocks were round and prominent behind her.

For no reason, Fouada suddenly jumped up. The woman squeezed into the seat in her place, huffing in irritation. Fouada pushed her way through the bodies, then hurled herself from the bus before it pulled away from the stop, her feet landing on the ground. She almost fell over but managed to stay upright and, looking up to see where she was, found herself in front of the rust-covered railings of the Ministry.

Like a bucketful of cold water in her face she realized where she was, remembering that she had intended not to go to the Ministry. But unknowingly her feet had brought her along her usual daily path, like a donkey before whom the door of the barn opens and who emerges alone and automatically into the field. And since it is automatic, it is very natural, like a baby emerging from its mother's womb.

She looked up at the gloomy building and saw it bulging out of the open courtyard, like her mother's stomach. Long wide cracks spread over its dark brown surface like stretch marks. She caught a strange smell, like the one she smelled in hospital maternity wards or in stale toilets. As she stumbled forward, the feeling of nausea intensified and she knew she was approaching her office.

* * *

The head of department was angry. He spoke loudly, saliva sprayed from his lips and a drop landed on her cheek. She left it there and did not wipe it off with her handkerchief, pretending to be unaware of it.

'You left your office before time yesterday, three and a half hours early!' she heard him say.

The word 'yesterday' resonated in her ear and without thinking she repeated:

'Yesterday?'

The director's thick lips curled in disdain and his shiny bald head nodded as he shouted:

'Yes, yesterday, or have you forgotten?' As if talking to herself, she said:

'No, I haven't forgotten, but I thought that it happened…' She swallowed the rest of the sentence '…a week or two ago.'

He continued speaking loudly, but she was not listening. She was wondering about the way people spend their time, how feelings of time do not always correspond to the number of hours or minutes that pass. Can the steady and continuous movement of the hands of a clock inside that limited, small circle be an accurate measure of time? How is it possible to measure something invisible and unlimited by something visible and limited? How do we measure something we don't see or feel or touch or taste or smell or hear? How do we measure something non-existent with something existent?

A thought occurred to her which she believed no one else had ever had. She felt a secret joy, the signs of which she hid from the head of department. She didn't know why or how she opened her mouth but suddenly she said to him:

'I've been working in this research department for six years now, and I believe I have the right to carry out research from today.'

As if she had delivered an insult, the director's bald head turned red and, sitting at his desk, he looked like an ape standing on its head, its behind in the air.

'Why are you smiling like that?'

She tightened her lips so as not to answer him, but instead blurted out:

'You may have the right to dock me for the time I was absent, but you have no right to ask me why I am smiling!'

She imagined that he would get even angrier and his voice get even louder, but he suddenly fell silent as if stunned by her unusual ability to answer back. His silence encouraged her to pretend to be angry and, raising her voice, she said:

'I do not accept that anyone, no matter who, should trample on my rights, and I know how to defend them!'

The redness of his bald head faded to a pale yellow, making it look like a melon.

'What rights of yours have I trampled on?' he exclaimed in astonishment.

Waving a hand in the air, she shouted:

'You trampled on two important rights ... first when you asked me why I was smiling, and second when you finished the question with the words 'like that'. The first right is my right to smile, and the second right is my absolute right to choose how I smile.'

His deep-set eyes widened, creasing the cushions of flesh around them, and he gasped in utter amazement:

'What is it you're saying, miss?'

Fouada was shaken by an inexplicable anger and without thinking snapped:

'And who told you I was a miss?'

His eyes widened still further.

'Well, aren't you?' he said.

Fouada thumped the desk with her fist and shouted:

'How dare you ask me such a question. What gives you the right? The regulations...?'

How had the scene changed so fast, so that now she, Fouada, was the angry one and had appropriated the right to be so? The head of department was now more afraid of her than surprised, and that fierce look with which he fixed his subordinates had vanished from his eyes to be replaced by a tame, almost respectful one, much like the one he gave the undersecretary and his immediate superiors. She heard him say in what would have been a gentle voice, had he practised the words over a number of years:

'It seems you're tired today. You're not yourself. I apologize if something I said offended you.'

He put his papers under his arm and left the room. She stared at his back as he went through the door. It was bent like an old man's, but not bent with age, rather with that premature curvature that afflicts civil servants from so much bowing and bending.

Leaving the Ministry that day, immediately she had left the rusty iron railings behind, Fouada told herself 'I will never go back to that dingy tomb.' She didn't pay much heed to the phrase for she had said it every day for the last six years. She set off for the bus stop to make her way home, but when she reached it her feet carried on walking down the street. She didn't know where she was going, just went on, aimlessly. She looked at the people striding quickly, purposefully and with determination towards a definite and conscious goal. She wondered at how they could achieve such a miracle, and at the utter ease with which they moved their legs. She spun around not knowing which direction to take and experienced herself as alone, inside a closed circle. No one turned with her, no one was with her, no one at all.

She raised her head and, with a start, saw the tall buildings with placards fixed to the walls. She suddenly remembered that she had come to a decision sitting at her desk that morning, a final, an irreversible decision. Yes, she would rent a small apartment and turn it into her own chemical laboratory. She drew herself up and stamped her foot forcefully. Yes, that was her decision and that was her intention, and neither of them would she relinquish.

Finding herself in Qasr al-Nil Street she strolled along it examining the buildings. From time to time, she stopped to ask a caretaker if there was a vacant apartment. At the Opera end of the street, she crossed over and retraced her steps, scrutinizing the buildings on the other side.

One caretaker she asked peered at her with his dark face and bloodshot eyes, then asked:

'Have you got a thousand pounds with you?'

'What for?' she said.

'There's an apartment going vacant at the beginning of the month, but the owner wants to sell the furniture to whoever rents it.'

'Is the furniture in the apartment?' she asked.

'Yes,' he replied.

'Can I see it?'

'Yes,' he said.

She followed him into the lobby of the building. He went to the lift, pressed number 12 with a finger, long and thin, like a black pencil with a white tip. Going up, she asked:

'How many rooms are there in the apartment?'

'Two,' he replied.

'And the rent?'

'It used to be six pounds a month.'

'Who's the owner?'

'An important business man,' he answered.

'Does he live in it?' she inquired.

'No, it used to be his office.'

The lift stopped on the twelfth floor. The caretaker went towards a large brown door bearing a small brass plate with the number 129 on it. Opening the door he went in, she following behind, into a small living room with a wide sofa whose seat sagged almost to the floor, two big, old chairs and a shabby wooden table. In the first room she saw a broad, blue, iron bed, a large chair and a clothes-stand. Entering the other room, she thought there might be a desk, but saw another bed, a wardrobe and a mirror. Turning to the caretaker, she asked:

'Where's the desk?'

His bluish lips curled back to show their moist red underside and he said gruffly:

'Don't know. I'm only the caretaker.'

Fouada wandered through the apartment and went to the window. From its towering height, the apartment overlooked the heart of Cairo. She could make out the main streets and the squares, the bridges and forks of the Nile. Fouada had never been up so high and Cairo seemed to her smaller than she had thought. The crowd that used to swallow her up, the buses that could crush her, the network of long, wide streets in which she could get lost – all now were remote, unreal, no longer a great city, but an anthill, crawling and scurrying without purpose, without significance.

She was strangely delighted by this diminution of everything while she remained the same size and weight, standing by the window; perhaps was even larger and heavier compared to what she could see below?

She was aroused by the voice of the caretaker saying: 'Do you like the apartment, lady?'

She turned to him and dreamily replied:

'Yes.'

Glancing at the iron bed, she said:

'But can't the deposit be reduced? This furniture isn't worth more than...'

The caretaker whispered in her ear:

'It's not worth anything, but these days the apartment ... this apartment won't go for less than thirty or forty pounds a month.'

'That's true,' she said, 'but even if I put myself on the market I couldn't find a thousand pounds.'

The dark face smiled, revealing surprisingly white teeth.

'You're worth your weight in gold!' he said.

This flattery pleased Fouada hugely in a way she hadn't felt for a long time and she smiled broadly saying:

'Thank you, uncle...'

'Othman,' the caretaker said.

'Thank you, Uncle Othman.'

They went back down in the lift. She shook the caretaker's hand, thanked him and was about to leave when he said:

'What do you want to rent an apartment for, lady? To live in?'

'No,' replied Fouada, 'it will be a chemistry laboratory.'

'Chemistry?' he exclaimed.

'Yes, chemistry.'

Again he smiled broadly and, as if he now understood, said: 'Ah, yes, yes, chemistry. A good apartment for it.'

'It's very good,' Fouada said 'but...'

The caretaker brought his lips close to her ear.

'You can come to an understanding with the owner. He might lower it to six hundred. You're the first one I've told this to, but you're a good person and deserve the best.'

'Six hundred?' Fouada said to herself. Could her mother give her six hundred? Uncertain, she looked at the caretaker.

'I can fix you an appointment with the owner if you like,' he said.

She opened her mouth to refuse, but instead said:

'Okay.'

'Tomorrow's Friday. He comes here every Friday to check the building.'

Smiling proudly, he added:

'He owns the whole building.'

'When will he be here? What time?' she asked.

'About ten in the morning,' he replied.

'I'll come at half past ten, but you must tell him that I don't have six hundred at the moment.'

'Pay what you have and the rest in instalments,' said the caretaker. 'I can fix it for you, he won't be too hard.'

With his mouth close to her ear again, he whispered:

'The apartment's been empty for seven months but you mustn't say you know this or he'll know that it was me who told you. You're the first one I've told this to, but you're a good person and deserve the best.'

Fouada smiled and said:

'Thank you, Uncle Othman. I'll repay you for this favour.

His answering smile was full of expectation.

* * *

Fouada arrived home before dark. Her mother was sitting in the living room wrapped in wool blankets. Om Ali, the cook, was with her. As soon as she heard Fouada enter, Om Ali got up, exclaiming:

'Thank goodness you've come.'

She enveloped her shrivelled body in a black wrap and tucked her small purse under her arm in readiness to go home. Fouada saw her mother's large eyes; a transparent shroud of pale yellow discoloured the whites. The tip of her nose was red as if she had caught a cold. She heard her say weakly:

'I've been worrying about you all day. Why didn't you phone?'

Sitting down at the table, Fouada said:

'There wasn't a phone nearby, Mama.'

'Why? Where have you been all this time?' her mother asked. Putting a spoonful of rice with tomato sauce into her mouth, she said:

'I was wandering the streets.'

Astonished, her mother exclaimed:

'Wandering the streets? Why?'

Swallowing her food she said:

'I was searching for a great discovery.'

Surprise creased her mother's face:

'What did you say?'

Fouada smiled, chewing a piece of grilled meat:

'Have you already forgotten your old prayer?'

And hunching her shoulders in imitation of her mother preparing to make a supplication and in her accent Fouada proclaimed:

'May the Lord help you, Fouada my daughter, to make a great discovery in chemistry!'

Her mother's parched lips parted in a feeble smile and she said:

'How much I want that for you, my daughter.'

Feeling happy, Fouada selected a slice of tomato sprinkled with green pepper and said:

'It seems that your prayer may be answered.'

Her mother's happy beam etched her wrinkles deeper:

'Why? Have they given you a raise in the Ministry? Or a promotion?'

The Ministry! Why did she have to mention it? Couldn't she at least have waited until she'd finished eating? Fouada felt the pleasure of eating disappear and that chronic pain began to creep into her stomach accompanied by a dry nausea that would not move. Without replying, she got up to wash her hands but again heard her mother say:

'Make me happy, daughter. Have you been promoted?'

Fouada returned from the bathroom and stood in front of her mother.

'What's the use of a rise or promotion, Mama?' she said. 'What's the use of the whole Ministry? You imagine the Ministry's something great, but it's only an old building on the verge of collapse. You imagine that when I leave here early every morning and come back every afternoon I've done some work at the Ministry, but you won't believe it if I tell you that I haven't done a thing, nothing at all, except write my name in the attendance register!'

Her mother stared at her with wide, jaundiced eyes and said sadly:

'But why don't you do anything? They won't be pleased with you for that and you won't get promoted.'

Fouada swallowed hard and said:

'Promotion! Promotion is given according to your birth certificate, according to the flexibility of your back!'

'The flexibility of your back?' her mother said in surprise. 'Are you in chemical research or in the sports department?'

Fouada laughed briefly, then put her fingers on her mother's mouth and said:

'Don't say research, it's a sensitive word!'

'Why?' her mother asked.

'Nothing, I was just teasing. What I mean is that I'm going to set up a chemistry laboratory.'

Fouada sat down beside her mother and eagerly explained what it would mean for her to have her own laboratory. She would carry out analyses for people and make a lot of money. Apart from this, she would do chemical research there and might discover something important to change the world. After this enthusiastic introduction, Fouada had to broach the tedious matter of finance, of asking her mother for money. Her mother had been listening closely and happily to everything Fouada was saying until the hints of requests for money. She understood that unmistakable tone in Fouada's voice that ultimately meant she was asking for something.

Finally, she said:

'That's very nice. All I can do is wish you every success, daughter.'

'But wishes alone aren't enough, Mama,' Fouada said. 'I can't open a laboratory on wishes. I need money to buy materials and equipment.'

Waving her veined hands, her mother said:

'Money? And where should the money come from? You know the well's run dry.'

'But you once said you had about a thousand pounds.'

All weakness vanished from her mother's voice as she replied:

'A thousand? There's no longer a thousand. Have you forgotten we took some of it to whitewash the apartment and to modernize the furniture? Have you forgotten?'

'Did you spend the whole thousand?' Fouada asked.

Tightening her lips, her mother said:

'All that's left is enough for my funeral.'

'Perish the thought, Mama' said Fouada.

In a frail voice and sighing feebly, her mother said:

'It's not far away, daughter. Who knows what can happen tomorrow. I had a bad dream a few days ago.'

'No... no... don't say such things,' exclaimed Fouada getting to her feet. 'You'll live to be a hundred. You're only sixty-five now, so you've still got thirty-five years of life ahead of you. And not just an ordinary life, but a happy and easy one because your daughter Fouada will achieve miracles in these years and money will rain down on you from the sky!'

Swallowing hard, her mother said:

'Why don't you save some money? I saved a thousand pounds from your father's pension, which is three pounds less than your wages. Where does all your money disappear?'

'My money?' retorted Fouada. 'My wages aren't even enough to buy one good dress!'

There was a long moment of silence. Fouada walked to the door of her room and stood at the doorway for a while looking at her mother swathed in woollen covers on the sofa. A funeral or a great discovery? Which of the two was more important or useful? She opened her mouth to make a final attempt.

'So you won't give me anything?' Without looking up, her mother replied:

'Do you want me to be buried without a coffin?'

Fouada went into her room and threw herself onto the bed. There was no hope left, nothing left, everything had vanished, everything was lost. The chemistry laboratory, research, Farid, the chemistry discovery. Nothing remained, nothing except her heavy, dejected body that ate and drank and urinated and slept and perspired. Of what use was it? Why was it the only thing that remained? Why it alone? Within that closed circle?

She stared at the white wall beside the wardrobe. There was something black on it, a square shape, a picture frame. It held the photograph of a girl in a long, white, bridal gown, holding a bouquet of flowers in her closed fingers, beside her a boy with a long face and black moustache. All her life, Fouada had seen this picture hanging in the living room but had never stood in front of it and examined it. Her mother had told her it was her wedding picture but she had only glanced at it from afar as if it were some girl other than her mother.

Only once had Fouada happened to stand in front of the picture and study it. That was a year or so after her father died.

Her history teacher had hit her over the hands twenty times with a ruler, twice on each finger. Fouada had gone home and complained to her mother and she had slapped her face for neglecting history. Then she went to the dressmaker's, leaving Fouada alone in the house. She didn't know why she had stood in front of the picture that day, but she wandered about the house, staring at the walls as though in prison. For the first time she saw the picture. For the first time she saw her father's face. She studied his eyes for a long time and imagined that they resembled her own. And like a knife in her heart, she suddenly realized that she loved her father, that she wanted him, wanted him to look at her with those eyes and to hold her in his arms. She had buried her head in the pillow on the sofa and wept. She cried because when her father had died she hadn't cried, hadn't grieved. At that moment, she wished her father were alive so he could die again, so that she could cry to put her conscience to rest. She dried her eyes on the sofa cover, got up, took the picture off the hook, wiped the dust off the glass, and looked at it again. It was as if the dust had veiled her mother's eyes from her because they now appeared clear and wide and held a strange look she had never seen before, an ill-tempered, tyrannical look. Fouada lifted the picture to hang it back on the hook but then took it into her room, hammered in a nail beside the wardrobe and hung it up. Then she forgot about it and hardly looked at it again.

Now Fouada closed her eyes to sleep, but felt something under her eyelids, something like tears, but burning. She rubbed her eyes, wiped them with the corner of the bed cover, laid her head on the pillow and pulled up the bedclothes to sleep. But the buzzing began in her ears, like the faint, endless ringing of a bell.

Remembering something, she jumped out of bed and dialled the five numbers on the telephone. The bell rang, loud and clear. The third night and Farid was not at home. Where could he be?

At one of his relatives'? But she didn't know any of his relatives. At one of his friends'? She didn't know any of his friends. She knew only him. She didn't know him in that traditional way, didn't know what his father did nor how many acres he might inherit from him nor how much he earned each month nor his position at work nor details like tax statements and deductions and passport number and date of birth. She knew nothing like that, but did know him in flesh and blood – the shape of his eyes and that unique thing that appeared in them, something with a life of its own. She knew the shape of his fingers, the way his lips parted in a smile, could distinguish his voice from all others, his walk from amongst hundreds, knew the taste of his kiss in her mouth, the touch of his hand on her body and his smell. Yes she knew, could isolate that unusual and particular warm smell that preceded him just before he arrived and stayed with her after he left, that remained on her clothes, hair and fingers, as if it were another person inseparable from her or as if it emanated from her and not from him.

But was this all the information she had about Farid? The shape of his fingers, the movement of his lips, the way he walked and his smell? Could she walk around searching for him everywhere, sniffing the air like a bloodhound? Why didn't she know more about him? Why didn't she know what his job was or where he worked? Why didn't she know where his family or relatives or friends lived? But he had never told her and she had never asked.

Why should she? He didn't ask her. They had been colleagues in the college of science. That was how it had all begun.

Hearing a sound nearby Fouada opened her eyes and saw her mother standing beside the bed. Her eyes seemed even wider and more jaundiced and her face more lined. She heard her say:

'How much do you need to set up a laboratory?'

Fouada swallowed hard and said:

'How much do you have left?'

'Eight hundred pounds,' her mother replied.

'How much can you give me?'

The mother was silent for a moment, then said:

'One hundred.'

'I need two hundred,' Fouada said. 'I'll pay it back.'

She got out of bed saying:

'I promise I'll pay it all back to you.' Her voice sad, the mother said:

'When? You haven't repaid your old debt.'

Fouada smiled and said:

'How can I repay it? You're asking me to repay you nine months' pregnancy, labour pains, the breast milk you fed me and nights awake beside the cradle! Can I ever repay you all that?'

'God will repay me for it, but you must return the hundred pounds you took last year.'

'Last year?' Fouada said distractedly.

'Have you forgotten?' her mother asked.

Fouada remembered that day a year ago. She had been sitting on her bed just as now when suddenly the telephone rang. She lifted the receiver and heard Farid's voice. He was speaking unusually fast.

'I'm speaking from home. Something urgent's come up. Can you get me some money?'

'I've got ten pounds,' she replied.

'I need a hundred,' he had said quickly.

'When?' she asked.

'Today or tomorrow at the latest.'

It was the first time Farid had asked her for anything, the first time anyone had asked her for anything. That day, she had been ill, with a splitting headache and couldn't move from bed, but suddenly her strength returned, she sat up and stared at the wall. It seemed to her that she was able to get up and search for that hundred pounds. Quickly she got up and dressed, not knowing from where she would get the money, only that she must go out and look for it. In a daze she wandered the streets, ideas rushed through her head – from relying on God to stealing and killing. Finally, she thought of her mother and hurried back home.

To get money from her mother was not easy, and only after inventing a big lie, which made her think her daughter's life depended on those hundred pounds, did she succeed. Those were historic moments, the moments Fouada put the money into her bag and rushed over to Farid's house. When he opened the door, she was shaking and panting. She hurriedly opened her bag and put a hundred pounds on the desk without speaking, overflowing with happiness.

Yes, she was happy. Perhaps it was the happiest moment in her life, to be able to do something for Farid, to be able to do something for someone, something useful. Farid looked at her with brown, shining eyes in which she saw that strange thing she loved but did not understand.

'Thank you, Fouada,' he said and put his arms around her. Instead of kissing her on the mouth, as he did every time they met in the house, he kissed her gently on her forehead and turned away quickly, saying:

'I must go now.'

Fouada cried that night when she got home. Couldn't he have stayed with her five minutes longer? Was he too busy even to kiss her? What could be so important to him?

Part Two

She sat on an old chair in the living room. The landlord sat opposite her. Between them stood the shabby table, on it a tray with two small coffee cups. His face was large and fleshy, a face one mistrusts the first time one sees it, something in the movement of the lips or eyes or something inexplicable giving it the appearance of lying or of deceit. Maybe it was that continuous, involuntary darting of his prominent eyes or the light tremor of his lips when he opened them to voice his rapid, mumbled words. She did not know exactly.

But should she judge people by their looks? Didn't she possess a scientific mind? Should she judge people according to her feelings and impressions of them? Why didn't she stop this foolish habit?

She saw his thin upper lip quiver as he spoke, revealing large yellow teeth.

'The rent of this apartment today is no less than thirty pounds a month,' he was saying.

She reached for a cup of coffee and said:

'I know, I know, but I only have two hundred. I'll pay it to you without taking the furniture. I don't need it.'

His bulging eyes flickered under his thick glasses, reminding her of a large fish under water. He glanced briefly at the caretaker standing by the door, then said:

'If you don't need the furniture, I'll reduce it to four hundred pounds.'

Swallowing a mouthful of bitter coffee, she said:

'I told you, I only have two hundred.'

Looking meekly at his master, the caretaker said:

'Please sir, she could pay two hundred now and the rest in instalments.'

The thin lips tightened into a smile and his fish-like eyes quivered as he said:

'All right, how much is each instalment?'

Fouada knew nothing about such dealings. She wanted the apartment; indeed, it had become the only hope in her life, almost the only salvation from that loss, that void; the only firm thread that might lead her to chemical research – perhaps to a great discovery. But this large fleshy face, those bulging eyes looking at her hungrily as if she were a piece of meat, would they be content with two hundred pounds in return for nothing? How would she pay off the rest? She would need to buy instruments and equipment in instalments. Where would she get it all? Then she had to pay the rent for the apartment every month and hire someone to receive clients and help clean the laboratory.

She hung her head, thinking in silence. Suddenly, she looked up at him. He was staring at her legs, greedily, and she automatically pulled her skirt down to cover her knees.

'I can't pay anything in instalments,' she said, picking up her bag and getting up to leave. He also got up and, as if embarrassed, looked down at the ground, mumbling in regret:

'I've never reduced the sum below five hundred for anyone and many people have come to me, but I refused to let the apartment for a long time. It's the best apartment in the building.'

'Yes, it is a nice apartment,' she said, making for the door, 'but I can't pay more than two hundred pounds.'

She walked towards the lift, feeling his glance burning her back. He opened the lift door for her and she went in, he behind her. He was large and broad-shouldered, with a prominent stomach and small feet. Before the lift descended, he said to the caretaker:

'Close up the apartment, Othman.'

The lift took them down. She saw his eyes examine her bust as though he were appraising it. She folded her arms over her chest and occupied herself by looking in the mirror. She was taken aback to see her own face. She hadn't seen it for a while, didn't recall having looked in the mirror for the past two days, since Farid's disappearance. She had perhaps glanced at her hair when combing it, but hadn't noticed her face. Now it looked longer than ever, the eyes even wider, the whites shot with red. Her nose was still the same, her mouth too, with that ugly, involuntary gap. She closed her lips and swallowed hard. The lift came to a stop on the ground floor. She was conscious of the landlord still studying her from behind his thick glasses. She opened the lift door and was rushing out of the building when she heard his voice behind her saying:

'If you please, miss…'

When she turned to him, he continued:

'I don't know why you want the apartment... to live in?'

'No,' she said in annoyance, 'to turn into a chemical laboratory.'

His upper lip again uncovered his large, yellow teeth and he said:

'That's wonderful. Is it you who will work in it?'

'Yes,' she replied.

His eyes flickered briefly, then he said:

'I'd like to give you the apartment, but...'

'Thank you,' she interrupted him, 'but as I told you, I only have two hundred pounds.'

He gazed at her for a moment.

'I'll take two hundred. You can be sure I would never accept it from anyone else.'

She looked at him in surprise and said:

'Does that mean you agree?'

He gave her a weak smile, his protuberant eyes – like those of a frog – swimming behind his glasses, then said:

'Only to do you a favour.'

Hiding her joy, she said: 'Can I pay you now?'

'If you like,' he replied.

She opened her bag and handed him two hundred pounds.

'When shall I sign the lease?'

'Whenever you like,' he said.

'Now?'

'Now,' he answered.

* * *

Fouada left the building and walked down the street grave-faced. She was overcome by unreal, dreamlike feelings, a mixture of total disbelief at getting the apartment and extreme fear of losing it; the fear one experiences on acquiring something valuable, thinking that one might lose it at the very moment of possessing it.

It seemed that what had happened was only a dream. She opened her bag and saw the lease folded under her purse. She took it out and unfolded it, pausing to look at some of the words: the first party, Mohammed Saati; the second party, Fouada Khalil Salim. Reassured that it was indeed real, she folded the paper, put it back in her bag and continued walking.

Something heavy lay on her heart. What was it that weighed her down? Wasn't she supposed to be happy? Hadn't she got the apartment? Hadn't her hope been fulfilled' Wouldn't she now have her own chemical laboratory? Be able to do research? Try to make her discovery? Yes, she should be happy, but her heart was heavy as though weighed down by a stone.

She had no desire to go home, and let her feet take her where they would. Then she saw a telephone, behind a glass door; pushing it open, she went in and was about to lift the receiver when a gruff voice said: 'You can't use the phone.' She went out to look for another telephone. It was one o'clock, Friday. Maybe Farid had come back, but in her heart she knew she would not find him. That uninterrupted, loud ringing was all she would hear. It was better not to call, better to stop asking about him. He had left her, had vanished, so why burden her heart with cares?

She saw a telephone in a cigarette kiosk and, pretending not to notice it, walked by, but then turned back and lifted the receiver with cold, trembling fingers.

The ringing tone pierced her head like a sharp instrument. It hurt her ear but she pressed the receiver closer, as if enjoying the pain, as if it was curing another greater and heavier pain, like someone who cauterizes their flesh with hot irons to rid themselves of a pain in the liver or spleen. The receiver remained pressed against her ear, seemingly stuck to it, until she heard the vendor say:

'Other people want to use the telephone too.'

She put down the receiver and continued on her way, head bowed. Where had he vanished? Why hadn't he told her the truth? Had it all been a deception? Had all her feelings been a lie? Why couldn't she stop thinking about him? How long would she roam the streets? What was the point of this futile, circling around like the hands of a clock? Should she not start buying instruments and equipment for the laboratory?

Raising her head, she saw a back that looked like Farid's. She stood rooted to the spot as though paralysed by an electrical current. But when she saw the man's face, in profile, she relaxed: it was not Farid. Her muscles seemed flaccid as they do after an electric shock; she felt unable to walk, that her legs were powerless to support her. Nearby was a small café with tables on the pavement, so she sat down on one of the chairs and glanced around her, half-conscious. Everything seemed familiar. Hadn't she seen it all before? The lame old man distributing lottery tickets? The dark-skinned waiter with the deep scar on his chin? The oblong marble table on which she laid her hand? The little, fat man at the next table drinking coffee, the thin brown lines on the cup? Even the tremor of the man's hand as he raised the cup to his mouth? All this had happened before. But she had never sat in this café, had never even been in this street ... but sitting there ... the lame old man, the waiter, the table, everything ... had surely happened once before: she didn't know where or when ...

She recalled having once read something about reincarnation and sceptically told herself that perhaps she had lived before in another body.

At that moment, a strange thought strayed into her mind: she would see Farid pass by in the street in front of her. It was more than a thought, an idea, it was a conviction. It even seemed that some hidden force had brought her to this particular café, in this particular street, at this particular moment, precisely in order to see Farid.

She did not believe in hidden spirits. Her mind was scientific and believed only in what could be put to analysis and into a test tube. But this unbidden conviction so dominated her that she trembled with fear, imagining that the moment she saw Farid she would fall to the ground struck by belief, like a blow from an invisible hand.

She tensed the muscles of her face and body, ready for the blow that would fall the moment she saw Farid walking amongst the people. Unblinking, her eyes scoured the faces of passers-by, her breath bated, her heart pounding violently as if to empty out its last drop.

The moment passed; she did not see Farid. She gulped, some calm restored, thanking God that he had not appeared, that she had not been struck down. Then she began to feel anxious that the prediction had not been fulfilled, that she would again fall into the abyss of waiting, of searching. She still hoped she would see him and went on staring into men's faces, scrutinizing each one. Some shared a feature or movement with Farid, and her eyes would settle momentarily on some similarity as though seeing a real part of Farid.

It was some time before Fouada became certain that her strange conviction was false. Her head and neck muscles slackened in disappointment, but also a faint relief crept upon her, the kind of relief that follows a release from responsibilities and belief.

Five days later, the laboratory was ready. It was Tuesday afternoon and Fouada was walking down Qasr al-Nil Street towards the laboratory carrying a package of test tubes and thin rubber tubing. She paused on the pavement waiting with others for the signal to cross the road.

Waiting for the green light, she looked up at the facade of the building opposite. Windows, balconies, doorways and spaces on the walls were covered with hoardings – bearing the names of doctors, lawyers, accountants, tailors, masseuses and other private professionals. The names, in large black letters on a white background, looked, she thought, like the obituary page in a newspaper. She saw her name – Fouada Khalil Salim – in black letters at the top of one page ... and her heart shuddered, as though what she read was the notice of her own death. But she knew she hadn't died; she was standing at the traffic lights, waiting for them to turn green, she could move her arms. As she swung her arms, one of them struck a man standing beside her with three other men. They were all looking at the front of the building, reading the hoardings. She imagined they were looking at her name in particular and shrank into her coat in embarrassment. It seemed to her that her name was no longer spelt out in letters of black paint but something intimate – like limbs – like the limbs of her body. With the eyes of the men examining her exposed name, she felt, in a confused way, that they were examining her naked body displayed in a window. When the lights changed, she slipped in amongst the other pedestrians to hide, remembering an incident from her first year in primary school. The teacher of religion, his nose thick and curved like the beak of a bird, stood before the class of young girls aged between six and eight expounding the religious teaching which stipulated feminine modesty. That day he said that a female must cover her body because it was private and she must not speak in the presence of strange men because even her voice was private. He also said that her name was private and should not be spoken out loud in front of strange men. He gave an example, saying: 'When, and only in extreme necessity, I have to mention my wife in the presence of men, I never utter her real name.'

Fouada, the young child, listened without understanding a word of what he said but instead read the teacher's features as he spoke. When he said the word 'private', she didn't understand what it meant, but she felt from his expression that it meant something ugly and obscene, and she shrank into her chair, grieving for her female self. The day might have passed peacefully, like any other

day, but the teacher of religion decided to ask her the meaning of
what he had said ... She got to her feet trembling with fear and,
as she stood, she did not know how, urine involuntarily ran down
between her legs. The eyes of all the girls turned to her wet legs;
she wanted to cry but was too ashamed.

* * *

Fouada was in her chemical laboratory. Everything around her was
new, washed and waiting: the pipes, the test tubes, the equipment,
the basins, everything. She went over to the microscope placed
on its own table with its own light, and turned the knob, looking
down the lens. She saw a clean and empty circle of light and said
to herself:

'Maybe one day, in this circle, I will find the object of my long
search.'

She felt a desire to work, so she put on a white overall, fixed the
pipes and lit the gas burner. The softly hissing light of the flame
was brilliant and she picked up a test tube with metal pincers,
washed it carefully so that no speck of dust should remain and
put it to the tongue of the flame to dry, then braced herself for the
research.

But she remained motionless, holding the empty test tube,
staring into it as if she had forgotten the object of the research,
feeling cold sweat creep across her forehead. A fundamental
question suddenly hit her, a question to which she had always
known the answer; but when she actually faced it and began to
think, the answer escaped her. The more she thought, the further
it escaped. She recalled the day a colleague had read her coffee

cup to predict future events. The friend reading the cup suddenly asked her:

'What's your mother's name?'

Startled by the unexpected question Fouada was taken aback. She couldn't remember her mother's name. Her friend insisted, and the more she pressed, the further away the name escaped Fouada's memory till, in the end, the reading had to continue without it. But Fouada remembered the name at the very moment the friend stopped asking.

She continued to stare into the empty test tube. Then she put it back on the rack and began to pace the room, her head bowed. Everything could disappear except that! Everything could escape her except that! For that to vanish was intolerable, unbearable! It was all she had left, the only reason for her to continue living.

She went over to the window and opened it. Cold air struck her face and she felt somewhat refreshed. 'It's depression,' she thought. 'I shouldn't think about research when I'm depressed.' She looked out of the window. The large sign hung from the railing of the balcony. The street was far below and people were going on their way without looking up, paying no attention to her chemical laboratory. It seemed that nobody would be interested in her laboratory, that nobody would knock at her door. She chewed her lips in anxiety and was about to close the window when she noticed a woman standing below and looking up at her window. All at once, she became excited. No doubt the woman was suffering from gout and had come for a urine analysis. She rushed to the outer room, on the door of which was written 'Waiting Room', and straightened the chairs. She looked at herself in the long mirror near the door and saw the white overall reaching to above her knees like a hairdresser's, glanced over her gaping mouth and looked into her eyes, smiling as she whispered to herself:

'Fouada Khalil Salim, owner of a chemical analysis laboratory. Yes, it's me.'

She heard the drone of the lift come to a stop, heard its door open and close, heard the clacking of heavy high heels on the tiled floor of the corridor. Fouada waited behind the door for the sound of the bell, but heard nothing. Very quietly, she slid back the peep-hole and saw a woman's back disappearing through the door of the neighbouring apartment. She read the small copper plaque on the door: 'Shalabi's Sport Institute for Slimming and Massage'.

She closed the peep-hole and went back into the inner room on the door of which was written 'Research and Analysis Room'. She avoided looking at the empty test tubes and began pacing up and down the room, then looked at the time. It was eight. Remembering that today was Tuesday, she threw off the overall, flung it on to a chair, then rushed out.

Last Tuesday he had not come – perhaps for an unavoidable reason? And here was another Tuesday. Would he come today? Would she go to the restaurant and find him sitting at the table? His back towards her, his face towards the Nile? Her heart pounded but inside it was that weight that hardened and contracted like a ball of lead. She would not find him, so why go to the restaurant? She tried to turn and head for home but couldn't. Involuntarily, her feet made for the restaurant like a wild horse that has thrown its rider and is galloping unrestrained.

She saw the naked table-top, the air whipping it from all sides like a rock in a violent and tempestuous sea. She stood for a moment grave-faced, then left the restaurant with head bowed and made her way home with slow and heavy steps.

* * *

Her mother was in the corner of the living-room praying, back to the door and face to the wall. Fouada stood looking at her. Her bowed back was bent forward, the raised hem of her robe exposed the back of her legs. She knelt on the ground for a few moments, then got to her feet and bent forward again, lifting her robe and uncovering her legs. Fouada saw large, blue veins protruding from the back of her legs like long winding worms and said to herself, 'A serious heart or artery condition.' Her mother knelt on the ground, turned her head to the right and whispered something, then looked to the left muttering the same words. Finally, she stood up supporting herself on the sofa, put her feet into her slippers and turned to Fouada standing behind her.

'In the Name of Allah, the Compassionate, the Merciful!' she intoned. 'When did you come in?'

'Just now,' Fouada replied, sitting on the sofa and sighing with fatigue. The mother sat down beside her and looking at her said:

'You seem tired.'

She was just about to say 'very tired,' but glancing at her mother's face and seeing the whites of her large eyes, clearly tinged with a yellowness she had never seen before, said:

'I've been working hard. Are you tired, Mama?'

'Me, tired?' said her mother in surprise.

'Your heart, for example,' Fouada replied.

'Why?' her mother said.

'I noticed varicose veins in your legs when you were praying,' she said.

'What's the heart got to do with legs?'

'The blood goes to the legs from the heart,' she replied.

Her mother waved her hand dismissively.

'It can go where it likes,' she said, 'I don't feel tired.'

'Sometimes we don't feel tired,' Fouada said, 'but the illness is hidden in our bodies. It might be as well to do an examination.'

Crossing her legs her mother said:

'I detest doctors.'

'You don't have to go to a doctor,' Fouada said. 'I'll carry out an examination.

'What examination?' her mother said in alarm.

'I'll take a urine sample and analyse it in my laboratory,' she replied.

Her mother gave a wry smile and exclaimed:

'Ah, I understand! You want to carry out an experiment on me!'

Fouada stared at her for a moment, then said:

'What experiment? I'm offering you a free service.'

'Thank you very much,' her mother said, 'I'm in the best of health and I don't want to delude myself that I'm ill.'

'It's neither a matter of delusion, Mama,' Fouada said in annoyance, 'nor of illness.'

'So what's the point of analysis then?'

'Confirming the absence of illness is one thing, analysis is something else,' she replied.

She fell silent for a moment, then more quietly said:

'Analysis in itself is an art which I take pleasure in performing.'

Her mother's upper lip curled in derision:

'What's the art or pleasure in analysing urine?'

As if talking to herself, Fouada replied:

'It's work that relies on the senses, just like art.' 'What senses?' asked her mother.

'Smell, touch, sight, taste…' Fouada said.

'Taste?' her mother exclaimed, staring at her daughter for a moment.

'It seems to me you know nothing about these analyses!' she said.

Fouada looked at her mother and saw a strange look in her eyes, like that in her wedding photograph, a hard, suspicious look, bitterly mistrustful of whoever was before her. She felt the blood rush to her head and found herself saying:

'I know why you refuse. You refuse because you don't believe in analysis.'

Without meaning to, she raised her voice and shouted:

'You don't believe that I can do anything. That was always your opinion of me, that was always your opinion of father…'

Her mother's mouth fell open in surprise. 'What are you saying?'

Raising her voice even louder, she replied:

'No, you don't believe in me. That's a fact which you've always tried to hide from me.'

Her mother gazed at her in utter astonishment and in a feeble voice said:

'And why shouldn't I believe in you…?'

'Because I'm your daughter,' Fouada shouted. 'People never appreciate the things that they have simply because they have them.'

Fouada lowered her head, holding it in her hands as if she had a bad headache. The mother kept staring at her, silent and apprehensive.

'Who told you that I don't believe in you, daughter?' she said sadly. 'If only you knew how I felt when I saw you for the first time after you were born. You lay beside me like a little angel, breathing quietly and looking around in wonder with your small shining eyes. I picked you up, lifted you to show you to your father and said to him: "Just look at her, Khalil." Your father glanced at you briefly, then said angrily: "It's a girl." Raising you up to his face, I said to him: "She'll be a great woman, Khalil. Look at her eyes! Kiss her, Khalil! Kiss her!" I held you so that your face almost touched his, but he didn't kiss you, just turned away and left us.'

The mother wiped away a tear from her eye on her sleeve, and continued:

'That night I hated him more than ever. I stayed awake the whole night looking at your tiny face as you slept. Whenever I put my finger in your hand, you wrapped your little fingers around it and held on tightly. I cried till daybreak. I don't know, daughter, what illness I had but my temperature suddenly rose and I fainted … when I came round, I found I'd been taken to hospital where they removed my womb and I became sterile.'

She took a handkerchief from the pocket of her *galabeya* to wipe away the tears which ran down her face, and said:

'You were the only thing I had in my life. I used to go into your room when you were up at night studying and say to you...'

She was weeping and put the handkerchief to her eyes for a moment, then lifted it and said:

'Have you forgotten, Fouada?'

Fouada was fighting off a sharp pain in the side of her head and was silent and distracted, as if half-asleep.

'I haven't forgotten, Mama,' she said faintly.

Gently, her mother asked:

'What did I used to say to you, Fouada?'

'You used to tell me that you believed that I would succeed and do better than all my friends...'

Her mother's dry lips parted in a weak smile and she said:

'You see? I always believed in you.'

'You only imagined I was better than all the other girls.'

'I didn't only imagine it,' said her mother with conviction. 'I was sure of it.'

Fouada looked into her mother's eyes and said: 'Why were you so sure?'

'Just like that, for no reason...' she responded quickly.

Fouada tried to read the expression in her mother's eyes so as to understand, to discover the secret of that conviction which lay in them, but she saw nothing. In a flash, she felt her irritation grow into anger and snapped at her mother:

'That conviction ruined my life...!'

'What...!' her mother exclaimed in astonishment.

Without thinking and as if her words were dictated by someone from the distant past, she said:

'That conviction of yours haunted me like a ghost. It weighed me down. I only passed my exams…'

She paused for a moment, looking around distractedly, then gulped, then went on, speaking quickly:

'Yes, only passed my exams for your sake. It used to torture me, yes, torture me, because I loved science and I could have passed by myself…' She put her head in her hands and pressed it hard.

Her mother was silent for a moment, then said sadly:

'You're depressed tonight, Fouada. What's been happening these past few days? You're not your usual self.'

Fouada remained silent, clutching her head in both hands as if fearing it would snap. A sharp pain split her head in two, while somewhere at the back something pointed made itself felt. She didn't know what it was exactly, but it seemed to begin to disclose the true reason for the mysterious sadness which sometimes came over her just when she'd had a happy moment.

And that reason was none other than her mother. She loved her mother more than anything else, more than Farid, more than chemistry, more than discovery, more than her very self. She was incapable of freeing herself from this love even though she wanted to, as though she had fallen into an eternal trap whose chains and ropes bound her legs and hands – from which she would never in all her life be able to release herself.

Unconsciously, she moved her little finger, ran it over her upper lip, then put it in her mouth. She began to chew it like a child whose teeth have emerged but who is still sucking its mother's breast. A long time elapsed as she sat on the sofa in the living room, her head between her hands, the tip of her little finger between her teeth. Her mother seemed to have left the room and she didn't know where she'd gone, but after a while she returned holding a small glass of yellow liquid. She extended the slender, veined hand that held the glass to her daughter. Fouada raised her eyes to her and the pent-up tears fell from them into her lap.

* * *

Fouada took great delight in washing the tubes, preparing flasks of alkalis and acids, checking the chemical analysis equipment and the spectrometer. She lit the burner, poured a sample of her mother's urine into the test tube and held it in a metal clamp over the flame. Standing like this, she realized why she had suggested that her mother give her a sample: she had wanted to use the new laboratory equipment.

The sample was free of sediment and since the heat solidified nothing, she turned off the burner, poured a drop of cold urine onto a slide, which she placed under the microscope, and looked down the lens. She saw a large circle inside within which moved small discs of different shapes and sizes. She moved the mirror to adjust the light and turned the knob of the magnifying lens. The large circle widened, increasing her field of vision, and the small quivering discs became bigger and looked like grapes floating on water.

She focused on one of the discs. It had, she thought, the form of an ovule. It was shaking like a living creature and inside it quivered two small dark discs, like a pair of eyes. As she stared at them her conscious, scientific mind was suspended and it seemed to her that they stared back at her with her mother's familiar look. Like an ovule – it was her mother's ... perhaps she herself was this ovule thirty years previously ... only her mother had not put it into a test tube and closed it with a stopper. It had attached itself to her flesh like a louse to the scalp and had eaten her cells and sucked her blood.

She remained, unmoving, like a dreamer, staring into the lens, time and thought lost as her imagination ran riot. She pictured, with shock and disbelief, her mother lying on a bed with her father beside her. She had never before imagined that her mother performed those acts that women did before having children, although certainly her mother had performed them, the proof being her own existence. She imagined her mother's form in such a position and pictured her the way she knew her, with a white scarf wrapped around her head, a long *galabeya* over her body, long black socks on her feet and woollen slippers too. Yes, she saw her in all these things lying on the bed in her father's arms, her lips sternly closed, a grave frown on her wide forehead, performing her marital duty – slowly and with the same dignified movements with which she performed her prayers.

The door bell was ringing. It had been ringing ever since she saw the 'ovule'. Dazed, she thought at first it was the bell of the next-door apartment or of a bicycle in the street. But it went on ringing. She left the microscope and went to open the door. The dark discs were still quivering before her eyes when she saw a pair of bulging eyes inside which darted two prominent black pupils. It seemed to her she was still looking down the microscope and she passed her hand over her eyes saying:

'Come in, Mr Saati.'

His massive bulk followed her into the waiting room with hesitant steps as if he didn't know why he had come. Looking around at the new metal chairs, he said:

'Congratulations! Congratulations! What a very nice laboratory.'

He sat down on one of the chairs, saying:

'I thought about calling in on you several times before today to congratulate you on the new laboratory, but I was afraid...'

He fell silent for a moment, his eyes uncertain behind his thick glasses, then he went on:

'I... I was afraid of disturbing you.'

'Thank you,' she said quietly.

Looking up, he saw the copper plaque and exclaimed:

'Research Room!' He got up, put his head round the door of the room and saw the new materials, test tubes and bowls and said admiringly:

'It's wonderful, wonderful! It really is a chemical laboratory!' She looked around somewhat surprised. She hadn't yet felt that she really possessed a laboratory or that it was a real chemistry laboratory. It seemed incomplete to her, many things were lacking. In genuine surprise she exclaimed:

'Honestly? Does it really look like a chemical laboratory to you?'

He looked at her in surprise.

'And you? Doesn't it look that way to you?'

Regarding her laboratory with new eyes, she said absently: 'We don't always see the things we have.'

He smiled, drawing back his upper lip and again revealing large, yellow teeth, and said:

'That's true, especially in the case of husbands and wives.'

He gave a short laugh, then sat down again on his chair while she remained standing.

'You seem to be busy. Am I holding you back?' he asked.

She sat down on a chair near the door.

'I was doing some research,' she said.

She smiled for no reason, perhaps remembering the shape of her mother's ovule. His intimate glances devoured her face and he said:

'I'll tell you something. Do you know you look like my daughter? The same smile, eyes, figure, everything...'

Fouada felt his gaze on her body and looked down in silence. To herself she whispered:

'He only wants to chat.'

'When I saw you for the first time,' he said, 'I felt that curious resemblance, felt I knew you ... maybe that's why I decided to give you the apartment.'

Yes, he just wanted to chat. Now he was talking about the apartment. What had brought him here? He had ruined her pleasure in analysing her mother's urine.

'In the past few days,' he continued, 'I thought about coming to help you prepare the laboratory, but I was worried that you might think badly of me. Women here think badly of a man who shows a desire to help, don't they?'

She was silent, suddenly preoccupied with something else, recalling an incident from her childhood when she played in the street with other children. There was a foolish old man who used to wander the streets and the children ran after him chanting: 'The idiot's here!' She would run with the other children and chant with them. One day, she ran faster than the others, leaving them behind and catching up with him. The old man spun round and gave her such a fearsome look that she turned on her heels and, imagining that he would chase and catch her, ran like the wind. From that day, she stopped chasing him with the other children and hid when she saw him, for it seemed to her that his fearsome, terrifying glance was for her alone.

Fouada couldn't think why she now remembered that distant incident, except that the eyes of the foolish old man had bulged like these in front of her. She looked around the laboratory as if suddenly discovering that she was alone with Saati in the apartment. Feeling frightened, she got up and said:

'I must leave now. I've just remembered something important.'

He got up saying:

'Sorry for interrupting you. Would you like a lift somewhere in my car?'

She rushed over to the door and opened it.

'No, thank you, it's not far.'

He went out and she locked the apartment and went ahead of him to go down by the stairs. In surprise, he said to her:

'Aren't you waiting for the lift?'

'I prefer to walk,' she replied, rushing down the stairs.

* * *

She walked along the street looking in the shop windows. Darkness was falling fast, the street and shop lights were already lit and she had no wish to go home. Walking alone, she peered searchingly into the faces of those who passed by, already addicted to this strange habit, the habit of comparing men, their features, their movements, their size, to Farid. She was also addicted to something even more bizarre: making predictions and then being convinced of the possibility of them coming true. As she walked along the street, she might tell herself: 'Three private cars will pass followed by a taxi. I shall look into the taxi and see Farid sitting there.' Then she'd start counting the passing cars and when the prediction was not borne out she'd bite her upper lip and say: 'Who said it would come true anyway? It's nothing but an illusion.' She'd go on her way and in a while, another, different prediction would occur to her.

At the end of Qasr al-Nil Street, a crowd had gathered around a car. She heard a voice say: 'A man's dead.' She found herself pushing through, panting and trembling, until she reached the man lying on the ground. She looked at his face. It was not Farid. Slowly, heavily she made her way out of the crowd.

She left Qasr al-Nil Street and headed for Suleiman Street. It was bustling with people, but she saw no one. Her thoughts were far away, perceiving the bodies around her only as part of the exterior boundaries that separated her from the vast, pulsating mass of the world, and knowing instinctively that such a body occupied such a sector of the street and that she must avoid colliding with it.

Then it seemed that some obstruction stood in her way. She raised her head to find a long queue of people across the street; and so she stopped too.

The queue gradually moved forward until she found herself in front of a ticket office. She bought a ticket and with the others went towards a large door in a dark hall. Torchlight was shone onto her ticket and she followed its circle of light until she reached a seat.

A film had just begun. On the screen, a man and a woman were embracing on a bed. The camera drew away from them to a man's foot showing from beneath the bed, then returned to the man and the woman who were still joined in a long kiss. Something crawled up Fouada's leg and, without taking her eyes off the screen, she brushed it away.

On screen the kiss ended and the man dressed and left. The woman said something, the other man came out from under the bed and the embracing began anew.

She sensed the crawling again. It didn't feel like a fly, more like a cockroach, for it did not flit around but crept slowly up her leg. Eager not to miss any of the film, she kept her eyes on the screen, reaching out in the dark to catch the insect before it climbed above her knee. But her fingers closed around something solid and in terror she looked at her hand to find that she had grabbed the finger of the man sitting next to her. She held on to his finger, glowering at him angrily. But he didn't turn to her, just kept looking at the screen in total absorption as if he did not see her, and as if his finger were nothing to do with him. She threw his finger into his face so that it almost jabbed him in the eye, but he continued to stare at the screen as though sleeping. She stumbled quickly to her feet and left the cinema.

*   *   *

Stretched out on her bed she stared at the ceiling, at that familiar, small, jagged circle where the layer of white paint had fallen. Feeling cold, she pulled up the covers and closed her eyes to sleep, but did not sleep. She considered reaching for the telephone … to dial those five numbers as she did every night before going to sleep, but she kept her hand still and pressed her head into the pillow, saying: 'I must stop this habit.' But she didn't stop. She knew there would be only that cold, shrilling bell, which had ceased to be a sound or air waves and become barbed fragments of metal that penetrated her ear, that scarred like fire.

And yet she had grown used to it. At the same time every night she dialled the same five numbers, pressed her ear to the receiver and invited that searing pain as if it comforted her, like a sick person cauterizing their body with fire to stifle another, more intense fire, or like an addict grown dependent on the taste of a poison who demands it every day.

The sound of the bell, the sound of her sobs, her sighs and heartbeats intermingled, indistinguishably. A conglomerate that manifested itself as one continuous, penetrating whistle like that which rings in the ears when there is total silence.

Very well! She waited for the bell every night as if it had become a new lover. She knew it was only a bell, but it came from Farid's telephone, rang in Farid's house, vibrated on Farid's desk at which they had often sat beside each other, reverberated against the divan on which they had often lain together, and moved the air which they had breathed in together and exhaled together.

The bell stopped. Farid's voice whispered in her ear. She felt his arm around her waist, his warm breath on her neck. She had not forgotten that he had been away from her so long, and yet she seemed unaware of everything, could remember nothing, not even that she had a head or arms or legs. All her senses had flowed away and all that was left of her were two swollen, inflamed lips.

She opened her eyes to look into his. But it was not Farid. It was another man with small blue eyes and thick eyebrows. The first man she had ever loved. She was a young child, she didn't recall how old she was at the time, but she did remember that as she grew older, she would open her eyes every morning to find her bed dry. She had hated being wet and thanked God that it was over. But God was not deceived by her thanks and soon afflicted her with another type of wetness, even more serious, for it was not colourless like before and had no sooner dried than it soaked the white bed sheet again. No, it was deep red and could be removed only by scrubbing so hard that her small fingers burned, and then, even after washing, it did not disappear completely but left a pale yellow stain.

She didn't know the real reason for it, for it was a haphazard wetness that appeared and disappeared as it pleased. She believed that somebody attacked her small body while she slept or that on her alone had fallen some malignant disease. She hid the catastrophe of her body from her mother and thought of going to the doctor on her own to reveal her secret. But once, her mother caught her washing the bedsheet at the sink. She was so ashamed that the earth spun and she tried to roll the sheet up.

She saw her mother's eyes looking at her from under a shadow she had never seen before. She reached out for the sheet and took it from her and saw the red patch on the white fabric, lying there like a dead cockroach. She tried to deny her disgraceful crime but her mother seemed to collude in it with her and was neither shocked nor angry, nor even surprised. It was as if she expected this misfortune to befall her and accepted it calmly and completely.

Fouada mistrusted this calm. It even terrified her, so much that her body trembled. So it was not a catastrophe. So it was not a unique, temporary sickness. It was something ordinary, quite ordinary. Her terror increased as her sense of its ordinariness grew. She had hoped it was something unique since unique things are bearable precisely because they are unique and not permanent.

Her small body began to change. She felt the change flow through her like a soft snake with a long, thin tail that flicked and flickered in her chest and stomach, stinging different parts of her body. The stings were both painful and pleasurable. How, she wondered, could these physical sensations be painful and pleasurable at one and the same time? But her body seemed to be wiser than she and was content with the pain and with the pleasure, happy with both side by side, embracing both with neither wonder nor surprise.

Her body changed suddenly and yet gradually. She felt and did not feel the change, like warm air entering her nose, or tepid water quietly pouring over her, which she bore without feeling its warmth since it was the same temperature as her blood.

She was surprised one day when she saw her naked breasts in the mirror. There was no longer the smooth chest she was used to seeing but instead two peaks, tipped by two dark raisins, that rose and fell with every breath, that jumped when she jumped as though, were it not for that thin layer of skin, they would fall off like oranges fall from a tree.

When she jumped, she felt something else jump behind her. She turned before the mirror to discover two other rounded humps held taut by fleshy skin at the lower part of her back. She remained studying her body for a while. It seemed to her to be that of some other girl, not Fouada, or that of an adult woman. She felt ashamed to look at those curves and protrusions that flaunted themselves disgracefully with every breath. But there was something besides shame, something deep and buried, something that wrapped itself in a thick mist, something like hidden pleasure or wicked pride.

Why did these old images stay in her mind alongside the image of the first man? Why did they persist when other more significant and more recent images had gone? But she believed that a chemical reaction happened in the memory cells, dissolving some images and highlighting or distorting others so that some parts remained whilst others were effaced. Yes, parts were eliminated. The lower half of the body of the first man in her life was effaced. Why? She didn't remember him having a lower half. He had a large head, small blue eyes, shoulders and long arms. How did he walk without legs? She didn't remember ever seeing him walk, for he was always at the window of his room. Taller people might have been able to see inside the room as they passed by in the street but she was small and could see only if she jumped up.

She deliberately played with her skipping rope under his window and every time she skipped, she would peek into the room. She could not see everything clearly because her head went down too quickly but she did manage to glimpse a painting hanging on the wall, a large suitcase on top of the wardrobe, a desk with books on it. She loved the coloured painting more than anything else and, jumping under the window one day, said to him:

'I want a coloured painting.'

'Come in and I'll give you a painting,' he said to her.

She could not go without her mother's permission, and her mother refused, saying firmly:

'You're too old to skip in the street.'

She threw herself onto her bed, shaking with rage. She hated her mother at that moment and envied her friend Saadia whose mother had died in childbirth. But she soon got up and tiptoed out, shoes in hand, and ran into the street.

Her heart was racing as she knocked at his door. She was happy because she would get a coloured painting, but she knew that the picture was not the sole reason for her happiness. She wanted to see his room from inside, wanted to see the shape of his wardrobe, his bed, his slippers. She wanted to touch his books and papers and pictures, wanted to touch everything.

He opened the door and she entered, out of breath. She stood by the wall shivering like a plucked chicken. He spoke to her but her voice was stifled and she could not answer. He came over to her and she saw his blue eyes close to her. She felt afraid. Close up, the shape of his face was strange, a sharp look in his eyes like that of a wild cat. He pulled her towards him with his long arms and she screamed, fearing that he would slaughter or stifle her. He slapped her face saying: 'Don't scream!' but she only grew more scared and screamed all the more. While trying to escape from his arms, she heard a rap on the door. He let go of her to open it and she nearly fell to the ground. There stood her mother, flesh and blood, in the middle of the room.

She opened her eyes to find herself lying on the bed shivering with cold. It was dark and the window was open. She imagined a ghost moving behind the window and trembled, even though she knew it was only the eucalyptus tree shaken by gusts of wind. She got up to close the window, then went back to bed and got in under the blankets.

Thinking that she heard breathing other than her own in the room, she peered out from under the covers and looked fearfully around. Her eye fell on a long shadow standing beside her wardrobe and she was about to scream when she realized it was only the clothes-stand with her coat on it. She closed her eyes to sleep but then felt the movement of something that seemed to come from under the bed. She wanted to reach out and turn on the light but she was afraid to put her hand out in case the ghost crouching under the bed grabbed it and so she stayed curled up under the covers, wide-eyed, until sleep coursed through her body as warm as blood.

* * *

The rays of the sun were filtering through the slats of the shutter when Fouada awoke. She remained curled up under the covers, wanting to stay there for ever. But she got up and dragged her body over to the mirror. Her face was sallow and seemed even longer than usual, her eyes larger, her lips paler, between them that ever-widening gap that made her teeth appear even more prominent. She gazed into her eyes for a moment, as if searching for something, then pursed her lips in displeasure and went to the bathroom. She took a hot shower and, feeling refreshed, smiled as she looked at her body in the mirror. She was tall and slender, with long arms and legs, and felt a hidden power in her muscles, an unspent power, an imprisoned power, which she did not know how to release. She dressed and went out into the street. The air was fresh, the sun bright and warm, and everything sparkled and quivered with animation. She strode along swinging her arms briskly in the air, feeling strong and energetic and greeting the new day eagerly. But where was she going? To that putrid tomb which smelled of urine? To that shabby desk at which she sat for six hours a day doing nothing? Would that strength and that eagerness dissipate into nothing?

She saw a horse pulling a cart, its hooves striking the ground with strength and vigour. She stared at the horse in envy. It spent its power pulling the cart, it released its energy, moved its feet happily. If she were a horse, she would be the same, pulling her cart, clattering on the ground with her hooves, perfectly happy.

When bus 613 came, she stood still and looked at it, motionless like a stubborn horse. No, she would not go to the Ministry, would not waste the day on nothing, would not waste her life signing the attendance register. For what? For those few pounds she took home every month? Sell her life for a few pounds? Bury her intelligence in that closed room with its stagnant air? Yes, it was that stagnant air that dissipated her vigour, the stagnant air that shut off her thoughts, killed them before they were born. She often had thoughts, research ideas often occurred to her, she often came close to making a discovery, but everything withered away in that room with closed doors and windows and sombre, dreary desks and those three mummified heads.

Another bus came. She almost got on but stood her ground and looked at it steadily. This moment came every day without her triumphing over it. If only she could manage today, she could manage every day. If only she could triumph once, that once would break the awful habit.

The bus was still there, but she stayed where she was and raised her head to the sky. Another moment and the bus would be gone without her and it would all be over. The sky would remain just as high and blue and silent. Nothing would happen. No, nothing would happen.

She took a deep breath and said aloud: 'Nothing will happen.' She put her hands into the pockets of her coat and walked off humming to herself. She looked about her in surprise and joy, like a prisoner emerging into the street for the first time after long years in prison. She saw a newspaper vendor, bought a paper and glanced at the headlines on the front page, then bit her lips. They were the same headlines she saw every day, the same faces, the same names. She looked at the date on the top of the page, thinking she was holding yesterday's paper or that of the previous week or year. She turned the pages, scanning them for a new subject or a new face but reached the last page without finding anything. She folded the newspaper and tucked it under her arm but then remembered having seen a familiar pair of bulging eyes in one of the pictures, eyes that looked like Saati's. She opened the paper again and, to her astonishment, her eye fell on the photograph of Saati himself. She read his name under the picture: Mohammed Saati, head of the Supreme Board for Building and Construction. Unconsciously, she ran her fingers over the eyes as if they protruded from the paper, even though the page was soft, smooth and flat.

She read the text under the photograph. It described in detail a meeting that Saati had held with the board workers, in words she seemed to have read so many times before. She had often read the name Saati and seen his picture. Fouada was amazed that she hadn't made the connection between all this and Saati the landlord whom she knew, but she never imagined that this same Saati could be the subject of an article in a newspaper. She looked again at the picture and the name, then folded the paper and put it under her arm.

The caretaker was sitting on his bench in the sun when she reached the building. He jumped to his feet when he saw her and ran towards her, holding out a small piece of white paper. She unfolded the paper to read: 'I will come by at six p.m. today. It's important. Saati.' As she entered the lift, her fingers toyed with the paper and unconsciously tore it to shreds, which she then tossed through the iron grille of the lift.

He would come by at six in the evening. Something important. What could be so important? What could be important from her point of view? The matter of research? Where Farid was? The collapse of the Ministry building? That was her life. Nothing outside that was important. But Saati knew nothing about research

or Farid or the Ministry, so what could be so important in his
visit?

She entered the laboratory, put on the white overall, arranged
the gleaming glasses and bowls on the table, lit the burner and
grasped the metal clamp in order to pick up the test tube. But
instead she left it in the wooden rack, upright, its empty mouth
open to the air.

For some minutes, she gazed at the empty test tube, then
sat down, head in her hands. Where to start? She didn't know,
didn't know at all! Chemistry had evaporated from her head. Ideas
crowded her mind when she read or carried out experiments in
the college laboratory or whilst she walked in the street or slept.
Where had all these ideas gone? They were in her head. Yes,
they were there. She felt them move, heard their voices. A long
conversation took place between them which culminated in
results that surprised her.

She often arrived at a new idea that made her almost mad
with joy. Yes, almost mad. She looked around in surprise and saw
people walking as if they were beings of a species alien to her.
And she? She was something else! In her head was something
not in the head of anyone else, something that would dazzle
the scientists, something that might change the world. A car or
bus might almost hit her and she'd jump onto the pavement in
fear and cautiously walk alongside a wall. Her life might be lost
under some wheels and with it the new idea for ever. She walked
faster, wanting to communicate the idea to the world before
something happened to her, almost running, then really running
and panting, then stopping and looking around her. Where, where

was she running? She suddenly found that she didn't know, didn't know!

She turned off the burner, removed the white overall and went out into the street. The movement of her arms and legs relaxed her, relieved the pressure in her head, released that pent-up energy inside her. She noticed a telephone in a shop and stopped suddenly. Why didn't they put telephones in less obvious places? Why did they have to display them like this? If she hadn't seen the telephone, she wouldn't have remembered. She reached out and lifted the receiver, put her finger in a hole and began to dial. The bell echoed in her ear, sharp, loud and uninterrupted. Quietly, she replaced the receiver and took some steps, then stopped abruptly, saying to herself: 'Is it Farid? Is Farid's absence the reason? Why has everything changed? Why has everything become unbearable?' When Farid was present, her life was the same, only Farid made everything bearable. She would look into his shining, brown eyes and feel that worldly things were without value. The Ministry was transformed into a small antiquated building, research became just another empty illusion, and discovery, yes even discovery, became another wan, childish dream.

Farid used to absorb her pain and her dreams, so that with him she was without either pain or dreams. With him, Fouada was someone else. Fouada without a past or a future, Fouada who lived for the moment, while Farid became her every moment.

How had he become her every moment? How had a man become her whole life? How could a person consume all her attention? She didn't know how it had happened. She wasn't the sort of woman that gives her life away to anyone. Her life was too important to give to one man. Above all, her life was not her own but belonged to the world, which she wanted to change.

She looked around anxiously. Her life belonged to the world, which she wanted to change. She saw people hurrying around, cars speeding about, everything in the world running without stopping. She alone had stopped and her stopping meant nothing to that pushing, rushing movement. What did her stopping mean? What could a drop in the ocean do? Was she a drop in the ocean? Was she a drop? Yes, she was and here was the ocean around her, its waves thrashing and wrestling and racing each other. Could a drop defeat a wave? Could a drop change an ocean? Why was she living this illusion?

She caught her breath and shrank into her coat, walking engrossed in thoughts with head bowed until she arrived home. She went in and threw herself down on the bed fully dressed.

* * *

She opened her eyes and looked at her watch. It was seven. She stretched her legs under the cover, feeling pain in her joints. She closed her eyes to go back to sleep, but could not. She had slept continuously for four hours, something she never did during the day. Then she remembered that it had not been continuous, she had awoken once at five o'clock. She hadn't forgotten the meeting with Saati at six, but had closed her eyes, telling herself that she still had another hour. She woke again at a quarter to six and moved her arms to lift the covers and get up, but instead had pulled them up over her head whispering to herself: 'What will happen if I'm a little late?' The next time she opened her eyes it was seven o'clock.

She stayed under the covers stretching, picturing Saati with his huge body and thin legs standing at the door of the laboratory, pressing the bell and getting no answer. She was pleased that sleep had rid her of Saati for ever.

These feelings filled her with energy. The ache in her limbs disappeared, she got up, dressed and went out. As she was going downstairs, she saw her mother open the peep-window in the door. Her pale face, criss-crossed with lines behind the narrow iron bars, looked like the creased and crumpled page of a book.

Fouada heard her weak voice saying: 'Are you going to the laboratory?' 'Yes,' she replied.

'Will you be late?'

'I don't know,' she replied distractedly. She wanted to ask her something but instead looked at her in silence, then descended the stairs and went out into the street.

The air was cold and dense but the darkness of the night was even denser. She walked along the street slowly and carefully as if about to collide with something, as if parts of the darkness had solidified, become obstacles she might walk into. She quickened her pace to get out of the dark streets and walk beside the flower garden, inhaling the scent of jasmine. Her heart faltered. Why did she still sense his smell? Why did she still feel his lips on her neck? Why did she still taste his kiss in her mouth? Why did these things remain with her whilst he himself had disappeared? Disappeared – flesh, bones, smell, lips, everything about him. So why did anything – these tangible memories of him – why did they remain?

But, did they remain? Wasn't this smell her own smell, this touch that of her own skin, this taste her saliva? Why did what was him and what was herself seem entangled and mingled? Was it possible that he was a part of her? Or that she was a part of him? She felt her head and limbs. Which part could it be? She felt her shoulders, chest, stomach. Suddenly she was aware of being in a broad, well-lit street and that many glances were on her. She hurried to the bus stop.

She took the bus to Tahrir Square and walked towards Qasr al-Nil Street. She saw the building in the distance and felt a hard lump move in her heart. The laboratory too had become something oppressive, those empty test tubes, waiting, with mouths open to the air and their transparent glass walls revealing emptiness, ranged in their wooden rack, flaunting their meaningless existence.

She opened the laboratory door and went in. On the floor was a piece of paper. She picked it up and read the reproachful words: 'I came by at six and did not find you. I'll drop by at nine. Saati.' She looked at the clock. It was half past eight. Just as she was making for the door, she heard the bell, hesitated and stood for a moment behind the door without opening it. The bell rang again and she called out: 'Who is it?' The caretaker's voice reached her and she took a deep breath and opened the door. With the caretaker were a man and a woman.

'They were asking for an analysis laboratory so I brought them here,' she heard the caretaker say.

She led them into the waiting room where they sat down. In the research room, she put on the white overall, then went out to them.

'We've come for an analysis to see why my wife's sterile,' the man said curtly.

He pointed to the woman who was sitting, head bowed, in silence.

'Have you been to the doctor?' Fouada asked the woman. The woman stared at her in silence and the man replied:

'I've taken her to many doctors. She's had analyses and X-rays but we still don't know what the cause is.'

'Have you also been examined?' Fouada asked him.

The man looked at her in astonishment.

'Me?' he snapped.

'Yes, you,' she replied quietly. 'The man can sometimes be the cause.'

The man got to his feet, pulled his wife up by her arm and shouted:

'What's all this rubbish! She's not going to be analysed here!'

He might have taken his wife and left, but the woman did not move. She stood, staring at her husband, wide-eyed and unblinking, as if she had died and frozen into that position. Nervously, Fouada went over to the woman and tapped her on the shoulder saying:

'Go with your husband, madam.'

As if there were an electrical charge in the touch, the woman started and clung to Fouada's arm with all her strength, crying in a strangled voice:

'I won't go with him! Help me! He beats me every day and takes me to doctors who put metal prongs in my body. They've examined everything, they've analysed everything and said I'm not sterile. It's him that's sick! Him that's sterile! They married me to him ten years ago and I'm still a virgin. He's not a man! In the dark, he doesn't know my backside from my head!'

The man pounced like a wild beast, hitting out at her with his hands, feet and head. The woman hit back. Fouada moved away from them in fear, muttering to herself:

'He's mad! He'll kill the woman in my laboratory! What shall I do?'

She rushed to the door and went out into the corridor to call someone. Suddenly, the door of the lift opened and out came Saati.

In panic, she said:

'A man's beating a woman in there.' At that moment, a piercing scream rang out and Saati rushed into the laboratory. The woman was on the ground with the man kicking her. Saati grabbed hold of him with one hand, slapped him across the face a number of times with the other, then threw him and the woman outside the room and slammed the door.

Fouada stood motionless, listening to their raised voices as they fought with each other on the stairs. She went to the door to see what the man was doing to the woman, but their voices had stopped and the corridor was quiet. She went to the window to watch them leave the building, thinking that the woman would not leave on her own feet, but was astonished to see the man come out followed by the woman walking quietly and with head bowed, as quiet as she had been before the incident. Fouada kept staring at her until she disappeared from view, then left the window and sank into a chair engrossed in thought.

Saati had been watching her, and when she sat down he also sat on a chair near her.

'You seem upset for the woman,' he said smiling.

She sighed and said:

'She's wretched.'

The prominent eyes flickered as he said:

'No more wretched than others you will see here in your laboratory, but you can't do anything for them.'

He pointed upwards and said:

'They have a god!'

'Is there a god that takes people's mistakes away from them?' she replied irritably.

She didn't know why she uttered the sentence for it was not her own. It was Farid's sentence; she had often heard it from him. The sentence reminded her of Farid and her heart sank. She bowed her head, silent and dejected. She heard Saati say:

'You seem to have been upset by the woman.'

She remained silent. He got up and took a few steps towards her, then said:

'You are kind to everyone...'

He paused for a moment, then went on in an agitated voice:

'... except me.'

She looked up at him in surprise. He gave an embarrassed smile and said:

'Why did you miss our appointment? Were you busy? Or is this the way all women are?'

The words 'all women' rang in her ear.

'I am not like all women!' she retorted.

'I know you're not like all women,' he said apologetically. 'I know that very well, maybe only too well!'

She opened her mouth to ask him how he knew, but then closed her lips. A long period of silence passed, then she found herself saying:

'What was the matter of importance?'

Sitting down, he said:

'Yesterday, I ran into the undersecretary of the chemistry ministry at a supper party. He's been a friend for many years and I remembered that you work at the chemistry ministry so I mentioned you to him.'

'He doesn't know me,' she said. Smiling, he said:

'He knows you very well. He described you to me in detail.'

'That's strange,' she exclaimed.

'It would be strange if he didn't know you!' he said.

'Why?' she asked.

'Because he's a man who appreciates beauty!'

She glowered at him angrily and said:

'Is that the important matter?'

'No,' he replied, 'only when I asked him about you, he told me that you were an excellent employee and have excellent reports.'

She smiled sceptically and he said:

'When he talked about you so enthusiastically, I had an idea. I need a chemical researcher in the Board.' 'What do you mean?' she said.

'I mean that I can transfer you to my place, in the Board.'

'To your place?'

'There won't be as much work as in the Ministry,' he went on. 'In fact, you won't have to do anything at all. The Board doesn't have a chemical laboratory.'

She looked at him in astonishment and said:

'Then why should I go?'

He smiled. 'To be in my office.'

She jumped to her feet, her head reeling. She glared steadily into his fish-flickering eyes and said:

'I'm not like that, Mr Saati! I want to work! I want to carry out chemical research! I'd give my life in order to work as a researcher!'

She fell silent for a moment, swallowed hard and then said:

'I hate the Ministry! Loathe it, because I do nothing there. I don't know how my reports can be excellent since I haven't done anything for six years! I won't go to the Board. I won't go to the Ministry. I'll hand in my notice and devote myself exclusively to my laboratory.'

His eyes clouded and he looked down. There was a long silence. Fouada got up, went over to the window then came back and sat on the edge of the chair as if about to get up again. He gazed at her fixedly from behind his thick glasses, a small muscle twitching under his right eye.

'I don't understand you at these moments when you are angry,' he said softly. 'Your eyes are full of buried sadness. Deep inside you there's a pain, I don't know why. You're too young to be so bitter, but it seems you've gone through harsh experiences in your life. But, Fouada, life shouldn't be so serious. Why don't you take life as it comes.'

He went over to where she was sitting and, feeling his soft, fat hand on her shoulder, she jumped to her feet and walked over to the window. He followed her, saying:

'Why waste your youth with such cares. Look,' he said, pointing to the streets, 'look how young people like you enjoy life, while you, you are here in your laboratory submerged in analytical work and research. What is it you're searching for? What is it you want that can't be found in that world down there?'

She looked down at the street. The lights, the people, the cars glittered and rippled with an animated, living movement, but the movement was far away from her, separate from her, like a moving picture on a cinema screen, describing a life other than hers, a story other than hers, characters other than hers. She was alone, isolated, constricted within a circle that often threatened to crush her body.

As if from far away she heard Saati's voice.

'You seem tired,' he was saying. 'Take off that white overall and let's go out for some air.'

'I've got a meeting tonight at the policy council,' he continued, looking at his watch, 'but I won't go. These policy meetings are very boring. So much talk and the same talk every time.'

She suddenly remembered the many newspaper articles and pictures of him.

'Apparently you have extensive political activity.'

'Why do you say that?' he asked.

'I seem to have read a lot about it.'

He laughed briefly, his thick glasses reflecting the light, and said:

'Do you believe what you read in the newspapers? I thought that people no longer believe anything that's written. They simply read the papers out of habit, that's all. Do you read the papers every day?'

'I read them and don't read them,' she replied.

He smiled, his teeth showing as yellow as ever.

'What do you really read?' he asked.

Sighing, she replied:

'Chemistry.'

'You talk about chemistry as though you were talking about a man you love. Have you ever been in love?'

As if cold water had been dashed in her face, she recollected that she was standing at the window with Saati beside her, the laboratory empty and silent. She looked at the clock. It was eleven. How had that happened? Hadn't she tried to leave the laboratory before he came? Then she remembered the incident with the man and the woman. But couldn't she have left the laboratory immediately after? She glanced at Saati. His portly body was leaning against the window supported by legs that were thin, like those of a large bird. His eyes – now like a frog's, she thought – darted behind the thick glasses. It seemed to her that before her was a strange type of unknown terrestrial reptile – that might be dangerous. She looked around in consternation and, taking off her white overall, went towards the door, saying:

'I've got to go home immediately.'

He looked surprised, then said:

'We were talking quietly. What happened? Did my question upset you?'

'No, no,' she said. 'Nothing upset me, but my mother's alone at home and I've got to get back immediately.'

Walking with her to the door, he said:

'I can give you a lift in my car.'

She opened the door saying:

'Thank you, but I'll take the bus.'

'The bus? At this time of night? Impossible!'

They went down to the ground floor. He walked ahead of her to the long, blue car and opened the door for her. She saw the caretaker leap to his feet respectfully. She hesitated for a moment, wanting to run away, but unable to. The car door was open and the two men were waiting for her to get in. She got in and Saati closed the door. Then he hurried to the other side of the car, opened the door, got in and started the engine.

The street was practically deserted except for a few people and cars. The air was cold and damp. She saw a man standing in front of a cigarette kiosk. Trembling suddenly, she was about to shout 'Farid!' when the man turned and she caught sight of his face. It was not Farid. She shrank into her coat, shivering with sudden cold. Saati glanced at her and said:

'Someone you know?'

'No,' she said faintly.

'Where do you live?' he asked.

'In Doqi…' she replied and gave him the street and house number.

The car crossed Qasr al-Nil Bridge. She saw the Cairo Tower standing erect in the dark like some huge alien creature, its flickering red eyes spinning round and round in its head. Watching the flickering balls circling around she felt dizzy and saw a double tower, with two revolving heads. She rubbed her eyes and the second tower vanished, leaving only one with one spinning head. Then the second one reappeared. Again she rubbed her eyes to make it disappear, but it remained. From the corner of her eye, she glanced at Saati and saw him with two heads. She trembled and hid her face in her hands.

'You're tired,' she heard his voice say.

Raising her head, she replied:

'I have a headache.'

She looked out of the window. The darkness was intense and all she could see now was a mass of blackness. Suddenly, there came into her mind something she had read about a man who used to chase women, take them to a dark and remote place and murder them. She glanced furtively at Saati – his bulging eyes fixed ahead, his thick and fleshy neck resting on the back of the seat, his thin, pointed knees ... When he turned towards her, she looked out of the window. The houses were dark and shuttered. No light appeared in the windows, nobody walked in the street.

Why had she got into the car with him? Who was he? She didn't know him, knew nothing about him. Was she awake or having a bad dream? She dug her nails into her thighs to make sure she was there.

The car seemed to have stopped. She trembled and edged over to the door. She heard Saati's voice say:

'Is this the house?'

Looking out of the window, she saw her house and exclaimed in relief:

'Yes, that's it!'

She opened the car door and jumped out. He also got out and walked to the front door with her. The staircase was dark.

'You're tired,' he said to her, 'and the stairs are dark. Shall I see you to the door of your apartment?'

'No, no, thank you,' she replied quickly. 'I'll go up by myself.'

He held out a podgy hand, saying:

'Shall I see you tomorrow?'

'I don't know, don't know,' she replied agitated. 'I might not go out tomorrow.'

His eyes glinted in the dark and he said:

'You're tired. I'll phone you tomorrow.' Smiling, he went on:

'Don't wear yourself out with chemical research!'

She climbed the stairs, her legs quaking, imagining that he was coming up after her. Many crimes happened on darkened staircases. She reached the door of the apartment panting, took out her key, her fingers shaking as she searched for the keyhole. She opened the door, went in and quickly closed it behind her. She heard her mother's regular breathing and felt calmer, but she still shivered with cold. She put on some thick woollen clothes and tucked herself into bed, her teeth chattering. Then she closed her eyes and lost consciousness.

* * *

In the morning, she awoke to hear her mother's voice saying something but what it was she didn't know. She saw her mother's eyes looking down at her anxiously and tried to lift her head from the pillow ... it was too heavy ... inside it something solid pressed and crushed against the bones of her skull, reverberating, like the sound of a machine, of clanging metal. She looked around the room, saw the wardrobe, the window, the clothes-stand, and the telephone on the shelf. She opened her mouth to speak but was silenced by a sharp pain in her throat. Her mother's lined face drew closer and she heard her say:

'Do you want the telephone?'

She shook her head.

'No, no,' she said hoarsely. 'Take it away, into the living room. I don't want it here.'

Her mother picked up the phone and held it to her chest as if it were a dead, black cat. Fouada heard her go into the living room, then return.

She buried her head under the covers, hearing her mother say:

'I heard you coughing in the night. Have you caught a cold?'

From under the covers, she replied:

'It seems like it, Mama.'

She moved her parched tongue in her mouth and felt a bitter taste slip down into her stomach. She wanted to spit it out and pulled a handkerchief from under the pillow, coughed and tried to clear her blocked nose. Something hard, like a pebble, scratched her throat; she sneezed and coughed but the pebble would not be dislodged. With each breath, it settled further down inside her chest.

Her mother said something and she replied 'yes' without knowing what it was and heard the feet shuffle out of the room. She made a small gap between the bed and the covers to let in air, but that let in a narrow shaft of light as well and she saw her hand under her head, a watch around the wrist. She glimpsed the figure the small hand pointed to and remembered the Ministry. She closed up the gap and night returned.

Yes, let the night return and stay. Let the light around her dim and let there never be day. What use was day, that endless cycle from home to the Ministry, from the Ministry to the laboratory and from the laboratory to home? What was the point of it all? What was the point of going around in circles? Of moving the muscles of the arms and legs? Of activating the digestion and blood circulation? She remembered Saati saying: 'What are you searching for? What is it you want that can't be found in this world?' She didn't want anything from this world, wanted nothing from it, not even money. What would she do with it anyway? What did a woman do with money in this world? Buy expensive dresses? But of what use were expensive dresses? She didn't remember one of her dresses, didn't remember Farid looking even once at them. She had never felt that her clothes had a value except to cover parts of her body.

And what beside dresses? What did a woman do with money in this world other than buy dresses? Buy jewellery and face powder? That white powder with which women cover their faces, to hide those blood vessels that run through living skin? What is left of living skin after its blood colour is blotted out? Only dull, dead skin, chalky white, etiolated.

What else besides powder and dresses and jewels? What did a woman want from the world? Going to the cinema? Visiting women friends? Gossip and jealousy and the pursuit of marriage?

But she didn't want any of these. She didn't buy make-up, didn't go to the cinema, had no women friends and did not pursue marriage. So what was she seeking?

She pressed her head into the pillow and clenched her teeth in frustration. What do I want? What do I want? Why don't I want those things that other women want? Aren't I a woman like them?

Lifting the cover from her face a little she saw her slender fingers and nails, just like her mother's. She touched her skin and body, the skin and body of her mother. She really was a woman, so why didn't she want what other women wanted. Why?

Yes, why, why? She didn't know. Was chemistry the reason? But was she the only woman to have studied chemistry? Was Madame Curie the reason? But was she the only woman to have heard of Madame Curie? Was it the chemistry teacher? But where was the chemistry teacher? She knew nothing about her, had heard nothing of her since leaving school. Did her life depend on a word spoken by some obscure woman? Was it her mother? But did her mother know anything about the wide world outside the four walls of the house? Was it Farid? But where was Farid? Who was he? She didn't know anyone who knew him, didn't know where he was, didn't know even if he had ever really existed. Maybe he was an illusion, a dream? He was absent and as long as he was absent, how could she distinguish dream from reality? If he had only left a note in his handwriting she could have been sure. Yes, with a piece of paper, she would have known, whilst with her head, arms and legs she could know nothing. Neither her body nor her head could know anything. Everything inside her head had been reduced to a meaningless, muffled clangour. Everything inside her had been catalysed into a dull, continuous hum, like that perceived when everything is silent.

Yes, there was complete silence deep within that body outstretched and incapacitated beneath the covers, silence and only silence. It was incapable of saying anything. The words that came out of its lips were not its own words but simply the random echoes of words heard before; the words of others, words that Farid, her mother, the chemistry teacher had spoken, or words she had read in a book. Yes, it repeated only what it had heard and read and, like a wall, could only voice echoes.

Her body under the covers was heavy and inert – like a stone – she was hot and sweated profusely. A warm, viscous substance poured from her nose. She pulled a handkerchief from under the pillow and blew her nose hard. It dripped like a worn-out tap. She was not a clean, dry wall, but an oozing, dripping wall – with a noxious, involuntary wetness.

She kicked the cover from her body, wanting to kick off her arms, legs and whole body, but it adhered, clung to her, remained attached to her, lying on top of her – an oppressive weight and obscene wetness, like the body of another person, a stranger.

A stranger, with all the strangeness of some person she might encounter in the street, the strangeness of the caretaker, of Saati. She shuddered. Yes, an utter stranger who swallowed food, not knowing what happened to it. Sometimes she heard a noise in her stomach, like the mewing of a cat, as if she didn't know what was happening there, where all that quantity of food went. Like a mill, it turned and turned and pulverized solid things. There was only that turning and the pulverizing and nothing else. Nothing else.

What else could there be? That illusion which beckoned through the mist? Test tubes from whose mouths a new gas danced? What could a new gas do? A new hydrogen bomb? A rocket with a new nuclear head? What did the world lack? A new means of killing?

Why the killing? Was there nothing else of use? Something to eliminate hunger? Disease? Suffering? Oppression? Exploitation? Yes, yes, here was the wall, echoing words it had heard from Farid. What do you know about hunger? About disease? What do you know about suffering or oppression? What about exploitation? What do you know about them and about that which you talk of to people whilst not even living with people? You look at them from a distance, study their movements and houses as if they were moving images on a blank screen. Have you ever been hungry? Have you ever seen a hungry person? That woman begging on the pavement of the Ministry, a young child in her lap, did you even see her? Did you look into her eyes? Wasn't it only her sun-beaten back you saw and didn't you envy her?

Do you know anything of this? Why then persist in this illusion? Don't you eat and drink and urinate and sleep like others? Why aren't you like others? Why?

Yes, why, why? Why aren't you like others, calmly accepting life as it is? Why not take life as it comes? Even these words are not yours. Didn't you hear this very same question from Saati yesterday in the laboratory? Do you store up all the words inside you? Even Saati's words? How stupid you are! Can't you say one word of your own?

Fouada awoke to the sound of her mother's voice. She saw her standing beside her, holding a glass of tea in her thin, veined hand. She stared at her long, slender, wrinkled fingers. Her own were as long and slender as her mother's and would become as wrinkled as hers with gnarled joints, like dry twigs. She looked up and saw her lined face, her dry lips parted, the same gap, the same teeth. Let the same lines cover her face too. Let her own legs become incapable of moving quickly, and her feet shuffle like hers.

She reached out weakly and took the glass of tea. Her mother sat on the edge of the bed looking at her. Why was she silent? Why didn't she say anything? Why didn't she raise her hand to the sky and repeat her old supplication? But the dream was gone, the illusion lost. She had not given birth to a natural wonder. Who had told her that she would? Why her in particular? Why her womb in particular? Millions of wombs gave birth every day so what had put this illusion in her head? Maybe she had inherited the illusion from her own mother, just as Fouada had inherited it from her. Some woman in the family must have imagined her womb to be different, must have begun it all. Someone had begun it, there always had to be someone.

She heard her mother say:

'What's wrong, Fouada? Why don't you speak?'

Her voice was so sad she wanted to cry, but she held back the tears and opened her mouth to say:

'I've got a bad headache.'

'Shall I get you an aspirin?' her mother asked.

'Yes,' she nodded.

As her mother went back into the living room the telephone rang. Fouada jumped out of bed, shaking. Was it Saati? She stood in the doorway looking at the phone. Her mother went over to answer it, but she shouted:

'Don't answer it, Mama! There's someone I don't want to talk to…'

But then, suddenly, she thought it might be Farid and rushed to the telephone. She lifted the receiver and gasped: 'Hello.' The oily voice of Saati came to her and she slumped into a chair, flaccid and lifeless.

Part Three

Fouada left the Ministry and walked alongside the rusty iron railings. Her head was heavy and her heart convulsed, inside it that hard, perpetual lump. She saw the woman sitting on the pavement, holding her child to her chest, empty hand reaching out. The street was noisy and crowded but no one noticed the outstretched arm. One pushed her aside to clear his path, another trod on her in his hurry. She heard the child crying as she passed by and saw that small skeleton with sunken eyes, prominent cheeks and a small pouting mouth trying in vain to suck a piece of brown wrinkled skin that hung from the woman's chest.

She put her hand in her pocket to take out a piastre, but kept it inside her pocket. She raised her eyes to the street. Long cars followed one after the other, within each a shiny head that reflected the light and a fleshy neck that resembled Saati's.

She took out the piastre and held it in her hand for a moment. What good was a piastre? Would it clothe the bones of that small skeleton in flesh? Would it cause the milk to flow from that shrivelled flap of skin? She chewed her lips. What could she do?

A chemical discovery to eliminate hunger? A new gas for millions to breathe instead of food?

She let the piastre fall from her fingers into the empty open palm. A piastre would do nothing, but let it be a passing charity, to ease her conscience, a trifling price to pay and forget.

Here were Farid's words again. His voice in her head had a sting. Her eyes searched for his brown, shining ones. There were many eyes around, so why his in particular? When she gazed, close, into his eyes she did not feel the astonishment she felt when looking closely into other eyes, even her mother's or into her own. When she stared at her eyes in the mirror, their familiar shape disappeared, as if they were the eyes of an unknown animal. But Farid's eyes had something strange in them, strange yet familiar, that grew more and more familiar and was not at all strange. When the distance between the two of them vanished and they touched, she felt utterly secure.

Was all that an illusion? Had her feelings so betrayed her? If her feelings lied, in what could she believe? Words of ink on paper? An official document with the Ministry seal on it? A certificate printed in duplicate? What could she believe if her feelings lied?

She stopped abruptly to ask: But what are feelings? Could she touch them? Could she see them? Could she smell them? Could she put them in a test tube and analyse them? Feelings, mere feelings, an invisible movement in her head, like illusions, like dreams, like some hidden force. Could her scientific mind believe in such nonsense?

She looked around, confused. Were feelings true or false? Why when she looked into Farid's eyes did she feel that he was familiar, and when she looked into Saati's eyes feel that he was a thief? Was that illusion or knowledge? Was it a random movement in the optic nerve or a conscious movement in the brain cells? How could she distinguish between the two? How could she distinguish the mistaken vibration of a pressed nerve from the healthy idea emanating from a brain cell? And how did a brain cell think? How could a small mass of protoplasm think? Where did an idea come from and how did it pass through her cellular tissue? Electrically? A chemical reaction?

She looked up to see what was around her and noticed the building with the white placard bearing her name in black letters. Her heart shrank. Test tubes with open mouths – empty – a tongue of flame burning the air, burning itself, that insistent whistle echoing in her ear when everything fell silent.

Yes, that was the laboratory. But it wasn't a laboratory any longer. It had become a trap, ensnaring her impotence, ensnaring her ignorance, ensnaring the silence and the nothingness in her head.

She passed the entrance to the building without entering, walked on a few paces, then stopped. Where was she going? Everywhere had become like the laboratory, a trap for impotence, silence and the whistle in her ears. Home and the Ministry, the telephone and the street, everything interlocked, undeviating.

She retraced her steps to the building, to go to her laboratory. There was no way out. The trap opened its jaws and she entered between them. Saati would come in a while. He would surely come, to the laboratory or wherever. He knew her every place: telephone number, house, Ministry and laboratory. He would come in his long blue car, with his bulging eyes and fleshy neck. He would surely come, for why didn't the earth lose its equilibrium, the test-tube rack shake and the empty tubes fall and break? Why did the earth turn so perfectly? Why was its equilibrium not disturbed, just once?

She had entered the laboratory, put on the white overall and now stood at the window watching the street and observing the cars as if waiting for him, for Saati. And she really was waiting for him. She saw the long blue car pull up in front of the building and Saati get out, with his portly body on thin legs.

As she dragged her feet to the door, she noticed her reflection in the long mirror beside it. Her face was thinner and longer, her eyes dulled and sunken into their sockets, the gape of her mouth even wider, her teeth even more prominent, just like her mother's.

She closed her lips to hide her teeth, clamping her jaws together to crush her teeth, or something else, between them. There must be something to crush. She ground her teeth making a metallic sound. When the doorbell rang, she made a sharp gesture with her fist and said: 'I won't open it…' and held herself quite still, inanimate. Again the bell rang; her breath quickened into a rapid panting. Then, quivering, she opened the door.

* * *

He was carrying a small packet in his cushiony hand. His upper lip lifted, revealing the large, yellow teeth, and his prominent eyes quivered behind the thick glasses.

'A small present,' he said, putting the package on the table and sitting down.

She remained standing, staring at the thin green ribbon tied around the packet.

'Open it,' she heard him say hoarsely.

He was giving her an order, had taken upon himself the right to give her orders, had paid the price of this right and had the right to use it. She looked at his eyes. They were quieter, as if he had begun to gather confidence in himself. He was giving her something, having paid a price for her, and was now able to buy something from her, anything, even the right to order her to open the packet. She remained on her feet, unmoving.

He got up and opened the package himself. He came over to where she stood, held out a box to her and said:

'What do you think of this?'

She saw something glittering against red velvet.

'I don't understand about these things,' she said distractedly.

He stared at her in surprise and said:

'That's a genuine diamond.'

He brought his face close to her and she saw his fish-like eyes, covered by a dark membrane that hid the natural sparkle.

He had perhaps paid a great deal of money, perhaps a hundred pounds or more, but what was it worth to her?

She had no use for such things, didn't wear rings or bracelets or necklaces. If even the skin that enclosed her body irritated her, how could she wrap other cords around her limbs? If she was aware of the weight of her own muscles and bones, how could she weigh down her limbs with metallic chains, of whatever kind?

He came closer still, repeating:

'The stone's a genuine diamond.'

She smiled in silence. He would never understand. To her a genuine diamond was useless. What was the difference between it and a piece of tin or glass? Does the earth make a distinction between things?

That familiar quivering had returned to his eyes.

'What gift would please you?' he muttered in a defeated voice.

She didn't know how to respond. What presents did Farid give her? Did Farid even buy her presents? She didn't remember him buying her anything. There was nothing that could be bought. What could he buy? His words? The tone of his voice? The light in his eyes? The warmth of his breath and the sweetness of his lips?

Saati put a soft, plump hand on her shoulder saying:

'What can I give you to make you happy?'

The muscles of her shoulder contracted to shrug off the weight of his hand. She turned around. What could he give her? Could he give her the elusive contents of the test tube? Could he give her that lost idea? Could he stop that uninterrupted and meaningless high-pitched humming in her head? Would she lift the receiver one day, the ringing stop and the voice of one for whom she searched reach her?

She looked at him. He was putting the box into his pocket with unsteady fingers. There was nothing he could do; what could she tell him? She took a few steps, head lowered, then said in a constricted voice:

'Let's go out. I'm nearly choking.'

* * *

The long blue car took them through the streets of Cairo. They remained silent until the car emerged into the countryside near the Pyramids, then she heard him say, almost brusquely:

'There's a secret in your life I don't understand. Why don't you open your heart to me?'

She glanced at him briefly, then fixed her eyes on the expanse of desert and said:

'I don't know if my life has a secret or a meaning. I just eat and sleep like any animal and do nothing useful for anyone.'

He half-sighed, half-grunted.

'Are you still at that stage?' he asked.

'What do you mean?'

'I went through that stage twenty years ago,' he said. He was silent for a moment, then went on:

'But I found out that real life is something else.'

'What do you mean?' she said.

Grimacing, he replied:

'Lofty principles always brought me into conflict with real life. They called me a non-conformist.'

'Who are they?' she asked.

'My colleagues at university.'

'Did you go to university?'

'I was a teacher with principles.'

'And then what happened?' she asked.

He laughed briefly, then said:

'Then I conformed.'

He turned to her, his eyes steady for a moment, and said:

'There was no other way.'

'Did you write any papers when you were at university?' she asked.

'I did seventy-three.'

'Seventy-three?' she exclaimed. 'How? That's impossible!'

Biting his lip, he replied:

'It was very simple. I only put my name to them.'

'And the real researcher?' she asked in dismay.

'He was a young man still trying to make it,' he said.

'But,' she shouted, 'didn't you do even one in-depth study of your own?'

'Impossible,' he said simply. 'Undertaking any real research takes a lifetime and ruins the chances for real life.'

She fell silent for a moment, grave-faced, saying to herself: 'Just as I thought the first time I saw him! The eyes of a thief! He stole seventy-three studies!'

'And then what?' she said.

'Then I became a great professor,' he laughed.

'And then?'

'A person's ambitions are limitless,' he said smiling. 'Then I went into politics.'

'And what do you know about politics?' she said.

'Everything. It's enough to befriend this or that one and to repeat slogans in an educated accent.'

She looked at the fleshy neck in disgust and said:

'And do you respect yourself now?'

'How does one respect oneself, Fouada?' he said in the same tone. 'Self-respect doesn't happen in a vacuum. It comes from the respect of others. And I, I am the head of the Supreme Board for Building and Construction, head of the political council. The newspapers write about me. I talk on the radio and television and give advice to people. The whole world respects me so how can I not respect myself!'

He pulled the car up by the side of the road and looking at her, said:

'Believe me, Fouada, I respect myself, but even more than that, I believe the lies I repeat in front of people. I have grown to believe them from repeating them out loud so often and so convincingly. What is a person, Fouada? What is a person if not a collection of feelings? And what are feelings if not the accumulation of life's experiences? Should I ignore all these experiences and inhabit a realm of principles and theories which cannot be applied to the real world? Should I, for example, do as Hassanain Effendi did?'

He fell silent for a moment as if reviving old memories, then continued:

'Hassanain Effendi was a colleague of mine at university. He believed that he had a new idea in his head and began a scientific study. He would buy test tubes out of his meagre wages, went all over to gather equipment, and then what happened?'

'What did happen?' she asked in concern.

He sucked his lips and said:

'His colleagues got in before him and registered superficial studies in order to get promotion while the senior professors were enraged with him for refusing to sell his name to anyone. Then they dismissed him on a trumped-up charge.'

'Impossible!' she exclaimed, shaking her head.

'I ran into him in the street a few months ago,' he said quietly. 'He stared ahead, looking dazed, and didn't recognize me. He was smiling, showing his yellow teeth, and his toes stuck out of his shoes. It was all very painful. Does anyone respect Hassanain Effendi?'

'I respect him,' she shouted.

'And who are you?' he said very softly.

'Me? Me?' she said angrily.

She felt her voice fading and that she was choking. She opened the car door and walked out into the desert. Saati got out after her and she heard him say:

'The truth is bitter, Fouada, but you must know it. I could lie to you, nothing would be easier. I'm used to it and practised at it, but I love you, Fouada, and want to spare you confusion and distress.'

He took her delicate, slender hand in his soft, fleshy one and whispered:

'I love you!'

She pulled her hand away and shouted angrily:

'Leave me alone! I don't want to hear a word!'

He left her and went back to the car. She walked alone in the desert and the humming began in her ear. Yes, let the humming go on. Silence was better than that sound. Let the meaningless, uninterrupted clamour fill her head, for it was better than those words. And you, Farid, you continue to be absent. What would you do if you were here? What would you do? What does a drop in the ocean do? What can a drop in the ocean do?

She spread her arms in the air and embraced the void. Yes, the void was better, nothingness was better. But how to become nothing? Her feet moved over the sand, her breath entered and left her lungs, the beats of her heart were still in her ears.

How could her body disappear? She stamped on the ground. Why can't I disappear? She held her breath to stop the air going in and out – pressed her hand to her heart to stop it beating.

It seemed to her that the air had stopped coming in, that her chest no longer rose and fell, and that she could no longer hear her heartbeats. She smiled. She had disappeared. But there was something heavy lying on her chest, something bitter burned her throat. A strange nauseous smell filled her nostrils and a soft, fleshy hand held hers. She tried to pull it away but could not find it. It had disappeared.

* * *

She opened her eyes and saw the wardrobe, the clothes-stand, the window and the ceiling with that jagged patch, and looked around bewildered. So she had not disappeared? This was her very same room, this her heavy head on the pillow and her body with its weight and density stretched out under the covers. This was the sound of shuffling feet approaching the room and this the brown, lined face looking in from the door. She saw the large eyes looking at her and heard the feeble voice say:

'What's the matter, daughter? What's the matter, Fouada?' She shook her head, saying hoarsely:

'Nothing, Mama, if only I were dead!'

'Why, Fouada? Death is for old people like me. You used to hate even the mention of it.'

'Farid,' she whispered.

'What?' her mother exclaimed in alarm. 'Is Farid dead?'

'No, no! He's only away, he'll come back,' she said shuddering.

She hid her face under the cover, swallowing the strangely bitter and acrid taste in her mouth. Where had it come from? She began to remember. She had been standing in the desert staring into space, had felt Saati behind her. He had put his arm around her waist and his eyes came nearer, growing larger and more prominent. She had felt his cold lips press on her lips, and his large teeth against hers. Her nostrils filled with a strange metallic smell like that of rusted iron, and her mouth filled with bitter saliva.

Yes, she saw and felt, but not clearly, not surely. It was all slow-moving and distant – like a nightmare. She had tried to hit him but her arm would not lift.

She reached beneath the cover and felt her arm. It was there and she moved it to pull the handkerchief from under the pillow and spat into it repeatedly. But the hot bitterness clung inside her mouth and she felt she was about to vomit. She threw back the covers and went to the bathroom, but the desire to vomit had passed. Almost viciously she scrubbed her teeth with brush and paste, and gargled, but the bitterness burned in her throat and was slowly seeping down.

Her mother's slender hand was on her shoulder.

'What happened to Farid?'

She raised her eyes. There was a strange look in her mother's eyes and she shuddered.

'I don't know. I don't know. Leave me alone, Mama.'

She returned to her room and sat on the edge of the bed, clutching her head in her hands. The telephone rang and she jumped. It must be him. His mean, coarse voice would come down the line. He would surely come. Why didn't the earth spin off-balance and the telephone crash and break? But the earth turned without fail, and the telephone would neither crash nor break. His voice would surely come through the holes in the receiver just as the wind comes through holes in the door. He would come without fail. His bitterness would burn her throat and his nauseous smell fill her nostrils. Why not dress and run away?

She hauled up her heavy body and dressed. Her mother's eyes watched her in silence, a strange expression in them. Stumbling to the door she paused to look at her... She could stay with her – wanted to stay with her – but she opened the door and went out.

Mindlessly she dragged her body through the streets. Her head was quiet, but not calmly, naturally quiet, but with a kind of paralysis, tranquillized, as if her brain cells were stilled by drugs.

She let her feet go their own way without directions from the head. Why always the head? Why wasn't the mind in the legs? The head does nothing more than be carried on the shoulders, then it rules and controls, while the legs do the work as well as carry the head, the shoulders and the whole body without ever being in control. Just as in life. Those who work and toil do not rule while the heads continue to be carried by necks, relishing the fruits and issuing controls.

Farid's words again. The tone of his voice, the movement of his hand, were still in her head. Why? When he was gone? How did his words, his movements, come to be creeping through her head once again?

She walked beside the flower garden. The scent of jasmine drifted to her. Farid's breath on her face with its smell, its warmth, and the touch of his lips on her neck returned. Her pale hand lifted – to touch his face – but it trembled in the air, then fell by her side.

The Nile was just as it always was, languid, eternal and infinite; its long, ruffled body, winding, languorous – like an aged whore, abandoned, content and without care. Fouada looked about her. Everything was abandoned, content, without care. And she? Couldn't she too be without care – carefree? Couldn't she become one of those mummified heads in the office? Couldn't she put her name to research she had not done like the smart, successful ones do?

Her eyes scanned the sky and earth. What had she wanted from the start? She hadn't wanted anything, hadn't wanted to succeed or shine. She had only felt, felt there was something in her that was not in others. She would not simply live and die, and the world remain the same. She had felt something in her head, the conception of a unique idea, but how to give it birth? The idea was awake, alive and struggling, but it did not emerge, seeming as if imprisoned by a thick wall, thicker than the bones of her skull.

She was all feelings, but how else does anything new begin? How did any discoverer who changed science or history begin? Doesn't it all begin with feelings? And what are feelings? An obscure idea, a mysterious movement in the brain cells. Yes. Isn't the beginning always a mysterious movement in the brain cells? So why mock her feelings? Why deny them? The first time she saw Saati, hadn't she felt that he was a thief? Had her feelings about the towering building and the long car betrayed her? Had the Supreme Board and the political council and the newspaper articles changed her first feelings? Despite everything, hadn't she continued to feel that he was a thief? Hadn't her brain cells picked up that invisible lie in the shiftiness of his bulging eyes? So why disregard her feelings?

She stood still for a moment and asked herself, had she ever before doubted her feelings? When had the doubt begun? When? She glanced around and caught sight of the door of the small restaurant and remembered. It was that night, that dark, gusty night when she entered the restaurant and saw the empty, uncovered table, the wind hitting it from all sides, like the buffeted stump of a tree.

Her feet approached the restaurant door apprehensively. Should she go in? What would she find? Perhaps, perhaps she would find him, perhaps he had come back. Her feet moved slowly, step by step towards the door. She paused to take a deep breath, then entered the long tree-lined passageway, knees quaking and heart pounding. She would come out of the passageway and look at the table and not find him. Better to go back right now. Yes, better to go back ... yet there was a hope that he was there, sitting at the table, his back leaning slightly forward, his thick black hair, his ears always flushed, his gleaming brown eyes in which that strange thing moved, that thing she sensed without seeing, something which made him *him*, his individuality, his particular words, thoughts and smell, made him Farid and not one of a million other men.

She turned to go back, but her feet moved her forward, down to the end of the passageway, then turned to the left. She stood with head bowed for a moment, unable to look up. Then she raised her head and her eyes met a brick wall. The table, everything, had gone; all she saw was a short wall in the open air like those walls that are built around the dead.

She heard a soft voice behind her ask:

'Do you want any fish?'

She turned to see a woman carrying a child. It was not a child, more a tiny skeleton, its small toothless jaws grasping a shrivelled breast that hung from the woman's chest like a strip of leather. The woman looked at her through half-closed, congested eyes and repeated in a weak voice:

'Do you want any fish?'

Fouada swallowed the bitterness in her mouth and said absently:

'There used to be a small restaurant here.'

'Yes,' the woman replied, 'but the owner lost his money and left the place.'

'And who took it?' she asked.

'The municipality,' the woman said.

'Who built this wall?'

'The municipality,' the woman replied.

Contemplating the wide open space, she asked:

'What did they build it for?'

Tugging at a dry breast and putting it between the child's jaws, the woman answered:

'My husband says the municipality built this wall to put its name on.'

The woman added:

'Do you want any fish?'

She smiled weakly and said:

'Not today. Perhaps I'll come back to buy another time.'

She left by the small door and walked down the street. There was no longer hope, no longer anything, only a brick wall, a short brick wall, good for nothing except the names of the dead.

No, there was only a wall. Was there nothing else? There was nothing. Everything had disappeared, as when a dream fades. What was the difference between dream and reality? If he had left a small note in his handwriting she could have known, a piece of paper with letters on it could have made the difference between dream and reality, whereas she, with her head and arms and legs, she could not.

She shook her head angrily. It was as heavy as stone, as if it too had become a wall. Was there anything else? Anything apart from a blank wall that returned an echo, returned what it heard and what it read? Could it say anything of its own? Had it ever said anything new ... that no one had ever said before? Did it not emit that uninterrupted, humming sound when all was silent?

The humming began in her head. Holding her head in her hands she sat on a stone wall. She stayed with head lowered for a second, then raised her weary eyes to the sky. Was it all a dream? Were her feelings an illusion? If her feelings lied, what was true? What could she believe? A name written on a wall? A name signed to a study? A word printed in a newspaper?

The sky ... was it the highest wall of all? Silent like any other wall? Raising her hands in the air she said out loud:

'Are you a wall? Why are you silent?'

A man walking in the street stared at her and approached, examined her with narrow, black eyes, then smiled a half-smile and said:

'I'll pay you only one riyal. Your legs are too thin.'

She looked at him, alarmed, then dragged her heavy body off the wall and let her legs carry her unthinkingly home.

* * *

The door of the house was open, the living room was full of people. Faces she knew and those she didn't looked at her curiously. She heard a loud sound like a scream and saw a face that resembled her mother's, but unlined. It was her aunt Souad, with her fat body in a tight black dress, who yelled: 'Fouada!'

She wrapped her short, fat arms around her. Many women surrounded her, screaming with one voice; the smell of scent rose from their black clothing. Half choking, she pushed the fat bodies away from her, shouting loudly:

'Get away from me!'

The women withdrew, bewildered. With heavy steps, she went slowly to her mother's room. She was lying on her bed, her head and body covered. Fearfully she approached and cautiously put out a hand to draw back the cover. Her mother's head wrapped in a white headcloth appeared, her face lined, eyes closed, mouth pressed tight, small gold earrings in her ears. She was sleeping as she always did, except that no breathing was perceptible. Fouada searched her face. Her features were changing bit by bit, as though collapsing into her face and clinging to her bones, the blood draining away.

A shiver ran through her body. Her mother's face had become like that of a stone statue, radiating an eerie coldness. She replaced the cover over the head, trembling. The screaming ran in her ears, uninterrupted and piercing. Dazed, she stumbled to her room, but it, too, was filled with faces she did not know.

She went into the living room. Strange eyes surrounded and encircled her. Screams echoed in her head. Without realizing, she walked towards the door, stood behind it for a moment, then rushed down the stairs and ran out into the street.

She didn't know where she was running, but simply ran, looking over her shoulder as if pursued by a ghost. She wanted to escape, to somewhere distant, where no one would see her. But he did not let her escape. He saw her running down the street, stopped the blue car, and ran after her. He caught her arm, saying:

'Fouada, where are you running?'

Gasping, she stopped and saw his eyes bulging and quivering behind his glasses. In a bewildered voice, she said:

'I don't know.'

'I phoned you an hour ago,' he said, 'and heard the news.'

Lowering his head, he added:

'I came to offer you my condolences.'

She wheeled round, the screams still ringing in her ears, the strange staring eyes crowding her from every direction. Burying her face in her hands she broke into tears. Saati helped her to the car, which took them from street to street. On the horizon the sun's last rays were fading. Across the sky, grey, tear-stained cloud-bodies were spreading. The car emerged into the open country and the desert glowed beneath the headlamps. She remembered her mother's face in the morning, waiting for her before she left the house. There had been a curious look in her eyes, a pleading look asking her to stay, but she had not seen that look as clearly she saw it now. Or had she seen it and consciously or unconsciously pretended not to? She had often pretended to ignore her silent looks, often pretended to ignore them. She had wanted to hurry and get out. Why had she hurried? Why did she go out? Where was she going? Why hadn't she stayed with her this last day? She had been alone, completely alone. Had she called out to her and she was not there to hear? Had she wanted some water and found no one to bring it? Why had she left her this day? Could this day ever return again?

The tears poured into her nose and throat and she opened her mouth for air, gasping, sobbing. The car had stopped. Saati sitting beside her was silent, looking at her long, pale face and staring fixedly into her green, distraught eyes. He put out his plump hand and took her trembling slender one.

'Don't be sad, Fouada. This is how life is. There's no life without death.'

He was silent for a moment, then said:

'What's the use of being sad? It only makes you ill. I'm never sad, or if it happens that I am, I think about happy things or listen to soothing music.'

He put out his hand and turned on the radio. A dance tune came out. The tears froze to a lump in her throat and, feeling she would choke, she opened the door and stepped out into the desert. A light cool breeze tightened her muscles, but her body was heavy. She moved her legs to shake off that oppressive weight but it bore down on her. She opened her mouth to scream, to expel the lump from her throat, but the muscles of her mouth expanded and contracted, expelling nothing. The lump slid into her neck, and its muscles expanded and contracted, then it moved to her chest and stomach; these muscles too began to expand and contract. But like the tentacles of some hydra-headed serpent the lump slithered into her whole body, until all her muscles expanded and contracted in rapid, violent spasms like convulsions. How desperately she wanted to rid her body of that choking, creeping thing.

The tune from the car radio rang through the silent desert. Her ears were deaf to it but it filled the air and entered her with every breath. Panting, she wanted to stop, to be still, but her muscles ignored her consciousness and her body began to tremble to the tune, discharging the venom from the pent-up energy and unconsciously revelling in the joy of dancing.

Yes, she had lost conscious control and was abandoned to the delight of the violent movement, yet one small point in her head, perhaps one single brain cell, still retained consciousness. It still knew that she was in the desert, that Saati was standing beside her, that she was extremely sad, that her mother was dead, Farid was absent, the idea of research was lost, her life in the Ministry empty.

She shook her head fiercely to separate out that one conscious cell, but it would not be dislodged. It had taken hold, solidified and began to rattle around her head, ripping through her languid brain cells like a pointed pebble.

The music stopped suddenly. Perhaps it had reached the end or perhaps Saati had turned off the radio. Her body crumpled onto the sand, breathless and soaked in sweat. When was the last time her body had been so drenched in sweat? When was the last time she had danced so wildly, uninhibitedly? Listened to Theodorakis? When was the last time Kazantzakis had said only madness destroys? Farid used to fight madness. He used to say that the madness of one individual means incarceration or death, whereas the madness of millions ... What does the madness of millions mean, Farid? Knowledge and hunger, he used to say. Hunger exists, only knowledge is lacking. And why don't they have knowledge, Farid? How can they, Fouada, when everything around them is either silent or lying?

She opened her eyes. She was lying on the sand beside a huge bulk with bulging eyes from which emanated something false and thievish. She heard a hoarse voice say:

'The most wonderful dance I've ever seen and the most beautiful dancer that exists!'

His arms were around her, filling her nostrils with a rusty metallic smell and her mouth with bitter, acrid saliva. She saw his bulbous eyes grow larger and more prominent, a strange frightening look in them. She struggled to turn, in terror, but saw only the desert and darkness. She tried to breathe but couldn't and with all her strength pushed him away from her, leapt up and ran. He ran after her.

Before her the spreading darkness, behind her that bulbous-eyed shadow, stalking her. It seemed that the flat desert in front of her was rising and spinning into two great, bulging eyes as she ran in a long narrow trench between them. The black convex bulk of the sky, too, had become great, bulging eyes, towering over and pressing down on her. She stumbled against something round and solid, fell to the ground and lost consciousness.

Lost consciousness except for that one conscious cell into which her five senses were polarized. She could still see, hear, feel, taste and smell. She felt a plump, fleshy hand on her chest, smelled a rusty metallic smell, tasted bitter, acrid saliva.

The cushiony hand became coarse, trembling fingers. The trembling did not stay in one place but crept lower, to her stomach and thighs. She saw his thick creased, fleshy neck like the trunk of an old tree out of which jutted small black buds which might have lived and developed but instead had died and decayed. His unbuttoned silk shirt revealed a hairless, fleshy chest, an unfastened leather belt hung around a bloated belly from which hung a pair of thin, hairless legs. His belly rose and fell with his spasmodic breathing and from inside him came a curious, muffled rattle like the groan of a sick animal.

A strange, heavy coldness enveloped her body, a coldness it had known only once before. She had been lying on a leather sheet surrounded by metal instruments – scalpels and syringes and scissors. The doctor picked up a long syringe and jabbed its needle into her arm. That same heavy coldness had coursed through her body as though she were plunged into a bath of ice and her body grew heavier and slowly drowned.

Only now there was no water beneath her but something soft ... like sand. Cold air entered her dishevelled dress, hot, bitter saliva gathered in her throat, the smell of something old and rusted invaded her nostrils. A panting, shuddering bulk lay beside her, its thin legs limp and shaking. She tried to open her mouth to spit but could not. Her eyelids grew heavy and closed.

* * *

She opened her eyes to see daylight streaming through the slats
of the shutters. She looked around in bewilderment. Everything
in her room was normal, the wardrobe, clothes-stand, window,
ceiling and jagged circle. She heard shuffling feet in the living
room, approaching her room. She looked at the door expecting
her mother's face to appear, but a long while passed and nothing
happened. Remembering, she leaped out of bed onto her feet.
Trembling, she went to the living room and apprehensively
approached the door of her mother's room. Was it all a dream?
Or was she really dead? She put her head round the door, saw
the empty bed and retreated in fear. She went to the kitchen, to
the dining room, to the bathroom but her mother was nowhere.
Dizzily she leaned her head against the wall. A solid lump whirled
in her skull, knocking against the bones. Bitterness scalded her
throat. Supporting herself against the wall, she staggered to the
sink and opened her mouth to spit, but the bitterness pressed on
her stomach and she vomited. The obscene, rusty smell emanated
from her mouth, her nose, her clothes. She undressed, stood
beneath the shower and scrubbed her body with a loofa and soap
but the smell clung to her flesh. It had entered her pores and cells
and into her blood.

Still clutching the walls, she returned to her room. Looking
around in distraction, her eyes settled on the face of her mother
in the photograph hanging near the wardrobe. Her mother seemed
to look out at her with large, jaundiced eyes, feebly pleading
with her to stay. She covered the face with her hand. Would her
mother never lose that accusing look? Had she not paid for her

sin? Wasn't she filled with that burning bitter taste? Wasn't her body steeped in that concentrated smell of old rust? Was there any grief greater than this? What was grief? How did people grieve? A loud scream clearing the voice and relieving pent-up feelings? Black clothing whose newness refreshed the body? Banquets and slaughtered meat stimulating the appetite and filling the stomach? Was there a dead mother who enjoyed more grief than this? Was there another mother whose daughter swallowed poison after her? Was there a mother's death greater than this death? Was there a greater filial repayment?

She went to bed feeling somewhat calmer and stretched out her arms and legs, but the heaviness was still on her body, the bitterness still burned. When, when would this heaviness relent and this burden lift?

The telephone rang. It was him. None other. There was only him left. There was nothing else left but to swallow poison day after day. Her insides would be eroded by the acrid burning, her body saturated by the concentration of old, cold rust. Only a slow death remained.

She put out a slender hand and raised the receiver. The hoarse, oily voice came through:

'Good morning, Fouada. How are you?'

'Alive,' she said listlessly.

'What are you doing tonight?' he asked.

'I don't know,' she said. 'I have nothing left.'

'What about me? I am left,' he said.

'Yes,' she said, 'there's only you left.'

'I'll pick you up at the laboratory at half past eight,' he said.

*   *   *

Walking out of the door she noticed something, something white and glistening behind the glass panel. She stepped back and peered into the mailbox. There was a letter there. Her body began to shake. She opened the box and picked up the letter with long, trembling fingers. She glanced at the large, square letters with their familiar flourishes. Her heart throbbed painfully. It was Farid's writing ... Dream or reality? She saw the stairs, the door and the mailbox. She put out a trembling hand to touch it. Yes, it was there, it was tangible. She fingered the letter. It was real paper with a thickness and density of its own. She put her fingers to her eyelids. They were open.

She turned the letter over, examining the corners and edges. There was nothing on it other than her name and address. She put it to her nose and met that distinctive smell of paper and postage stamp. She opened the envelope and took out a long sheet of paper, covered with writing:

Fouada...

How many days have passed since our last meeting, since that short night that bore the first winds of winter. You were sitting before me, the Nile behind you, in your eyes that strange glint which said: 'I have something new' and your slender fingers drumming on the table with a quiet that hid the volcano beneath. You were silent and I knew you were in pain. After a long silence you said: 'What do you think, Farid? Shall I leave the Ministry?' I understood you. At that moment, you wanted me to say: 'Yes, leave it, come with me.' But, you remember, I said nothing. I always felt that your role was different to mine. Your role is to create something new if you're given the chance, whereas my role is to create the chance for people to create something new. And what is new? Changing the old? And what does change create? Isn't it thought? Do you remember that small child who did the rounds of the tables in the restaurants? Do you remember his wrinkled hand when he held it out for a piece of bread or a piastre? People pitied him and gave him a piastre without thinking. If only they thought about what a piastre does! If only they thought why he was hungry! Yes, Fouada, it's thought, the idea that emerges from the head. Does an idea emerge from the head without expression?

Your role is to create the idea and mine to create the expression. Alone, I can do nothing. My role is neither as easy nor as convincing as the words appear to be. It's a sort of madness, for how do stifled, muted mouths express themselves? How can a voice penetrate through dense, stone walls? It's a sort of madness, but the madness of one individual can create nothing, only collective madness... do you remember that old conversation?

All right, I am not alone. There are others with me. All we have is that simple, dangerous role, and those simple, natural words which were born with the first human ... to think and to express. Nothing except these words for us to say and write. No cannons or rifles or bombs. Only words.

After we separated that short night, I walked alone down Nile Street, thinking about you, feeling you were in pain, that deep inside you a new idea was struggling to come out, fighting alone against a high wall ... in the Ministry, at home, in the street and in your skull. Yes, Fouada, there's another wall in your head, one you were not born with, but which day by day was erected out of long silence. I said to myself that night as I walked: 'It is only a short wall, it will collapse finally, when the other walls collapse.'

I did not reach home. A man stood in my way. I think he was not alone, there were others, perhaps many, all armed. I had nothing. You remember, I was wearing a brown shirt and trousers. They searched my pockets and found nothing. Are words put in a pocket? They grabbed me and put me in irons, but the words were carried in the wind. Can they catch the wind and put it in irons?

The walls surround me, but you are with me. I feel your small, soft hand on my face and see your green eyes looking into mine, that imprisoned, new thing appearing in them that wants to be born but cannot. Do not grieve, Fouada, and do not weep. The words are in the wind beyond the walls, alive and entering hearts with the very air. A day will surely come when the walls will fall and voices will once again be freed to speak.

Farid

THE
CIRCLING
SONG

NAWAL EL SAADAWI

FOREWORD BY FEDWA MALTI-DOUGLAS

Foreword

Prolific writer, ardent fighter for women's rights, challenger of patriarchy, feared by most and loved by many, without doubt the most prominent and prolific female author in Arabic: Nawal El Saadawi, trained as a doctor and psychiatrist, has the uncanny ability to place her finger on the hot buttons that inflame Arab readers.

Anyone who puts pen to paper has a favourite book among all the books to his or her name. It is no surprise that, for the prolific Egyptian physician–author Nawal El Saadawi, hers should be *The Circling Song*.

The Circling Song is a translation of the Arabic novel *Ughniyyat al-Atfal al-Da'iriyya*, rendered more correctly into English as *The Children's Circling Song*. The presence of the children is not accidental, since this haunting and masterful narrative revolves around a song sung by children holding each other's hands to form a circle without a beginning or an end. The children run in this never-ending circle as they sing a song that is itself repeated endlessly. The intrusive narrator provides the reader with a lesson on the Arabic language, in which meanings and genders can be changed with one dot or one letter. The twins, Hamida (the female) and Hamido (the male), are the central protagonists who display beautifully this ambiguity in the Arabic language.

Hamida steals a piece of candy, which she sucks as she lies in bed. The store-owner chases her and rapes her. This violation sets the narrative into motion as first the mother suspects that the blood she sees on her young daughter's clothing signals menstruation. But when Hamida's belly grows in size, the mother understands that the blood represents something else. She sends her daughter away on a train. This first rape, caused by a stolen piece of candy, is followed by a second rape, this one in the city where Hamida arrives by train. Impelled by hunger she grabs some bread, and this stolen food leads to her second rape, this time by 'the government'. When Hamida is raped a third time, she is a servant assaulted by her master because she has eaten a small piece of meat.

The confluence of eating and rape brings us into the universe of the corporal as it intersects with the political (the second rape) and the social (the third rape). The coming together of these three elements is not unusual in Saadawi's fiction.

We see the identical confluence, but with a clear religious component added, in *Woman at Point Zero*, where the doctor narrator is entranced by an imprisoned prostitute's narrative. The prostitute, Firdaus, we learn, was also raped, by her uncle, a traditionally educated man. She is then married to a much older religious man. A miser, he beats his wife because he has found a piece of food in the garbage. She runs away to an uncle's house where she is informed that men, especially religious ones, beat their wives. She escapes, but this time into prostitution.

As *The Circling Song*'s Hamida exits the train in the city, her brother, Hamido, is boarding a train at the instigation of his father, who declares to him that 'only blood washes out shame' – the blood being, of course, female.

In another Saadawian tale, a short story entitled 'A Story from a Woman Doctor's Life', a third-person narrator introduces the text: 'Dr S. wrote in her diary.' Dr S. in this unusual framing proceeds to recount the story. A young girl is sitting in her clinic, flanked by a tall young man, her brother. The brother entreats the doctor to examine his sister, wishing to reassure himself about her, 'since we are marrying her off to her cousin next week'. The girl cuts her brother off, insisting that she does not love this man and does not wish to marry him. The brother, however, responds that she does not want to marry him for 'another reason, Doctor... I think you understand', a clear allusion to the possibility of her having lost her virginity.

Observing the fright in the young girl's eyes, the doctor asks the brother to leave the room in order that she undertake the examination. Alone with the doctor, the young girl begs her to save her from this brother, who would kill her. The doctor decides that she cannot examine the patient without her permission. She tells the young woman that she will inform her brother that this is outside her purview. The patient objects, insisting that her brother will simply take her to another doctor. She then asks the doctor to claim that she examined her and that she was 'honourable'. Her brother, she adds, will kill her otherwise. She is in love with another man and will marry him in a month, swearing to the doctor that nothing dishonourable occurred between them.

Examining her conscience and her medical codes, the doctor in the story calls in the brother and declares to him that his sister is honourable. As she explains it later, she believes that the girl is indeed honourable. 'Medicine can only distinguish between disease and non-disease. It cannot distinguish between honour and dishonour.' The brother is made to apologize to his sister for doubting her and the two leave. The doctor then writes her own oath: 'I swear that my humanity and my conscience will be my rules in my work and my art', adding 'I put down my pen and felt an ease I had not felt for a long time.'

The framing technique here is more an introductory preface to the doctor's written words. If it were absent, however, it would not alter the essential plot of the story. Hence, its presence is quite eloquent. This doctor needs a third-person narrator as an intermediary who introduces the actual writing process itself. The recording of the story in writing differs from oral and epistolary framings, although like them it requires mediation. Like the other protagonists whose sagas needed to be narrated by the doctor, Hamida and Hamido, from the countryside, are individuals who would not have access to the written word. The woman doctor is once more the means through which silent voices can tell their stories.

With the brother–sister combo, El Saadawi has put her medical finger on a deep societal problem. Brother–sister jealousy is pervasive in Arabo-Islamic culture. So pervasive, in fact, that the noted Arab folklorist Hasan El-Shamy has boldly argued that brother–sister sexual attraction and subsequent jealousy are so powerful in Arab culture that they replace in its psychological centrality the Oedipus conflict in Western society. This brother–sister relationship appears in texts ranging from the medieval to the modern, from the literary to the philosophical.

The sister in this Saadawian short story is frightened by her brother. Twice she repeats to the doctor that her brother will kill her. This is not an unrealistic expectation on the part of the young girl, as her Saadawian literary cousin, Hamida, demonstrates. The girl's honour is the motivating force behind the visit to the doctor. The female body must be certified as honourable before it can be handed on to the would-be husband. But this male knows little about women's solidarity. He is attempting to control a woman's body, which becomes a pawn in intricate social gender games. The doctor, however, is able to defeat this man's desire and give the young woman back her body. Medicine as social power for the female comes to the rescue.

In the Saadawian short story, the brother's concern for his sister's virginity is pre-eminent. Her body is a commodity whose honour, if absent, will surely lead to her death. The Syrian male writer Zakariyya Tamir savagely attacks the marital customs that turn the female into a commodity in his short story 'The Eastern Wedding'. There, the price of the young girl is agreed on, so much per kilo, and she is taken to the marketplace and weighed in. Tamir comes close to Saadawi, who even in *Memoirs of a Woman Doctor* likened the vocabulary used in the marriage ceremony to that used in the rental of an apartment, store, or other property. The marriage-as-commerce metaphor is repeated when the narrator of

Memoirs wonders if people expect her to sit and wait while some man decides to come and buy her as one buys a cow. Woman's body is a commercial object whose value is linked to its 'honour'.

Dr S's new oath with which she closes her case history calls for humanity and conscience not only in her work but in her art as well. Medicine and art are once again brought together in an eloquent proclamation. But it is through medicine that she has saved a sister from the death threats of her brother. Social justice becomes fused with the physician's art, understood in the broadest sense.

The story of Dr S., like *Memoirs of a Woman Doctor*, shows us the potential power of an upper-class woman in Egyptian society. She may be able to save herself. She may sometimes be able to save others. But what we glimpse in these medical narratives, and what is more clearly revealed in other Saadawian narratives, is another female type: the lower-class woman who loses control over her body and who, if she attempts to regain it, will meet with physical destruction. This is certainly the case for Hamida in *The Circling Song*.

The simple phrase 'only blood can wipe out shame', which links a corporal element, blood, to a social element, shame, is one so embedded in Arabo–Islamic culture that it takes on an enormous importance, as it is transformed and shortened to 'honour killing'.

Fedwa Malti-Douglas
Martha C. Kraft Professor, Indiana University

Author's Introduction

Among the novels I have written, *The Circling Song* is one of the closest to my heart. I wrote it at the end of 1973 – in November, I'm quite sure – when I was going through a period marked by an enigmatic, internal sadness. Egypt's ruler at that time was extremely pleased with, and proud of, his victories; he was surrounded by a large entourage of men, and some women, all of whom applauded him for whatever reason, and perhaps without any reason.

It was not clear to me what the principal source of my melancholy was, but there certainly were some external reasons that contributed: being deprived of my position and summarily dismissed from my job the year before (in August 1972) because of some of my published writings; the confiscation of my books and articles; and the inclusion of my name on the government's blacklist. Meanwhile, every morning I saw the face of Egypt's ruler printed on newspaper and magazine pages, and I could hear his voice reverberating from various loudspeakers.

No affiliation or contact linked me with politics or the ruling establishment, or with the ruler. I was writing all the time, and carrying on my medical practice on a part-time basis. But a relationship of sorts developed between the ruler and me (from one side, of course); it was an association based on hatred. I had not experienced hatred before in that way: at the time, most of my relationships were ones built on affection.

From time to time, I visited my village, Kafr Tahla. There I would feel a sense of relief and relaxation as I sat in my father's very modest old house, which was almost bare of furnishings. I would smell the fragrance of its dirt floor, newly sprinkled by my cousin Zaynab to keep the dust down. I would see the faces of the children, both girls and boys, looking like flowers just as they open, covered with flies as bees cover a blossom. I would hear them singing as they played atop the dung heaps.

One of their songs was 'Hamida had a baby...' I used to hear them frequently as they sang it, and I had heard it many times before as a child, as one of them. I don't know why, when I heard them singing it this particular time, the song inspired me with the idea behind this novel.

The idea was vague and cryptic, and profound; it kept me from sleeping for several days, or perhaps weeks. Then I began to write. Carrying my papers inside a cloth tote bag and wearing my leather sandals – since they had flexible, rubber-like soles – I would leave my house on Murad Street in Giza, just across the river from Cairo. It would take me about half an hour to traverse Nile Street, cross the Cairo University Bridge, and reach my destination: a small, outdoor garden café by the Nile, since demolished to make way for the Fire Department. Seated on a bamboo chair, a little bamboo table before me, I would gaze at the waters of the Nile and write.

I wrote the first draft of the novel in a few weeks, and rewrote it in a few days. As I wrote certain sections, I could feel the tears on my face. When Hamida (or Hamido) felt tears, I felt my own. I was sure that my novel would amount to something, for as long as I was crying real tears along with the characters of the novel, then surely this work was artistically alive, and would have a similar effect on those who read it.

Whenever I heard the microphones and broadcasts bellowing out their joyous songs, my sadness would grow. I didn't know which of the two emotions held more reality: the joy of the world around me, or the sadness inside. I felt that this world and I were utterly incompatible, and the novel was simply an attempt to give that incompatibility concrete form.

I couldn't publish this novel in Egypt, of course, since I was on the government's blacklist. So I tried to publish it in Beirut. At that time, Beirut was like a lung which gave many writers – men and women prohibited from publishing – the ability to breathe.

Dar al-Adab published the novel in Beirut two or three years – I don't remember exactly – after I had written it. In Egypt, naturally, the critics ignored it. Perhaps they even avoided reading it, for this was the treatment they had consistently given my other books. Thus, the novel came out in an atmosphere of silence, and it has lived in the same silence to the present. But people did read it, because the publisher in Beirut reprinted it more than once, and because one of the publishers in Egypt also has published it several times (since 1982). But the critics in Egypt maintained their silence, while the novel continued to be published and read in Egypt as well as in other Arab countries.

Meanwhile, I had forgotten this novel completely and had written other novels in a very different style. Yet the characteristics and structure of this particular novel lived on in my imagination, like a dream that one has once had. I wanted to write another, perhaps a more ambitious novel that would draw upon the same way of writing. And from time to time I would meet a woman or man who had read it, or receive a letter from a reader – sometimes a woman, sometimes a man – making a comment about this novel along the lines of 'This little book has released so many of my innermost feelings! Why don't you always write in this style?'

But every idea has its own particular mode of expression, and I made no attempt to impose this style on different thoughts or ideas.

One day when I was in London, the publisher of this novel asked me if I had a new novel which could be translated and published. I don't know why this particular work came to mind immediately – this novel which had been published in Arabic for the first time more than a decade before in Beirut. I realized that I was very fond of *The Circling Song*, and that it was like the sort of close relationship which one does not forget no matter how many years pass. I hadn't read the novel for ten years, as I don't like to read my books after they are published, but the translator of this novel gave me a copy of the translation for me to review. The strangest thing happened: it seemed as if I were reading it for the first time. I would stop at certain sections, surprised, as if the writer were another woman, someone other than me. Indeed – and how peculiar this seemed – I felt actual tears coming whenever Hamida (or Hamido) cried. And this is how I knew that the translation was as I wished it to be.

Nawal El Saadawi

Every day, and at whatever time I left the house, my gaze was met by a ring of little bodies, winding round and round, circling continuously before my eyes. The children's thin, high-pitched voices spiralled palpably up into the sky. The rhythmic orbit of their singing was synchronized with the movement of their bodies, fused into a single song, comprising one stanza which repeated itself in a never-ending, unbroken cycle, as they turned round and round, and round:

Hamida had a baby,
*She named him Abd el-Samad,**
She left him by the canal bed,
The kite swooped down and snatched off his head!
Shoo! Shoo! Away with you!
O kite, O monkey snout!
Hamida had a baby,
She named him Abd el-Samad,
She left him by the canal bed,

---

* Male name, literally 'Servant of the Everlasting', but *sumuud*, from the same root, also suggests 'defiance' and 'resistance'. According to the author, this song is sung by peasant children, and accompanied by a ring dance; as they reach the line 'Shoo! shoo!' they may throw stones outward from the circle.

The kite swooped down and snatched off his head!
Shoo! Shoo! Away with you!
O kite, O monkey snout!
Hamida had a baby,
She named him Abd el-Samad...

The children would repeat the song, so rapidly that the first line sounded before the echo of the last had died down, and the last line seemed to follow fast on the tail of the first. Because they were circling and singing uninterruptedly, it was impossible to pick out the song's beginning or end by ear. And since they were grasping each other tightly by the hand as children are wont to do, one could not tell by looking where the circle began and where it ended.

* * *

But everything does have a beginning, and so if I am to tell this story I must begin. Yet I do not know the starting point of my tale. I am unable to define it precisely, for the beginning is not a point that stands out clearly. In fact, there is no beginning, or perhaps it would be more accurate to say that the beginning and the end are adjoined in a single, looping strand; where that thread starts and where it ends can be discerned only with great difficulty.

Here lies the difficulty of all beginnings, especially the beginning of a true story, of a story as truthful as truth itself, and as exact in its finest details as exactitude itself. Such exactitude requires of the author that he or she neither omit nor neglect a single point. For, in the Arabic language, even one point – a single dot – can completely change the essence of a word. Male becomes female because of a single dash or dot. Similarly, in Arabic the difference between 'husband' and 'mule', or between 'promise' and 'scoundrel', is no more than a single dot placed over a single form, an addition which transforms one letter into another.

So I must begin my story at a well-defined point. And a well-defined point is just that and nothing else. It cannot be a dash or a circle, for instance, but rather must be a real point in the full geometrical sense of the word. In other words, scientific accuracy is unavoidable in this work of art which is my novel. But scientific accuracy can corrupt or distort a work of art. Yet perhaps that corruption or distortion is exactly what I want, and what I aim for in this story. Only then will it be as truthful, sincere and real as 'living life'. This is an expression upon which I insist; I write it deliberately, with premeditation: it is not a haphazard or accidental choice. For there are two kinds of life: 'living life' and 'dead life'. 'Dead life' is that which inhabits a person who walks through life without sweating or urinating, and from whose body no foul substance emanates. For foulness, corruption and rot are necessary corollaries of 'living life'. A living person cannot hold back the urine in his bladder indefinitely or he will die. Once he is dead, though, he can keep his foulness bottled up inside. He then becomes what might be called a 'clean corpse', in a scientific sense. From an artistic point of view, however, inner corruption is more deadly than foulness which is allowed to escape into the world outside. This is a well-known fact or phenomenon of nature, and it is for this reason that the smell of a dead body is much more foul than the odour of a body which is still alive.

* * *

I fancied (and my fancy, at that particular moment, amounted to fact) that one of the children who were circling round as they sang in unison suddenly moved outside of the circle. I saw the small body come loose from the steadily revolving ring, breaking the regularity of its outline. It moved off like a gleaming speck, or a star that has lost its eternal equilibrium, detached itself from the universe, and shot off at random, creating a trail of flame, like a shooting star just before it is consumed in its own fire.

With an instinctive curiosity, I followed his movement with my gaze. He came to a stop so near to where I stood that I could see his face. It wasn't the face of a boy, as I had thought. No, it was the face of a little girl. But I wasn't absolutely certain, for children's faces – like those of old people – are sexless. It is in that phase between childhood and old age that gender must declare itself more openly.

The face – oddly enough – was not strange to me. So familiar was it, in fact, that it left me feeling bemused, and then my surprise turned to disbelief. My mind could not accept the sight before my eyes. It is just not plausible that, leaving home in the morning to go to work, on the way I should run head-on into another person only to discover that the face which met my gaze was none other than my own.

I confess that my body shook, and I was seized by a violent panic which paralysed my ability to think. Even so, I wondered: why should a person panic when he sees himself face to face? Was it the extreme weirdness of the situation in which I found myself, or was it the almost overwhelming familiarity of the encounter? At such a moment, one finds everything becoming utterly confused. Contradictory or incompatible things come to resemble each other so closely that they become almost identical. Black becomes white, and white turns to black. And the meaning of all this? One faces, with open eyes, the fact that one is blind.

I rubbed my eyes with trembling fingers, and looked at the child's face again, and again, any number of times. Perhaps I have been gazing into that face ever since. Maybe I am still looking at it, at this very moment, and at every moment, as if it is following me around as closely as my shadow, or clinging to me like a part of my body, like my own arm or leg.

* * *

Panic, by its nature, breeds loathing, and I cannot deny that I felt an instant hatred for this face. Some people might think I'm not speaking sincerely when I say this. Perhaps they will ask themselves how one can loathe his own face, or body, or any part of his body. No doubt those people have a point – after all, they're more able to see me than I am able to see myself. This is not a unique or personal tragedy: in fact, everyone suffers from it, for one is always most visible to others – whether frontally, in profile, or from the rear. While others know what we look like from behind, we can only look ourselves in the face – and that by means of a mirror.

The mirror is always at hand, positioned like another person standing between one and oneself. Even so, I have no animosity towards the mirror. As a matter of fact, I am practically in love with it. I adore gazing into it at length – staring into it, actually. I love to see my face. The truth is that I never tire of looking at my face, for it's a beautiful face, more beautiful than any other face I've ever seen on this earth. Moreover, every time I look at it, I discover new aspects of its beauty that almost bewitch me.

Not everyone will feel ill at ease with my frankness. But candour is not always welcome; in fact, it is rarely so. Nevertheless, I have promised myself to tell the truth. Speaking candidly is hard work, I know, and persisting in it requires ever-greater efforts and more and more sacrifices. One must give up trying to be attractive or acceptable at every moment; one must even accept that people may find a certain degree of ugliness in what we are or in what we say and do. Sometimes they may find us so ugly that we become repulsive to them. But this is the struggle demanded of freedom fighters, and also of anyone who wants to produce a good work of art, which is what I am trying to do.

What particularly dazzled me about this face were the eyes, and the eyes alone. Eyes are what I adore in a person most of all. And I believe (although my conviction may lack scientific foundation) that the eyes of a person are extremely sensitive organs, that in fact they are the most sensitive of all, followed closely (and this is natural) by the reproductive organs. But what drew me most to the eyes was a certain light that seemed to shine in all directions, reflecting itself in all nooks and crannies, like the purest of fine-cut diamonds. It was certainly a confusing gaze, one that defied easy appraisal, for it wasn't a one-dimensional look with a clear meaning. It wasn't a look of sadness, or an expression of joy, a look of reproach or of fear. No, it was not a single look. It was a look composed of many looks, even if on the surface it seemed uniform. For soon enough the first look disappeared, to be followed by the second and third, each enveloped in turn, like the turning pages of a thick book or the folds of a length of fine weaving, successive layers piling themselves one atop the other.

My attention was so fully captured by the eyes that I noticed no other features of her face – neither nose, nor cheeks, nor lips – nor did I notice the tiny hand which rose in the air, waving to me with a gentle and familiar gesture as though she had known me all along.

'What's your name?' I asked her.

'Hamida.'

The voices of the children rose in unison, accompanied by their winding movement and circular song, circling ceaselessly so that one could not tell the beginning from the end.

Hamida had a baby,
She named him Abd el-Samad,
She left him by the canal bed,
The kite swooped down and snatched off his head!
Shoo! Shoo! Away with you!
O kite! O monkey snout!
Hamida had a baby

I laughed, as adults normally do when they are trying to be playful with children.

'Are they singing for you?' I asked.

But I got no answer. She had vanished during the brief moment when my head moved as I laughed. I just barely caught a glimpse of her small back, bending slightly as she disappeared inside a dark wooden door on which was mounted a wooden human hand that served as a door knocker.

I didn't bother with the door knocker, as strangers to a household usually do when they are facing a closed door. I knew my way, despite the massed darkness that always squats in the entrances to these houses, a gloom made even heavier by the sun's setting long before. To my right, I saw the nanny-goat's head peeping out from behind the wall; to my left was a small step leading into a room, merely a slight elevation. Still, as I crossed it, I stumbled – just as I have every time – and almost fell on my face. I would have done, had it not been for my body's practised agility and its remarkable ability to regain a threatened balance.

I spotted her. She was lying on the reed mat, deep in sleep. Her eyelids were half closed, and her lips were parted just enough to let through the deep breaths of a sleeping child. Her arms were coiled around her head, and her right hand was closed over a penny or perhaps a halfpenny coin. Her long *galabeya** was hitched up over her thin, tender-skinned legs as far as the knees, and her little head quivered in a minute, hardly perceptible movement. Her small jaws were pressed lightly together, giving the impression of bliss dissolving in her mouth: a piece of candy, concealed beneath her tongue.

There was no moon, and the night was gloomy. The lamp, lit since early evening, had now become but a feeble wisp of light; either its wick had burnt out or the oil had been depleted. And

---

* An ankle-length gown or robe which is cut to hang loosely; it is worn traditionally by both men and women, although the style, colours and cloth differ.

as I stood there, a sudden, strong, hot gust of wind extinguished the faint tendril of light. The wind had burst in from the direction of the door, which actually wasn't a door at all, for the room possessed only that small, slightly raised threshold. But now that the lamp had gone completely out, the darkness had become so dense that one could not distinguish the floor from the walls, or the walls from the ceiling. Nothing at all was visible in the heavy blackness – nothing, that is, except a large object that filled the doorway completely, the only light now coming from two small round apertures set high in that wooden block, holes which emitted a piercing yellow light stained with the redness of still-glowing embers.

In that moment falling between the last threads of night and the first strands of day, not even the half-light which makes the way for dawn had emerged. In the darkness, his large, bare foot stumbled on the slight rise of the threshold. But his tall, broad body regained its balance, and he sprang forward, pantherlike, on tensile feet. He moved on, slowly and cautiously, stepping over something that looked very much like the backless leather slippers worn by men in the countryside.

Like the eyes of a wildcat whose sharp vision and sweeping night sight have not been tamed to dullness, those piercing, reddish-stained apertures made certain that she was on the mat. When his coarse, flattened fingers reached out to lift the *galabeya* from her pale thighs, she was still deep in sleep, enjoying the sound slumber of childhood. The dream, though, had shifted: the sweet had melted to nothing beneath her tongue, and the shopkeeper was demanding the penny. She opened her fingers;

her hand was empty. The shopkeeper snatched up his stick and began to run after her.

As small and light as it was, her body could fly through the air like a sparrow. No doubt she would have been able to stay ahead of the shopkeeper (aah, had she only been a real sparrow!). But a feeling of heaviness came upon her, suddenly and just the way it happens in dreams. She felt her body grow sluggish; it seemed to have turned into stone, into a statue whose feet are planted on the ground and whose arms are fixed in place with iron and cement. Her thighs, pulled apart, seemed to have turned into marble, and her legs, held stiffly in the air, were split wide open. The blows of the stick rained down between her thighs with a violence she had never known before.

She screamed, but no voice came out. A large, flat hand clapped down over her mouth and nose, stifling her. She became aware that a large body smelling of tobacco was pressing down onto her: this wasn't a dream, she realized. Although her eyes were nearly closed, she could make out the features of the face clearly enough to recognize their resemblance to those of her father or brother, one of her uncles or cousins, or another man – any man.

Like all children, when Hamida woke up each morning her mind was clear of the previous night's dreams. Sparrowlike, she would hop up from the mat and run to her mother with the happy cries of a child who greets the new day with a well-rested body and an empty stomach, eager for even a morsel of bread baked to such hardness that it can crack baby teeth, or a single gulp of milk straight from an udder, or a lump of old, fermented cheese scraped from the bottom of the clay jar.

That morning was no different from any other. But this dream had not been laid to rest, forgotten. Harsh fingers had left red and blue marks on her arms and legs, and she could still feel a pain between her thighs, while the aroma of tobacco clung to her skin.

Thinking it a fever, her mother bound Hamida's head in a kerchief and left her to lie on the mat. Hamida slept the entire day and through the night. She awoke the next morning believing the dream forgotten, as if it had evaporated in the air or been lost in the past, in fact as if it had never been. She jumped up from the mat with her usual energy, except that she felt a slight heaviness in her legs which soon disappeared as she dressed for school and scampered off with the other children.

I could always distinguish Hamida from the rest, for her school pinafore was made of a coarsely woven, faded cream-coloured calico. Moreover, on the back was a stain that had been red a few days before, for as she sat in class, a spot of blood had seeped through her knickers. Her mother, who was always warning her to be ready for this event, had shown her how to put the rough cotton towel carefully between her thighs, for she was no longer a little girl. How often she had heard her mother's comment: 'I was your age when I got married – and my breasts weren't even showing yet.'

Whenever Hamida twisted around and saw the stain on the pinafore, she could feel the embarrassment beading her small, even forehead like sweat. She would dash home to take off the pinafore, replacing it with her *galabeya*. Squatting by the metal basin, she would wash out the garment, for it was her only school pinafore. Then she would hang it out on the line, in the sun, so that it would be dry before the next morning.

One day the pinafore became tight. Only with difficulty did she squeeze her body into it, especially from the front, over her belly. Bearing a strange expression that Hamida had never seen before, her mother's eyes came to rest on her belly. It was such a sombre, frightening look that it sent a light shiver through her small body. Her mother's large fingers closed around Hamida's skinny arm.

'Take off your pinafore!'

Hamida obeyed. She put on her *galabeya*, and huddled by the wall, finding a sunny patch in which to sit. Usually, her mother called her to lend a hand with the kneading or baking, or the cooking, or sweeping the house. Or her father, or one of her uncles, sent her to the shop to buy tobacco. One of her aunts might hand over a still-nursing baby, to be cared for until she returned from working in the field. Or the neighbour would sing out from her rooftop, asking Hamida to fill her earthenware jar from the river. Her brother, or an uncle, would toss his dirty socks and pants at her for laundering. At sunset, the girls and boys of the neighbourhood would crowd around her. They would all scurry down to the street and play hide-and-seek, or cops and robbers, or 'the snake's gone, gone', or 'a grain of salt', or 'Hamida had a baby'.

But today, nothing of the sort happened. They left her alone, sitting in the sunshine. She couldn't find any way to pass the time except to stare at the path of the sun's disc across the sky. When it set, after a stretch of time, she remained there, sitting stolidly in the darkness, her small body trembling. She sensed something out of the ordinary, but didn't know what. Something dreadful was happening around her, in the darkness, in the dead silence, and in the eyes, everyone's eyes. Not even the chickens who were always about, crowding and pushing to get near her, approached as they normally did. The big black tomcat who usually came up to rub himself against her stopped at a distance and stared at her, his dilated eyes apprehensive, his long, sharply tapered ears held rigid.

Hamida's head drooped over her knees. She dozed off for a moment, or perhaps it was several hours later that she came to, suddenly conscious of long fingers taking hold of her arm. Alarmed, Hamida started, and would have screamed had it not been that her mother's hand was suddenly clapped over her mouth. Her mother's faint voice sounded more like a hiss:

'Come on, follow me, on your tiptoes.'

As there was no moon, and the half-light that just precedes the dawn had not yet appeared, the night was dark. The entire village was asleep, still and silent in that moment falling between the last hour of the night and the beginnings of day, just before the dawn call to prayer. Her mother's large, bare feet almost ran over the dusty ground, with Hamida following so closely behind that she could almost touch the hem of her mother's gown.

She was just meaning to open her mouth to ask the question in her mind when her mother came to a halt at a squat wall which separated the main country road from the railroad. Hamida knew this wall: she often hid behind it when playing hide-and-seek. Her mother handed her a familiar-looking rectangle of black cloth: it was a *tarha*.

Hamida settled the *tarha* over her head so that it hung down over her body, covering her neck, shoulders, chest, back and belly. Now she looked just like one of the village women. As her mouth formed its question, the train whistle sent a shiver through her mother's body. A harsh tremor shook the ground beneath the woman's feet, and just as harshly her large fist plunged forward suddenly, pushing into her daughter's back, pushing Hamida towards the train. Again, her whispering voice was lowered almost to a hiss:

'The train doesn't wait for anyone. Go on, run away!'

Hamida leapt towards the approaching train, but then stopped to turn around momentarily. She saw her mother, standing exactly in the same place, as if rooted to the spot, impassive and motionless. The black *tarha* which enveloped her mother's head, shoulders and bosom was utterly still. Her chest showed not the slightest rise or fall, nor did any part of her show the tiniest movement. Even her eyelashes were frozen in place; she looked like a statue, a real one carved from stone.

The train was now coming into the station: a massive black head emitting smoke. The strong beam of its one large eye exposed the station. It also exposed Hamida, as she stood there out in the open. Hastily, she took cover behind a post. The train slowed, its cars colliding against each other, its iron wheels screeching against the iron rails, producing such a loud and brazen sound as it came to a stop that Hamida thought the noise must have awakened everyone in the village. She rushed towards the train, pulling the edges of the *tarha* around her face to disguise herself as best she could.

She extended one small foot towards the steps leading up into the train. She had never ridden in a train before. There was a gap between platform and stairs, and her leg fell short. She pulled back her foot and glanced around in panic. She feared the train would start moving before she could manage to climb on. Seeing a throng of men and women boarding the forward carriage, she hurried over to stand behind them. She watched closely as, one after another, they ascended the steps. Every single one of them, she could see, took hold of an iron handle beside the doorway before placing a foot on the first step. She hadn't noticed that handle before. Hamida stuck out her right arm, clutched the handle as tightly as she could, pulled her body forward until her foot reached the step, and disappeared inside the carriage.

She sat down on the first seat that met her eyes, noticing that it was next to a window. As the train began to move slowly, she peered outside. She poked her head further out of the window. Her neck stiffened as she saw her mother, still standing in the same spot, impassive and motionless, everything frozen in place: *tarha*, head, chest, eyelashes, everything.

On the point of calling out, Hamida reminded herself that it was no longer her mother whom she could see, but rather the statue of the peasant woman that had stood at the entrance to the village for many years – how many she did not know. She could not remember a time when she had not seen it there. It must have been there forever; it must have been there even before she was born.

Her head still outside the window, she regained her breath in a few gasps. It was the first time she had experienced the feel of tears on her face or their taste in her mouth. But she did not move, not even to wipe off her tears on the sleeve or hem of her *galabeya*. She let them run down her face, and when they reached the inner corner of her mouth she licked them off without visibly moving a single facial muscle. She didn't make a sound or flicker an eyelid; not even her eyelashes trembled. Everything had gone pitch black. The train dissolved into the blackness and blended into the night, like a drop melting into the depths of the sea.

* * *

As Hamida's train pulled away, Hamido was still lying inert on the reed mat. Although his eyes were closed in sleep, he could see his father's eyes in the faint light. His father stood tall and straight, like the trunk of a eucalyptus tree which has sent its roots deep into the earth.

An oppressive chill ran through Hamido's small body, numbing his arms and legs as if he were caught in a troublesome dream. He lay motionless, his steady gaze directed at that tall, impassive phantom. Somehow, he knew that something serious had happened, or soon would. He held his breath and vanished completely under the grimy, blackened coverlet, his small fingers pulling it taut around his head. His right ear, atop the hard pillow, trembled in time to the beating of his heart, which seemed to issue from his head rather than his chest.

At any moment he expected those long fingers to reach out and strip off the bedcover, exposing his head. The wide-open eyes would settle their gaze on his, filling his eyes with whatever it was that was so ominous. But the coverlet remained in place, pulled tightly over his head. In the silence he could hear his own heartbeat resound in the room. And despite the darkness, he could see the movement of his chest, so slight as to be almost invisible, like the ever-so-delicate stirring of treetops on a still and moonless night, unrelieved by a single breath of moving air, when the darkness, like his grimy bedcover, has wrapped itself over sky and earth, in that brief moment hidden on the boundary of night and day, before the threads of dawn begin to appear and the darkness creeps away. The gloom lifts slowly, like a huge fish swimming in an endless ocean where lie the village's small mud huts, huddled together in the depths like a huge heap of black dung.

When Hamido opened his eyes, daylight already filled the room. What he had seen was nothing but a dream; he was absolutely sure of it. He jumped up from the mat and ran out into the street. His friends, children of the neighbouring families, were playing as usual in the narrow lane extending along and between the mud-brick façades. Each child held fast to the hem of the next one's *galabeya*, forming a dancing, whistling, train. Then they would break apart and play hide-and-seek, concealing themselves behind the dung heaps, inside the animal pens, behind a large earthenware water jar inside one of the houses, or inside the mouth of an oven.

He saw Hamida amongst the children, running for cover behind a pile of dung. She squatted so that her head would not show above the mound. But he could see her white thighs, and between them a thin strip of rough brown calico. Even though she attempted to hide her crop of soft black hair in the dust so that no one would see her, Hamido spotted her at once. This time, he was the seeker, so he bounded off at a run, his bare feet stirring up a whirlwind of dust as he headed towards her.

He fixed his eyes on the dung heap, pretending not to see her. He advanced on tiptoe, slowly, cautiously, and swerved as if to conceal himself behind the heap. Then he sprang – a single jump, a panther's leap – and grabbed her by the hair. His other hand shot out with lightning speed and he let it rest on her thigh for a few moments. Then his small, stiff fingers pulled at her knickers, but Hamida kicked and butted him, as she did whenever the seeker caught her. She managed to free herself of his grasp, and ran to hide behind another dung heap.

Hamida was not the only one to play hide-and-seek, for all the village children joined in the game. When any of the girls ran to hide, and squatted to conceal themselves, their small white thighs were bared and their cheap, dirty knickers showed, looking like thin black strips between their thighs. The seeker – whoever it was – would grab at the strip, trying to pull the knickers down. But the girl knew how to aim a practised kick, with one or both feet. The seeker would not give in either, but would fight her with the same methods. A battle in miniature would ensue, an almost imperceptible skirmish, for the dung heap concealed the pair of small bodies. But four tender little feet could be seen, jutting out from behind the pile, the girl's foot indistinguishable from the boy's: in childhood, feet – like faces – are sexless, especially if the feet are bare, for only shoes define their gender.

Her kick propelled Hamido backwards, and he toppled over on to his behind. He recovered quickly, though, and so did she;

as he got to his feet, he caught sight of her face. It wasn't Hamida. His eyes swept the area, peering at all the children in turn. He ran to the house to search for her – in the animal pen, in the mouth of the oven, behind the water jar, under the mat. He came out of the house at a run, looking for her – behind the dung heaps, behind the tree trunk, shimmying up the date-palm, under the embankment of the village's irrigation canal. Daytime slipped away, night began to fall, and still he had found no trace of her.

He paused on the canal embankment, peering into the gloom. His solitary shadow was reflected on the surface of the sluggish, mud-laced water. The shadow was that of a child, but his face no longer bore any resemblance to the smooth, soft, sexless faces of children. Had the water's surface been clear, with the tranquil purity of fresh water, perhaps it would have yielded an unclouded mirror and reflected his face to better advantage. Like all irrigation channels, however, this canal eddied with mud, its slow-moving surface obstinately pursuing a zigzagging course, meandering and twisting into wrinkles like the skin of an ancient face.

His eyes seemed to have widened and aged, as he stared fixedly, impassively, into the darkness, not blinking once, even his eyelashes frozen in place. For the first time, a large tear lay motionless on the surface of his eye. Before, his tears had always been children's tears, moving constantly, flickering with the fitful light of glimmery stars. In childhood, the flicker of tears and the flicker of smiles blend into one and the same glimmer.

But no one would have made a mistake at that particular moment. It was Hamido who stood with his body planted on the canal embankment. It was not a child, and this large tear was not the tear of a child. It was a real tear, tangible as it rolled over the face, and salty as it crept into the mouth.

This was real salt, for tears, like all body fluids, contain salt. And Hamido did not know how to live without Hamida, for she was no ordinary sister. Hamida was his twin. And there are two types of twins, those who develop from two embryos living in one womb, and those who grow from a single embryo which produces male and female. Hamido and Hamida had been one embryo, growing inside one womb. From the beginning they had been one cell, a single entity. Then everything split into two, even the tiniest features, even the minute, tiny muscle under each eye. No longer could anyone distinguish Hamido from Hamida. Even their mother used to confuse them.

But Hamido knew he was something other than Hamida. He was aware that ever since their birth his body had been separate from hers. The resemblance was strong, though, and it was so easy to mix them up that sometimes he himself became confused and thought he was Hamida. Concealing himself behind a wall, he would raise his *galabeya* until he could peer between his thighs. When his eyes fell on that small, narrow cleft, he thought himself Hamida; then, a stick held tightly in a huge hand would swing down over his head, causing him to pull his *galabeya* hastily down over his body and cry. His tears, though always real, vanished quickly as children's tears do. Spotting the stick that had been tossed on the ground, he would scurry over and pick it up, jamming it into the deep pocket of his *galabeya*. From time to time, he would reach into his pocket to finger it. Its hardness penetrated his fingers and moved on, into his arm, his shoulder, his neck, and when he tightened his neck muscles, his head would be thrown back, repeating the movement his father was wont to make with his head. He would try to speak from his throat, producing a coarse, oppressive timbre that echoed his father's voice.

Whenever Hamida heard her brother speak with his rough intonation she knew that the stick was in his possession. She couldn't see it, of course, but knowing he had it hidden somewhere beneath his *galabeya*, she would take flight, Hamido following at a run. To the casual observer, they would seem to be at play, but Hamido was not a child, and he had something hidden in his *galabeya* pocket, something hard which hung down his thigh like an alien limb.

And should Hamida glance in his direction and see his face, she would not know that it was Hamido standing there. The surprise would stop her in her tracks – or perhaps it was fright that caused her to freeze on the spot, as if she were a statue. Hamido's open palm would move over the sculptured surface, touching the stony eyelids, and poking a finger between eyelid and eye, just like any child exploring the head of a new doll – especially one of those big ones with hair and eyelashes so real that it could almost be alive.

Never in his life had Hamido held a doll, whether large or small. Peasant children don't play with shop-bought dolls, or rag dolls made at home, or toy trains, or paper boats, or balls, or anything else. In fact, they don't know what playing is. After all, playing is for children, which they are not. They are born full-grown, like insect larvae, which no sooner know the touch of the earth than they fly, or like the worms which reproduce

and grow in fermented cheese: as soon as the new worm separates
from its mother, one can hardly tell the young worm from the
old one.

Hamido caught sight of Hamida's face; as she walked towards
him from afar along the canal embankment, his heart pounded with
the primal joy of children. But as she drew nearer, he recognized
his mother's black *tarha*, encircling her head and falling over her
body. He ran to her and rested his head against her belly: when
Hamido stood tall next to his mother, his head came up no further
than her waist. He filled his nostrils with his mother's distinctive
smell, blending into the odours of bread baking, the soil of the
fields, and sycamore figs. He loved sycamore figs. Whenever
he spotted his mother returning from the fields, sycamore fruits
wrapped in her *tarha*, he would run to her. Seating herself beside
him on the ground, she would give him the figs, one by one, after
blowing the dust from them.

His mother pushed him away with one hand. But he pressed
himself against her, stubbornly clinging to her body and managing
to insert his head beneath her left breast. It was precisely here
that he loved to rest his head when sleeping next to her at night.
Although she would position herself on the other edge of the mat,
at a distance from him, he habitually awoke in the middle of the
night, and, not seeing her beside him, would crawl over and bury
his head under her breast.

She did not always push him away. Sometimes, her arms
came out and encircled him, pressing him to her so fiercely that
she would hurt him. Through him would run a mysterious, vague
feeling that she was not his mother – nor was she an aunt, nor

any relation at all – but rather a stranger, her body alien to his. He would feel an unfamiliarity that made him shiver, generating a tremor that ran from surface to depths, convulsing his body like the shivering of a fever.

The tremor shook him so violently that he wrapped his arms around her, but he felt her big strong hand – strong as his father's – pushing him away, pushing him so forcefully that he nearly fell into the embankment's waiting grasp. He lifted his face to look at her, and saw instead the ageing, dilated eyes of his father, red capillaries running over their white expanse. His shivering grew more violent; he was so scared that he opened his mouth to let out a scream, but was prevented by his father's great hand, clapped over his mouth, and his father's coarse voice that now sounded more like a hiss:

'Follow me.'

As there was no room, and the half-light which just precedes the dawn had not yet appeared, the night was dark. The entire village was asleep, still and silent in that moment falling between the last hour of the night and the beginnings of day, just before the dawn call to prayer. His father's large, bare feet practically ran over the dusty ground, with Hamido following so closely behind that he could almost touch the hem of his father's robe.

He was just meaning to open his mouth to ask the question in his mind when his father came to a halt at a squat wall which separated the main country road from the railroad. Hamido knew this wall: he often hid behind it when playing hide-and-seek. His father handed him a long object, rigid and sharp, which gleamed in the darkness like a knife.

Hamido jammed the knife into his *galabeya*, and it fell deep
into his pocket, where it hung down alongside his thigh. He felt
its sharp, pointed tip against his flesh; the muscles of his thighs,
legs and feet contracted, and he stood rooted to the ground. The
piercing sound of the train whistle made the ground beneath him
shake, so that he had to plant his feet even more firmly on the
ground, resisting any movement, as if he were an intractable wild
horse. But his father's large, powerful hand pushed into his back,
and his coarse voice, kept low, came out once again like a hiss:

'Only blood washes out shame. Go on, follow her!'

So Hamido plunged towards the approaching train, but
then stopped to turn around momentarily. He spotted his father,
standing exactly in the same place as before, as if rooted to
the ground, impassive and motionless, eyelids unmoving, the
capillaries on the whites of his eyes frozen in place, like threads
of blood drawn on a painting with a careful hand.

* * *

Just as her brother boarded the train, Hamida was stepping down
onto the station platform. It seemed as if she were sinking into an
ocean, a turbulent sea with waves not of water but of humanity:
men, women and children, all wearing sturdy leather shoes. And
long lines of cars, which to Hamida looked like trains, went by
in a steady stream, moving along gleaming streets that showed
no dirt, branching out in all directions only to intertwine and
then diverge once more, endlessly, like a tree sending its crown
high into the heavens and plunging its roots deep into the earth.
And the houses here were packed together in a single, enormous,

towering mass that entirely obscured the sky. The commotion, the sounds of people and car horns, were deafening, and Hamida could no longer hear a thing. But her bare feet were moving over the asphalt as if of their own accord, one foot behind the other, in that natural movement one learns from earliest childhood. As she did not know her way, Hamida might have gone on in this mechanical fashion indefinitely. She had no idea where her path had started, or whence it might take her. But her movements were interrupted by a heavy leather shoe that trod on her left foot and almost crushed it. She staggered back momentarily, only to find an enormous car bearing down on her. Her mouth open to its widest, Hamida shrieked; her voice, stifled for so long, let go in a long, shrill scream which lasted as long as two or three normal screams, or ten or a hundred or a thousand successive screams all merging into a single, unbroken sound that went on and on as though it would continue for all time.

The terrific din swallowed up her scream as the waves of the sea swallow a drop of water, a bit of straw, a butterfly, or a newborn bird not yet able to fly. No one heard her voice, and her scream changed nothing. Around her, the world surged on, like a roaring cataract that tears apart crocodiles and leaves the splintered remains of ships in its wake, its pulverizing waters unaffected all the while, and its surface remaining as white as ever.

Hamida hobbled on her wounded foot to a sheltered corner next to a wall that seemed relatively remote from both vehicles and people. She leant her head back against the wall and stared before her, into the hazy vagueness that seemed to envelop everything around her, as if she were engulfed in a dream – or a nightmare –

from which she would awaken shortly, to jump up from the mat like
a little bird. She made to support her weight on her hand in order
to spring up. But her palm brushed against her belly, and suddenly
the haze lifted. Things fell into place, becoming intelligible not
through the rational faculty which takes in new facts, but with that
instinctive, mysterious understanding which issues from an utterly
fatigued body in moments of rest or extreme languor.

She fell asleep right where she was, and awoke hungry. She
noticed a bakery just next to the spot she had chosen, and out in
front – very near indeed – sat row after row of carefully arranged
loaves. She reached out a skinny arm; her fingers closed around a
loaf and brought it to her mouth. She was just closing her teeth on
it when a large hand gripped her arm.

She inhaled sharply, her chest rising up so that her small
breasts showed, just like two olives, beneath the wide-cut
galabeya; her protruding belly, inflated like a child's balloon,
revealed itself too. The black *tarha* still covered her head and
hair and fell over her shoulders as far as her lower back, coming
to an end just above her small, rounded buttocks.

Her gaze travelled upwards in alarm until it met a pair of eyes
staring straight at her. She tugged at the *tarha*, bringing it across
to half-hide her face, as she had seen the women of her village do.
Only a single eye was visible now, dilated and black, its look of
bafflement still alight with the innocent sparkle of childhood: the
gleam of an eye that had always been closed, and was now opening
for the first time onto the infinite world. A taut, circular muscle
– like a severed question mark – surrounding the eye intimated
alarm, and over the cornea dry tears had deposited a film which

hung there like a light cloud. She sensed a new feeling creeping over her face, moving from the bridge of her nose towards one eye: a realization that she was a female, with a femininity not yet complete. No one had acquainted her with herself; it was she who had discovered this, on her own, a few minutes before, finding herself to be a newly, ripening fruit, fresh and still coated with dew.

Eluding the large hand, she managed to slip off at a run. The figure charged behind her. She turned into a street and hid behind one of its many doors. Poking her head out, she saw no one there and believed herself safe. But the long arm appeared from somewhere behind her and grabbed her by the neck, and a rough, brutal voice pierced her ears.

'I've got you now, thief! You're under arrest! Come on, now, walk ahead of me, to the police station!'

She gave in, leaving her thin white arm to his grasp. The hand clutching her was coarse and large, its joints protruding and its bones unnaturally curved, with veins bulging beneath the skin. Under the stubby fingernails ran a layer of dirty black. Her eyes crept up the long arm: over each broad shoulder marched a horizontal row of five brass buttons, separated by a burly neck encased in a high collar blackened around the inner rim with dirt dissolved in sweat. The collar encircled his neck with perfect fit, then descended over his chest in a line of ten brass buttons. During her stretch of compulsory schooling, Hamida had learnt some rudiments of arithmetic, and she began counting the buttons. Five over each shoulder, that makes ten on the shoulders, plus ten more on the chest: that makes twenty buttons in all.

Midday had arrived, and the sun was now blazing hot. Its red disc was reflected in the round brass buttons, giving them the likeness of twenty suns that made one's eyes water at a mere glance. Unable to go on looking at them, she dropped her gaze to the ground. But the surface beneath her bare feet seemed aflame; she had never felt such heat underfoot before. His high boots struck the ground with a strange metallic sound, like iron grating against iron. His stride was long, each foot planting itself firmly on the asphalt. The feet rose into long legs inside trousers of heavy cloth, with a deep, vault-like pocket in which was hiding a sharp, hard implement, hanging down along his thigh.

They turned off the broad thoroughfare into a narrow side street, the long fingers still encircling her arm. But now the five fingers had become only four. The fifth had disengaged itself from the rest, moving upwards on its own, over the soft arm, cautiously, stealthily, until it buried its coarse black tip into the soft childlike armpit that as yet bore no sign of hair.

She tried to pull her arm away. But the four fingers contracted, closing around her upper arm more tightly, digging into the soft flesh, while the fifth finger emerged from beneath her armpit, straining until its pointed black snout reached as far as the soft rise of her breast – still just a bud – bearing down on it with cautious, trembling, jerky pressure which became firmer at the bend of a street, or behind a wall, and relaxing or stopping altogether whenever they were walking down the middle of the street; and occasionally, as they passed a throng of people, that fifth finger would retract itself quickly and join its four brothers.

A foul odour suddenly filled her nostrils, she found herself in a dark, narrow alley. She saw him come to a stop before a small wooden door. He drew a key from his pocket, unlocked the door, pushed her inside ahead of him, and closed the door.

At first she could see nothing, for the place was pitch dark. He lit a small kerosene lamp, which at once revealed a bare, tiled floor, with just a little rug in one corner that reminded her of the mat at home. It was a cramped room, and had only a single, small, iron-barred window high in the wall, a clay water-jug perching on its sill. In the faint light, the walls of the room looked a grey colour, overlaid with the sort of black tint produced by soot from a gas burner. On a nail in the wall hung a suit of heavy cloth. From its chest and broad, padded shoulders, yellow brass buttons gleamed in the darkness like eyes, open and feverish with a viral liver infection. On the floor sat one huge, high-topped boot, looking like a headless animal, and beside it was tossed a pair of white, baggy pants, the rear yellowed and the belly gone blackish, giving off the smell of old urine.

She raised her head from the tiled floor and saw him standing there, naked. His broad shoulders had become narrow – bony, even – and his collarbone protruded sharply. The sturdy trouser legs had given way to thin and bowed limbs; his massive feet, which before had rested so far above the ground, now had nothing to separate them from the tiles. The sharp, rigid implement concealed in his pocket had become visible.

She caught her breath with a gulp, her surprise imbued with a panic that she resisted instinctively. But he threw her down on the floor, his bulky finger tearing at the neck of her *galabeya* so that the threadbare garment ripped in half down the front, revealing no underclothes below.

'Who are you?' she asked, her voice cracked and weak.

'I'm the government.'

'The Lord keep you – let me go.'

He answered in the same coarse, imperious tones. 'Go where, girl? You're already condemned.'

Everything began to happen with the extreme rapidity of panting breaths, of muscles contracting and expanding, an extraordinary speed which occurs only in dreams. But this time no confusion marked the dream: instead of a shopkeeper beating her with his stick, there was before her a male creature with a rough moustache that rubbed coarsely across her face, a smell of tobacco which stifled her, and a chest of thick hair, matted and plastered to the skin by a sticky, viscous sweat.

Suddenly everything stopped: a moment of stillness akin to the moment of death. She lifted her head from the tiled floor and looked about her. She saw him lying on his back, eyes closed, utterly still. She thought perhaps he had died, when a faint snore began to issue from his gaping mouth, soon rising to become like the gurgling of an ancient waterwheel turned by an ailing bull. She raised herself quietly and composedly from the floor, pulled the two sections of her torn *galabeya* over her chest and stomach as best she could, and tiptoed to the door. She twisted her head back calmly, and saw the twenty yellow eyes, wide open and staring at her. Hastily, she opened the door.

The broad main street was visible ahead of her. She took off along it, running with all the strength she could summon, fleeing without a moment's pause.

* * *

That very moment, Hamido had stepped down from the train. Now, his back to the south and his face turned northward, he stared straight ahead, gazing at the many faces crowding the area outside the Bab al-Hadid railway station, Cairo's old central depot. His bare feet padded over the asphalt; beneath the ample folds of his *galabeya*, the knife swung down close to his thigh like an artificial limb or an organ newly implanted in his flesh.

The knife's sharp tip bumped against the flesh of his thigh, and he shivered, the tremor passing through his neck and head. He staggered, and almost fell among the heavy leather shoes surrounding him, but he tautened his leg muscles and kept his balance. His eyes lost themselves in the vast, buffeting ocean: rising with the buildings' towering summits, falling with the sun's rays reflected on the gleaming asphalt, circling with the movement in the immense traffic circle, at the centre of which stood a huge stone statue with a human head. Around it moved row after row of people, and flags, and cars, round and round, uncoiling and branching off into numerous straight lines, only to intertwine once again, pouring into another traffic circle, and then branching off, the branches splitting into still more branches, separating, then mingling again, and dividing, endlessly.

He shaded his eyes with his hands and leant his head back against a lamp-post. He couldn't fight the drowsiness which was overwhelming him, and he dozed off standing up. A muted sound awakened him. Glancing around, he noticed that the boulevard, submerged in the evening gloom, was now calm and empty of people and vehicles. His sharp eyes bored into the darkness, and he caught sight of a spectre running in the distance, its feet bare, its long *galabeya* not loose enough to hide the visible swelling over the stomach.

'Hamida!' He gasped her name out, sending a rush of pent-up breath through his barely parted lips, then took off over the asphalt, his left hand raised protectively before him, slashing at the darkness, and his right hand plunged into his pocket, fingering the sharp hardness of the knife-blade. The spectre stopped in a darkened corner. With slow, wary footsteps, Hamido drew nearer, until there was no more than a single stride between them. He heard the rough voice, coming in a whisper that was more like a hiss.

'Only blood washes out shame.'

He pulled the weapon from his pocket and hid it behind his back. Suddenly, a moving searchlight exposed the darkened corner, and he saw his mother's face beneath the black *tarha*. He screamed; the sound rang out in the night and the light came to a stop on his face. Someone drew near; in the darkness he couldn't see the figure's eyes. But he could see eyes on the shoulders and over the chest – two rows of eyes, round and staring, giving off a yellowish light.

His lips formed their question, but a large, coarse palm landed on his temple, followed by a second slap across the other temple. He lifted his arm to resist the blows, but it was arrested by five tightly encircling fingers. He brought his other arm upwards instinctively protecting himself, when there loomed in the air a cudgel-like wooden arm that came down on his head.

Hamido opened his eyes to a violent headache. Probing his head, amidst the hair he stumbled on the wound, already crusted over with dry blood. He scratched at the scab until it fell, landing beside a huge pair of boots rising to high leather tops, surrounded by a trouser-fold of heavy cloth. The legs seemed awesomely long; he realized they stretched up eventually into a stocky chest. Down the front and across the shoulders were fixed two rows of round yellow buttons which reflected a faint lamplight.

The enormous boot trod on the clot of dried blood, trampling it brutally underfoot. With the thud of the boot on the floor, there rose in the air a harsh voice.

'Your name?'

'Hamido.'

The sharp razor passed across the skin of his head: his thick hair tumbled into a pail, along with his *galabeya*. The sun of early morning was slanting in, and he saw the shadow of a tall, broad-shouldered person following him across the floor. The shadow came to a stop. He moved; it moved. He struck the floor with his foot and heard a strange metallic sound, not one that he had ever heard his own, bare, foot make. He looked at his feet, and there he saw the enormous, heavy boots, rising into high leather tops. He saw trousers of heavy cloth. Inside trousers and boots were his very own, actual, skinny legs, which extended upwards into a broad squarish chest, bolted with a row of brass buttons, and then into broad shoulders padded with cotton, or perhaps with straw.

In his new boots, he paced the ground, taking slow, timorous steps. Inside each boot rested a small, bony foot, clenched and compressed under the thick leather, its toes thin and white, bloodless and motionless, dead or nearly so, the entire foot absolutely still inside the boot. It was the boots which gave movement to those feet, lifting and lowering them, carrying them over the ground step by step. With every step over the asphalt, the iron-studded soles produced a dull thud, metallic and slow, like the sound made by the hoof of a sickly calf as it is driven to the slaughterhouse.

He stopped; so did the black shadow, sketched so meticulously on the ground. The utter smoothness of his shaven head reflected the sun, and his eyes were no more than holes emitting a penetrating light. His neck muscles were stretched taut and his back muscles tensed; beneath the tight wall of his abdomen lay a distended emaciated stomach, fed only on black smoke, black saliva, and an end of dry bread, baked to hardness, which he dipped in treacle and ate with a slice of onion, or a bit of pickle which stung like a bitter cucumber, to balance out the sweet taste of the treacle. Then he would neutralize the bitterness with black smoke, sucked in through nose, mouth and gullet to fill his chest and create pressure on his stomach until he could belch like one whose belly is full.

A thin whip stung him on the nape of his neck; his feet moved automatically over the ground. Right foot first, then left foot – iron cleats thudding against asphalt with a regular beat, like the hour striking or the heart beating, lub dub lub dub. Left right left right.

'Halt!' The strong, harsh voice resounded through the air. The boots on his feet collided against each other noisily. His legs and thighs came together tightly, muscles contracted. His right hand plunged into his pocket and came to rest over the killing tool, its hardness extending along his thigh and ending in a tapered and punctured metal head.

'Attention!' shouted that grating voice.

The fingers of his right hand closed around the implement – four fingers only, the thumb moving away to rest alone over the hammer. He had one eye trained on the fixed point halfway between the open eyes.

His mouth dropped open and he began to pant. But a strong hand slapped him across the stomach, and the harsh voice pierced his ear.

'Close your mouth. Hold your breath.'

He obeyed. The rough, commanding voice sounded.

'Only blood washes out shame!'

And he pulled the trigger.

He heard a loud report, a sound he had never heard before, and saw a body fall to the ground. From beneath it ran a red stream which he recognized at once as ewe's blood. For today was the feast-day, and here he was, still upright, his stance unchanged, staring at the pair of open eyes, still and lidless eyes, fixed in a cold, dead stare, eyes that had dilated with terror. The terror shifted to him; beneath the full *galabeya* his thin legs began to shake, and he ran to bury his head in his mother's bosom and weep.

He rubbed his face against his mother's chest, wiping away his tears. He looked up. There were his father's eyes, covered with the tiny red capillaries. There were the brass buttons over the chest and shoulders, with their own unique gleam, and the hoarse voice, with its frightening, peremptory harshness.

'Crying like a woman, hunh?'

And Hamido returned to his position in the rank. He stood erect, his eyes reflecting the redness of the sun directly overhead – for their blackness had fled, beneath the lid, under the shade, to a secure and moist place. The asphalt blazed, and seemed to melt in the heavy heat. He felt that the heels of his boots were digging into the asphalt, in the way that they would bore into the soft, muddy ground.

Hamido stopped for a second to pull up his boot tops. Lagging one step behind his row, he felt the stinging blow of the whip on his nape, and bounded forward to get in line. But instead he tripped and fell on his face.

His boots slipped off just as he was toppling over. The burning air thrust its way into his chest in the shape of a spoken word, uttered in a voice that he realized was his own. He became aware that it was his own body, and no one else's, that had fallen to the ground, and that the regular beats pounding on his inner ear were in fact issuing from his own chest. He felt proud of his ability to distinguish his body from that of the ewe.

Pride showed in his eyes, although his face was still to the ground. Spittle flew from the coarse mouth, coming to rest on the back of his head. And it was followed immediately by a familiar curse – an epithet pertaining to female genitalia – and then by a fierce kick with the blunt toe of a heavy boot, which landed in his back, directly over his kidney.

This sort of kick with the hard snout of a boot did not carry the same force every time, though, for I used to see Hamido clambering to his feet afterwards and running to join his rank. But today was the feast-day. And the big chief – his master – was to attend the celebrations in person, not through a delegate, as he usually did. Naturally, any mistake whatsoever – even a slight misstep – would be unforgivable. On this particular day, a slip of the foot was not a mere slip of the foot, but rather was immediately transformed into something else, something far more serious. A misstep would distort the rank. And when one rank gets out of order, naturally the others become misshapen too. And this spells disaster right through.

Thus, everything went awry, becoming blurred and jumbled before Hamido's eyes. This was due not only to a deficiency in his powers of observation, but also to a lack of time. For, on such an important day as this, time is limited indeed, and the pace of life quickens to become a series of gasps. No one is able to breathe naturally, for everyone must gasp for breath if things are to remain as they should.

Like everyone else, then, Hamido panted, and as he did so a certain eye caught sight of him. Somewhere in the vicinity, there is always an eye which takes notice of whatever is going on. Observing things, staring with uninhibited intrusiveness into the lives – or deaths – of others, it gives the living no space to enjoy life, nor the dead respite in which to enjoy death. Hamido brought his legs together with a rather shy and fumbling movement (for meanwhile he had acquired a certain amount of diffidence), clearing the way for the procession of vehicles. But since time was so short, his right leg had no time to draw back as it should have, quickly; extended into the road, barefoot, his stiff toes quivering visibly, there it was in full sight of everyone.

Baffled, the procession stopped before this unprecedented and never-to-be-repeated scene. For the history books make no mention of any such incident of this type. Yet perhaps this is not so surprising, for what is recorded as history and what actually occurs in real life are two different things. And in this particular case, what actually occurred was so momentous that it deserved to find a place in history. But, being what it is, history does not open its pages to the recording of momentous events – especially if their hero is Hamido.

Hamido did not feel that he was a hero, despite the crowd which gathered around him: for in no time, an overwhelming number of people had collected. The empty spaces between buildings filled up with bodies; heads obstructed doors and windows; people left their offices and bureaus, and locked their shops, crowding into tightly compressed rows to enjoy the spectacle. I don't think anyone lagged behind – whether little or big, male or female, upper class or lower class – for all wanted to amuse themselves. To seek pleasure is, after all, a universal pastime, and legitimate on condition that it takes place in secret.

Hamido was still on the ground, in the same position, his eyes closed; for death, of course, has its effects. Even so, he saw lots and lots of men around him (for the vision of the dead is sharper than that of the living). He knew they were men by their shaved heads, the rubbery tubing and brass buttons on their uniforms, and of course by the hard killing tools hanging down alongside their thighs.

He tried to open his mouth to defend himself, to tell his story, beginning it with the day his mother gave birth to him. But the big chief – his master – was present, and in his presence time is restricted. There isn't time enough for anyone. In any case, it is in the nature of things that the judgement must be issued first, and signed or imprinted with the thumbprint or sign of the accused to show that he is aware of its contents. Furthermore, the accused must follow the directives spelled out in the ruling. Only after all of this has been done will there be sufficient time for anything else – such as an appeal in which the condemned can claim innocence.

Thus, with all due promptness, Hamido's sentence was issued. In fact, it filled up an entire page of the official register. The law specified that Hamido must read the police report before putting his signature or thumbprint to it, for this would indicate his compliance with the contents. The words were unclear and not easy to read though, for the handwriting was poor and the report had been written in great haste. Hamido had difficulty making out the script, especially since he had not learnt to read or write, but he was able to pick out a word or two in each line. It amazed him that the police had shown such an ability to transform him from an unknown soldier into a hero – even if his heroism was so far outside the norms governing these things that wiggling his bare toes in his big chief s face had come to be considered, in his case, as a gesture of rebellion. Hamido was no longer able to contain or conceal his pride, and he began wiggling his toes, with slow and dignified movements that were full of an almost regal self-esteem.

All those present raised their hands to applaud – including the big chief, his master, who was in the front row. (The movements of the big chief, like the movement of history, cannot afford to ignore the masses.) And when his arms swung upward to applaud, the sandwich stuffed with ewe's meat, which he had concealed under his arm, fell to the ground. A lame child who was crawling among the crowded rows of people, carrying small sacks of toasted seeds for sale, snatched the sandwich away immediately.

Hamido smiled, even though he understood nothing of what was happening around him. The scene had not been intentional; he could take no credit for it. Moreover, it had been imperfectly executed, showing a lack of experience, and deficient in the requisite cultural background and perusal of The Heritage. Hamido had not read the many volumes pertaining to our Cultural Heritage; specifically and most significantly, he had not studied the tales of platonic love, derived from the era when love was clean and pure and people were honourable, back in those days when their sex organs had not yet been created.

But then Adam had committed The Great Crime (as Hamido's mother had told him), and lo and behold, there appeared an ugly organ growing between his thighs. It was a divine revenge – a just one, according to Hamido's mother. At this point in his musings, a question occurred to him that had never come to his mind before (perhaps because his body was now dead, and thus he could give his soul the right to think of sacred subjects). That question was the following: how had Adam committed the crime before this organ had been created for him?

Hamido made an attempt to rid himself of this speculation, for thinking about such matters could only be considered an immoral practice, especially in the presence of the big chief, his master.

Hamido stole a quick glance between his thighs, but did not find the member in question. Instead, and in its place, he found a small cleft which reminded him of the cleft he used to see on Hamida's body. He thought there must be some mistake: perhaps the bodies of the dead had been confused, and in the final sorting they had given him a woman's body. Mistakes are bound to occur in the final sorting: the civil servant who is responsible for the procedure has poor eyesight due to pulmonary tuberculosis. To make matters worse, he is the only one assigned to this task. (The budget doesn't allow for any expansion in personnel.) This civil servant is charged with transferring names from the initial to the final sorting lists. But the letters of some names are similar, particularly as certain names given to females can be distinguished from male names only by the single-letter, feminine ending: Amin becomes Amina, Zuhayr turns into Zuhayra, Mufid goes to Mufida, and Hamido becomes Hamida. In other words, with a mere stroke of the pen, man becomes woman.

Sometimes, Hamido loved being a woman, while at other times he resisted it strongly. For in those days women were charged with certain humiliating tasks normally performed by servants, like wiping a man's shoes when he came out of the lavatory, or giving him a glass of water as he lay on his back belching out loud (and belching out loud was the prerogative solely of men) or washing out his smelly socks or his underpants, which were even smellier because of the urine and the short supply of soap and water.

Hamido did try to rectify the situation. But this was not easy even in the best of circumstances, since he always had to establish that he was *not* a woman. Every time, they summoned the medical examiner, who would strip off Hamido's soiled pants with grumbling displeasure and look between his thighs, insolently. Sometimes, the examiner would not verify it simply by looking, but would insist on extending his elegant hand, with its carefully pruned nails, to examine the shrivelled and terror-stricken member. Measuring it from all angles with a finely calibrated plastic ruler, he would then take out his Parker fountain-pen and record the numbers in a notebook specifically designated for this purpose. He despatched these numbers inside an envelope sealed with red wax to the police's Department of Citizen Identification and Documentation.

Now, in this department reigned complete bedlam. Fingerprints were confused with footprints, and both with prints of other parts of the body. First and last digits were mixed up; portions of numbers were dropped and misplaced, while other portions were blotted out. This was due to the bad quality of the ink, for it was adulterated (corruption was widespread at that time: an entire bucket of water might well be added to a bottle of ink).

As a result, and in this fashion, Hamido's status remained undefined for quite a number of years, during which time no one would come to a decisive opinion, and no one would summon him for re-examination. He began to believe that the subject had been forgotten, that the incident might as well never have happened. He started to walk the streets confidently, even going into a barber's shop one day to have his long beard shaved off. He sat down on the comfortable swivel chair, gave his feet a relaxed shake, drew out an old newspaper from the pile on the table, and riffled its pages indifferently. But no sooner had he turned to the last page than his eyes widened in surprise. There was his own picture, printed at the bottom of the page among those of female suspects. Prostitution was not prohibited in those times, so they arrested him and returned him to service.

* * *

At that time, Hamida had found her way to an honourable profession (for in those days, 'honour' meant domestic service). She learnt the first lesson which such service demands: that one must call females by the term 'my mistress' and address males as 'my master'. She became aware that her master and mistress grew more satisfied with her the lower she hung her head when passing before them, and her upper half began to take on a permanent stoop. The house protected her from the street, and in the street a man lay in wait, never ceasing to pursue her.

The kitchen was her life. More specifically, her life was the humid square patch in front of the basin, her small hands plunged in the water running from the tap, day and night, summer and winter. Her black eyes faced the wall, gazing from beneath a crust of dried tears that was dissolved from time to time by a blazing look, sharp as a sword, that pierced the wall and passed through into the dining room. That expression penetrated all the way to the round dining table surrounded by nine mouths, opening and shutting upon bulging jowls, jaws grinding, teeth clacking like the cogs of a mill-wheel.

In the basin, stacks of empty plates collect, covered by a film of congealed fat; the garbage pail is filled to the brim with

untouched leftovers, while the sink drain becomes clogged with
the half-chewed leavings.

At midnight, after mopping the kitchen floor, she crams a
chunk of bread into her mouth, and gnaws on a bit of skin or a
piece of bone that holds remnants of marrow. She settles herself,
wet *galabeya* and all, on the wooden bench behind the kitchen
door, her swollen, reddened fingers still oozing a yellow fluid with
the warmth of blood. Her ears track the aggressive male hissing
that emanates from the bedroom, followed by a submissive female
moaning and the creaking of wooden bed joints.

As she sleeps, the fatigue drains from her body, the pain
in her hands and feet abates, and her breathing settles into an
intimate peacefulness through which glide familiar images that
have lain dormant in some dark interior. A spent wisp of light still
dances through those recesses, casting a faint glow that gives the
walls the appearance of mud-brick, with its interspersed gleam of
yellow straw. The walls climb to the round, window-like aperture
and drop to a floor covering which looks very much like that
familiar straw matting. On one edge lies her mother, the black
tarha wrapping her head, one hand pillowing her temple. On
the nearer edge sleeps Hamida, lids half-dropped: the eyes of a
child who has fallen asleep to the tones of a frightening bedtime
tale. Her lips are half open over tiny, translucent teeth which
have sprouted recently in place of baby teeth. Her breaths have
the sweet, childlike smell given off faintly by closed blossoms
just before the dew falls and dawn arrives. Beneath the full-cut
galabeya her breasts show like two tiny buds that have emerged
just moments before, to be compressed suddenly under the large

hand, flat as an axe blade, which has begun to creep stealthily underneath the *galabeya*, raising it from the small legs and thighs. Everything becomes compounded into a single object, a single heavy stick in the shopkeeper's hand, striking blow after blow, over her head and chest and then between her thighs. And she screams voicelessly, and she cries alone in the night in stifled sobs, and swallows her tears before dawn. Early in the morning, before anyone has awakened, she spits her tears into the lavatory, straightens up resolutely, and peers into the mirror at her tear-washed eyes, raised questioningly.

But no one answers her questions. No one responds to her slightly stooped back, her festering, swollen fingers, the cracked soles of her bare feet ascending the service stairs. The servants' stairs spiral crookedly; at every twisting bend is a dark crevice wide enough to hold a secret crime, and a garbage bin that has overflowed, filling the floor with flies and tiny cockroaches which crawl under the bottoms of doors into the elegant, well-appointed flats.

Yet an observer would see no marks of servitude upon Hamida as she climbs or descends those stairs. And what are the emblems of servitude? Tears have rinsed her eyes clean, and her gaze is directed upward: and nothing matters but the eyes. Everything else may well be ulcerous and oozing pus; Hamida may well be sunk up to the knees in garbage – animal leavings, for her masters are among the carnivorous, and dead flesh carries a smell more putrid than that of dead vegetation. Hamida stamps the odour underfoot, and holds her head high, and comprehends what no one else seems to understand.

What Hamida realizes is that one's garbage increases as one's position in society rises. It is in the nature of things that the stomach which consumes more from its upper orifice expels more from below. And naturally, as her master's stomach is indisputably the largest stomach around, his refuse is the most abundant. The servants lug it to the bins, and armoured vehicles cart it off to a distant spot in the desert, where it collects in the shape of a high pyramid, to be gazed upon by bedazzled tourists.

Small pyramids of garbage mark every street corner, visited from time to time by rats, stray dogs, and small cats whose round, gleaming eyes gaze upwards as if they are children, and whose paws – festering like Hamida's fingers – search swiftly and nimbly for a piece of bread and something to soak it in which has not yet gone rotten.

Clasped around something, Hamida's fingers emerged from the refuse bin. She opened her hand to see what it was, but a sudden light fell over her palm, and she ducked behind the wall. The light followed her, casting a long shadow across the floor: a close-shaven head, shoulders broad and outlined by a row of yellow buttons. Recognizing him at once, she gasped loudly, and opened her eyes to the rough voice of her master.

'Hamida!' She saw the ewe coming through the door, driven by the butcher, and realized that today was the feast-day commemorating her mistress's death.

Her gaze met the ewe's eyes. The ewe planted all four legs firmly on the floor and refused to move. Hamida stared into the black spheres surrounded by pure white. Blanketing the whiteness was an unexpected gleam that moved over the surface of the eyes, glittering, like a large, immobile tear which neither evaporates nor falls. Her eyes widened in surprise, with the consternation of one who has raised her head suddenly, only to see her own eyes in a mirror which had not been there before.

The butcher tugged the ewe by means of a short rope wound around her neck. The ewe followed him, but twisted her neck to the rear so that she still faced in Hamida's direction. The butcher's large, coarse fingers closed round the neck. The ewe's small hooves, front and back, lashed out at him. Four strong hands came out and pulled her forelegs and hindlegs apart. Now she lay stretched out on her back, her wide black eyes open in terror, searching in the eyes around her for her mother's eyes. Not far away, her mother stood motionless, eyes calm and steady, lashes unmoving, the black *tarha* quiescent over her head, shoulders and chest.

A long, slender muscle extending the length of the small, lean thigh trembled, and the tremor moved to the top of the thigh. It perched there, on the obtuse angle, looking like a child's open, panting mouth, its lips soft and rosy, dewy with a transparent saliva akin to children's tears, revealing beneath them the red hue of blood. The delicate tongue began to tremble, like the tongue of a little bird being slaughtered.

She raised panicky black eyes once again to search for her mother's eyes amongst those crowding around her. Her mother looked at her with alien eyes, with a look cold as a knife-blade. She shifted her eyes to the ceiling, averting them from the blade, but the knife was coming ever nearer, little by little, until a lightning-quick movement split her in half.

Hamida did not feel the pain. Her eyes remained dry, and she abandoned herself to the dirt floor, lying there passively, while from beneath her thighs came a long ribbon of blood, its dark red hue glistening in the sunshine. Ants appeared from nowhere to accumulate thickly over the blood-ribbon curved and inanimate like the back of a dead snake. She blew at the ants to scatter them, and sneezed as the dust penetrated her nose, ejecting the tears which had congealed in her throat. She reached out and covered the ants in dirt. Now that the blood had been buried, the previously level patch of floor was slightly mounded, like a grave. She pressed the sole of her foot over the protruding gravesite, trampled the uneven floor with both feet, paced over it with all her reclaimed strength. At the bend in the wall she twisted to look behind her. Finding no one there, she raised the *galabeya* from her legs. The familiar appendage was not there; in its place she found a small cleft, which looked just like that old, closed-up wound.

The familiar roughness of that voice reached her ears. 'Hami-i-ida.'

Hurriedly, she lowered her gown, hoisted the full water bucket and poured it over the ewe, cleansing her neck of the congealed blood. She hosed water into the ewe's slit gullet, and the spray gushed from her mouth and nose like a fountain. The seven children laughed in delight: for today was the feast, the ewe had been slaughtered, and the utensils, serving dishes and plates lay ready on the table.

The dinner hour arrived, and everyone sat down to eat; everyone, that is, except the mother, who had died in the bedroom, and Hamida, who was still hoisting the bucket, pouring water onto the dead body, filling her small palm with shampoo and rubbing it into the thick coat, inserting her small finger to wash the large ear. She raised the closed lids and washed the eyes, and then the nostrils. She cleaned the mouth and neck, the black hair under the ewe's legs, and her underbelly.

She washed the animal's thighs carefully, from below and above and in between. Her eyes wide in surprise: the space between was smooth and sealed shut, showing no appendage. At the uppermost part lay a long cleft that looked like an old wound.

Her trembling fingers moved down to the hind legs; she pushed the loofa into the cloven hooves, to which remnants of soil still clung: black and clayey soil, streaked with yellow lines, like the straw with which animal pens in the village are strewn.

She heard the same harsh, commanding tones, coming from outside the door this time.

'Don't waste your time on the hooves, we'll give them to the butcher as alms.'

She grabbed the morning newspaper from the top of the bookcase and wrapped the hooves in it. On the front page she noticed a photograph. A crowd of round, fleshy faces filled the picture, and in the middle she recognized her master's features. They were sitting in a circle. The plates before them were full, piled high, pyramid-like; gleaming knives were plunging downwards methodically over the pyramids, which dwindled regularly and very rapidly until they had disappeared and only crumbs remained on the plates.

She thought the pyramids had faded away. However, when she scrutinized the newspaper with great care, she found them unchanged: piled high, tall, and tapering to sharp points. But now they were in another part of the picture, in another position between table and chairs, rising from below on two thighs to ascend as far as the obtuse triangle at the base of the ribs, directly under the heart.

Hamida's fingers slid over the smooth, slippery heart. The knife in her hand trembled as she cut the great artery and split open the heart so she could wash it from inside. How often she had done this with the hearts of chickens, rabbits and geese – but the ewe's heart was much larger, and still very warm, its muscles yet pulsing, sending its hidden, trembling oscillation through her fingers. The trembling moved into her arm, and then into her chest and all the way to her heart, which was beating more rapidly now.

From inside the split heart fell a deep-red clot of blood, which slipped over the marble edge of the basin and fell onto her foot. As she stooped to remove the clot, her eyes were caught by a long, thin, red ribbon that ran along her calf. She thought it was an artery, but in fact it was moving downwards over her skin rather than beneath. She touched it with her fingertip, and brought her finger to her eyes: it was wet with real blood.

As she straightened up, her alarmed eyes met her mother's: eyes empty of fright, cool as a brackish lake, silent as the grave, staring fixedly at her with the gaze of the dead. The lids dropped over the deceased eyes; the cover dropped over the head and body. She heard her mother's faint voice coming from afar, as if from beneath the ground.

'You've come of age, Hamida.'

Her mother handed her a pair of knickers made of brown calico. Hamida put them on under her *galabeya* once and for the last time, for as it happened she did not remove them with her own hands. Rather they were stripped off by other hands, by coarse and flattened fingers that bore a strange odour permeated by the scent of tobacco. Hamida knew the smell of tobacco: she used to buy it from the shop for her father or brother, or one of her uncles, or some other man from the family. It made her sneeze and cough whenever she brought it close to her nose.

When she coughed, the corners of her mouth would puff out like those of her father, and she would imitate his rough voice, and stand in the large entrance area of the house, just as he did, throwing her head back conceitedly as he did, inflating her jowls and placing her right hand firmly on her hip.

Were one to catch a glimpse of her at that moment, one would think her Hamido. She herself used to believe she was Hamido. She would stride over the ground firmly, hitch up her *galabeya* over her thin hard legs, and run towards the boys, shouting 'I'm Hamido.' They would play cops and robbers, or the train game, each of them grabbing the hem of the next, and taking off across the ground, whistling.

The whistle grows loud in the night. Hamida's small body shakes as she stands near the train. The darkness grows dense behind her, taking the shape of a large hand pushing her forcefully in the back, propelling her forward. Hamida darts off in the darkness, but almost immediately the darkness splits to reveal ten yellow eyes gleaming like brass buttons, and a sharp white blade hanging concealed alongside the long legs. She wraps her black *tarha* around her head and shoulders, chest and belly, and slips off in the evening blackness as if she herself is a piece of the night. But the legs run behind her, carrying their sharp blade, and the large feet advance with a sound that reverberates like the clash of iron against iron.

* * *

Hamido was still in the service. In the heel of his shoe was embedded an iron cleat which struck the asphalt slowly and heavily, like the hoof of a mule afflicted with sunstroke. The sun was afire: for it was an August noon in Cairo. Hamido's head, shaven utterly bald, seemed to attract the flaming red disc, for it clung to his pate. His eyes and nose had been reduced to boreholes that flung out the fire accumulated inside his skull. Ears, mouth, anus – all the orifices of his body shot out the red fire in hot, tiny lumps, congealed to hardness like old, clotted blood.

As he stared at the round, red disc, it turned into two red discs, inside each one a gleaming black sphere, like the pupil of an eye, surrounded by a circle of pure white, as children's eyes are. He stared at the pair of eyes: recognizing their particular shine, he shouted. 'Hamida!' He pulled the rigid implement upward from next to his thigh and aimed it exactly at the fixed point, halfway between the two eyes. He heard his father's rough voice.

'Fire.'

He fired.

The body fell, smeared with blood, the eyes open and fixed, gazing skyward. The gods had crowded the skies, seating themselves, one leg crossed over the other. Their upper legs dangled from amongst the clouds (and thus were visible to the naked eye) swinging with a regular horizontal movement, like that of a clock pendulum. The sun had disappeared and night fell; the music came on – the national anthem, in celebration of the victory. Palms were raised in applause, bearing the dead body upwards. The nose of the deceased brushed against the sole of a foot – belonging to one of the deities – and smelled the familiar odour emitted by feet whose owners do not wash them. The dead person averted his nose from the gods; the clamorous shouts ascended, and the black sheath split to reveal the badge of martyrdom in the battlefield of honour.

The dead person extended his hand, which was soiled with stains gone black (since the blood had dried) to receive the badge. Another hand – a clean, carefully manicured one – shot out and snatched the medal away. The dead person brandished his arm, sketching his anger in the air; the darkness was filled with searchlights, bulging from their sockets, their yellow glow spherical, looking like brass buttons.

Hamido's lips parted in bewilderment. His dead body fell among long legs, between which hung the hard killing tools; his bare foot was crushed beneath the high, heavy boots with their tall uppers. The ground became doughlike, and his other foot plunged in. Then his legs sank in – up to the knees, halfway up his thighs, as far as the top of his thighs, to the middle of his belly. Little by little, he was sinking as far as the middle of his chest. The earth's grip closed around his neck, and his head went limp over the ground. He found the earth warm and tender, just like his mother's chest, so he buried his head between her breasts and managed to insert his nose under the left breast: his favourite, old, safe place. But his mother distanced him with her strong hand, as forceful as his father's. He lifted his head and saw his father's large hand, its long fingers grasping the badge, his wide, black eyes with their tiny red veins stared straight at Hamido. Hamido reached out; despite the dense crowd which constricted space and movement, his hand remained suspended in the air. Eyes stared at his bloodstained fingers, and no one shook his hand. (In those days, people scorned the slain and respected the slayer.)

Hamido was not a killer. It was he who had determined the point halfway between the two eyes and sighted, and he who had pulled the trigger, and he who had killed. But he slayed without becoming a slayer. For the slayer it is who carries the shame, yet whose own hands remain unsullied.

This shame was not Hamido's shame, though. All he had to do was to wash it away. (The distribution of special areas of expertise was one of the marks of progress, and so some managed shame and disgrace while others took care of the washing procedure.)

He pours the water from the bucket and washes everything carefully: hair, head, arms, legs, folds of skin around the hooves. He hears the imperious voice, coming from somewhere inside the house:

'Take the hooves – that's your share.'

So the hooves are lodged inside one of the daily newspapers, to enter history under the rubric of 'alms'.* Hamido carries them

---

* Specifically *zakat*, in Islam the religiously prescribed obligation of giving alms to the poor; it is considered one of the five 'pillars' or basic practices that all Muslims are required to carry out to the best of their abilities.

off under his arm, and walks along the street, visibly proud of them. From time to time, he peeks under his armpit, and there he sees the thick, black coat parting to reveal a white, bloodless face, and the dead eyes dilated and turned skyward.

With an instinctive curiosity, Hamido stared into the sky. He noticed a lone, fiery star, as its long, thin tail moved shining over the blackness like a line of fresh blood which has not yet coagulated. Then a breeze came up and dried the blood, and the star turned black, and the sky became one motionless and impervious mass.

Hamido's head sank onto his chest; from his eyes trickled a hot thread, which descended to slip into the corner of his mouth, running beneath his tongue with the familiar, salty flavour of pickling juice.

He clamped his jaws together and swallowed the bitter fruit. There was nowhere he could take sanctuary from the loathing he felt. It was attacking him through all the passages and outlets of his body, injecting its bitter, salty taste through the cracks in his skin and the orifices of his body, accumulating in his recesses day after day, year after year, so that his insides took on the putrid sliminess of a jar that has long stored old, fermented cheese. Filling his mouth with black smoke, he would expel the air from his lungs and swallow nothing but smoke.

Hamida knew the smell of smoke, as she used to buy tobacco from the shop. But this time the smell was different, mingling with another, unfamiliar one. It reminded her, though, of the smell of the toilet after her master had shaved his beard. As her small fingers handed him the towel, she could see his eyes in the mirror: white and black alike dilated and radiating a brassy yellow light.

The light finds her and comes to a stop, even though she is hiding behind the kitchen door. Her small body shrinks inside her damp *galabeya*; her shoulders are uneven, the left one higher than the right. Her torso sags to the right from the weight of the vegetable basket, pulling her right arm down.

The toes of her left foot barely graze the blazing asphalt, while her right foot just brushes it with the back of her bare heel. An observer would think her lame. But Hamida is not lame: she is just hungry. So she reaches into the basket; her slim fingers slip under the greens until she feels the touch of the fresh meat. She tears off a strip of flesh and crams it between her teeth, quickly, before anyone can see her.

Hamida's teeth are tiny and white, but they are sharp, able to cut through raw meat and crunch the bones. These are primitive teeth, grown centuries ago, before the invention of knives and forks and other modern implements. (It was because of these implements that her master's teeth had lost their strength and his gums had been stricken with pyorrhoea.) Her eyes, too, are primitive and strong, able to spot objects from a great distance, and her ears can pick up any sound, no matter how far away. (Her master had also lost this ability, due to the secret police's discovery of modern hearing aids.)

Hearing a voice, Hamida raised her eyes, and saw her mistress's head peering out of her heavily decorated window high in the towering edifice. Because of the great elevation, her mistress's head was the size of a pinhead. Yet Hamida could see it clearly, and she took note of the fleshy muscle contracting beneath wide, hairy nostrils. She realized, from the way the hairs were trembling, that her mistress had picked up the smell of the meat she'd ground under her teeth. Hamida denied it, of course, but unfortunately for her, a tiny piece of meat had lodged between two teeth. Her mistress's tender-skinned fingers snatched it out with a pair of tweezers. In the full blaze of the sun, she donned her prescription spectacles, and examined the minute scrap as it lay on her open palm.

On this particular day, her mistress did not beat her. After a heavy lunch, a quarrel had broken out between master and mistress. It ended in agreement on the principle of women's equality to men in the supervision of servants. Thus, it fell to her master to carry out the beating this time.

Hamida lay down on the kitchen floor. Hearing heavy footsteps, she shut her eyes and waited. She felt the long fingers with their carefully trimmed nails lifting the damp *galabeya*, baring her small legs and thighs and buttocks, as far as the middle of her back and belly. Giving off a brassy shine, the yellowish eyes stared at the belly, throwing their citrine light over it: a belly stretched taut, its muscles contracting forcefully, falling to primitive thighs that could move in any direction, resisting and kicking out with full force. Her little foot propelled itself forward into the stretch marks of his flabby, protruding stomach. He grabbed her foot, and for the first time actually became aware of the shape of a woman's foot. This one had toes, five toes, each separated from the other. Her mistress's foot lacked toes; or, to be more accurate, her mistress's toes were stuck together, like a camel's hoof, in a single soft mass of flesh.

His hands crept over the legs. He felt the strong movement of the muscles pulsing under his palm. Her mistress's muscles never moved. Still and silent, they offered no resistance, as if his fingers were plunging into a sack of cotton (which wasn't surprising, as her mistress had already died, some time before, in the bedroom).

The movement of this living flesh dazzled him, as if he were a hog who suddenly comes out of a waste area in which it has existed on the remnants of carcasses for years. He shuddered deliriously, and his clothes fell from him. His warm body brushed the cold tile floor, still wet from being mopped. His lax, flabby muscles contracted, and an electric current flowed along his spinal column. Life stirred in all his senses; the broad nostrils of his trembling nose stole a whiff of garbage from beneath the basin. He inhaled as deeply as he could, filling his chest with the putrid odour. The smell ran through his body and with it ran an old memory, from the days of childhood, of the first time he had experienced sexual pleasure.

But Hamida was cowering in the corner, clinging to the wall, a tremor spreading over her body, and along with it an old memory of her first beating. Her panic-stricken black gaze was fixed on the stout bamboo stick. He had hidden it beneath his clothes, or perhaps behind his back, and now he whipped it out and raised it in her face, erect and hard. In a flash, he aimed it at the fixed point halfway between her eyes. And pulled the trigger.

Hamida screamed. Her voice reverberated through the dark, silent night like the sound of a bullet being fired. Her mistress tossed from side to side inside her silken shroud. A few light sleepers bounded out of bed and turned on the lights. Closed windows and doors were opened, and necks were craned.

But the commotion led to nothing. The kitchen comprises four walls, a ceiling and a door; on the door is mounted a steel lock and chain. Everything returned to normal. Lights were extinguished, windows and doors shut and locked. All things were closed and locked. Stillness prevailed, and the darkness collected over the kitchen tiles, growing denser in the corner behind the door, in the shape of a naked little body beneath which ran a long, thin, thread of blood, as a pair of tearful, wide eyes shone childlike through the darkness.

* * *

Since early childhood, Hamido had been able to recognize this particular glow from a distance, and, like starlight, it had always drawn him. A solitary star lies wakeful and vigilant in a uniformly black, impermeable sky, while Hamido marches alone over the asphalt road, through the darkness, eyes uplifted towards the star, arms folded across his chest so that the old, black splotches of blood on his hands are visible. The sepia tones of tobacco stain his fingers, darkened under the nails to the colour of soil. His coughing fragments the night, and his white spittle bisects the darkness, landing on the asphalt in a ball, like a lump of white flesh streaked thinly with blood that comes to rest next to his feet.

They picked up his bloody trail, seized him, and returned him to service. The doctor lifted his calico drawers with fastidiously groomed fingertips, averting his face as the dead body's odour wafted through the room. He wrote out the diagnosis with his Parker pen: 'Suitable only for domestic service.' So Hamido became a house servant in the old style.

They took away the things in his custody: the iron-cleated leather boots, the suit and its cotton- and straw-padded shoulders, the yellow brass buttons – five across each shoulder and ten over the chest – and the wide leather belt from which hung his sheath, sheltering the blade that was sharp as a knife.

Hamido probed at his body in the darkness. He discovered that he was wearing the old, full-cut *galabeya*, which now fell over his thighs loosely as would a woman's *galabeya*. His shoulders, now bony and no longer perfectly horizontal, were like the pans of an unevenly weighted balance. His right hand hung lower than his left, dragging with it the whole right side of his head and body. There's a simple and well-known explanation for this infirmity: house servants used to hoist vegetable baskets with their right hands. These baskets were always heavy, for they were filled to the brim with potatoes and tomatoes and artichokes. And in the bottom lay the slaughtered flesh, its warm, red blood seeping through the white waxed paper, its heart still quivering with an imperceptible movement, its ebony-coloured eyes open and looking upwards, tearful as they shone out in the darkness like the eyes of a child.

Bewildered, Hamido stared at the child's eyes. They didn't have the characteristic glow of children's eyes; their shine was brassy, more like that of adults' eyes. The child clambered onto Hamido, thighs hugging his back and knees perched over his neck, one calf to each side, the heels of his shoes against Hamido's stomach.

The little one swung his legs as children do when riding donkeys. Hamido moved forward on hands and knees, the child on his back quivering in delight, a bamboo switch held tightly in his hand. The sun sat exactly halfway between the eyes, and the street was a mass of blazing red asphalt, overlain by fiery, crimson pebbles. When a flame-coloured pebble penetrated his right knee, Hamido paused to cough; the muscles of his chest were unable to contract and expel the pebble.

He hung his head, so that it nearly met his chest and he truly came to resemble an infirm donkey. The toe of the child's shoe, sharp as the tip of a knife, punched him in the belly, and he let out a cry. But his stomach muscles were unable to contract and expel the scream. He wrapped his arms around his stomach to protect it from the shoes, but then the child attacked him, biting him in the calf.

The fangs entered his flesh, and seemed to pierce his bones all the way to the marrow. He clenched his jaws and swallowed the pain. The agony accumulated in the bone marrow, hard and jagged like a piece of gravel. The child shrieked in delight and swung the toe of his shoe into the chip of gravel; it flew into the air and came to rest inside Hamido's belly, which was as warm as his blood-filled chest, or as his shaven head, which carried not a single hair to shade it from the sun.

The fire moved through his body. He submitted to it completely, letting it attack him from all openings. Assuming once again the bearing of a sickly donkey, he crawled forward, the burning taste of hatred invading him through the pores of his body to accumulate in its cavities, hardening and growing crimson, until it would have looked like a live coal. He reached down to pull out the killing tool, and his fingers bumped against his inanimate thighs, their muscles hanging lax beneath the *galabeya*. He hid behind the kitchen door and raised his *galabeya*. Rather than finding the hard implement alongside his thigh, he was startled to see the cleft, black and scabbed-over, just like the old wound. His head fell over his chest.

The peremptory voice boomed out her name. Hamida extracted a hammer from behind the kitchen door. Her damp *galabeya* clung to her body, and a mark in the shape of a shoe was etched into the skin of her stomach. Under her stomach wall, hatred was growing like an embryo, rolling into a dough-like ball, rising day after day, swelling with water, fermenting and giving off its own particular scent.

The security apparatus picked up the smell, for there is always a security apparatus with watching eyes and sniffing noses somewhere nearby. Hamida held her breath and wiped the palms of her hands before stretching out one small hand to offer the glass of water from as far away as possible. Her master's neat, manicured hands closed around the crystal goblet. He averted his face from the smell, but it was so penetrating that it reached the dead nose of her mistress in the bedroom, causing the relaxed hairs in her nostrils to stiffen until they were sharp as pins.

Hamida denied it, of course. But her body was the crime. They took the body away and left her the crime. Like bees sucking at a flower blossom, they take draughts of the nectar and then reject the sucked-out remains. They tossed away the remains with a strong fling of the hand. The hand thrust into her back, feeling more like a kick. The road was dark, the night black, and she stared into the gloom. She recognized her mother's fist in her back, so she lifted her gaze to meet her mother's, and was on the point of calling out to her. But her mother was standing there motionless, even her eyelashes frozen in place.

Hamida walked by the stone statue and left it behind. Silence spread through the night and she realized that she was alone. She sat down on a stone bench by the Nile and filled her chest with the river's sad and sluggish air. The sadness entered her chest with the night-time gloom, and she knew that she had been born motherless, that her paternal grandmother had been a slave in her master's court and had died by her father's knife.

She let her body go limp on the bench, opening her pores to the attack of grief, which poured in to fill her completely and give her strength. Only rarely does sadness give; and then it earmarks a special kind of person for its giving, one who is able to exchange the offering. And Hamida was able to give herself completely to sadness. She could devote herself exclusively to it and live from it: eating and drinking it, digesting it so that its juice ran in her blood, to be sifted by her intestines and then secreted by her pores. It would trickle over her body like glistening threads, which she would lick off and swallow once again, to be digested once more, and secreted yet again.

To any passer-by, her erect stance, alone in the night, would suggest a Ramessid statue. A tongue of water moves over its cheeks, neck, shoulders, thighs and feet, moving so gently that the motion cannot be sensed. The moisture remains on the skin, not evaporating despite the dry night breeze, but rather entering the pores, returning whence it came, to its origins in the mother's womb. For it is sadness and cannot be mistaken for anything else. She and the everlasting embryo in her womb live for each other, and it comes and goes at her bidding. Whenever she wishes its emergence, it becomes her child – a natural child, not like the artificial children who from birth possess certificates inscribed in ink. In their bodies, black ink runs in place of red blood. Their sexual organs are amputated, their hair is uprooted from their heads, and alongside every thigh hangs a toy pistol.

Her child has no familiarity with pistols, or dolls handmade of rags or straw, or any other toy: playthings are for children, and he is not a child. He is born standing on two feet; scrambling among the piles of manure, by himself, he laughs. It is this laugh which distinguishes him from children, for it is a soundless laugh that produces no movement in the facial muscles. His small eyes, though, are each coated by a tear which gives them a particular lustre. Beneath the tear a point of light diffuses, like a solitary star, wakeful and vigilant in a moonless sky.

Hamida walked through the night searching for her child. She circled the dung heaps. She looked behind the garbage bins. Next to the wall she spotted a little body huddled into a ball. She recognized him at once, and reached out into the darkness to enfold him to her chest. The darkness was cut by a yellow light and the brass eye appeared: always there is an eye watching, round and lidless, like a snake's eye, while the tail behind it is long and soft. The softness did not deceive her, though; she looked behind the tail. She saw the killing tool, hidden there, hanging alongside the thigh. It was not a male snake. Yet, even though she saw a female viper, Hamida knew that anything which kills must be male, and she screamed out to her child: 'Watch out for him, he'll kill you!'

The fangs entered the spindly leg. Like a long, thin tail, the blood flowed out, wetting her little toes, and running down to the soles of her feet. She raised her head, and saw her mother's wide, jet-black eyes fixed on her own eyes, looking at her mutely, the black *tarha* covering head and chest and belly. She opened her mouth to form her question, but the large palm was clapped over her mouth. Her breathing, the slight breeze, the rustling of the trees: all became a soundless, impermeable, black mass. The black *tarha* melted away into the night as a drop of water melts into the ocean.

But the legs pounded along behind her, towering above her like a high wave that followed her into the sea, constantly checking her position, plunging with her to the depths, and floating with her, a pair of corpses, on the surface. The wave lost itself with her in the middle of the ocean, then reappeared on shore, colliding with her against the edges of the rock, getting lost in the white foam, swaying with her between ebb and flow.

The flow was weak; the ebb was weaker. For the sea was not a sea after all, but rather the River Nile; its waters lay sluggish in the river bottom, their movement slow and heavy, like a half-paralysed foot that lies immobile once it is lowered to the ground. Hamido pulled the foot upward, though, with all his strength, using all the muscles in his thin, bowed leg. Raised above the ground, the foot became fixed there, and would not descend again. But the ground pulled it back with all its force so that it fell heavily, like a foot carved from stone.

It was early morning; the sun was still slanting across the ground, and his shadow was sketched over the earth: long, thin, as bowed as a rainbow. The head was shaven and the shoulders uneven, one higher than the other. One leg was longer than the other, too: this was the frame of a lame man. Laughing, the children behind him were clambering onto his back.

The children's voices and screams hurl themselves at him from somewhere above his head, and their feet pound over his back like the wheels of a train. Each one grasps the hem of the next, and they whistle, and the whistling ascends in the air. Each of them runs to hide from the seeker – behind a dung heap, in the animal pen, or behind the lamp-post.

The lamp-post stretched so far into the sky that it seemed stuck fast to the moon. The moonlight fell onto Hamida, turning her face, arms and legs white as she stood concealed behind the lamp-post. Her entire body shone pale, smooth and hairless. Only the roots of her plucked body hair protruded, becoming rigid with a shiver that spread across her skin.

She extended a white hand and touched her skin. Only her body could give her reassurance, for nothing outside it was reliable or secure: the world beyond consisted of strange bodies harboured in corners, behind walls and doors, in the darkened bends of streets, everywhere. Although the angles might seem smooth and innocuous from the outside, as if nothing lay within, when the sides of the triangle parted and the legs drew apart, the killing tool would emerge, clearly visible, hard and erect.

Hamida screamed, but the sound that emerged did not have the familiar timbre of a cry of fright or a plea for help. As a matter of fact, Hamida was not asking for anyone's help, since she knew that the road was empty of people. She was well aware that its windows and doors were shut and its lights extinguished. It was an area devoid of sounds, of voices, of everything.

No, it was not a scream for help, but it was sharp and long, going on and on as if it were in fact millions of screams coming together, welded into a single scream as endless as the night, and bonded in place with millions of the black particles from which the darkness and silence are made.

Nor was it a scream of alarm or fear. Hamida had no fear of the dark, or of silence, or even of death, for she was part of the darkness and her voice was the silence. And death has lived with her. She has borne it like a second body clinging to hers, like a second person, dead and living inside her. It occupies the emptiness within, enfolding its arms and legs, stretching itself out, its scent spreading outwards through her eyes and ears, from her nose and mouth, wafting from every opening in her body. At night, when the gloom intensifies and solitude weighs heavier, she reaches out and feels him beside her, clinging to her; in her embrace his breaths mingle with hers, the heat of his body indistinguishable from her warmth.

Hamida planted her hand on her back, and a feeling of safety came over her. Were one to see her warm, soft, gently curved body from the rear, one would mistake her for a child. But as she turns around and her eyes grow visible, one sees unmistakeably that she is old. The faces of the elderly, like those of children, are sexless, but her growing belly, expanding with the live embryo, identifies her as a woman. One would be at a loss to determine her age, for Hamida is ageless. Such is the status of children born in defiance of the government employee who determines birth dates. They live untouched by the government, unaffected by history, unmarked by time and place. They do not pass through the stages of childhood, youth and old age as do ordinary human beings. They live on, beyond old age, notwithstanding the government employee who records dates of death. Like the gods, they are spared the boundaries of time, and they live forever, sharing a single, extended existence unmarked by developmental stages.

Born as adults, they grow old without experiencing childhood or adolescence, and then move suddenly from old age to infancy, or from childhood to adolescence. They pass by in a single fleeting second, faster than the eye can see, for the human eye cannot fathom their essence. Such creatures appear as child, youth and old person at one and the same time and place. Sometimes they walk the roads when already dead, and when their smell is virtually unbearable. Yet the human eye remains incapable of distinguishing them from the living. Even wrinkles hold little significance in such cases, because they appear not as wrinkles but rather as the natural laughter lines which show on a child's face when it laughs forcefully but inaudibly.

Hamida was still standing behind the lamp-post, her face swollen, round and white as flour beneath the light, her wrinkles concealed by powder, and her cracked lips – chapped by hunger – glazed with a bloody, red crust. Her chest protruded from the opening of a torn gown, and her belly jutted out below. Her cracked heels were visible inside backless, slipper-like shoes. Her hair, as thick and black as a piece of the night, covered her head and chest, encasing her entire body in blackness. From within the blackness her white neck arched out, like a healthy tree trunk showing above the forest horizon, signalling that its roots are sunken deep into the moist ground.

An observer would think her a woman of the night, even though she was not a woman and the time was not night. The sun was directly overhead, at the exact midpoint between the eyes. Hamida was staring at the blazing red disc, unblinkingly, without the slightest twitch of a facial muscle, staring with all the patience she could summon. She saw him clearly at the centre of the circle, like a rainbow: long, thin and stooped, passing before her eyes with his characteristically slow gait, one shoulder higher than the other, one leg longer than the other – the frame of a lame man. She recognized him immediately and almost shouted out 'Hamido'. But she feared that her hiding place behind the lamp-post would thus be revealed, that he would recognize her swollen belly and pull out the killing tool.

She clamped her lips together and held her breath. But he smelled her anyway, for her odour was strong and penetrating, like that of the dead. He came to a stop, and stuck his long, thin hand behind the lamp-post, but it found nothing to grasp. 'Hamida.' The barely audible voice was familiar, an imitation of her own voice, in fact. He bent his trunk into a skilfully crafted imitation of her shape – for there had been great progress in craftsmanship, industry and technology. So skilful was his portrayal, that Hamida was confused into thinking the voice was actually hers and mistaking the body as her own. She emerged from behind the lamp-post confidently, walking out with head bent, as usual.

But as she lifted her head, her gaze clashed with the yellow eyes. So terrified was she by this surprise that she saw double. Then the four eyes multiplied with lightning speed, until yellow eyes surrounded her: ten marching down the chest and five along each shoulder, giving off a brassy yellow light.

The metallic voice bounced across the asphalt like the clanging of iron against iron.

'What's your name?'

'Hamida.' Her voice was barely audible.

The razor-blade moved over her head, her soft, thick hair fell into the pail. The razor dropped to her body, and passed over her skin, uprooting the hair. When it reached the pit of her lower stomach, moving through the patch of black hair it stumbled upon the tiny white bud that looked like a newborn bird. It plucked the bud from its roots, leaving in its place a deep wound in the flesh, like the scabbed-over cleft. (In those times, this surgical operation was called 'purification'; its goal was to 'purify' the human being by removing any remaining sexual organs.)

Hamida lay on the cement floor, surrounded by four cement walls, her arms and legs rigid and bound together into a single bundle. Between her thighs hung the iron padlock of a hard metal belt. (This has entered history as the chastity belt.) Its chain clanked dully against the cement floor whenever she moved a limb.

Beneath her, a pool of blood seeped through the cracks in the floor. The walls were splashed with blood in the shape of human fingers: old, black blood, like spots, millions of them, stains left by every age and race and sex: children, men, women, old folks, white, black, yellow, red. Everyone had a particular stain, an individual one shaped like the imprint of a hand.

Hamida stuck a small fingertip into the cleft; it came out wet with blood. She wiped it on the wall, imprinting her mark on the cement, like a personal signature. (Illiterate people – the likes of Hamida – all seal official documents this way.) Black, bloodstained fingers reached out to imprint their seal on the documents – millions of documents, bearing millions of seals, all black, their lines crooked and spidery like the legs of cockroaches, or flies, or locusts. Millions of insects, diffusing over the earth, night and day, on to bridges and city walls, at the bend of every street, behind every house and every wall, inside every crevice in the earth, their bare and shaven heads poking out across the surface of the ground while their skinny, bowed bodies remain inside the fissures. Their insides are hollowed out, empty of internal organs, devoid of livers, hearts, stomachs, intestines. The vast, empty cavity becomes a secret storage place packed tight with hatred. (In those days, only this spot was beyond the reach of the security apparatus. More recently, the military have made great advances; in the field of medicine, for example, they have invented x-ray equipment which reveals foreign bodies inside a human being, and an electronic speculum which is placed in the anus to reveal the contents of the internal cavity.)

X-rays fell upon her swollen belly, showing the cavity full to the brim with hatred, layer upon layer upon layer, millions of fine layers, like thin sheets of near-transparent metal massed on top of each other to form a solid bulk of hard metal. The doctor probed at her with his soft, carefully manicured fingers and let out a shout.

'Gunpowder!' The pickaxes rained down, breaking apart the earth, turning over the soil, inverting the very fissures they had made. They stumbled on the gunpowder stores, one and all. (History has celebrated the victory of x-rays over cancerous protrusions in the body.)

But cancer is a sly disease, more cunning than history, and the tumour continued to grow deep inside the earth. When Hamida placed her hand beneath the womb, she felt the tumour, warm to her hand, giving off the heat of her body, and was reassured. She sniffed the familiar fragrance on her fingers – a scent reminiscent of the dung heap, the garbage bin or the lump of dead flesh. She breathed it in fully: for it was the odour of her life.

Hamido turned his head in her direction, attracted by the odour they shared. Conceivably, he could have distanced himself and fled, but instead he approached her, by virtue of their shared lot. He halted beside the corpse, unrolling his tall frame and sketching the long, thin, crooked outline of his shadow on the asphalt. The white blade hung visibly alongside his thigh, its black, blood-like stains in evidence. He filled his chest with the night air, and realized that he had been born motherless, that his paternal grandfather had been a soldier in the army of Muhammad Ali* and that he had been slain in prison.

---

* Muhammad Ali (1769–1849): Born in Kavalla, Macedonia, he came to Egypt in 1801 as a soldier in an Albanian contingent attached to the Ottoman Turkish army. Triumphant in the power struggles which followed the French, then British, evacuation of Egypt, he was named Pasha/Ottoman Viceroy of Egypt in 1805 and ruled until 1848. Founder of the dynasty that ruled Egypt until just after the 1952 revolution, Muhammad Ali instituted reforms aimed at expanding Egypt's military power; these reforms, centring on education as well as industrial and agricultural development, had the effect of strengthening the country's economic base.

He knew suddenly – and as if it were an ancient verity as certain as death – that prison was his destiny. He offered no resistance, but let his body go limp in the iron grip. During the years of captivity, he had been drilled in the principle that relaxing the body lessens the strain it must undergo. Indeed, the tension had drained from his opened pores, from his eyes and ears and nose and anus. Now, nothing would seem quite as brutal, whether it was the beating, or the feeling of his body puffing up, or the branding by fire (at least, prior to the discovery of electricity).

His body falls limply to the ground, and he stretches out as fully as he is able. From beneath him stream thin trails of blood that slip into the crevices in the ground. The walls bear black stains that look like blood, every one in the shape of five fingers and a palm. Millions of stains, left by every age, every race, every sex: children, men, women, old people, white and black, yellow and red. And every one has his own particular, distinguishable stain.

Hamido rose from the floor, supporting himself against the wall, and imprinted his mark on the cement like a personal signature. (Those convicted – the likes of Hamido – seal police reports this way.) Black, bloodstained fingers reach out to imprint their seal on the police reports – millions of reports, stacked and heaped like corpses on Judgement Day (before the discovery of buses made such a crush of bodies an everyday occurrence). These bodies were aligned horizontally and arranged side by side in alternate directions – head next to rear and rear next to head – and so closely packed that they covered every inch of floor and ceiling. They were tightly compressed and so congealed together that no air could possibly penetrate, and no one could stretch out an arm or leg.

Hamido closed his eyes, opened his mouth, and moaned. The others followed his example, and millions of voices rose in the gloomy vastness, manufacturing the silence of night. The silence was so dense and heavy that it created a pressure on his ears, causing him to open his eyes. A pair of feet, the soles badly cracked, were almost touching his face. He recognized them at once and whispered, imitating her voice: 'Hamida.' But she did not answer: she was dead, her body sprawled on the ground, her face to the sky, the white moonlight falling upon it to give it the round and swollen aspect of an inflated bladder.

She opened her mouth and moaned (due to the pressure of urine). Millions of moans rose in the dawn and created the national dirge (which they used to call the national anthem).

Hearing the anthem, Hamido realized that morning had come. He dragged his legs out from under the iron girdle and walked to the latrine – the only place in the world where he felt optimistic. From behind the wall, he would exchange a few words with others, while his lower half would send out a thread of urine, as thin and bowed as his frame, its odour as piercing as his. At this, he would feel suddenly and surprisingly mirthful; observing the yellow threads of water around him, glistening in the light like victory arches, he would let out a great roar of laughter.

The loud guffaws would ring out from the latrine, millions of them, for the numbers increased day after day. And in those days, all equipment was susceptible to breakdown, except that of reproduction and the wireless, of course. The sound would spread as any sound does, and at the same speed (by means of one of the instruments available at the time), to enter the large pair of ears like a sharp pebble. A clean, manicured finger would poke itself into those ears, and the sharp pebble would fall into his chubby, fleshy palm. Gazing steadily at the designated civil servant, he would inquire:

'Are they laughing?'

The civil servant would lower his eyes, as civil servants usually did in the presence of the big chief, Hamido's master:

'No, milord, they're just urinating.'

Hamido was still standing in the latrine. The thread of water had not yet expended itself when he saw the civil servant coming to carry out an inspection. He felt afraid; and fear, like death, is an organic being, composed of flesh and blood. He sensed the blood draining from his head, limbs and internal organs, seeping downwards to collect at the pit of his stomach, in a single point that swelled to become as distended as his bladder. The civil servant still stood before him, legs planted apart insolently, eyes fixed steadily on him with the courage of civil servants in the absence of their master, mouth open to show ulcerous gums, afflicted with pyorrhoea (like his master's gums).

He felt a sharp pain low in his belly. He turned around. They were tightening their grip, and bodies were pressing in on him from every side, leaving no open space, yielding no room at all. The only empty space he could see was the ulcerous open mouth, so he aimed the ribbon of water at it and emptied all the fear from his body.

Hamido opened his eyes. He could feel the pool beneath him, its warmth like that of his body and its piercing smell akin to that of his life. He realized that he was still alive and was quite hungry. He reached out, extending his hand into the shallow bowl. Millions of small black insects swarmed out, buzzing around him gleefully, some flying, others scuttling, still others crawling. A few clung to the ceiling and perched on the walls; others disappeared inside the cracks, and one alighted on his open palm.

He looked between its legs. Seeing there the old, scabbed-over wound, he knew it was a female, and that she was dead. He clapped his other palm over her, and she died again. He cracked her dead extremities and the recorder picked up the sound. (A tape recorder of the latest model, the size of a chickpea, had been fixed inside one of his body parts.) He cracked the toes of his own right foot with pride and self-esteem. His passage through history had significance, and this was why, when lenses were trained on the state's employees, he saw terror shading their eyes. For any movement they made would enter history instantaneously – even a mere cracking of a knuckle (due to the brittleness of one's joints after the age of forty) or a finger raised to brush away a fly that has perched on one's nose.

He gave his toes an innovative, creative shake. In spite of everything, he loved authenticity and originality, and despised imitation. What an accumulation of imitative, inauthentic, ape-like movements history has recorded! Identical faces, identical fingers and toes, one imitation after another, one imitation over and over again. An accumulation that grows ever vaster, higher and higher, just like a pile of manure. Every day the cow lies down, and every dawn his mother collects the dung, dumping it in a sunny place. By the next day it is dry, and on its way to becoming firmly rooted in history.

Finally, the treacle appeared, a congealed mass at the bottom of the bowl, which settled at the base of his stomach like a lump of tar. He chewed at a bit of onion, offsetting the sour taste of the bitter cucumber. He lit a wad of tobacco and filled his chest and stomach with smoke. Now he felt something akin to fullness, and belched in a loud voice that intimated self-confidence. (At that time, only males experienced this.)

Hamida heard the sound, and in it she recognized the smell of tobacco. After all, she used to buy tobacco from the shop for her father or brother or uncle or some other man from the family. The shopkeeper would hand her a sweet, which she would pop into her mouth, hiding it under her tongue. When he demanded the penny from her, she would open her hand and find nothing; she would open her eyes and find the lamp, like a wisp of light, flaring up only to die out at a single gust of wind. And darkness would fill the door, like a tall, huge body, solidly dark except for two round holes at the top of the head from which pierced a red light, the colour of the pre-dawn.

'Who are you?' she whispered, in a frightened, nearly inaudible voice.

He answered in the same tones. 'Hamido.'

She closed her eyes so that he would not recognize them; she let his long arms enfold her, and his hot breaths warm her. It was winter, and her ears, so soft and small, were like shells of ice.

He whispered, expelling a hot breath into her ear.

'Who are you?'

She remained motionless, her ear still below his mouth, and gave no response. She pretended to be asleep; she hid her head in the thick hair on his chest. When she felt the large fingers raising the garment from her body, she held her breath. Her chest no longer rose or fell. She had turned into a corpse.

But in the morning, the slanting sun fell on her eyes. She saw the lank form beside her, noted its thin and crooked shape. His shoulders were uneven, resembling hers; his fingers were swollen and festered from washing dishes, like hers, and the fingernails were just as black. She knew at once that it was her own body, so she hugged him with all her strength, and pressed her chest to his, and felt the outlines of the leather wallet just beneath her left breast. She was hungry, so she slipped the wallet from his pocket quickly, before anyone could see her.

She hid behind a wall and opened the wallet. She saw her portrait: encased in the black *tarha*, she resembled her mother on the night of her wedding. She found a directive in her father's handwriting, reminding him to wash away the disgrace, and four pounds and a *bariza**.

The *bariza* bought her a meal, and with two pounds she purchased a mini-dress (the sort of shrunken dress popular in those days among chaste and virtuous wives, since the only parts of their sacrosanct bodies exposed by such garments were the arms, shoulders, bosom and thighs). With the remaining two pounds she bought a pair of open-toed shoes with spike heels. (The emergence of open-toed shoes in that era was aimed at revealing the blood-red nail varnish worn by women; but these shoes had backs so that the cracks in women's feet resulting from domestic service would be hidden.)

---

* In those days, a ten-piastre coin or note.

Hamida walked down the street, teetering on her high heels, her arms, thighs and throat bare, her dress cut low to reveal her breasts. She had come to resemble her mistress, and although she walked right by the *shawish* (the widespread term for policemen in those days) he did not arrest her. In fact, as she passed before him undeterred, he lowered hishead, and kept his eyes on the ground. (This was called 'averting the glance' and was practised before matrons of unblemished reputation. He had learnt the manoeuvre during his years of training.)

Holding her head aloft, she moved on with swaying, tottering steps. She swung her bare shoulders, the left one appearing to be higher than the right. Her left breast was higher than her right breast (due to the swollen wallet concealed beneath her left breast) and her buttocks, one higher than the other, shook as she continued on her way.

She drew a few steps away from the policeman and ran her hand over the wallet. Its leather had the soft feel of saliva trickling over one's fingers after eating a sugared pancake. A stream of warm blood was moving from her left breast to her belly and on to her thighs and feet, and then ascending to her head, ears and nose, and falling once again to her heart, following its normal, repeating circuit and sending into the motionless cells a new impulse that gave her a pleasurable sensation.

She worked her jaws, and chewed the pleasure until it melted into her saliva and she swallowed both. The pleasure mingled with her blood and circled from head to foot, from feet to head. Her head began to spin, and she leant back against a lamp-post. Her lids drooped, so that the street grew dark and the sky turned black and moonless. The circular blue light fell over her face, and she recognized it at once. (Her master always painted the headlamps of his car blue to avoid being seen or recognized by anyone during his nightly rovings.) He opened his door and got out, walked round and opened the door for her, waited until she was seated, shut the door and circled round the car again, reached his own door, opened it, sat down, and shut the door. (Her master had been trained in this circular motion in the Faculty of Arts and Protocol.*)

Her spike heels were plunged into thick carpeting, soft as dough, and her shoes came off, revealing her cracked heels. She hid them under the silken coverlet. Her body had settled into a horizontal position on something soft – softer than dough – and she relaxed the muscles in her buttocks, which her long period of standing behind the lamp-post had strained. Her body began to sink into the dough: feet, legs, thighs, chest, all the way to the neck. Only her head remained visible, sticking up over the surface.

Her head began to sink gradually: chin, mouth, nose. Her eyes dilated with terror as she realized she could get no air. And terror is an organic being, composed of flesh and blood. It was personified before her now in the shape of a strange, misshapen creature with the head of a human being and the body of an ape. Its head was bare, shaven to sleekness, its chest a forest of hair, its buttocks as bare and smooth as its head, the skin on its backside

---

*A pun on the several meanings of *adaab*, as 'etiquette', as 'morals', and as 'arts' or 'humanities' in the context of higher education. The singular, adab, means both 'literature' and 'good manners'. *Kulliyat al-adaab* is the faculty of arts in a university.

showing the same transparent blood-redness as the face. The creature had reddish lips, parted to show a long, sharp tongue, just like a white blade with a hard metallic edge, at its tip a darkened hole in which death was lying in wait.

She screamed – her suppressed, inaudible scream – and dropped her eyelids over the terror. But it crept into her throat (through the lachrymal canal which connects eye and ear) and sat there, rolling up into a lump. She tightened the muscles of her throat and spat as forcefully as she could, so that thin threads poured fountainlike from her mouth, nose and ears.

Her master laughed with a childlike delight that propelled his fleshy cheeks upwards so that his eyes were squeezed completely shut. She realized that he would fall asleep in a moment. (The royal salute had rung out, announcing the end of the jamboree.) As his snoring filled the air, she undid the golden buttons on his chest and lifted out the heavy leather wallet that had been pressing against his chest.

Opening the door quietly, she got out and made her way – slowly and assuredly – to her own car, which she unlocked with a gleaming silver key like the one her mistress had had. The car slipped over the soft asphalt like a graceful skiff gliding through the water. She passed alongside the policeman, his stance as erect as the lamp-post. He quivered (as if an electric shock had shot through him) and raised his right index finger to touch his left ear (a sacred movement in those days which symbolized love of country).

She stuck her head outside the car window. The moonlight fell on her face. The road was empty except for the lamp-posts, standing erect along both sides of the road. To the right, arms were raised high, and to the left, a finger was held to every ear.

She recognized the black stains on the finger, and whispered: 'Hamido!' But Hamido heard nothing, and remained stiffly upright, his head raised to the sky and one black finger to his ear. (Those travelling abroad used to see this memorial to the unknown soldier erected at the entrance to every capital city.)

Hamida stretched out her hand and grabbed his. His fingers were like hers, and the lines on his palm resembled hers. In a rush of sympathy – for their lot was a shared one – she tried to bend his arm downwards. But the stone arm, raised wearily, would not move. She raised her eyes and noticed that the wide ebony eyes shone with a real tear, a childlike one. The tear fell on to her cheek, still hot, and crept into the corner of her mouth and under her tongue, bitter to the taste. She swallowed it. Another hot tear fell on to her cheek and ran into her nose, just as bitter, so she swallowed it. Grief began to attack her from all sides, through every pore and orifice, pouring into her nose, mouth and ears like a soft powder. But the particles were sharp, like pieces of splintered glass, and they ripped apart the thin membranes that lay at the back of her nose, mouth and bronchial passages. She coughed silently, and from her chest oozed a white fluid that ran through a long narrow channel connecting heart to throat to nose to ears to eyes. She was ejecting mucous from her eyes, and spitting tears from her nose and mouth and ears, white substances jetted through with hairlike streaks of blood.

She raised her face to the moonlight, which had become intensely white and devoid of blood streaks. Her features were strange; in fact, it was their contradictory nature that attracted attention. The chin was small, rounded and soft like that of a child, while the forehead protruded, rough and wrinkled like an old person's brow. The lips were virginal, parted in a deprivation not to be satisfied – like the lips of chaste wives. The cheeks bulged with a sharp and insatiable gluttony – like the cheeks of respectable husbands. The nose was straight and upturned in self-pride, with the insolence of criminals and those outside the law, while the ears were small, submissive and motionless, like those of government employees. The eyes were black and wide, bearing a primitive and shameless look, uplifted and steady, not averting their glance as the eyes of modest women do, as they gaze downwards, bashful and ashamed of their impertinent thoughts.

Strange features they were, and utterly contradictory. Even stranger, the contradictory nature of the features harmonized with the features themselves, in a balanced and familiar manner. In fact, the harmony and balance were so remarkable as to attain a degree of appeal whose very unfamiliarity captured attention. It was as if these features marked not one face but two or three or four, or as if the face was not even a face but something else.

This was a something else that stirs up confusion and bewilderment, and anxiety, and indeed even anger. Naturally, a person grows angry if, looking into the face of another, he sees not the other person's soul but rather his private parts. And, naturally too, one's anger intensifies if the form of these private parts is unfamiliar or unnatural. For it is in the nature of things that private parts have a shape which inspires shame and offends honour – as well as carrying the odour of filth (not unlike the smell of sweat,

urine, or any of the body's other poisonous discharges). But for
them to have a sweet scent is strange indeed, for this indicates that
the body is retaining its sweat and poisons. Very soon its insides
will become putrid and give off the odour of filth. The face, though,
will remain clean and white, adorned by features that demonstrate
nobility as well as ancient and respectable family origins (and
other such refined characteristics, as delineated clearly in the
faces of noble people – the likes of her master).

Her master's face turned in her direction as she stood in
the moonlight. Her dark and wide-open eyes returned his long
gaze, not averting or dropping their gaze. He was so angry that
he wanted to spit in her face. But he had grown so accustomed
to concealing and suppressing his anger that it could no longer
motivate any facial movement, except for a sudden contraction of
one small muscle at the angle of his nose, which pulled his lips
apart in what would seem – to the naked eye – to be a smile.

Since she had no other appointment, she climbed into the car.
They passed along the facade of his chief residence in Zamalek*.
She saw her mistress gazing down from the high, heavily
ornamented window. Although her head was the size of a pinhead
(because of the great elevation) he could see her. Hiding his face
with his right hand, he stepped on the accelerator and the car
shot off before anyone could spot him. He drove slowly along Nile
Street and crossed the bridge; now he was entering the quarter of

---

* An island in the Nile at Cairo which has been a well-to-do residential and business area
since the turn of the twentieth century, and where many of the foreign embassies have been
sited. Traditionally, Zamalek has had a relatively large proportion of foreign residents, and
has often served as a symbol of wealthy urban Egypt with its foreign alliances.

Bulaq,* where he had his secondary residence. (Every respectable husband at that time had a secondary residence in addition to the main one, and the number of his secondary residences increased in proportion to his rise in position.)

He stripped off his clothes promptly (as is the habit of those involved in important matters), then raised his foot and placed it on the edge of the bed, his other foot remaining on the floor. (He had been trained to stand on one leg during his years of public service.) By coincidence, at this very moment she turned towards him; she found not the killing tool but rather the old, closed-up wound. One might have expected her to register surprise, but apparently she had seen nothing to disconcert her, for she swung her head back towards the wall indifferently. There, inside a gilt frame, she saw her mistress in military garb. Her mistress's eyes were settled upon the naked heap, and she followed its movements with the sedate, even grim, look of a magistrate, all the while snapping photos from every angle. (NB These pictures have been preserved in the archives of the Bureau of Intelligence.)

Thus, Hamida's face became well-known indeed. Whenever she peered from the car window, necks were craned in her direction – though heads were lowered, of course. Her face was plastered on walls, and erected at every street corner. That was where she used to stand and wait, and sometimes, when the waiting seemed to stretch out endlessly, she would look up and see her picture hanging there, lips parted in an expansive smile,

---

* An old port on the east bank of the Nile, opposite Zamalek and just north-west of the old city of Cairo, which in the nineteenth century became an industrial area. Since, it has developed into a densely populated and largely working-class residential and business area of the city.

while from the corner of her mouth, a long, white thread of warm saliva ran upwards to the edge of her nose and then edged towards the space between nose and eye.

With the palm of her hand, she would wipe the moisture off her face and then wipe her hand on the wall. There, sketched on the wall, would appear the palm and five human fingers. As the night breezes blew over it and the sun rose on it, the hand would dry out, turning into black stains the colour of old blood.

The sun's rays fell over Hamido's eyes as he slept upright beside the wall. He opened his eyes and saw the palm and black, extended fingers. Her fingers were like his, and the lines on her palm resembled those on his. His lips parted, calling out: 'Hamida!' He pulled the killing tool up, from alongside his thigh, but just then he caught a glimpse of the shining silver key dangling between her fingers, and realized that she was his lady mistress. He hid the implement in his pocket in the blink of an eye, let it hang loosely behind his thigh, and stood in his place erect, the muscles of his back taut and his right arm raised, his eyelids relaxed and dropping over his eyes like a curtain.

When the sound of the car had grown distant, he opened his eyes to see its tapered back bisecting the darkness which then swallowed it. He relaxed his back muscles, let his arm fall, and felt at ease. He filled his chest with the night air, and tried to remember what he looked like as a child – the shape of his features when he smiled or laughed – but he could recall nothing. There was no childhood to remember, no smile, no laughter.

He heard his own heavy footfall on the ground: right, left, right, left. Lub dub lub dub. Slow, regular beats, interposed by periods of silence as black as death. He coughed and spat out a lump of blood-tinged saliva. The bamboo switch fell onto his back; its sting told him he was naked and had not yet died. He lost his sense of optimism and spat again. Hearing the commanding tones of that familiar voice, he pulled the implement from its black sheath, and sighted carefully on the point midway between the two eyes. The harsh voice shouted,

'Fire!'

He fired.

The tall, crooked body dropped; a long thread of blood streamed from a hole exactly at the midpoint of the knobby protrusion on the centre brow. The blood cut across the figure's eyes, cheeks, nose and lips, to circle his small, rounded, child-like chin.

He was not one child, but rather thousands or millions of children, whose bodies had tumbled onto the asphalt. Every child's face was marked by a long thread of blood that ran from eyes to nose to mouth and the reverse. The sun fell over the asphalt, the sky turned a pure blue, and the gods came into sight, massed together, sitting in rows, one leg over the other, smoking from a waterpipe.

Hamido stretched out his leg; it collided with another leg. He extended his arm; it bumped against another. He was drowning in a sea of dead bodies. He began to swim, using both arms and legs, through the vast ocean. He stopped for a moment to catch his breath, and turned around to find out where he was or who had brought him here. He remembered nothing except that he had been a child, and that a strong fist had pushed him in the back and hurled him into the sea. He saw the hand sketched on the wall: a large palm like his father's but with fingers that were swollen and cracked like his mother's. His lips parted; he shouted 'Mama!' His mother's black eyes looked at him, the black *tarha* covering her head and neck, shoulders and belly.

She was standing not far away, her tall frame motionless, the rise of her chest firm and still next to his head. He put his head on her chest, and buried his nose between her breasts. But his mother's strong hand pushed him away, causing him to glance up in her direction. There he saw his father's wide eyes, the red streaks gleaming like thin snakes over the whites, and he heard his father's coarse voice.

'Only blood washes away shame.'

He approached his father, staring steadily into his eyes. The red streaks over the large whites trembled. (A person takes fright if he sees an open eye gazing at him unblinkingly, for such a stare means that the eye is examining him thoroughly to see him as he really is.)

His father backed away, and, with just one step to the rear, the lamplight fell squarely on to his face. He brought one big palm upwards to hide his face, but the light exposed his tall, large body as he stood there, blocking the door. He blew at the wisp of light, and it went out. The darkness now became so dense that it was impossible to distinguish the floor from the walls, or the walls from the ceiling. His large, bare foot stumbled on the slight rise of the threshold. But he regained his balance, and sprang forward panther-like on tensile feet. He moved on, slowly and cautiously, stepping over something which looked very much like the backless leather slippers worn by men in the countryside.

Hamido shrieked, his voice childlike; but his body was not that of a child. His hand plunged into his pocket, which was as long as a sheath, and drew out the hard metal implement. He determined the spot halfway between the white circles, over which the red threads glistened, and sighted. He held his breath, and shut his eyes, and pulled the trigger.

He opened his eyes and saw the tall, bowed body stretched out in the sun, its dilated eyes turned upward and its right arm dangling to the side, grasping something. Hamido opened the fingers, and the penny fell into his palm. He closed his hand over it, and went to the shop to buy tobacco. He bought a sweet and put it in his mouth. He turned to go back, but the shopkeeper asked him for the penny. He opened his closed hand and found nothing. The shopkeeper snatched up his stick and set off behind Hamido at a run.

As small and light as it was, his body could fly through the air like a sparrow. No doubt he would have been able to stay ahead of the shopkeeper (aah, had he only been a real sparrow!), but a feeling of heaviness came upon him, suddenly and just the way it happens in dreams. He felt his body grow sluggish; it seemed to have turned into stone, into a statue whose feet are planted on the ground and whose arms are fixed in place with iron and cement. His thighs, pulled apart, seemed to have turned into marble. In each foot was rammed a nail, as if he had been crucified. The bamboo switch swung into the air, long and thin and curved like a bow, and rained down on something soft and warm, like living flesh.

* * *

When Hamido opened his eyes, daylight was filling the room. He thought for sure that what he had seen had been nothing but a dream. He jumped up from the mat and ran out into the street. His friends – all children of neighbouring families – were playing as usual in the narrow lane extending along the mud-brick facades. Each child grasped the next one's hand, forming a ring that circled round and round. The thin, high-pitched sound of their singing orbited with the movement of their bodies, yielding a single song, comprising one stanza which repeated itself in a never-ending, unbroken cycle:

> *Hamida had a baby,*
> *She named him Abd el-Samad,*
> *She left him by the canal bed,*
> *The kite swooped down and snatched off his head!*
> *Shoo! Shoo! Away with you!*
> *O kite! O monkey snout!*

Because they were circling and singing uninterruptedly, it was impossible to pick out the song's beginning or end by ear, just as it was impossible to tell by looking where the circle began and where it ended. For they were children, and when children play they grasp each other by the hand to form a closed circle. But everything does have an end, and so I must end this. Yet I do not know the end point of my tale. I am unable to define it precisely, for the ending is not a point that stands out clearly. In fact, there is no ending, or perhaps it would be more accurate to say that the end and the beginning are adjoined in a single, looping strand; where that thread ends and where it begins can be discerned only with great difficulty.

Here lies the difficulty of all endings, especially the ending of a true story, of a story as truthful as truth itself, and as exact in its finest details as exactitude itself. Such exactitude requires of the author that he or she neither omit nor neglect a single point. For even one point – a single dot – can completely change the essence of a word in the Arabic language. Male becomes female because of a single dash or dot. Similarly, in Arabic the difference between 'husband' and 'mule', or between 'promise' and 'scoundrel', is no more than a single dot placed over a single form, an addition which transforms one letter into another.

Hence the importance of a well-defined point – that is, a real point in the full geometrical sense of the word. In other words, scientific accuracy is unavoidable in this work of art which is my novel. But scientific accuracy can corrupt or distort a work of art. Yet that corruption or distortion is exactly what I wanted, and what I aimed for in this story. Only then would it become as truthful, sincere and real as 'living life'. For some of the time, life may be dead, like that life which inhabits a person who walks through life without sweating or urinating, and from whose body no foul substance emanates. One who is truly alive cannot imprison his foulness within, or else he will die. Once he is dead, his face will become purest white, while his insides remain putrid, stained by the rottenness of death.

I fancied (and my fancy, at that particular moment, amounted to fact) that one of the children who were circling round as they sang in unison suddenly moved outside of the circle. I saw the small body come loose from the steadily revolving ring, breaking the regularity of its outline. It moved off like a gleaming speck, or a star that has lost its eternal equilibrium, detached itself from the universe, and shot off at random, creating a trail of flame, like a shooting star just before it is consumed in its own fire.

With an instinctive curiosity, I followed his movement with my gaze. He came to a stop so near to where I stood that I could see his face. It wasn't the face of a boy, as I had thought. No, it was the face of a little girl. But I wasn't absolutely certain, for children's faces – like those of old people – are sexless. It is in that phase between childhood and old age that gender must declare itself more openly.

The face – oddly enough – was not strange to me. So familiar was it, in fact, that it left me feeling bemused, and then my surprise turned to disbelief. My mind could not accept the sight before my eyes. It is just not plausible that, leaving home in the morning to go to work, on the way I should run head-on into another person only to discover that the face which met my gaze was none other than my own.

I confess that my body shook, and I was seized by a violent panic which paralysed my ability to think. Even so, I wondered: why should a person panic when he sees himself face to face? Was it the extreme eeriness of the situation in which I found myself, or was it the almost overwhelming familiarity of the encounter? At such a moment, one finds everything becoming utterly confused. Contradictory or incompatible things come to resemble each other so closely that they become almost identical. Black becomes white, and white turns to black. And the meaning of all this? One faces, with open eyes, the fact that one is blind.